NO. AR.

MVFOL

# THE RACE TO KANGAROO CLIFF

# ALEXANDER McCALL SMITH

# THE RACE TO KANGAROO CLIFF

*Illustrations by*
## IAIN McINTOSH

DELACORTE PRESS

Text copyright © 2018 by Alexander McCall Smith
Interior illustrations copyright © 2018 by Iain McIntosh

All rights reserved. Published in the United States by Delacorte Press,
an imprint of Random House Children's Books,
a division of Penguin Random House LLC, New York.
Originally published in hardcover by BC Books,
an imprint of Birlinn Limited, Edinburgh, Scotland, in 2018.

Delacorte Press is a registered trademark and the colophon is a trademark of
Penguin Random House LLC.

Visit us on the Web! rhcbooks.com

Educators and librarians, for a variety of teaching tools, visit us at
RHTeachersLibrarians.com

*Library of Congress Cataloging-in-Publication Data*
Names: McCall Smith, Alexander, author. | McIntosh, Iain, illustrator.
Title: The race to Kangaroo Cliff / Alexander McCall Smith ;
illustrations by Iain McIntosh.
Description: First edition. | New York : Delacorte Press, [2018] | "Originally published
in hardcover by BC Books, an imprint of Birlinn Limited, Edinburgh, Scotland, in
2018"—Copyright page. | Summary: The students and crew aboard the School Ship
Tobermory head to Australia to take part in a tall ships race, but an unexpected change
of course brings a different kind of adventure.
Identifiers: LCCN 2018021321 (print) | LCCN 2018032440 (ebook) |
ISBN 978-0-399-55407-0 (ebook) | ISBN 978-0-399-55405-6 (trade hardcover)
Subjects: | CYAC: Sea stories. | Sailing—Fiction. | Boarding schools—Fiction. |
Schools—Fiction. | Adventure and adventurers—Fiction. | Australia—Fiction.
Classification: LCC PZ7.M47833755 (ebook) | LCC PZ7.M47833755 Rac 2018 print) |
DDC [Fic]—dc23

The text of this book is set in 12-point Cambria.
Interior design by Trish Parcell

Printed in the United States of America
10 9 8 7 6 5 4 3 2 1
First Edition

This
book is for
Roderick
McCall Smith

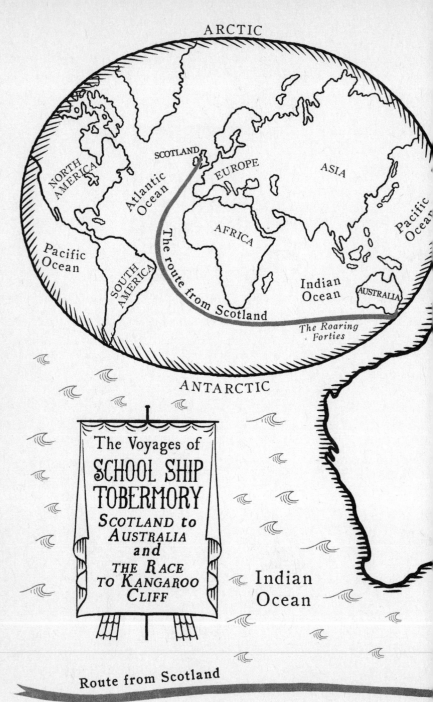

## CHAPTER 1

*An unusual rescue*

"Iceberg ahead!"

Those two words were enough to make the hairs on the back of Ben's neck stand on end.

They were shouted out by Badger, Ben's friend with whom he shared a cabin on board the *Tobermory,* a training ship and boarding school. Badger gave his warning when they were both on watch duty—their job was to look out for signs of ice, or anything else that could be a danger.

They were standing together at the prow, the very front of the ship. Above and behind them, secured to the towering masts, were the rigging and the great expanse of sails that drove their course. The wind was light, although it had blown strongly earlier that morning, and the ship was traveling slowly. That was just as well, as the last thing you wanted to do was find yourself going too fast when there were icebergs.

Ben strained his eyes. The early-morning fog, thick and clammy like a cold white potato soup all about them, made it impossible to see very far. "Are you sure?" he asked his friend.

Badger nodded. "It was over there," he said, pointing to the bank of swirling fog. "The fog's hiding it now, but I'm sure it was there." He paused. "Or pretty sure."

"One hundred percent sure?" Ben pressed him.

Badger hesitated. "Ninety percent," he replied. "Or eighty . . ."

"Should we tell the Captain?" asked Ben.

Badger hesitated again. Nobody wanted a false alarm, but nobody liked crashing into an iceberg. He made up his mind. "I think we should warn him," he said. "It's always better to be safe than sorry. You go, Ben—I'll stay here and keep a lookout."

Ben ran back down the deck toward the Quarterdeck, where Captain Macbeth, the skipper—and school principal—was standing with some of the teachers and the student crew.

Captain Macbeth

"Badger thinks he saw an iceberg," Ben informed him.

Captain Macbeth had been talking to Miss Worsfold, but he cut off his conversation when he heard Ben's report.

"An iceberg, you say? Where?"

"Dead ahead," said Ben. "But a fogbank has swallowed it up and we can't see it any longer."

The Captain lost no time. Shouting out his instructions, he changed the course of the great ship, causing all but a few of the sails to lose their wind and flap loosely about. Almost immediately, the ship was slowed down.

"You come with me," said Captain Macbeth to Ben. "We'll find out what's to be seen up there."

They joined Badger at his post.

"Any further sightings?" asked the Captain.

Badger was about to say, "No, sir, nothing," but stopped himself, as ahead of them, off their starboard bow, the fog had cleared. Appearing from behind its swirling cover was the steeply rising shape of an iceberg. It was not large, by the standards of such things, but it was quite bulky enough to cause serious damage to any ship that collided with it.

"There it is!" shouted Badger.

"Yes," said the Captain. "I see it now."

Looking through his telescope, the Captain was able to tell that the iceberg was hardly moving and that if they kept on their current course they would not get too close to it.

"Well spotted," he said to Badger. "These things can easily sink a ship."

The Captain looked again at the iceberg. Something had caught his attention.

"Well, well," he said. "Now, there's a sight you don't see often."

Ben asked him what he had seen, and the Captain's answer was to pass him his telescope. "Take a look at the bottom right-hand corner," he said.

Ben focused the instrument. For the most part, all he could see was white, but then, as he adjusted the eyepiece, something else came into focus—something that was small and both black and white. He blinked, and looked again. *Surely not,* he thought, and yet, as he looked again he realized that his first impression had been correct. It was a penguin. There was a penguin on the iceberg—a tiny marooned penguin standing on the edge of the ice, looking back at him across the expanse of cold water.

"It's a penguin!" exclaimed Ben. "There's a little penguin on the iceberg."

By now they had been joined by others who had been working nearby and had come to see what the excitement was all about, including Poppy, an Australian girl who was a close friend of Ben's sister, Fee. Other friends, Angela Singh and Thomas Seagrape, passed around the telescope. They all expressed surprise at seeing a penguin in such a lonely and improbable place.

"It can happen," said the Captain. "I've seen penguins trapped on ice floes before. So I suppose they can end up on icebergs, too.

"It might have hopped up on it just before that chunk of

ice separated itself," he went on. "Then, before it knew it, the ice could have drifted off."

"Poor creature," said Thomas Seagrape. "It must be miles and miles from all the other penguins."

For a while there was a silence. Ben imagined they were all thinking the same thing, but he was the one who put it into words. "Will it die?" he asked.

The Captain frowned. "I'm afraid it won't be able to survive much longer all by itself. So . . . well, yes, I'm sorry to say, it probably will die."

Again there was a silence. The ship was moving slowly and the ice was drifting along at much the same pace. For a while, at least, they and the little penguin were companions in the middle of this vast ocean.

It was Thomas Seagrape who spoke next. "Can't we rescue it?"

All eyes turned to Captain Macbeth. He looked at the students: it was clear that he was wrestling with an answer. They had a lengthy journey ahead of them, and it would take at least an hour to lower a boat and row over to the iceberg, rescue the penguin, and then bring it back to the ship. An hour may not seem like a long time, but when you are crossing a great ocean, an hour's delay may mean that you miss the wind or wander off your course.

And yet there are more important things in life than being on time.

"Are you really keen to do that?" asked the Captain.

The answer came in a chorus of voices—saying the same thing: yes.

"In that case," said the Captain, giving his orders quickly, "Poppy, you get a crew together to row over to the iceberg. Thomas, you go and tell Miss Worsfold that I would like her to skipper the boat across."

With a broad smile on his face, Thomas Seagrape saluted briskly and set off. For her part, Poppy immediately appointed Fee and Angela to her boat crew, along with Badger and Ben. They all went to fetch their life jackets and their warmest sea clothing. Rowing up to an iceberg would be a chilly business, Poppy warned them. She had never done it herself, but just one glance in the direction of the great chunk of ice was enough to tell her that this was so.

Miss Worsfold spoke to them before they climbed down the gangway to the lowered boat.

"We're setting out on a dangerous mission," she said. "I want everybody to be extra careful, as the water round here is really cold. If anybody falls in, then we'll be in serious trouble. You don't have much time in water this cold before your muscles stop working. Does everybody understand that?"

They nodded.

"Now, when we reach the iceberg," said Miss Worsfold, "it might be very difficult to get onto it. Icebergs are slippery and you'll need to have a good sense of balance. I'll go myself, but I'll need a volunteer to come with me."

The teacher looked around her. "Poppy," she continued, "you'll have to stay on the boat, as you'll be in charge of the oars. Is there anybody here who's ever done any ice-skating?"

Fee put up her hand. "I have, Miss Worsfold."

"Would you like to come with me, then?" asked Miss Worsfold. "You'll have developed a bit of balance on the ice rink."

Fee nodded. She was happy to assist, and she listened carefully as Miss Worsfold explained how she planned to catch the penguin. "They're trusting birds," she said. "Usually you can walk right up to them. But we'll take a fishing net—just in case."

They were ready to depart, and one by one they made their way down to the large rowboat that was bobbing up and down at the side of the ship. Above them, lining the ship's railings, were most of the other students. When the ship had slowed down, they had realized that something was happening and had all come to witness the rescue in progress. Although excited, they were quiet as they watched the boat, commanded by Miss Worsfold and rowed by Poppy and crew, move away from the side of the *Tobermory*.

The iceberg had drifted a bit closer to the ship, and it did not take them long to row across to its side.

"Ship oars!" commanded Poppy when they were close enough.

This was the instruction to stop rowing, and it brought the small boat to a stop. They were within touching distance of the iceberg, and Poppy was able to toss a rope across to its side. At the end of this rope was a small grappling hook that dug into the surface of the berg once the rope was given a tug. This anchored the boat and enabled Miss Worsfold and Fee to step out onto a flat section of the floating chunk of ice.

It was a tricky business walking toward the penguin, and once or twice Fee had to stretch out her arms on either side to regain her balance. The penguin was not far away, on a shelf of ice just above the surface of the water, and it watched them passively as they approached.

"I don't think it's frightened," whispered Fee.

"Neither do I," agreed Miss Worsfold. "And I don't think we'll need our net."

They approached the marooned bird very slowly, Miss Worsfold holding out a hand toward it as if offering food. Her hand was only a few inches away when there was a sudden splash in the water just beneath the place where the penguin was sitting. And at the same time, there was a loud noise—something between a bark and a snarl.

Miss Worsfold and Fee looked down into the water with horror. There, its head projecting from the surface, was the largest seal either of them had ever seen. And as they

stared at it, the seal opened its mouth to reveal a set of massive curved teeth.

Miss Worsfold acted quickly, pushing Fee back from the edge of the ice. Then, scooping up the surprised penguin, she shouted out to Fee to follow her back to the waiting boat.

Once they reached the boat, Miss Worsfold passed the penguin to Poppy, who placed it carefully in the small wooden box they had brought to transport it. The penguin did not struggle, seeming to be quite happy to go along with this unexpected rescue attempt.

As the boat made its way back to the *Tobermory*, they heard a loud cheer come across the water from the ship. Everybody on board had seen what had happened and was applauding the bravery of the rescue crew.

Miss Worsfold sat in the boat and wiped her brow. "That was a narrow escape," she said, her voice revealing the fear she had just experienced. "That wasn't an ordinary seal, everybody—that was a leopard seal."

Fee shivered at the thought. They had been within striking distance of one of the most dangerous creatures in the sea—a creature that would be quite able to make a meal of you if it found you in its waters. If they had waited a few seconds longer, the seal could have launched itself up out of the water and sunk its teeth into the closest human leg. And if that had happened, then the unfortunate victim would have been dragged down into the icy water below. It did not bear thinking about.

The Captain welcomed them back on board. His first officer, Mr. Rigger, who also taught knots and sailing skills, had already prepared a small hutch for the penguin. This was placed near the stern, in a position where the penguin would get lots of fresh air and would be able to shelter from the wind. Cook had already found a couple of fresh fish that had been placed in a small bowl just inside the hutch. It was as fine a home as any penguin could hope for—and was much better than the perilous sanctuary that the iceberg had provided.

Cook had also prepared a mug of warming hot chocolate for every member of the rescue crew. This was served downstairs in the mess hall, and as they sipped at the welcome hot drink, Miss Worsfold explained what had happened.

"I think the penguin had become a bit weak," she said. "He would have been sitting on the iceberg, too frightened, perhaps, to dive for fish. And the reason he was frightened—well, we discovered that, didn't we, Fee?"

Fee shuddered at the memory of that great mouth with its wicked-looking teeth.

"You see," continued Miss Worsfold, "I think the penguin was not the only passenger on that iceberg."

Poppy drew in her breath. "You mean the seal lived on it too?"

Miss Worsfold nodded. "That leopard seal had probably decided to hitch a ride on the iceberg. It would have been all right, because they are very efficient hunters and there would have been plenty of fish swimming around the ice below. But what it really wanted to eat, I should think, was a tasty meal of penguin. And that was about to happen when Fee and I happened to drop in."

"So you saved the penguin from becoming a meal for a leopard seal?" asked Badger.

Miss Worsfold said that this was so. "I think we were just in time," she said.

"I'm glad," said Badger. But then he realized they could not keep the penguin on board forever—they would have to find a home for it. But they were not going to sail farther south to Antarctica. They would have to find somewhere else for it.

Badger asked Miss Worsfold what they would do with the penguin. She confessed that she had not thought too much about that, but she imagined there were zoos in

Australia, where they were heading, that would be able to offer it a comfortable home. "It will get everything it needs," she said. "A pool to swim in, lots of fresh fish each day, and—for the hot weather—a refrigerated enclosure in which to spend the night."

Miss Worsfold had more to say about penguins—and about the other creatures that lived at the cold ends of the world. "They're finding it a bit difficult these days," she said. "Polar ice caps are melting, and that means their territory is shrinking."

Poppy had read that polar bears, in particular, were suffering. "They don't have enough to eat," she said. "And they're getting caught on ice floes."

Miss Worsfold nodded sadly. "It's a hard time for our fellow creatures," she said. "Not only for polar bears and penguins, but also for elephants and wolves and tigers . . ."

"But at least we've saved one penguin," said Badger. "And that's a good thing?"

Miss Worsfold looked a bit more cheerful. "You're right, Badger." She paused. "And would you like to be in charge of the penguin feeding schedule?"

Badger said he would, but only if Fee would be in charge with him. "She's the one who rescued him," he said. "With you, of course, Miss Worsfold."

Fee was happy to be involved. She would do Monday to Wednesday, while Badger would do Thursday to Saturday. Poppy could cover Sunday, if she agreed, which she did.

"That's fixed up, then," said Miss Worsfold. "Speak to Cook about fish. There's enough in the freezers, so our penguin shouldn't go hungry." She was about to say something else about fish but stopped. "Our penguin . . . I think we'll have to find a name for him."

"Or her," said Poppy.

"Yes, I suppose we don't know right now which is which. But I think Cook will be able to tell us."

Fee was puzzled. "Cook? Does he know about penguins?"

"Not especially," said Miss Worsfold. "But he's always been a keen bird-watcher. He'll know."

"Can't we have a name that suits both a boy and a girl penguin?" asked Poppy.

"Such as?" said Miss Worsfold. "Any ideas?"

It was Ben who said the first thing that came into his mind. "Feathers," he said. "How about Feathers?"

Everybody agreed that Feathers was a good name for the penguin and that it did not matter whether he was a he or she was a she. The important thing was that he (or she) had been saved from being a leopard seal's lunch.

"We could call the leopard seal Jaws," suggested Poppy.

That night as Badger and Ben lay in their hammocks after lights-out, Badger asked Ben a question.

"Would you prefer to be eaten by a shark or a seal, Ben?"

Ben replied that he did not think it would make much difference. "It would hurt pretty badly either way," he said.

"Or a whale?" Badger asked. "I wonder what it would be like to be swallowed by a whale."

"It would be very dark," said Ben. "But at least you'd be able to breathe. And then, when the whale opened his mouth, you could swim out again."

"I'd prefer not to get too close to any of those," Badger mused. Remembering where the ship was headed, he asked Ben what were the animals he hoped he would *not* meet in Australia.

"One of those very poisonous spiders you find there," said Ben in the darkness. "I don't much like the sound of them."

"Or a saltwater crocodile," suggested Badger. He had been reading about Australian wildlife and he had not liked what he read about their crocodiles. "It's the most aggressive crocodile in the world," he went on. "It will even chase you on land."

"I'll keep a good lookout," muttered Ben. He was beginning to feel sleepy, and was not sure that he wanted to drop off with thoughts of crocodiles in his mind. That would be a surefire way of ensuring that he had nightmares about being pursued by giant scaly creatures.

But Badger had more to say. "It doesn't matter if you

keep a good lookout," he warned. "You can't see them, you know. They're just below the surface of the water, and you don't always notice them until it's too late."

"Oh, well . . . ," Ben said. "You can't stop doing things just because of crocodiles. . . ."

And with that he fell asleep and did not hear what else Badger had to say—which did not matter too much, as Badger himself was tired by now and had little to add about crocodiles or anything else.

# CHAPTER 2

*Where are we going next?*

How was it that Ben and Fee and sixty other young people should find themselves on a sailing ship on the far southern oceans rescuing—of all unlikely things—a stranded penguin? The answer is that they were at school—which is where just about everyone of their age has to spend a lot of time—but in their case their school happened to be a ship.

The *Tobermory*, in fact, was one of the best-known school ships in the world. It was based in Scotland, on the island of Mull, and it took young people from many different countries. What they had in common was the desire to learn about ships and the sea while at the same time doing all the usual things that you do at school. This meant that it would be easier—if they wanted it—to become sailors when they grew up.

Ben and Fee, twins who had just celebrated their thirteenth birthday, had joined the *Tobermory* because their parents, who were famous marine scientists, had to be away a great deal. Because of this, they could not go to an ordinary school, but had to find a boarding school where they would stay while their parents were far away on the family research submarine.

Ben MacTavish

"I'm glad that we chose the *Tobermory*," said Fee to her brother. "Not all boarding schools can be as much fun as this."

Ben agreed. "I love being here," he said. "I like everything about it."

He liked the Captain—Captain Macbeth—who had a friendly dog called Henry. He liked the Captain's assistant, Mr. Rigger, with his famous mustache that could act as a weather vane and would let you know where the wind was coming from. He liked Matron, who had been a famous diver in the Olympics before she met and married Cook, who made possibly the best sausages in the Northern

Fee MacTavish

**Mr. Rigger**

Hemisphere. And of course he liked all the friends he had made since he joined the school.

His main friend was Badger, with whom he shared a cabin. While Ben came from Scotland, Badger was an American boy whose parents lived in New York. His father was extremely busy and traveled a great deal for work so had little time to spend with his son. This saddened Badger. Badger would have preferred to grow up seeing more of his father. But he never complained. Badger was like that—he looked for the positive side of things.

Badger was a good friend. Ben liked his cheerful attitude and his special talent. That talent was the ability, when he was speaking to you, to make you feel that of all the people in the world, you were the one he really wanted to be talking to. Ben had noticed that some people let their eyes wander when they spoke to you. Badger never did that.

**Matron**

Ben's sister, Fee, had a special friend in Poppy, who came from Australia. "Plenty of people who

Badger

are good at things make you feel small," Fee had explained to Ben. "They push you aside and do things much better than you can. Poppy never does that. She shows you how to do something and then you do it together. That makes you feel proud to have done something that you otherwise might not have been able to do." Poppy was helpful and a great new friend.

There were other friends in the group. Thomas Seagrape, who came from an island in the Caribbean, knew a lot about the sea. His mother was the skipper of a ship that ran between Jamaica and nearby islands. Ben liked Thomas not only because of his big smile and his kindness, but also because he was brave.

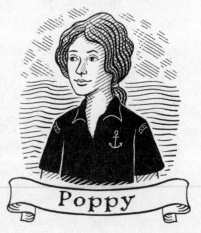

Poppy

Tanya had been a stowaway who had been allowed to stay on board ship because of the Captain's good heart. He realized that if he sent her home, she would have had to

Thomas Seagrape

return to her wicked uncle and aunt, who ran a dog kennel in Scotland and who made Tanya work for no pay. Her father was a sailor who had lost touch with her, but she hoped that she would find him somewhere on the world's great oceans.

Angela Singh came from India and was good at mathematics and history, but tended to be a bit nervous about everything else. Angela was becoming more courageous, as encouraged by Poppy.

"Don't think too much about what might go wrong," Poppy had advised her. "Just take a deep breath and do what you have to do."

On board ship you are more or less bound to have one or two people who are not so nice. In this case it was three, and their names were William Edward Hardtack, who was Head Prefect of the Upper Deck; Geoffrey Shark, who was extremely pleased with himself and

Tanya Herring

Angela Singh

with his fancy hair style; and Maximilian Flubber, whose ears flapped backwards and forwards whenever he told a lie, which was quite often.

There was not much anybody could do about this group.

"They're like bad weather," said Poppy. "You have to put up with bad weather, and so you have to put up with Hardtack and Co. It's just the way it is."

"They're not going to spoil anything for me," said Fee.

"Nor for me," agreed Angela.

But that was easier said than done. The trouble with people like Hardtack, Shark, and Flubber was that spoiling things for other people was exactly what they liked to do.

The voyage to Australia came a short while after the *Tobermory* had returned from sailing around the Caribbean Sea. That had been a particularly exciting trip. Once they had returned to Tobermory, the port after which the ship was named, the students themselves wondered what would be their next destination.

There were plenty of rumors.

"I've heard we're going to sail to Hong Kong," said Badger one morning at breakfast.

William Edward Hardtack

Maximilian Flubber

Geoffrey Shark

Poppy looked surprised. "Oh yes?" she said. "Well, I heard that it was going to be South America—Chile in particular."

"No," said Tanya. "I saw Matron studying a chart of the seas around India. I bet it's going to be India—because why else would Matron be looking at that chart?"

Thomas Seagrape had an altogether different theory. "I heard Cook talking about how to get to San Francisco. He said something about the Panama Canal. So I think we're going all the way to the west coast of America."

Poppy laughed. "Let's face it," she said. "We've all heard different things and the *Tobermory* can't be going to all those different places. Why don't we . . ."

"Ask the Captain?" suggested Fee.

"Exactly," said Poppy.


At dinnertime one day, when Captain Macbeth came to the mess hall to address the whole school, he asked whether anybody wanted to ask any questions.

At first everybody was silent. Then a hand went up. It was Badger's.

"Yes, Tomkins?" said the Captain.

Badger stood up and cleared his throat.

"I was wondering," began Badger. "I mean, quite a few of us were wondering where we'll be going next."

Captain Macbeth smiled. "Oh you were, were you?" he said.

Badger nodded. "It's just that . . . it's just that it's good to know where you're going to be."

The Captain turned to Mr. Rigger, who was standing at his side, and said, "That seems like a perfectly good reason."

Mr. Rigger nodded. "I'd say so, Captain."

The atmosphere in the mess hall was electric with anticipation.

"It's going to be in the Southern Hemisphere," said Captain Macbeth.

Mr. Rigger nodded. "Southern Hemisphere," he echoed.

The Captain was enjoying himself. "I can reveal to you that it's a continent."

Hardtack called out, "Antarctica."

The Captain shook his head. "No, not Antarctica."

Fee was particularly good at geography, and so she realized that there were not many other choices. She put up her hand.

"Are we going to Australia?" she asked.

"Yes," said the Captain. "That's exactly where we're going." And then he added, "And we shall be leaving next week."

The Captain then went on to explain why Australia had been chosen as their destination. "Australia's a wonderful country," he began. "It's worth going there just to see it. But there's something more. There's going to be a tall-ships race out here, starting in Queensland and heading all the way up round the tip of the continent. I was asked if we would take part, and I said we would. I thought you might enjoy a spot of racing."

At this announcement, a loud cheer rang through the mess hall. A number of people had been hoping that Australia would be the *Tobermory*'s next destination

Poppy was especially pleased by this news. She came from Alice Springs, right in the middle of Australia, where her parents ran a sheep farm. If the ship called in at Sydney or Melbourne, she was sure that her mother and father would make the long journey to meet them. She would then be able to show them around her school, which she had been keen to do ever since she started. She liked the idea of being able to introduce her friends on board to some of the things that in her mind made Australia one of the best places on earth. She would show them kangaroos and wallabies; she would take them camping in the bush and brew up a pot of tea in her billy can; she would take them to see people who knew how to throw a boomerang properly; she would take them to a beach where they could go surfing.

Not everybody was happy. As they filed out of the mess hall, Poppy found herself close to William Edward Hardtack and his friends. "Boring, boring," muttered Hardtack. "Who wants to go to a place that's covered with eucalyptus trees? Who wants to go to a really boring place like Australia?"

"Not me," said Geoffrey Shark.

"Nor me," added Maximilian Flubber, his ears beginning to twitch.

Poppy felt her cheeks flush with rage. "Excuse me," she hissed. "Have you ever been to Australia, Hardtack? Or you, Shark? Or, Flubber, you too—have you ever been there?"

"Never wanted to," snapped Hardtack.

"Too many people like you there," said Shark.

This made the other two laugh.

"You're ignorant," said Poppy, struggling to control herself.

Chuckling over what they thought of as their witty remarks, the three boys disappeared down the corridor.

"Ignore them," said Angela Singh. "I can't wait to see Australia—and I think just about everybody else on board feels the same." She had a question, but she couldn't quite bring herself to pose it. She wanted to ask about spiders and snakes, but she knew that everybody was aware of her worries about such things, and so she said nothing.

Poppy looked at her friend—and smiled. She could guess what Angela was thinking.

"And you mustn't worry about . . ." Poppy lowered her voice. "About funnel web spiders and so on—Australia's a pretty safe place."

Angela swallowed hard. "Oh, I wasn't worried," she said.

"Of course you weren't," said Poppy kindly. But both girls knew that what each of them had just said was, in fact, the opposite of what they really felt.

# CHAPTER 3

*Flubber slips*

They had to get to Australia first, and that involved a long sea voyage. Captain Macbeth explained it to them on the day before they were due to weigh anchor and set off.

"As you know," he said, "Australia is on the other side of the world from Scotland, and that means it will take us at least eight weeks to get there."

Everybody looked at one another as they absorbed this news.

"Eight weeks at sea!" Fee whispered to Poppy. She wondered what it would be like to see no sign of dry land for that long. And would their supplies of food hold out for such a length of time, or would they have to catch fish to keep them going?

Poppy smiled. "We'll get used to it. And time will pass quickly enough—it always does when you're on a ship."

The Captain went on to describe their route. They would take the same course used by sailing ships in the days of clippers—the fast ships that sailed between England and

Australia back in the eighteen hundreds. That would take them down the middle of the Atlantic Ocean, past the bulge of South America, and then straight across to Australia.

"The winds we want to catch down there," Captain Macbeth went on, "are called the Roaring Forties."

Miss Worsfold had talked about these winds, Fee remembered, in one of her geography lessons. The name the Roaring Forties said it all. The *Forties* referred to the winds' latitude—how far they were south of the equator—and *Roaring* was what high winds did.

Mr. Rigger took over from Captain Macbeth to explain that the farther south they went, the shorter the route—and the better the winds. "But," he added, "going that far south increases the chance of finding ice. So we shall have to be careful."

"Extremely careful," agreed the Captain. "Remember the *Titanic*."

The *Titanic* had been a famous passenger liner that hit an iceberg on her maiden voyage and sank as a result. The ship company had boasted that she was unsinkable, but that had been proved to be untrue: the *Titanic* had gone to the bottom of the sea, along with many of her unfortunate passengers. Hitting an iceberg was the same as hitting a mountain, and few ships could survive unharmed.

These warnings, though, did not spoil the excitement, and over the few days that remained before they set off, the mood on the *Tobermory* was an excited one. All classes were suspended while the ship was prepared. Everything was washed, polished, and double-checked. Ropes were coiled, rigging tightened, and decks scrubbed until not a speck of dirt remained, and then scrubbed again. Supplies were brought aboard from onshore: bags of rice and flour, crates of canned beans and sausages, sacks of potatoes, great blocks of butter ready for use—everything that would be needed to make three meals a day for the full ship's company.

"There are no corner shops at sea," Cook was fond of pointing out. "So if we run out of anything, we can't just nip out and buy it!"

This meant that everybody had to have enough shampoo and toothpaste to last for many weeks. Matron would give you more if you ran out, but not without making you listen to a lecture about not having planned things properly.

At last the *Tobermory* was ready to leave the small harbor that shared her name.

On the morning of their departure, Badger was washed and dressed by the time Ben woke up. As a special treat for his friend, Badger had gone off to the galley, where morning tea was served from a large urn, and brought a mug back to Ben.

"Time to wake up," he said once he was back in their cabin. "Here's your mug of tea in bed—I mean, in hammock."

Ben rubbed the sleep from his eyes and accepted the mug of steaming tea.

"You're really kind, Badge," he said as he took his first sip of the hot liquid.

"It's what friends are for," Badger replied, smiling. "Besides, I woke up at least an hour ago and was too excited to go back to sleep."

"I think I was dreaming about the Roaring Forties when you woke me up," said Ben. "I dreamed that there were massive waves and the ship was tilting right over."

"That's what it's going to be like," Badger said. "Only, it won't be a dream."

They sailed down the coast of Ireland, through the Irish Sea, and then out into the open Atlantic. The Atlantic is one of the great oceans of the world, and only seagoing ships, tough and well made, can stand some of the conditions found out there. The famous Atlantic swell is one of the tests awaiting sailors—these are vast mountains of water that travel from one side of the ocean to the other, lifting up and then dropping whatever floats on them. Then there were the waves themselves, which can be as high as a house, towering above ships and sometimes breaking with immense force, crushing whatever is below them under tons of cascading water.

On the *Tobermory*, new rules were now issued by the Captain.

"When you're on deck," the Captain announced to the student sailors as they left the protective cover of Ireland, "if the sea is rough, you must—and I mean *must*—have life-lines clipped on to your life jackets at all times. Anybody found on deck in such conditions without a lifeline will have to answer to Mr. Rigger and me. And we shall not be lenient—I can assure you of that. Isn't that so, Mr. Rigger?"

Mr. Rigger nodded gravely. "I've seen people swept off deck," he warned. "If they'd been wearing lifelines, they would still be with us." He paused. "Instead, they're down in Davy Jones's locker."

"That means they drowned," whispered Poppy.

Ben gave an involuntary shiver. He could imagine what it must be like to be swept overboard and realize that you may not be rescued. The trouble with going overboard in high seas is that you could very quickly disappear behind a large wave and people on board may not spot you. He shivered again. He would wear his lifeline—he was certain of that.

For their first few days in the Atlantic, the ocean behaved. Although there was a small swell—nothing much more than little hillocks of water—the sea seemed calm and everyone was wondering what all those dire warnings had been about. But then, on the third day out, the school awoke to a sky that was filled with dark gray clouds. The wind was rising now, and it was beginning to whistle through the rigging, making a long, low moaning sound— rather like an animal in distress.

The Captain gave the order for life jackets to be worn and for lifelines to be attached. Mr. Rigger checked everybody before they went on deck, sending anybody who had forgotten to put on a life jacket back down below to find one. Up on deck, it was the turn of Poppy, Fee, and Angela to be on watch. Poppy was at the helm and Fee was standing immediately beside her. Angela was in charge of watching the compass, giving Poppy a warning if she needed to steer the ship back on course.

It all happened quickly—as things at sea so often do— and this time it started with a remark from Poppy at the wheel.

She had spotted Maximilian Flubber crossing the deck, on his way to join Geoffrey Shark and William Edward Hardtack, who were on starboard watch at the time.

"Flubber!" shouted Poppy. "Your life jacket! Did you

take it off? Where is it? Captain says we're all to wear life jackets and have safety lines until this wind dies down."

Flubber halted in his tracks and stared at Poppy. Then, cupping his hands so that he could be heard against the wailing of the wind, he shouted his response: "Mind your own business!"

Poppy felt the anger well up within her. It *was* her business, because if Flubber were to be washed overboard when she was on the helm, she would have to steer the ship around to rescue him. No, she had every right to tell him to put on his life jacket.

"Flubber," she said. "I'm at the helm and I'm telling you—put on your life jacket!"

Flubber laughed, and although nobody was thinking this at the time, if things had turned out just a little differently it could have been the last laugh of his life.

Flubber continued to saunter across the deck, and did not see the large wave building up off the side of the *Tobermory*. This was a rogue wave—the name given to a large wave that comes from an unexpected direction. A large-enough rogue wave can sink a ship if it hits it in the wrong place. This wave did not do that, but it did break over the deck of the *Tobermory*, flooding it badly, washing various ropes and buckets over the side of the ship and into the angry sea below—and sweeping Flubber off his feet.

Shocked and surprised, Flubber might easily have been washed off the deck altogether and into the open sea had he not managed to grab on to the railings as he headed off the side. This left him half on the ship and half off it, clinging on to the steel railings with all his strength, shouting for help at the top of his lungs.

The crash of the waves and the howling of the wind drowned his cries, with the result that Hardtack and Shark did not hear him. Nor did they see him, as they were looking out to sea in the opposite direction when this happened. Poppy saw him, though, as did Fee, and they both gave a shout.

"Flubber! Flubber's going overboard!"

Not far away, Badger heard this shouting and looked up. On the other side of the deck he saw two hands gripping on to the railing and two arms below that, hanging on for dear life. Without a second's hesitation, Badger launched himself across the deck, wading through the last of the draining wave to reach his imperiled shipmate. As Badger reached the side, Flubber was just about to let go. Fortunately, he still had a few ounces of strength left in him, and this kept him from disappearing into the sea.

"Hang on!" shouted Badger as he took hold of Flubber's wrists. "Hold on—I'm going to pull you back aboard."

Badger tensed his muscles, and then, with a supreme effort, he gave as strong a yank as he could manage. This brought Flubber back onto the deck, wet right through, panting and spluttering every bit as much as if he were a fish plucked from the water.

Mr. Rigger now appeared. He had heard Poppy and Fee shouting and had come up on deck to see what was happening. Peering down on the sodden bundle that was Maximilian Flubber, he spoke firmly to the rescued boy.

"Why no life jacket, Mr. Flubber?" he asked. "Didn't you hear the Captain warn you?"

Flubber sat up and tried to wipe the salt water out of his eyes.

"I was on my way to fetch it, Mr. Rigger," he said. "Then this great big wave came. I promise you that's what happened."

It was a lie, of course—Flubber was always telling lies—and his ears started to wiggle, as they always did when he lied.

"Is that so?" Mr. Rigger asked Badger. "Was Flubber going to get his life jacket?"

Badger did not know what to say. Nobody likes to tattle, but at the same time, nobody—except people like Flubber—likes to tell a direct lie.

"Well?" said Mr. Rigger. He stared at Badger, waiting for the boy to answer, but Badger remained silent.

Flubber spoke. "Can I get up, Mr. Rigger?" he asked. "I've got water in my ears and I need to get it out."

Mr. Rigger sighed. "Listen to me, Flubber, you could have been drowned right before our eyes. Never, ever forget your life jacket when the wind and the sea are in this bad mood. Remember that."

Flubber rose to his feet. Mr. Rigger looked at Flubber and Badger; then he went back to what he was doing.

"That was close," said Badger.

Flubber was dismissive. "I was never going to drown," he said. "People like me don't drown. It's you guys who drown because you're useless swimmers."

Badger ignored this provocation. He knew that there was no point arguing with Flubber. Rather, he would give a full report to the Captain so that he might know exactly what was going on. If he wanted to punish Flubber, then that was the Captain's business, and William Edward Hardtack would be unable to blame him. Of course, Flubber should have thanked Poppy, Fee, and Badger, but he didn't.

By now, Hardtack and Shark had come across to find out what had happened.

"You okay, Flubs?" asked Hardtack. "These people bothering you?"

Badger drew in his breath. He had saved Flubber's life, and now they were beginning to threaten him.

Flubber looked down at the deck. He did not look at Badger as he spoke. "It's all right, Tacky," he said. "I'm fine."

Hardtack gave Badger a warning glance, and then led Flubber back to where Shark was standing. Badger went to join Poppy and Fee, who were still standing at the helm.

"I can't believe it," said Poppy. "Flubber should have thanked you for saving his life. He didn't say a word, did he?"

Badger shook his head. "No, he didn't."

He was right, of course—Flubber had not said so much as the smallest thank-you. But that evening when they were all in the mess hall having their dinner, Flubber appeared behind Badger's chair and whispered something in his ear.

"I meant to say thank you," he said. "And I would have said it if it hadn't been for . . ." He left the sentence unfinished.

"If it hadn't been for what?" asked Badger.

Flubber gave a nervous look in the direction of the table where Hardtack and Shark were sitting.

"If it hadn't been for Tacky," he said. "He didn't want me to."

For a while, Badger said nothing. But Flubber's words made him think. Perhaps Flubber was weak and Hardtack was strong—and Hardtack knew that he could bully him into doing his bidding.

Badger looked into Flubber's eyes. He saw weakness there—and fear.

"You have a choice, Flubber," he said quietly. "I know that it can't be easy being Hardtack's friend."

Flubber looked back at him with gratitude. "Thanks, Badger," he said, his voice so low as to be almost inaudible. "I'll remember that."

## CHAPTER 4

*Surf dog*

Off the coast of South America the winds died down and the sea, responding to these changed conditions, became friendlier. Instead of huge rollers traveling from horizon to horizon, there were small, well-behaved waves that you could barely feel on a big ship like the *Tobermory*. It was warmer, too. The wind farther north had been cool and sometimes even cold; now it was like the breath of a large animal on the skin—a comfortable blowing that would never make you shiver or seek shelter. The sun added to this good feeling—it shone without interruption from dawn until dusk, dancing on the surface of the water with golden shoes.

Ordinary lessons had begun again in the classrooms down below. Miss Worsfold started her geography lessons, which introduced everybody to currents and the effect they had not only on ships but also on the weather.

"There's an important current called El Niño," she explained. "It flows off the other coast of South America, but it's responsible for droughts and floods all over the world."

She drew a picture on the board.

Miss Worsfold

"That's a big current," she said. "There are smaller, weaker currents all around us, and if you're a sailor, you should know about them. Why?"

Angela Singh put up her hand. "Because they can give you a free ride," she said. "A boat can go much faster if it lets a current help it along."

Miss Worsfold nodded. "Or more slowly," she said, "if it goes against the current. That's more like walking uphill."

Currents came into other lessons, too, such as the mathematics class that Mr. Rigger taught each morning.

"Let's imagine," he began, "that there's a current of one-point-two knots going east to west. Let's imagine, too, that you're on a ship following a course west to east—that is, against the current. The wind is pushing you along at six knots an hour and you sail for five hours." He paused, looking out over the heads of the class. "How far will you have traveled at the end of those five hours?"

Badger raised his hand.

"Twenty-four miles," he said.

"Wrong," said Mr. Rigger.

Badger looked puzzled. "But six multiplied by five is thirty. Then you take away one-point-two multiplied by five, which is six, and you get twenty-four. Twenty-four miles."

Mr. Rigger shook a finger. "You're forgetting something."

Poppy suddenly realized what it was that Badger had forgotten. "*Nautical* miles!" she burst out.

Mr. Rigger clapped his hands together. "Exactly," he said. "A mile is 1,760 yards or 1,609.34 meters. A *nautical* mile, which is the same as a knot, is . . ."

"1,852 meters," supplied Angela Singh.

"That's right," said Mr. Rigger. "That means that the correct answer to our question is twenty-four *nautical* miles, which is a bit farther than twenty-four miles."

From the back of the class there came a sniggering sound, heard by Badger but not by Mr. Rigger. Geoffrey Shark muttered, "Stupid! Anybody would have known that it was nautical miles and not ordinary miles. Stupid, stupid, stupid!"

Badger bit his lip. He was sure that Shark would not have been able to work it out himself and was in no position to laugh at others.

"Ignore him," whispered Poppy. "Just ignore him."

"I'm glad Badger's not navigating the *Tobermory,*" came a loud whisper. This was from Maximilian Flubber.

This was too much for Poppy, who spun round in her seat and glared in Flubber's direction. "Have you forgotten who saved your life?" she hissed.

Flubber turned away. For a moment he looked ashamed, but then his usual expression returned to his face. Yet Ben, at least, thought there was a chance that the unpleasant threesome of Flubber, Shark, and Hardtack might not be as united as they would like people to believe. He felt that sooner or later one of them—possibly Flubber—would realize Hardtack was just dragging them down and that unless they made a real effort to get away from his influence, things would just get worse. Even if Flubber or Shark realized this, knowing something was not the same as acting upon it. Could Flubber or Shark ever take that important first step of telling Hardtack to his face that they wanted nothing to do with his tricks and plotting? Ben was not sure, but he thought they would not.

The *Tobermory* made its way down the coast of South America. Now they were off Brazil, the largest country on the continent, and would follow the Brazilian shore until the time came to turn off sharply to the east and head for Australia. They knew that once they did that, the Roaring Forties would lie ahead of them. That part of the voyage would be tough, but they had their sea legs and would be able to cope with the deck going violently up and down for days on end. They had calm waters and a view of beaches and jungle to keep them happy this part of the trip.

Henry, the Captain's dog, was a popular member of the

crew. He had no real duties, although he would sometimes be used to warn smaller boats if they were in the way of the *Tobermory*. In that case, Henry would sit up on the prow of the ship and bark loudly, warning others that they risked a collision if they did not give way to the large sailing ship. Usually other sailors appreciated this warning and would wave cheerfully to Henry, who would give an encouraging bark in response.

When he was not acting as lookout in this way, Henry would sometimes take up a position at the rail and look out wistfully over the sea. It was no secret what he was doing on these occasions. A few voyages earlier, the story went that Henry had rescued a mermaid and brought her to safety on the *Tobermory*. Was Henry looking out to sea in the hope of finding another mermaid?

That was the story, but of course, like so many stories you hear at sea, it simply was not true. Nobody has ever seen a mermaid—not a real one—and there was no photograph to prove that mermaids existed. The safest thing to do, when there are no photographs, is to conclude that people are just making things up or passing on a story that has never been checked.

It was a Saturday morning. There were no lessons, and the students of the *Tobermory* were allowed to pass the time in whatever way they liked. The ship was sailing along in a gentle and comfortable way, and although there had to be a few people on watch, helping with the lines or handling the helm, most were able to play chess or cards, or draw in their sketchbooks, or write letters home.

Henry was sitting halfway along the main deck, his tail stretched out behind him, enjoying the warmth of the sun on his dark wet nose. He was not thinking of anything in particular—dogs often think of nothing at all—although every now and then he formed a mental picture of his dinner and imagined that he could already smell the gravy that would be ladled into his bowl that evening, and his tail wagged with pleasure whenever it came to him.

It was while Henry was daydreaming in this way that a school of flying fish was disturbed by the passage of the *Tobermory* through the water. Flying fish are a strange sort of fish, even if one sees a lot of them out at sea. Most fish cannot fly, just as most birds cannot swim underwater. These fish, though, are equipped with a small set of flippers that can act as wings when the fish launch themselves out of the water. Once they do that, these stubby wings flap at high speed, making a whirring sound, just as if they are powered by a loud clockwork motor. It is a sort of *bbbzzz* sound.

Miss Worsfold had explained about flying fish.

"They can't breathe out of the water," she said. "So they don't want to stay in the air too long."

"Then why do they do it?" asked Mike Wood.

"It's because something's chasing them," she said. "When a bigger fish comes after a shoal of flying fish, the one thing they can do that the bigger fish can't do is launch themselves out of the water, fly a little way, and then drop back into a different bit of water. It's all about escape."

As Henry lay on the deck and the students busied themselves with their various hobbies, down below in the water a hungry barracuda—a big fish with sharp teeth—decided that a small cluster of flying fish would make a good midday snack. The flying fish, panicking at the sight of the barracuda, hurled themselves out of the water, began to flap their wings as fast as they possibly could, and set off through the air above the surface.

What they did not notice was the *Tobermory* immediately in front of them. But it was too late to turn back, and so they simply flew slightly higher and shot over the deck of the great sailing ship, heading for the water that they knew would lie on the other side.

Henry, who had been drowsing, suddenly saw a cloud of flying fish directly above his nose. No dog could ignore a challenge like that, and he went scampering after them, barking furiously and determined to catch one, if not two, of these insolent creatures. The flying fish were too fast for Henry and he was unable to clamp his jaws around them. But he was also unable to stop himself in time, and shot off the edge of the deck, following the flying fish in a perfect arc down toward the water.

It was Angela who noticed this happening. She shouted out at the top of her voice and was heard by quite a few others. They all looked up to see what was going on, and were rewarded with the sight of poor Henry flying through the air, dropping down to the water below. And then they saw—and heard—the splash as the poor dog ended up in the sea.

Henry, of course, was a good swimmer, and there was never any danger of his drowning. But it was still not easy to pick him up, as he was soon caught up by a wave that was heading toward the shore. And not only that—floating about in this wave was a small wooden plank and, seeing this, Henry clambered up onto it to use it as a surfboard.

It was a marvelous sight, and there were howls of laughter from the deck of the *Tobermory*. Captain Macbeth heard the noise and came up from below to see what was going on. At first he was alarmed to see his dog in the water, but then, when he saw Henry surfing, his face broke into a broad smile.

It was a simple matter to stop the ship and launch a small boat—captained by Mr. Rigger—to row off to pick up Henry. They had to row all the way to the shore, though, as the plank surfboard had carried Henry at some speed and had deposited him on the edge of the beach, where the waves made a white line of foam and froth.

When he came back on board, he was given a hero's welcome.

"You know," said Mr. Rigger as he watched Henry being dried in a large towel Matron had provided, "I thought I'd

Down below in the water a hungry barracuda decided that the small group of flying fish would make a perfect midday snack....

No dog could ignore such a challenge....

It was a marvelous sight, and there were howls of laughter from the deck of the *Tobermory*....

come across everything there was to see on the oceans, but now ... well, Henry is the very first surfing dog I've ever seen."

Hearing his name mentioned, Henry uttered a bark. A dog's bark can mean anything, but the meaning of this one seemed clear enough: *Please don't underestimate what I can do!*

## CHAPTER 5

### *Shark takes a shower*

They made it across the Roaring Forties much more quickly than they had anticipated, even allowing for the time they'd spent rescuing Feathers the penguin from his dangerous iceberg. That was not the only ice they saw—they narrowly avoided hitting a large chunk one night when the moon went behind a cloud and it was difficult to see what lay ahead. Fee and Angela were on watch at the time and they were both known for their sharp eyesight. Poppy and Badger were at the helm when this happened, and they were able to swing the ship sharply to starboard and just miss the ice floe with a cable or two to spare. A cable is a measurement used at sea and is just over six hundred feet or one hundred and eighty-five meters. That may sound like quite a lot, but at sea, when you're travel-ing at speed and not able to turn all that quickly, it is not much.

Just a day or two before they reached Australia, there was one incident. It had to do with water, which is one of the most precious things on any ship when it is at sea: fresh water. There's any amount of salt water all about you, but you can't drink salt water. So sailors have to watch their supply of fresh water and make sure it lasts until the next time they can fill up with water in a port.

Like any big ship, the *Tobermory* had large tanks down below in which fresh water was stored. Pipes led up from these tanks to the kitchen and then on to the basins and showers in the washrooms. The kitchen staff looked after drinking water, decanting it into large containers from which everybody could fill their individual water bottles. They also filled jugs that were placed on the table at meal-time, allowing students to have a glass of water with their meals.

Fresh water was needed in the washrooms because you can't wash in seawater, nor can you brush your teeth in it. Washing in seawater leaves you covered in salt and feeling sticky; only fresh water will make you properly clean.

Standing under the shower for a long time may make you feel nice and clean, but it uses a large volume of water.

Poppy had explained all this to Fee when she showed her round the ship shortly after Ben and Fee had first joined. "There's a very important rule when it comes to showers," Poppy had said. "No shower longer than two minutes."

Fee frowned. "Two minutes isn't long."

"No, it isn't," said Poppy. "It's really just in and out."

"But why?" asked Fee.

"We need to conserve water," Poppy explained. "There are lots of people on board. If everybody had a long shower—say, ten minutes—we'd run out of water way before we reached the next harbor."

Fee loved long showers, but she understood that these would just not be possible on board. "I'll be careful," she promised.

"Good," said Poppy. "Because if we ran out of water, then we wouldn't have anything to drink." She paused before continuing, "There's a famous poem. It's called *The Rime of the Ancient Mariner.* Do you know it?"

Fee shook her head.

"It's about a ship that runs out of water," said Poppy. "It goes like this:

> *"Water, water, everywhere,*
> *And all the boards did shrink;*
> *Water, water, everywhere,*
> *Nor any drop to drink."*

Fee shivered. "If we ran out of water in the middle of the ocean," she said, "what would happen? Would we die of thirst?"

Poppy shrugged. "If it didn't rain, maybe. However, if it rains you can collect water in a canvas tarpaulin. You rig it up above the deck and it collects all the rainwater. You can get quite a bit that way. Rainwater is not full of salt like ocean water."

Fee was relieved. But Poppy went on, "*If* it rains . . . And it doesn't always rain. How much rain have we had in the past few days?" She paused for a few moments before answering her own question. "None. So if we ran out of water now, it wouldn't be good."

Fee was always careful with fresh water after that—as was everybody, as they heard often enough from the Captain and Matron about the need to conserve supplies. Fee attended Matron's special classes on how to wash your hair in forty-five seconds (if you had long hair) and thirty seconds (for short hair). There were also lessons on how to clean your teeth using less than half a cup of fresh water and how to wash your clothes in a bucket.

All the water tanks had gauges on them, and it was part of the duties of the morning watch to check the levels on these gauges, record them in a book, and report them to the duty officer, who was one of the teachers. When the *Tobermory* was still three days from Australia, it was the turn of Ben and Badger to check the water levels in the main freshwater tank. Because they had been at sea for so long, the two secondary tanks had been used up and the ship would be dependent on the main tank for the rest of the voyage. The Captain had calculated, though, that there would be enough water to see them through, and nobody was worried about a shortage.

The Captain held up a hand. "Calm down," he said. "Take a deep breath—and then tell me what the trouble is. What water are you talking about?"

"The main tank," said Badger. "We were checking the level this morning—"

"As you should be," interjected the Captain. "You're on this watch, aren't you?"

"Yes," said Badger. "So we checked and the gauge was almost at zero. There are only about fifty gallons left."

The Captain frowned. "Which tank are you talking about? One of the secondary tanks?"

Badger shook his head. "No, the main tank, sir. The secondary ones are already empty. The main tank is down to fifty gallons, and if people have their showers this morning . . ."

He did not finish. The consequences of that did not have to be spelled out to the Captain.

As captain of the ship you have to be able to make decisions—and make them quickly. Without losing a moment, Captain Macbeth rushed to a switch near his desk and pushed it. This was the general alarm, which sounded throughout the ship. Everyone had been trained to react to this by making their way up to the main deck, bringing their life jackets with them. It was also a firm rule that you came immediately and that you did not waste time changing or combing your hair or searching for the things you might like to take in a lifeboat.

The main water tank was down in the bilge—the lowest part of the ship. It was put there because there was enough room for it, and although water does not flow uphill, there was a large electric pump that took the water to the upper decks. It was dark down in the bilge, and the only way to see was to use the powerful flashlight kept near the door for exactly this purpose.

Ben took this flashlight and lit the way down the ladder into the bilge.

"I don't like it down here," he confessed to Badger. "It makes me feel a bit . . ."

"Scared?" supplied Badger.

"Yes, I suppose so." It is not easy to admit to people that you are scared, but Ben knew that Badger was not the sort of person to laugh.

"I'm scared too," said Badger reassuringly. "I get scared when it's dark and when there are all sorts of odd sounds."

It was dark where they were—and there were all sorts of odd sounds. These were the creaking and groaning of timbers that are the constant soundtrack to a boat at sea. There were creakings and groanings, as well as other sounds that were more difficult to interpret. There was a buzzing sound and a whistling, and something that sounded just like footsteps, although that was impossible, as they were the only people down there.

*Unless the ship is haunted,* thought Ben. He thought that, but did not say it. He had heard some talk of that, but he knew that people often made up these stories just to frighten one another. This was definitely not the time to raise the possibility.

They made their way down to the bottom of the ladder. Ben played the beam of light over the short walkway that led to the side of the main water tank. They could already see the gauge illuminated in the darkness, although they could not read the figures until they reached the tank. Badger bent down to read the gauge. Ben heard a sharp intake of breath—a gasp.

"Almost empty," whispered Badger. "Only . . . only . . ." He struggled to make out the markings on the gauge. "Only fifty gallons left."

"Fifty gallons!" exclaimed Ben. "That's impossible, Badge. Take another look."

Badger craned his neck to get a better view. "No," he muttered after a while. "It's almost all gone."

Ben leaned forward to take a look himself. He hoped that Badger had got it wrong, but when he looked at the gauge, it told the same story. "Knock on the side of the tank," he said to Badger. "See if it sounds empty."

There is a big difference between the sound that a full tank makes and the sound an empty one makes. One sounds like a solid block of wood—the other sounds like a drum. This sounded like a drum.

"It's definitely almost empty," said Badger. "Listen to that."

They tried it again, and there was no doubt in the of either of them: the main water tank was almost pletely dry. If everyone went to wash their hands breakfast, it would soon be depleted.

The two boys looked at each other. "We go and te Captain right away," Badger said. "Because . . ." He l at his watch, and Ben's heart sank. They were up because they were on watch; everybody else wa about to get up and would be going to the washroo a shower. Unless they stopped that, the ship's wate ply would be totally exhausted within a couple of utes.

With only the flashlight to guide them, they scra out of the bilge and up the ladder as quickly as they manage. Then, even though the ship was moving ab such a way that they would normally not run, they ran as fast as they possibly could to the Captain's cal

The Captain had only just got dressed and was straig ing his tie when the two boys knocked loudly at his He was surprised to see them, and he knew immed that there was something wrong.

"A problem?" he asked.

"Yes," blurted out Badger. "The water . . . We looke see, and we—"

"It was really low," said Ben, who was still panti catch his breath.

If it rains, you can collect water in a canvas tarpaulin....

"The tank's almost empty," whispered Badger.

TAP
TAP
TAP

"Calm down," said Captain Macbeth. "Take a deep breath—and then tell me what the trouble is...."

Ben and Badger knew why he had done this. If people were still in their hammocks, or even if they were on their way to the washrooms to take their morning shower, they would go straight up to the deck. This was the best way of stopping the showers from being used.

It was quite a sight. Most of the people who came up onto the deck, bleary-eyed from having been woken up so abruptly, were still in their pajamas. There were one or two, though, who had got up early and who were already dressed—and one or two of them looked as if they had already had a shower.

"Pay attention!" shouted the Captain once the last of the stragglers had appeared. "We are facing a serious water crisis—nobody is to use the showers or the basins. Anybody who wants drinking water should apply to Cook. The toilets may be used as normal—they flush with seawater."

After the Captain had finished his announcement, there was a buzz of excited chatter. A water crisis? Why was there a water crisis when everything had seemed to be fine the day before? Nobody had said anything then about the tank running dry. Ben and Badger went to join their friends, who were eager to find out what had happened.

"Are you absolutely sure you were reading the right gauge?" asked Poppy. "You're sure you weren't looking at one of the other tanks?"

"Absolutely sure," confirmed Badger. "We both looked, didn't we, Ben? Just to be sure."

Ben nodded. "We also knocked on the tank to see if it sounded empty—and it did. It was just like a great big drum."

"We're in serious trouble, then," said Poppy. "We're miles from Australia and the nearest fresh water."

Tanya shook her head sadly. "What will happen when Cook's supply of drinking water is used up? What then?"

Breakfast was a somber affair. Although everybody was trying to put a brave face on it, they all knew just how serious their situation was. Cook did his best to appear cheerful, but it was clear that he was worried. He usually chatted in a friendly way with people when they came to collect their food, but that morning he was silent.

Nobody said anything at the table either. And what was there to say? Talking could make you thirsty, and so it was probably best not to talk. But if nobody said anything, then everybody might think thoughts that would make them even more worried. It was a difficult position to be in.

Then suddenly a boy from another table came up and whispered into Badger's ear. He was from another deck and his name was Bartholomew Fitzhardy. He was popular and was also one of the most skillful sailors in the school. He was not the sort to exaggerate or make up stories.

"I want to tell you something," said Bartholomew.

"Well, I'm listening," said Badger.

Bartholomew looked over his shoulder. "Not in here. Outside—on deck."

Badger looked puzzled, but he could tell that it was important. "Can Ben come?" he asked. "He knows how to keep a secret."

Bartholomew hesitated for a moment, but then he nodded. "All right. I'll go out first—you and Ben wait a few minutes and then come. I'll be on the port side—near the life belt locker."

Badger leaned over toward Ben and told him they would need to go up on deck in a few minutes. Ben nodded; he had guessed that Bartholomew wanted to talk to Badger in private, and he was glad that he had been invited too.

A few minutes later they left their table in the mess hall and made their way out on deck. Bartholomew was waiting for them exactly where he said he would be.

"What's up?" asked Badger.

Bartholomew spoke quietly. There was nobody else around, but he still seemed to be anxious about what he was about to say.

"Last night," he said, "I took a shower really late, just before lights-out. It was a quick shower and I had dried off and changed into my pajamas and dressing gown at the end of it. I turned off the lights in the washroom because I guessed that nobody else would be coming in after me. But as I came out the door, I bumped into Geoffrey Shark. He had his towel with him and his toiletry bag, and I realized that he was going to have a shower." He paused. "In fact, I *knew* that he was going to have a shower because he said to me, 'I hope you've left me some hot water, Fitzhardy.' You know how rudely those three talk. It was like that."

Badger waited for Bartholomew to continue.

"Well," Bartholomew went on, "when I got back to my cabin I realized that I had left my sponge bag in the washroom. It has my toothpaste in it and my soap, so I didn't want to leave it there overnight. I went back, and when I reached the washroom door, I met Shark. He had finished his shower and was going back to his cabin. He was carrying my sponge bag, though, and he said to me, 'You left this behind, Fitzhardy—I was going to bring it to you.' I thanked him and turned to go back to my cabin. As I did so, though, I thought I heard the shower running inside. I thought it was somebody else who had come to take a shower after Shark." He paused, lowering his voice. "I realized that Shark had turned the lights out. The switch is outside, and *he turned it off.* I didn't really think about it because I was so tired, but now that I do, I realize that Shark must have left the shower running *all night.*"

"All night!" Ben drew in his breath.

"That must be why we've got no water," said Bartholomew. "Shark let it all run down the drain."

Badger winced. "I suppose he didn't mean to."

"No," said Bartholomew. "He may not have meant to, but it is his fault, isn't it? It's his fault that we have no water left. He was careless. I feel bad too—I didn't check." He shrugged. "I'm not sure Shark knows."

Ben looked at Badger. "What are we going to do?" he asked.

"We're going to keep this to ourselves for the time being," he said. "I want to talk to Poppy and the others. In the meantime, Barty, I think you should keep quiet about this, and don't feel bad. It's Shark, not you."

Bartholomew nodded. "I just felt I had to tell someone, and you are usually someone who knows the best thing to do," he said. "I won't tell anybody else."

"Good. Keep it that way for now," said Badger.

## CHAPTER 6

*Stealing water*

That morning, Poppy and Fee were on helm duty for a half watch, with Mr. Rigger as duty officer. The winds had become much lighter as they neared Australia, and the seas were calm, so there was not much to do but follow the course for land. It was, in fact, rather a dull task for those at the helm, and would have been even duller had they not had rather a lot to think about. And those thoughts were all about water.

If you've ever been really thirsty and not been able to fill yourself a glass of water or get to a drinking fountain, then you will know that the last thing you want to think about is water. That just makes it worse. But that morning, as the *Tobermory* made its way toward Australia with only fifty gallons—or less now—of water in her tanks, water was the only thing people were thinking about.

Mr. Rigger was normally one of the most cheerful of the teachers, but this morning Poppy and Fee did not see so much as a trace of a smile on his lips. Even his mustache, normally a fine feature of his appearance, seemed discouraged and was drooping badly.

Poppy asked him directly, "How bad are things, Mr. Rigger?"

Poppy wondered whether he had heard her question. But then Mr. Rigger spoke. "By my reckoning, we've got at least three days to go before we get to the closest port. There's a place down in southern Australia that we could put into—it's the closest port—but unless the wind picks up . . ."

He did not finish his sentence, but sighed in a way that indicated he had nothing further to say—or at least nothing that would make anybody feel any better.

"But what about water?" asked Fee.

"Cook has put what we have into bottles," Mr. Rigger said. "There'll be one bottle between three people. All will have to share."

It would be a small sip in the morning and one at night—at the most—if the bottle was to last three days.

Mr. Rigger nodded miserably. "It's very little," he said. "But we have no choice."

Poppy looked up at the sky. "If it rains, we'll be all right," she said.

Mr. Rigger tried to look cheerful. "Yes," he said. "You're right, Poppy. I'm sure it'll rain."

They knew, though, that Mr. Rigger was just doing

his best to make them feel better. That was his job, after all—to get the best out of the crew.

Mr. Rigger asked probably the most awkward question—but he was not to know that.

"I wonder why we ran out of water," he began. "Hard to understand. You don't know anything about this, do you?"

He addressed the question to both of them. They both looked away—Fee looking to port, and Poppy looking to starboard. Mr. Rigger noticed this. He was an observant man—as all sailors tend to be—and he could tell that his innocent question had hit home.

"It could have been anything," said Poppy. "It could have been a leak."

It was not a good answer. It was not a lie—Poppy would never want to tell a lie—but it was not a helpful answer. It was not a lie because it *could* have been a leak. It was not a leak, of course, but it *could* have been one.

Mr. Rigger was looking at her intently, and Poppy felt herself blushing.

"Do you know what caused it?" Mr. Rigger asked. "You should tell me if you do."

Poppy glanced at Fee, who looked down at the deck in confusion. Feeling uncomfortable, she nodded her head. "I'm not sure if I know in the sense of being one hundred percent sure, but—"

"But we sort of know. We heard something about what might be the reason," interjected Fee.

They both felt uncomfortable because, as in any school, there was a feeling on the *Tobermory* that you did not tattle. Everybody knew that there were times when you *had* to tell the teachers about something even if you knew it would get somebody into trouble. If somebody was doing something dangerous, for example, or somebody was bullying somebody else, then you had to tell the Captain or one of the other members of the staff. But it was not always easy to tell on somebody who had done something wrong.

"You *sort of* know?" asked Mr. Rigger. "Well, in my mind you either know something or you don't. There can't be any sort-of knowing."

Poppy thought about this before she answered. "We've been told something," she said at last. "We've been told that..." She hesitated. "We've been told that somebody left a shower running all night."

Mr. Rigger looked grave. "I see," he said. "Well, that would drain the tank, I suppose."

"Yes," said Poppy. "But he probably didn't mean it."

Mr. Rigger considered this. "No," he said. "I suppose he didn't. Still, it was extreme carelessness."

"Yes," said Fee. "It's just the sort of thing that Shark—"

She stopped herself, putting a hand to her mouth as if to catch the words. But they were already out, and the one thing you can never do with words is put them back in your mouth.

"Shark?" said Mr. Rigger.

Neither girl spoke, and that was enough to confirm it.

"That boy," muttered Mr. Rigger, shaking his head. "We should have realized." He was going to say something more, but he stopped himself. As a rule, teachers did not discuss students with other students, but every so often something came out to show what they were thinking.

"What are you going to do?" asked Poppy.

Mr. Rigger was still shaking his head. When he stopped, he said, "There's no good crying over spilled milk."

"Or water," muttered Poppy under her breath.

Mr. Rigger had heard. "Or water—yes, precisely." He stroked his chin. "I don't know if there's much point in punishing him. It was carelessness, but he probably didn't know he was being careless." He looked at Poppy. "I don't want you to worry about being thought of as an informer. I don't want you to get into trouble with that bunch."

Poppy said nothing, but she was secretly pleased.

"I've an idea," said Mr. Rigger. "Perhaps we should give Shark the chance to own up. It would be a good idea for him at least to say sorry for his carelessness."

"He's not like that," said Poppy.

"Shall we see?" said Mr. Rigger. "Not everybody is completely bad."

"William Edward Hardtack is," said Fee.

Mr. Rigger shook his head. "No, even him. Even William Edward Hardtack will have some good in him." He paused.

"I'm going to have a word with Geoffrey Shark. I'm going to ask him if it has occurred to him that he might have left the shower running. And then I'll see what he says."

"He'll lie," said Poppy. "He always does. And Flubber, too."

"We'll see," said Mr. Rigger.

As the day wore on, people began to feel the impact of the strict water rationing that was now applied. Having been issued their precious bottles of water, people kept a close eye on the level, making sure that nobody had more than his or her fair share. Ben and Badger were sharing with Thomas Seagrape, and each of them, of course, was careful not to take more than a small sip when the bottle was handed over. But there were arguments elsewhere: Angela Singh, who was sharing with a set of twins known for their selfishness, Molly and Lolly, complained that they had taken large gulps rather than sips and had finished almost half the bottle in one sitting. And poor Bartholomew Fitzhardy spilled half of his bottle when he put it down without checking that the cap was screwed on properly. That did not go down well with the people he was sharing with, who said the water that had been spilled should be treated as his and therefore he was not entitled to any further sips. Ben felt sorry for him and he agreed with Badger and Thomas that Bartholomew could be given a sip of their water.

By and large, everybody behaved well in the emergency except for . . . Well, it was inevitable that if there was going to be any bad behavior, William Edward Hardtack and his gang would be mixed up in it somewhere. And this behavior was really bad—so shocking, in fact, that people found it hard to believe.

Miss Worsfold, who taught classes on marine biology, was of course interested in all sorts of fish and had in her cabin a large fish tank. In this she kept a number of small, highly colorful tropical fish. People were allowed to visit these fish from time to time, and just about the whole school had been introduced to them and been permitted to give them a small helping of fish food.

When she returned to her cabin later that afternoon Miss Worsfold saw to her surprise that the tank was only half full: somebody had drained water out of it. Fortunately, her fish were still alive, but they were now obliged to swim backwards and forwards in the small quantity that remained. They were not at all happy with this situation, and some of them looked as if they were gasping for oxygen.

Word soon got around the ship as to what had happened.

"Who on earth would do something like that?" asked Fee. "Imagine stealing water from fish!"

Nobody said anything, but it was clear that everybody was thinking the same thing. But nobody had seen anybody going into the staff cabins, and so any suspicions that people entertained had to be kept to themselves. But then something happened that solved the mystery . . . and in a way that nobody would have guessed.

It was at dinner. Everybody was feeling extremely thirsty. A little more water had been found by melting some ice that had been discovered in the ship's large freezers, but that was only enough to give everybody a small glassful. That managed to relieve the worst symptoms of thirst and it resulted in people's feeling a bit more cheerful at dinner. Clouds had been spotted on the horizon, and that also helped raise the mood a bit.

"They look like rain clouds," Mr. Rigger had observed. "With any luck, we might get some rain tonight."

Mr. Rigger was good at predicting the weather. It was something to do with his mustache, people said: not only could it act as a weather vane, but it could also detect approaching storms. If a storm was in the offing, it would bristle, rather like a cat's tail might do when there is static electricity about. That was what it was doing now, which Badger said was a really positive sign. If it rained, then the tarpaulin funnel erected on deck would soon fill the tanks down below with fresh rainwater.

But at dinner that night it was not rain that people talked about, but what happened to Hardtack and his friends shortly after the meal was served. They had just taken their seats at their table when William Edward

Hardtack suddenly gave a loud groan and wrapped his arms around his stomach. No sooner had this happened when Maximilian Flubber emitted a similar groan, to be followed by Geoffrey Shark, who did the same thing.

"Look at Hardtack," whispered Poppy to Fee. "I'd say that he has a rather sore stomach."

"And his pals, too," said Fee. "Look—Flubber's turned green."

By now the whole school was riveted by what was happening at Hardtack's table. Everybody saw when Hardtack rose to his feet, followed by Flubber and Shark, and then led the way, half running, half stumbling, toward the door.

It was Poppy who first guessed what had happened. "That's it," she exclaimed. "They drank the water from Miss Worsfold's fish tank. And it would have been full of fish food."

Badger's mouth dropped open in astonishment. "Of course," he said. "Of course that's what must have happened. You know what they feed fish? Ants' eggs. That stuff they give fish is actually ants' eggs."

"So when they drank the poor fishes' water," Fee joined in, "they were actually drinking a lot of ants' eggs too. No wonder they don't feel well."

It was hard not to laugh. Nobody would have wished illness on Hardtack and his friends, but discomfort and nausea—well, that was another matter.

Mr. Rigger had seen what was happening and had

followed the three boys to check up that they were all right. When he came back a few minutes later, Poppy asked him whether he thought the sudden departure of Hardtack and his friends had anything to do with Miss Worsfold's half-emptied fish tank. He did not answer directly, but Poppy could tell that her guess was correct.

"Put it this way," said Mr. Rigger. "Whoever drank that water will not do anything quite so selfish again—at least, not in a hurry!"

It rained that night. As the wind rose, sheets of heavy rain swept across the world of waves and foaming water that lay all about the *Tobermory.* And as the rain fell, it was collected in the spread-out tarpaulin and taken in pipes down to the tanks below. These were soon full—all three of them—giving the ship enough fresh water not only to reach Australia, but also to travel up the coast toward Queensland.

"The emergency's over," announced the Captain the next morning. "You may all have showers, wash your hands, and fill your water bottles—all those things are now allowed."

Geoffrey Shark was not punished for his carelessness, which could never be proved. "However, I think he may have learned a lesson," said Poppy. "And Flubber and Hard-tack learned a lesson too."

"I hope so," said Badger. "But you never know. You may

think that they've become better and then all of a sudden and with no warning they do something nasty."

Poppy thought about this. She suspected that Badger was right, but she was unwilling to give up entirely on Hardtack, Shark, and Flubber: there was still plenty of time for them to show another side to their character—and perhaps Australia would bring that out. Time would tell.

## CHAPTER 7

### *Boomerang*

They arrived in Sydney early in the morning. The ship had been sailing all night, and Poppy and Fee were on the watch ending just before sunrise. They knew they were close to land, and that the bank of fog off their port bow was concealing Sydney, with its famous Harbor Bridge and its opera house. They both wanted to stay on deck to see these when the fog lifted, but there was a rule that those who had been on the last watch of the night had to go to their cabins to get some sleep. They went down below, climbed into their hammocks, and quickly fell asleep, rocked by the motion of the ship as it completed the last few miles of their journey.

By the time the two girls awoke, the *Tobermory* had sailed past the protective arms of land at the entrance to Sydney Harbor. Without wasting any time, they joined the rest of the crew on deck, watching as the famous skyline revealed itself to them. Poppy was particularly excited, as Australia was home to her and she knew that her parents had traveled in from Alice Springs to be there to welcome them.

"There's the bridge," she called out excitedly. "I've climbed that. They take you up and they hook you to a wire so that you can't fall."

Fee gazed at the famous bridge, a high arc of steel crossing the two sides of the harbor. From a distance, it looked like a steel rainbow.

"You went up *there*?" she asked, imagining what it would be like to be at the top of the great structure.

The ship was moving through the water slowly, the sails having been dropped and the ship's engines turned on. A sailing ship like the *Tobermory* always attracts attention, and smaller boats were coming out to meet her, circling her playfully, their crews waving a welcome. Several boats sounded their horns in salute, and the *Tobermory* replied with hers—a long, low sound that echoed off the shore and its buildings.

When they reached the right spot, the Captain ordered the anchor to be lowered. With a loud clanking sound, followed by a splash, the anchor disappeared into the sea, the heavy links of its chain rattling behind it. Once it had reached the seabed below, more chain was let out to make sure that the ship would not tug itself free. With the anchor set, the Captain was able to order the switching off of the engines. Suddenly there was silence, and it was in this silence, with the sun-filled Australian sky above them, that everyone stood on deck and gazed at the scene before them. Fee felt as if she had to pinch herself. *I'm really here in Sydney.*

The Captain had to notify the authorities of exactly who was on board and who would be stepping ashore, and only once he had done this would it be possible for the boats to take people in. Soon that was sorted out, and the first of the boats made the short journey to the nearby quay.

Poppy and Fee were in the second boat, along with Angela, Ben, and Thomas. Mr. Rigger rowed this boat, and said that he would drop them off before returning to the ship for more passengers. Poppy could hardly contain her excitement. When she saw her parents waiting on the quay she almost upset the boat with her waving.

"Careful!" shouted Mr. Rigger. "You'll have us all in the water." But he smiled as he shouted the warning, as he knew the reason for her excitement.

Once ashore and united with her parents, Poppy introduced her friends. They all made their way to a café for lunch. Over the meal, Poppy gave her mother and father a full account of everything that had happened on the voyage—including the rescue of Feathers, Henry's experience of surfing, and the episode with the near-empty water tanks.

Poppy's father frowned as she told him of the selfishness of Hardtack and his friends. "I know people like that," he said. "You don't want them around you in the Outback, where we all have to rely on one another."

"Do you think they'll ever change?" asked Poppy's mother. She turned to her husband. "Remember that fellow who was in that group that got lost? He made off with the food and water, thinking he'd get back to town by himself."

"He left them out in the bush?" asked Poppy incredulously.

"Yes," said her mother. "He went off by himself. He didn't care about the others."

"And what happened?" asked Badger.

Poppy's mother waited for a moment. They were all caught up in the story. "What happened? Well, he tripped over a rock and broke his ankle. He dragged himself to the shade of a tree and waited. There was nothing else he could do."

"But you can't last long out there," added Poppy. "It's far too hot."

"That's right," said her mother. "Meanwhile, the others wandered around, becoming more and more lost, until one of them worked out where to go. They were well on their way home when they came across the fellow who'd run off with their supplies. He was still lying under his tree, looking pretty far gone. They picked him up and carried him home to town. He was too weak to walk, but they saved his life."

"He was lucky," observed Ben. "He thought he'd save

himself, but he ended up being saved by the people he'd left behind."

"That's true," said Poppy's father. "And worth remembering. You may think you're all right on your own, but you never know when you're going to need other people to help you."

After they finished their lunch, Poppy went off with her parents for some private time while the others explored the streets around the harbor. There were interesting shops, and having had nothing to spend their pocket money on for weeks, they were all able to afford something. Ben and Badger bought wide-brimmed Australian bush hats; Fee treated herself to a pair of Outback boots; and Angela and Thomas bought themselves boomerangs. Once back at the quay, they signaled to Mr. Rigger, who was standing on the deck of the *Tobermory* admiring the view. He returned their signal and rowed across the harbor to collect them.

"I see you've bought boomerangs," he said as they climbed into the rowing boat. "Do you know how to throw them?"

Both Angela and Thomas shook their heads. Thomas had seen a film of somebody throwing one, though, and he thought it looked quite easy. Angela had been reading the small instruction leaflet that came with the boomerang. This made it look simple, but instruction leaflets often do that—and she was not so sure.

Mr. Rigger laughed. "I've been in Australia before," he said. "Would you like me to show you?"

Both Angela and Thomas agreed. Mr. Rigger was good at showing you how to do things and they had confidence in him.

Once back on the *Tobermory,* they gathered around Mr. Rigger for the demonstration. "You hold it like this," said Mr. Rigger, grasping the end of the boomerang in his right hand. "Then you draw your arm back like this. And then . . ." They watched with bated breath as he suddenly hurled the boomerang into the air. Angela, whose boomerang it was, gasped. She had chosen it carefully for the designs painted on it—an Australian scene, complete with koalas and kangaroos—and for all her confidence in Mr. Rigger's ability, she had to watch her precious souvenir flying at high speed over the water. It had as yet shown no signs of coming back, and she was sure that sooner or later it would lose momentum, fall into the sea, and be lost. But just as she was about to protest, the flight path of the boomerang suddenly started to curve to the left.

"Look," said Thomas, "it's coming back."

Almost as if being controlled by some hidden force, the boomerang began to return to the *Tobermory.* As if by magic, it swooped up to and over the deck, still wobbling in its curious way, but more slowly. Angela was worried that it would not stop—that it would spin over the deck

and disappear on the other side—but she had not reck-
oned for Henry. The Captain's dog had been sitting near
the mainmast enjoying the sunshine when he suddenly
saw a strange flying object coming toward him. No dog
could resist the temptation of such a target, and Henry
leapt up, launched himself into the air, and with flawless
judgment caught the boomerang in his jaws.

This feat was greeted by a great cheer from all who had
witnessed it.

"Well done, Henry!" shouted Angela, relieved that her
trophy had not been lost forever.

Henry wagged his tail and made his way over to Mr. Rigger to drop the boomerang at his feet. Rewarded with a pat
on the head and the promise of an extra dog biscuit that
evening, Henry trotted back to his place near the mast.

"You see," said Mr. Rigger with a wink. "Easy, isn't it?"

Later that day, the entire ship's company gathered on deck
to say goodbye to Feathers, the rescued penguin. Although
there were plenty of people who wanted the penguin to
stay—and one of these, indeed, might have been Feathers
himself, as he had become quite comfortable on board—
the Captain had decided that it would be much kinder to
the bird to arrange a new home for him with other penguins. Fortunately, the large zoo on the other side of the
bay was home to a colony of penguins, and the director
had been willing to give Feathers a new home.

"Penguins are sociable creatures," the director explained when he came on board the *Tobermory* with two assistants and a portable penguin carrier. "They're never really happy on their own. They miss the company of other penguins."

Everybody could understand that, and so when they said goodbye to Feathers, although they felt sad, nobody felt that sending him to the zoo was the wrong thing to do.

"I'll send you photographs," said the director. "And we'll make sure that there's a notice outside his enclosure saying that he was rescued by the crew of the School Ship *Tobermory*."

From inside his carrier, Feathers could be seen peeping out at his friends. Henry came up and gave the bars of the carrier a lick.

Standing on the Quarterdeck so that everybody could see him, Captain Macbeth addressed the school.

"Members of the ship's company," he began. "We have had an exciting voyage, but now we are here in Australia and about to begin the next stage of our adventure. Tomorrow morning, at first flight, we shall sail out of Sydney Harbor and begin our journey up the coast of Australia. Our destination is the Great Barrier Reef, where we shall spend a day or two before going into harbor at a town called Cairns.

"Cairns is where the tall-ships race begins, and once

that happens I want every single one of you to concentrate on the business at hand—which will be a race. For two weeks there will be less schoolwork, as you will all be busy with the demanding task of trimming our sails and otherwise ensuring that the *Tobermory* sails as fast as she possibly can. That is going to be a hard task, as we are up against some of the best tall ships in the world. They are not going to give us an inch of ground—they will fight to win this race right up to the end.

"You might be wondering what lies ahead," the Captain continued. "I would like to be able to say to you that it will all be easy, but the one thing a captain must never do is mislead his crew. So I shall tell you instead that it's going to be really tough. And at times it will be dangerous. There are things you are going to have to be extremely careful about. There are great crocodiles, the saltwater crocodile. They live as easily in fresh water as in the sea. Look out for those and remember they are among the most dangerous creatures in the world. Then there are jellyfish that can give you a sting that can do a lot of damage. There are sea snakes that are the most venomous snakes in the world. I want you all to take great care not just from time to time when you think there may be danger about, but every single minute of the waking day."

The Captain paused to let his words sink in. At the mention of crocodiles there was a buzz of conversation as people sought reassurance from their friends and deck prefects.

But not everybody took the warning seriously. "Crocodiles!" sneered William Edward Hardtack. "I'm not scared of them. They're just overgrown lizards."

"That's right," said Geoffrey Shark. "If I see a crocodile up there, I'm going to make it into a handbag for my mum!"

"Hah!" said Maximilian Flubber, not to be outdone. "I'd like to meet the croc that would dare take me on."

Hearing these remarks, Badger shook his head in wonderment. How could anybody be so stupid as to talk like that about one of the most dangerous creatures on earth? He had read all about these Australian crocodiles, and he knew what a threat they were. Only a few months ago the newspapers had carried the story of a teenager who had been taken by a saltwater crocodile when he had been fooling around on the banks of a river. Crocodiles are *very* interested in people and like to get *really* close to them. In fact, crocodiles like people so much that they like to have them *inside* them.

Poppy had come back from her outing with her parents in time to hear the Captain's talk. She told her friends that everything the Captain said was true, and that if Flubber thought he knew better than the Captain, he was in for a nasty surprise.

"Australia's a great place," she said to Fee. "Some people

get the wrong idea and think it's full of things that will bite or eat you given half a chance; that's not really true, but there are times when you have to be careful." She paused. "Most creatures will get out of your way if they possibly can."

Fee thought about this. She was comfortable enough with most creatures, but she was not too keen on spiders. The trouble with them, of course, was that they were so small that most of the time you did not even see them. And she was not so sure that they would get out of the way—didn't they walk over you if you happened to be where they were going? And hadn't she read somewhere about a girl who had discovered a nest of spiders *in her hair*?

Tanya was more frightened of snakes. She asked Poppy whether she had ever been really close to a snake—and what was it like?

"Oh, we see snakes all the time in the Outback," said Poppy. "There's a snake called the brown snake—you see lots of them. Sometimes they even come into our house."

Tanya shuddered. "Inside the house?" she asked in a shocked tone. "Actually inside?"

Poppy smiled. "It's not that bad," she said. "They don't come in and sit at the table and try to eat your breakfast, or anything like that."

Tanya did not think this was funny. Nothing about snakes was funny in her view.

"They just slide around on the floor," Poppy continued.

"They like to curl up in cool places—under the bathtub sometimes, behind the cupboards, that sort of thing. You usually see them in good time."

"And then?" asked Tanya, her jaw quivering.

"And then my dad comes and takes them outside. He uses a special pole with a hook at the end. He picks them up and puts them down on the grass."

"And if they bite you?" asked Tanya.

"You try not to let them," said Poppy calmly. "But if one of those brown snakes bites you, you're in trouble. We have an antidote to their poison in the fridge, but you get pretty sick. You can die, if you're unlucky."

"I'd die of fright," said Tanya. "Just seeing a snake would be enough."

"If you think brown snakes are dangerous, you should see the western taipan," Poppy added.

Tanya did *not* want to see a western taipan, and would have preferred not to talk about them, but Fee was interested.

"That's even more poisonous?" she asked.

Poppy nodded. "If that bites you, you've got no chance," she said, "but fortunately they're rare. There's just a small part of northern New South Wales and Queensland where you find them."

Tanya's hand shot to her mouth. "But isn't Queensland where we're going?"

"Not that part," Poppy reassured her.

Fee had had enough of snake talk. "Let's talk about other animals," she said. And then she added, "Like the duck-billed platypus . . ."

Poppy smiled. "All right, but there's one thing I need to tell you: the duck-billed platypus has a poisonous spike on its tail. They look cuddly, but I wouldn't get too close to them."

Tanya groaned. "I'm staying on board ship," she said.

"Fair enough," said Poppy. "But don't fall in."

Tanya waited for an explanation.

"Great white sharks," said Poppy simply.

CHAPTER 8

## The giant clam

It took them almost a week to sail up the coast of Australia to the Great Barrier Reef. It would have taken them even longer had the winds not been so good, but with a strong breeze on their beam they were able to make better progress than the Captain had imagined. They sailed as quickly at night as they did during the day, checking their position by the stars as they traveled, going on to plot their course on paper charts in the large chart room. The skies were clear from dusk onward, great sweeps of dark velvet with the constellations scattered about them like silver dust.

Mr. Rigger was the expert on the stars, pointing out the Southern Cross and other constellations that could tell you exactly where you were if you had the right tables to work with. "Don't rely on your GPS," he warned. "Things can go wrong."

"Anything can happen at sea" was one of Mr. Rigger's favorite sayings—and, like a number of favorite sayings, it was absolutely right.

Mr. Rigger asked a question. "And just what can go wrong with your GPS?"

"The battery can go flat," said Poppy. "Without any power, you can't pick up the signal from the satellites."

"Good answer," he said. "We rely on batteries, don't we? And then, when they go flat, we don't know what to do, do we?"

William Edward Hardtack put up his hand. Badger turned to watch him. Hardtack could usually be relied upon to come up with some smart remark.

"Yes, Hardtack?" said Mr. Rigger.

"We recharge them," said Hardtack with a smile. "You plug them in and recharge. Simple."

Maximilian Flubber and Geoffrey Shark both giggled, but were silenced by a look from Mr. Rigger.

"I suppose you think that's funny, Hardtack," Mr. Rigger said.

Hardtack pretended to look surprised. "No, sir," he said. "I mean it seriously. Don't you recharge after your battery runs flat? I do that with my phone, sir—and with everything else. I recharge. Then they work. It's like magic, sir—but it's really just electricity."

Again Flubber and Shark giggled. Then Shark said, "Hardtack's right, Mr. Rigger. If your battery runs flat, you plug in and recharge." He paused. "I could show you, if you like, sir."

Mr. Rigger rarely lost his temper, but it was clear that he

was being pushed. "If you find this so amusing, Hardtack, perhaps you might care to go and tell the Captain all about it. How about that?"

This worked. Talking back to Mr. Rigger was one thing; showing disrespect to the Captain was quite another. Nobody—not even Hardtack—would try that.

"So," continued Mr. Rigger, now that Hardtack had been silenced, "the reason why you wouldn't be able to take Hardtack's advice would be that . . ."

Fee put up her hand. "There's no electricity when you're a hundred miles from anything."

"Exactly," said Mr. Rigger. "And apart from having a flat battery, your GPS might be broken. . . ."

"Or dropped into the water," suggested Ben.

"Yes," said Mr. Rigger. "You'd be surprised to know how many people drop important things down crevasses or over the side of mountains, or in thick snowdrifts. It happens all the time." He paused. "So it's useful to have other means of knowing where you are."

Turning to Ben, Badger said, "Do you ever get the feeling that what somebody's saying to you is really a warning about something that's going to happen?"

Ben thought about it for a moment before nodding his head. "Yes," he said. "I think I do."

Poppy and Fee were both on watch when the first signs of the Great Barrier Reef appeared on the horizon. To begin with, Poppy thought her eyes might be playing tricks on her, but when Fee called out, she knew that she had not been mistaken.

"Something up ahead," called out Fee. She had gone to stand by the rail on the starboard side of the ship, while Poppy stayed on duty at the wheel. "Can you see it?"

Poppy shouted out that she thought she could. And at the same time, from up in the crow's nest, came Badger's voice at full volume. "Reef ahead!" he shouted. "Fifteen degrees off the starboard bow."

Mr. Rigger appeared from down below, followed a few minutes later by the Captain himself.

"Reef ahead off the starboard bow, Captain," reported Poppy. "About five nautical miles away."

Captain Macbeth had his telescope, and he pulled it out to its full length and focused in the direction of the reef. "That's it, sure enough," he said. "Well navigated, everybody."

Orders were given to reduce the amount of sail. Almost immediately, the great boat responded and slowed down in the water, almost gratefully, like a runner who has reached the end of a long race.

The Captain took the helm from Poppy, who stood down and was congratulated on her fine steering. He and Mr. Rigger discussed their best approach and gave orders to the new watch coming on duty. More canvas was to be taken down and the restraining ropes on some of the sails were to be slackened. The ship was barely traveling at walking pace as its bow pointed directly at the waves breaking over the distant coral.

They had to be careful. A reef will cut straight through the hull of even the strongest ship, and once that happens the ship is doomed. What they had to do was get as close as they could without running the risk of going aground on any of the coral outcrops. Then, once they had anchored, they would be able to approach the reef itself in one of the smaller boats—a much safer way of moving among the little hillocks of coral that made up the barrier.

Captain Macbeth found just the right spot to anchor. As he gave the command for the anchor to be lowered, a great clanking of chains came from down below. With a noisy splash the anchor hit the water, followed by yard upon yard of heavy chain. Once enough chain had been laid, the noise stopped, although the boat was still being blown by the wind. The chain, now lying on the shallow seafloor down below, was pulled tight by the movement of the boat as the anchor settled. With a shudder, the *Tobermory* came to a halt, straining against the anchor and its chain, but not moving so much as an inch backwards or forwards.

The Captain called everybody on deck and told them the plans.

"We're going to spend the rest of the day here," he announced. "Everybody will have the chance to snorkel, and those of you who have passed your basic diving certificate can do scuba diving with Miss Worsfold."

Badger turned to Ben and gave him a high five. "That's us," he said proudly.

"And me," said Poppy, her voice full of excitement.

They were some of the few students who had taken Miss Worsfold's course when the *Tobermory* had been in the Caribbean. This had involved studying the rules of diving with an oxygen tank, as well as two short practice dives. There had been few places in the course, as the scuba diving equipment on the *Tobermory* was limited, and those who were chosen for a place on the course considered themselves lucky. There would be a chance to use those skills again—and in one of the most exciting places of all to dive—a living coral reef with all that went with it: fish, turtles, and . . . sharks.

Miss Worsfold called the divers to a meeting. There were ten of them altogether—eleven if she herself was counted. This included not only Poppy, Ben, and Badger, but also Bartholomew Fitzhardy, one of the best sailors on board and one of the most popular, too, and Amanda Birtwhistle, who was known for being an expert navigator. Thomas Seagrape was also a member of this group. Thomas had a lot of experience with diving at home in the Caribbean and could hold his breath underwater for longer than anybody else on board.

Miss Worsfold went over the safety rules.

"Never dive by your-self," she said. "That's one of the most impor-tant rules there is. If you have somebody with you, then they will be able to help you if you get into trouble."

There were other rules. One was about paying attention to how long you had been down. "You can get carried away," she warned. "You're enjoying yourself so much that you forget how long you've been underwater and then, all too soon, you discover you've used all your air."

Amanda Birtwhistle

Everybody listened carefully to this briefing. They would never break any of the rules, they thought. Never . . .

At last it was time to go. The people who weren't doing scuba diving were being taken off to do snorkeling over the reef, swimming on top of the water while breathing through a small tube rather like a periscope. They felt a bit envious of the scuba divers, but they would still be able to get a good view of the fish beneath them and they would all have a chance to learn scuba diving at some point in their time on the *Tobermory.*

They fitted into one of the smaller boats that was equipped with an outboard engine. Miss Worsfold was in charge, and once everybody was on board she put the engine into gear and began the crossing to the reef. The water rapidly became shallower, until it was probably not much more than twenty feet deep. It was sandy on the bottom, but now there were coral formations as far as the eye could see, some of them reaching almost to the surface.

Miss Worsfold stopped the boat. "Time to get into your gear," she said.

They helped one another clip their oxygen cylinders onto their backs and put on their flippers. Miss Worsfold inspected everybody to check that no mistakes had been made. "Mistakes are best dealt with before you get into the water," she said. "The last thing you want is to discover your mistakes when you're way down below."

Poppy and Amanda Birtwhistle were to be dive partners. Amanda was pleased about this as Poppy was a good swimmer and, most important, she was clearheaded. Poppy never panicked, even in a dangerous situation, and she was physically strong, too. There would be no need to be nervous with Poppy at your side.

Yet Amanda was still a bit nervous as they waited their turn to drop backward into the water. She knew that this was probably not the best time to ask a question about sharks, but she felt that she just had to.

"Do you think there are any . . . any sharks around here?" She tried to make her voice sound normal, but it went high when she got to the word *sharks.*

"Sharks?" replied Poppy. "Oh, I don't know. There may be."

Poppy had intended this answer to be reassuring, but its effect was anything but.

"*May be?*" echoed Amanda.

Poppy tried to sound unconcerned. "Well, you can never tell. It's possible, yes...."

Amanda's voice quavered. "P-possible that there are sharks?"

Poppy looked at her friend. She did not want to alarm her, but she also did not want to lie. She could say that there were no sharks, and that Amanda need not worry, but she knew this would not be the right thing to do. So, as calmly as she could, she said, "There can be sharks anywhere, Amanda—anywhere in the sea—and even in some rivers that are close to the sea."

Amanda's voice sounded tiny. "Oh," she said.

"But you have to remember some things about sharks," Poppy went on. "First, sharks are often shy creatures. Most of the time they don't want to get close to people at all. They keep their distance."

"*Most* of the time?" said Amanda. "That means that *some* of the time they like to get close."

Poppy thought about this. "All right," she said at last. "*Some* sharks are not all that shy."

"Like great whites?" asked Amanda, her lip trembling at the thought of those large and dangerous sharks.

"Yes," said Poppy. "I wouldn't call them shy. But remember, there are lots of other sharks that are much shyer than great whites. Reef sharks, for instance. They don't attack people—most of the time."

Amanda absorbed this information. "*Most* of the time," she said. "*Most* of the time . . ."

"And the other thing," Poppy said. "The other thing is that sharks usually don't like shallow water, and the water around here is really shallow, isn't it? Look down there—you can see the sand quite clearly."

Amanda glanced over the side of the boat. She could see the sand at the bottom, but it seemed to her that it was a good way down. There was plenty of swimming room for sharks, she thought.

The first of the divers went into the water, rolling backward in the way that divers do. Ben and Badger went in, followed by Bartholomew Fitzhardy and Thomas Seagrape. Then it was the turn of Poppy and Amanda. Poppy made a thumbs-up sign to Amanda and fell backward into the water with a splash, her friend following her a moment later.

The water was wonderfully clear. As Poppy looked about, she was able to see far into the distance, into a vast green world through which light filtered down from the surface. She saw, down below, outcrops of coral—tiny mountains around which brightly colored fish swam in lazy shoals, drifting in the flow of water, darting here and there for some tiny scrap of food or to escape from some larger fish approaching them. Waving fronds of seaweed made tiny forests, occupied by cautious, half-hidden sea creatures. She saw a large crab, its pincers held out before it, scuttling sideways across the seafloor below. She spotted a fish with a nose like a needle stretching out in front of it, the nose almost as large as the body.

Amanda stayed close to Poppy, feeling more secure if she had her friend firmly in sight. She was feeling less nervous now and was enjoying the feeling of weightlessness that a diver experiences. At the same time, she was aware that there was a current, and that if she stopped moving her arms and legs she would drift away really fast, as if carried in unseen arms.

Poppy pointed and Amanda nodded and followed her to the colorful mound of coral.

They were both caught up in the fascinating world of the coral reef. Poppy had found a tiny cave—no more than two hands' breadth wide—that some brightly colored fish were using as a hiding place. For her part, Amanda was watching a school of small striped fish and was keen to see what they were up to. Neither noticed that slowly but surely the two of them were being separated by the action of the current. Poppy was not moving very much, keeping her position by moving her flippers up and down like paddles; Amanda, though, was drifting along with her school of fish, so absorbed in what she was watching that she did not notice how far the current was carrying her.

After a few minutes of examining the coral, Poppy turned around to look for Amanda. In a moment of shock, she realized that the other girl was not there. Moving away from the coral, she scanned the underwater landscape around her. Not far away she saw two of the boys swimming together toward a coral face. But that was all.

Poppy thought Amanda could not have been gone for more than five minutes, so she was bound to be somewhere nearby. If she had drifted away, then she would have gone in the same direction as the current. By looking at the way the fronds of seaweed were floating, Poppy was able to work out where that would be.

She knew she should not go off on her own to find Amanda: that would be breaking the rule that you did not dive by yourself. What she should do, she felt, was get the two boys she had just seen to join her in her search. Swimming as fast as she could, she made her way over to join them.

The two boys were Thomas Seagrape and Bartholomew Fitzhardy. When Poppy swam over to join them, they waved cheerfully and pointed at the fish they were studying.

It was frustrating for Poppy: the one thing you cannot do when you are diving is talk, and so she had to communicate by signals. Pointing behind her in the direction in which she thought Amanda might have drifted, she made a series of frantic movements with her hands. They had all been taught basic diving signals, but now, in this emergency, Poppy found that she could not remember them. Through the glass of their diving masks, Poppy could see at first puzzlement on the faces of Thomas and Bartholomew, but this soon changed to concern. Thomas remembered his signals and made the sign for *okay* with his fingers and thumb. That prompted Poppy's memory, and she made the signal for *swim in this direction.*

All three of them were strong swimmers, and they were soon shooting through the water, scattering the surprised fish about them, heading down the current. As they went, all of them scanned the water ahead, hoping to see a line of bubbles rising through the water: that would be the first thing they would see of their missing friend.

It was Thomas who spotted her first. Grabbing hold of Poppy's arm, he made the diving signal for *look over there*—pointing two fingers, forked into a V. Poppy looked: a short swim away, rising up like a stream of silver, were bubbles of air. And as the swimmers got closer, they saw the figure huddled on the seabed, in much deeper water. It was Amanda. But what was she doing? From where they were, it seemed that she was struggling with something, her arms waving urgently.

It took barely a minute for them to reach her and see what had happened. Amanda was struggling to free herself, but it was not until they were on the scene that they realized the struggle was with a giant clam. This sea crea-ture had closed its wide, serrated shell onto a strap from Amanda's cylinder harness, and try as she might she was unable to free it. The clam itself was immense—about half the size of a person—and as far as it was concerned it was staying put, anchored to the seabed, no matter what any-body else might think.

Thomas was the first to reach Amanda's side. Seeing him, she stopped struggling and pointed to the clam and the strap that was so firmly wedged in its jaws. As Poppy and Bartholomew looked on, Thomas pulled as hard as he could on the trapped webbing. It would not budge, nor did it make any difference when Bartholomew added his strength and joined the tugging match.

Thomas realized that there would be no way of opening the clamshell—it was far too powerful for its jaws to be prised apart. That meant the strap would have to be cut, and that would require a knife. Turning to Poppy, he made a sawing motion with his hands. She understood what he meant, and shook her head. Bartholomew did the same: neither of them had a knife of any sort, let alone the strong diving knife that would be needed for a task like that.

Thomas thought. If the strap could not be cut, then the only thing Amanda could do would be to abandon her air cylinder altogether. If she did that, though, she would then have to shoot up to the surface as soon as possible, as she would no longer have any air to breathe. The difficulty with that, of course, is that when you have been that deep underwater, you have to stop on your way up and let the body adjust to the change in depths. If you do not do this, then you can get something called "the bends"—a very dangerous condition that comes about when bubbles form in the blood or muscles. The only way to avoid the bends is to take the final part of the journey to the surface very slowly, and that would be Amanda's problem: How could she go up slowly when she had no air to breathe?

These were the thoughts that were going through Thomas's mind—and also through Poppy's. She had thought of exactly the same problem, and she wondered how they were going to get around it. She stopped herself. An answer had come to her. It was a simple answer, and she was sure that it would work. But how to communicate it to Thomas when nobody could say anything other than emitting a chain of jostling bubbles?

Poppy decided to try her own sign language. Gripping Thomas's arm, she pointed to the strap and then to Amanda's air tank. After that she gestured away from Amanda, hoping to send the message about the abandonment of the tank. Thomas watched her closely, but it was clear that he had not yet sensed what she wanted to do. Poppy continued, pointing to her regulator—the mouthpiece through which divers breathe—and taking it momentarily out of her mouth and passing it to Amanda before putting it back in again.

Suddenly Thomas understood, as did Amanda. Now Thomas had to detach Amanda's air cylinder and then accompany her on a slow ascent to the surface. The first part of that was easier said than done, as there were complicated fasteners that had to be dealt with, but eventually it fell loose. They could see that Amanda was nervous, but Thomas immediately took his regulator from his mouth and offered it to her. Reassured that she would not be left airless, Amanda took a deep breath and began to swim slowly upward, supported by Thomas on one side and Poppy on the other. After a few strokes they stopped and Thomas passed his regulator back to her to allow her to take another breath. They made their way slowly but safely to the surface.

Once at the top, Amanda gasped in a lungful of fresh air and immediately expelled half of it in a shout of joy.

"Thanks!" she shouted. "You saved my life!"

Bartholomew and Poppy laughed. Thomas, who was always modest, shook his head. "No, I didn't. You would have been fine."

Amanda knew this was not true. "No, I wouldn't have. I was beginning to panic. I wasn't thinking straight."

Poppy noticed that the boat was now heading toward them. "Miss Worsfold's on her way," she said.

"Good," said Thomas. "I hope she has a diving knife."

When Miss Worsfold arrived, she helped all four of them into the boat and listened as Poppy gave an account

Ben and Badger were the first to go, rolling backwards into the water the way that divers do.

Amanda took a deep breath and began to swim gradually upward, supported by Thomas on one side and Poppy on the other....

The sea creature had closed its shell on a strap from Amanda's cylinder harness.

of what happened. "Thomas was the hero," she said. "He saved Amanda."

Miss Worsfold looked at Thomas and smiled. "Well done, Thomas," she said. "That was good thinking. If Amanda had come straight up, she could have gotten the bends." Then she frowned. "Mind you, there's still a valuable piece of equipment down there—we'll have to do something about that."

Thomas lost no time in volunteering. "I'll go straight down again," he said. "As long as you can lend me a diving knife."

Miss Worsfold nodded. "I can, but I think I should come with you."

Poppy's face fell at this. "Couldn't I go with him, Miss Worsfold?"

Miss Worsfold hesitated. But then she said, "You will be careful, will you?"

Both Thomas and Poppy reassured her that they would be careful. There had been enough emergencies for one day and they did not want to create another. After they had each checked their equipment, they rolled over backward into the water and began to swim down again to the bottom. The clam, of course, had not moved; its jaws were still tightly shut and it was paying no attention to the shoal of small, brightly colored fish that were nibbling at the lips of the shell. Taking Miss Worsfold's diving knife from its sheath, Thomas soon cut through the nylon strap that was caught in the clam's jaws. Making the *all okay* signal with his left hand, Thomas retrieved the abandoned air cylinder and he and Poppy slowly returned to the surface, pausing halfway to allow the nitrogen in their systems to dispel.

"Well done," said Miss Worsfold with a smile as they dragged Amanda's air cylinder into the boat. Then her expression changed. "You know, I'm going to have to report this incident to Captain Macbeth."

Poppy looked anxious. "But everything worked out all right," she said. "Amanda wasn't hurt—nobody was."

Miss Worsfold frowned. "That's not the point. The Captain has to know about every incident involving safety. That's the rule."

Poppy looked away. Amanda had broken the rules by going off on her own. Or was it her own fault for not keeping a lookout as to where Amanda was? She did not want to get Amanda into trouble, but it looked as if the choice of whom to blame was between her and the other girl.

She made one last plea to Miss Worsfold. "Can't we just forget about it, Miss Worsfold? Just this time? And I promise you, it'll never happen again."

Miss Worsfold shook her head. "No, Poppy, we can't," she said. "Rules are not there to be broken. I'm sorry, but I'm going to have to ask both of you to come with me to the Captain's cabin once we get back to the *Tobermory*."

## CHAPTER 9

### *A lie*

Fee did not see Poppy that day until they were well on their way to Cairns, where the tall-ships race was due to begin. It was shortly before lunch, a time when those who were not on duty at the helm or attending to the sails were allowed to do whatever they wanted to do. Some people did nothing, contenting themselves with sitting in the sun, while others played cards, or wrote up their personal logbooks—the diaries that everybody was required to keep throughout the voyage. Yet others washed their clothes or rinsed the salt out of their hair, or wrote postcards home to mail at the next port. There was always something with which to fill the time.

Fee found Poppy sitting by herself at the foot of one of the masts, shaded from the sun by the shadow cast by the main boom. She saw at once that there was something unusual about her manner—Poppy was usually cheerful and enthusiastic; now, though, she looked downcast and worried.

Fee lowered herself to sit next to her friend. "Something wrong?" she asked.

Poppy shook her head. "I'm fine," she said. "I'm just fine."

But Fee could tell that she was not. She wondered whether Poppy was upset at having to say goodbye to her parents in Sydney. You can get used to being away from home—almost to the point of not thinking about it all that much—but then something brings it all back to you and you start to feel homesick. "You can tell me, you know," she said. "Are you missing your mum and dad?"

The question seemed to surprise Poppy, who looked up sharply. "Missing them? Of course I miss them. Everybody misses home, don't they?"

"So, is that what's making you look so miserable?" asked Fee.

Poppy looked down at the deck once more. It seemed that she was debating whether or not she would take Fee into her confidence. Then she raised her eyes, and Fee could see that she was close to tears.

"It's so, so unfair," said Poppy. "It wasn't my fault, you know. It wasn't my fault at all."

Fee had heard that there had been a diving incident—on a ship news gets around like wildfire—but she did not know the details. Was this what Poppy was talking about? But surely Poppy had nothing to do with what happened, thought Fee. Hadn't it all been to do with Amanda's getting caught by a giant clam—or something equally unlikely?

She waited for a moment to see if Poppy was going to say anything more. When she did not, Fee asked her to tell her exactly what occurred. Was it true that Amanda had almost drowned because she put a leg into the jaws of a giant clam?

Poppy frowned and shook her head. "It wasn't like that at all," she said. "I've heard those stories of divers being trapped that way—but you can't, you know. It would be hard to fit your leg inside—but you could get a belt or a strap caught. That's what happened to Amanda."

Fee shivered. The idea of being caught all that way down and being unable to get up for air was the very worst nightmare.

"Thomas saved her life, you know," Poppy continued. "We both looked for her and then he shared his air while she came up. He was a real hero."

Fee agreed. But why would anybody have blamed Poppy for this? "What has it got to do with you?" she asked.

Poppy explained. "Miss Worsfold told us that we had to report to the Captain," she began. "It seems there's a rule that he has to be told about every incident. So we went along—Thomas Seagrape, Amanda Birtwhistle, and I— and told him what had happened."

"And what did he say?" asked Fee.

"He sat and listened," answered Poppy. "Then he shook his head. Like this." She demonstrated.

"Why?" asked Fee. "Was he cross with you? Because I don't think that he—"

Poppy did not let her finish. "You know how he looks when you've done something you shouldn't have?"

Fee did. The Captain had a way of looking disappointed—as if you had somehow let him down. He did not look like that very often, because he was a kind man and tried to put people at ease, but sometimes his irritation showed.

Poppy continued with her story. "He asked why Amanda was by herself when she first saw the giant clam."

"And why was she?" asked Fee. She knew enough about diving to know that you never dived by yourself if you could avoid it.

Poppy replied that she thought Amanda had drifted off because she was not paying attention. "Not that I'm blaming her," she added. "It's really easy to do that if you're looking at fish. The fish swim off—you follow them—and before you know it, you're far away."

"So it was her fault," said Fee. "In a way, that is. As you say, it happens quite easily—but it was still her responsibility to look out for it."

Poppy nodded. "I didn't move," she said. "Amanda was the one who allowed herself to drift." She paused. "But she lied about that."

Fee drew in her breath. "She said she didn't drift?"

With a further nod of her head Poppy confirmed

Amanda's lie. "Before I could say anything, she told the Captain that she had signaled to me that she was going in that direction and that I had signaled her back to say I was following."

"And she didn't?"

"No," said Poppy. "She didn't. I'm absolutely positive she didn't."

Fee asked what happened next.

"I couldn't believe my ears," said Poppy. "I looked at her, and she just looked back at me as if to challenge me to deny it."

"And did you?" asked Fee.

"I tried to," said Poppy. "But then the Captain held up a hand and told me to keep quiet. Then he shook his head again and said that it sounded to him as if we had both failed to pay attention and that we were both to blame."

The unfairness of this shocked Fee. From what she had heard, it was all Amanda's fault and Poppy had done no wrong. She was astonished that Amanda Birtwhistle, who was generally liked, should tell such a lie to get herself out of trouble. That was the sort of behavior one might expect from somebody like William Edward Hardtack—but not from somebody like Amanda.

"The Captain gave us a lecture," Poppy went on, "about safety. Then he said that as punishment we would not be allowed to dive for the rest of the voyage. He said we were lucky not to have had a tragedy on our hands and he hoped we had learned our lesson."

Fee was eager to hear what Poppy had said to Amanda afterward.

"When we left the Captain's cabin," Poppy said, "I asked Amanda what she had been thinking about. I told her that what she had said was a complete lie and it had gotten us both into trouble."

"And what did she say to that?" asked Fee.

"She denied it. She said she had not told any lies and that she had signaled to me and I had signaled back. She said that I must have forgotten." Poppy paused. "But you know what? I think she was just carrying on with the lie. She wouldn't look at me as she spoke—and that's always a sign. If somebody won't look at you, it's because they're ashamed."

Fee was silent. Being on board a ship with a lot of other people taught you various lessons. And one that she was learning—and learning rather quickly—was that although it was a good thing to trust people, there were times when your trust could be misplaced. Poppy had trusted Amanda, only to discover that the other girl would be prepared to make up a completely false story in order to get herself out of trouble. *How could anybody do such a thing?* she asked herself. The answer, it seemed, was that some people can do things like that quite easily. You might like to think they would feel bad about it, but it seemed that not everybody felt that way. It made Fee sad to think this, because she wanted the world to be a fair place—but sometimes, she decided, it was anything but fair.

Cairns was not far away. By midafternoon the *Tobermory* sailed into the large bay in front of the town and dropped anchor. The rattling of the great anchor chain as it snaked down into the water was normally a welcome sound, as it meant that there could be swimming or exploring, or any of the other things that were laid on by the staff. Of course, diving lessons were popular, as Matron had been a champion diver and liked nothing more than to demonstrate her skills and help others master the art of entering the water without too much of a splash.

But as they sailed into Cairns Bay there was something else to attract their attention. There, lined up at anchor and bobbing up and down with the gentle swell, were four large sailing ships—their competition in the great race that was to start in Cairns and finish in Darwin, far away on the northern coast of Australia. Distances are huge in Australia, and it is a long voyage between those two towns. Just how long it would take depended not only on the wind, which was unpredictable, but also on the skill of the crew. A strong wind in a favorable direction is not much use if the people on board do not know how to take advantage of it, and so a race such as this would be a real test of helming—or steering—the boat, of trimming the sails so that they pick up every ounce of push that the wind will give, of using the currents to help, and of the ability to keep going, day and night, without taking your eye off the task at hand.

Once the anchor had dropped and had dug into the sand below, Mr. Rigger called everybody to a meeting on deck. The Captain came up from his cabin and addressed all assembled. He congratulated them on a good voyage—nothing was said about the diving incident—and then he went on to point to the other sailing ships at anchor around the bay.

"Every one of these ships," he said, "is a training ship—just like the *Tobermory*. And each of them is crewed by people just like you."

Everybody glanced at the ships across the bay, imagining what the other people would be like. Fee asked herself whether each ship would have its equivalent of Hardtack and Co.? Would each have a teacher who could dive as well as Matron or an officer with a mustache like Mr. Rigger's?

The Captain was now pointing to the largest vessel in the group of ships. This was flying a large black, red, and yellow flag.

"Where's that ship from?" asked the Captain. "Anybody know?"

Ben was not sure, but thought he would guess. "Holland?" he called out. "I think that's the Dutch flag."

It was a perfectly reasonable guess, but it brought a

hoot of derision from Geoffrey Shark. "Dutch flag?" he shouted. "You need glasses, MacTavish! Can't you tell the German flag when you see it?"

"Maybe he doesn't know the difference between Holland and Germany," called out Maximilian Flubber.

There was some laughter at this, but not much. Ben glowered back at Shark and Flubber, his ears burning with embarrassment.

"None of that, please!" snapped the Captain. Looking directly at Shark, he continued, "MacTavish made a reasonable suggestion, Mr. Shark. But perhaps you'd care to tell us what the flag on that other ship is." He pointed at a ship lying beyond the German vessel. "Well, come on, Geoffrey: you tell us."

Shark's eyes narrowed. "France?" he ventured.

This brought a hoot of laughter from quite a number of people.

"No," said the Captain. "Wrong. That's a Russian ship." He paused. "Don't be too quick to laugh when other people get the answer wrong."

Ben felt a bit better now that Shark had been told off, but there was not much time to think about this as the Captain was describing the strengths and weaknesses of the other entrants in the race. The German boat would be the main competition; the *Tobermory* should be able to hold its own against the Russian boat, which was heavier and therefore slower than the *Tobermory.* The other two boats were from Australia and New Zealand, and although they were sleek and fast, they were smaller and might find the going heavy when faced with large seas.

"If we want to win," Captain Macbeth concluded, "we shall have to give everything we've got." He paused and looked out over the heads of the ship's company standing before him. "Are you prepared to do that, everyone?"

There was only one answer, and they gave it. "Aye, aye, sir!" This was the naval way of saying yes—and they meant it.

With the main business of the meeting over, Bartholomew Fitzhardy asked Captain Macbeth whether people could go swimming. The Captain smiled when he heard the question. "Not if you want to stay alive," he said.

Badger looked puzzled, and the Captain explained. "Crocodiles," he said simply. "I believe I warned you about them before. This is crocodile territory, I'm afraid."

"But this is the sea," Bartholomew protested. "And look, there are plenty of boats about."

The Captain shook his head. "These are saltwater crocodiles," the Captain reminded him. "Out on the reef it's safe enough, but inshore is a different matter. It may be rare for them to be in the harbor here, but they could be. And I don't think it's worth taking the risk. So no swimming until we're well away from these northern Australian waters."

It was disappointing, as it had been a hot day and

people would have welcomed the chance to cool down in the water. But the Captain's advice was good and all listened. Or most of them did. Flubber, who earlier on had implied that he was not scared of what he had called "overgrown lizards," smirked when the Captain forbade swimming and gave his friends Hardtack and Shark a knowing look. Poppy noticed it, and whispered to Fee, "They're planning something."

"Who?" asked Fee.

Poppy nodded in the direction of Hardtack and his friends. "Those three."

Fee raised an eyebrow. "Do you think they'd be stupid enough to go swimming?"

"They might be," said Poppy. "Those three have done some pretty stupid things in their time."

"If they do," Fee whispered to Poppy, "it could be the last mistake they make."

Poppy sighed. "I wouldn't wish a crocodile attack on anybody—even Hardtack. So I just hope they're not going to do anything dangerous."

Fee did not say anything. She had a bad feeling. Sometimes those bad feelings of hers were wrong and nothing happened—but at other times they were a warning of what really lay in store. She was not sure what it would be this time, but as she thought about it, she had another bad feeling, and when you have as many bad feelings as that, there is good reason not to ignore them.

# CHAPTER 10

## *Swimmers in the water*

Poppy found it hard to get to sleep that night. She was finding it difficult to forget what had happened in the Captain's cabin that morning, when Amanda Birtwhistle had so unfairly landed her in trouble. It is never easy to be punished, but if the punishment is for something you just did not do, it is even harder. Poppy was astonished that Amanda should think she could get away with her false story. She could fool others, perhaps—because nobody else had seen what happened—but Amanda must have realized that Poppy herself knew the truth. Did she not mind that? How could she look herself in the mirror and not cringe with embarrassment at the thought that the face looking back at her was a dishonest one?

Poppy had found herself standing close to Amanda when they were both lining up for dinner in the mess hall. The other girl had avoided her—in fact, she had pretended not to see Poppy at all—and that simply confirmed what

Poppy already thought: Amanda was ashamed. And well she might be.

Fee had spotted what was going on. "Amanda's trying not to look at you," she whispered over the dinner table.

Poppy nodded. "I noticed that," she said.

"I wonder if she's going to pretend not to see you for the rest of the trip," Fee speculated. "What if you're both on helming duty at the same time? What if you're both turning the wheel together?"

Poppy had to smile. "That could be hard. She would have to pretend she was steering with a ghost."

"Or if you bumped into each other in a corridor," Fee went on. "She'd have to pretend that there was nobody there. Or if you spoke to her . . ."

"She'd have to act as if she were deaf," said Poppy. "She'd have to say, 'Did somebody say something?'"

It was all very well, of course, for the two girls to joke about Amanda's behavior, but Poppy felt really hurt by what had happened. She toyed with the idea of going back to see the Captain and telling him that what Amanda had said was untrue, but she thought this would not make any difference. The Captain was always prepared to listen, and everybody knew that he was a fair man, but what could he do in these circumstances? He was being given two completely different versions of events, and had no way of telling which one was the truth. No, there was no point in speaking to him, because at the end of the day it would make no difference.

By lights-out time, Poppy felt no better. Lying in the dark, she stared up at the cabin ceiling and went over everything in her mind, getting crosser and crosser by the moment. Then she tried not to think about it, but this did not work very well. She thought of where they were—of the other ships in the harbor and the small powerboats they had seen coming out to inspect the new arrival—but whenever she did this Amanda seemed somehow to come into the picture. She saw Amanda at the wheel of one of the small boats, looking up at the *Tobermory* and pretending not to see her. She saw Amanda climbing up the rigging of the German training ship then looking back toward the *Tobermory,* but very deliberately not catching her eye.

She would have liked to switch on the light and read. That was always a good way of stopping yourself from thinking thoughts you did not want to think. But if she did that, she might wake Fee up, and she wanted to avoid that. So she closed her eyes once more and tried again to think about something that had nothing at all to do with her life on the *Tobermory.* She thought of home, of the farm near Alice Springs and of how they gathered the sheep for shearing—but then one of the sheep seemed to be avoiding her, and when she looked more closely she saw that it looked remarkably like Amanda Birtwhistle....

And it was then that she heard the noise.

At first she thought it was the sound of small waves lapping at the side of the boat. This sound was always present, but at times it became louder if the wavelets grew bigger for some reason. This could be caused by the wake of a passing boat or by a sudden gust of wind, and it would soon pass. But this sound did not fade away, and Poppy decided there was more to it than that. Somewhere down at the side of the boat, more or less immediately below their porthole, somebody—or something—was splashing around in the water.

Slipping out of her hammock, Poppy crossed the cabin to investigate. In the darkness, the porthole was a faintly glowing circle. There was a full moon that night, and outside the sea was bathed in silver moonlight dancing on the surface of the water. Poppy strained her eyes but was unable to see very much, other than the sea and, in the distance, the twinkling lights of the sleeping town. Suddenly, though, she became aware of a figure beside her: Fee had woken up and was now also out of her hammock.

"I heard a noise," said Poppy. And then, apologetically, "I'm sorry if I woke you up, Fee—I didn't mean to."

"I was awake anyway," said Fee. "I heard something too."

Just at that moment the noise repeated itself. "There," said Poppy. "Did you hear that?"

Fee nodded. "It was a sort of splashing sound," she said.

Poppy hesitated. It was strictly against the rules to

go up on deck at night without permission. There was a good reason for this: if you went up there in the darkness and fell overboard, nobody would see you. That was a rule that everybody understood and obeyed. Yet what if that splashing sound was being made by somebody who needed help? Surely that would be good enough reason to break the rules and see what was happening?

Her cabinmate must have been asking herself much the same question, as when Poppy turned to her, she simply nodded her head. "I think we should go and look," Fee whispered.

Together they made their way out of their cabin, taking great care to close the door behind them as quietly as possible. Then they crept along the corridor and up the companionway that would take them out onto the main deck. Nobody saw them go and nobody heard them.

The day had been a hot one, but the air was now a bit cooler. Above their heads, competing with the moonlight, were fields of tiny stars, and for a moment both girls simply gazed in wonder at the unfamiliar night scene. On the other side of the bay, they saw the mast lights of the other ships move gently from side to side with the slight rocking motion of the sea.

Poppy pointed to the side of the ship from which the noise had come. Then, creeping toward the edge of the deck, they peered over railings. At first they saw nothing but the sea, with the moonlight dappling the surface, but then, as their eyes became accustomed to the darkness, they made out three shapes in the water.

Poppy gave Fee a nudge. "Somebody's swimming," she whispered.

And then they heard a voice. It was not a loud voice, and they only heard it because they were on the deck immediately above it. But it was loud enough for them to make out exactly what was being said.

"Come on, Geoffrey," said the voice. "Let's swim all the way round the ship."

"All right," came the reply.

And then, "Wait for me," said a third voice.

Poppy and Fee looked at each other in astonishment. There was no mistaking who it was down there in the water: William Edward Hardtack, Geoffrey Shark, and Maximilian Flubber. And just as they came to this realization, they saw the rope ladder that had been slung over the side just a little farther down the deck. This reached all the way to the water and must have been the way the boys had climbed down for their forbidden swim.

As Hardtack and his friends began to swim toward the bow of the ship, Poppy touched Fee's elbow and pointed back toward the companionway. Without saying anything to each other, the two girls moved away from the railings.

"What are we going to do?" asked Fee, her voice dropped to a whisper.

Poppy thought for a moment. "They're being really,

really stupid," she replied. "Everybody knows that you should never swim in the sea at night. It's the most dangerous time there is. That's when sharks—and saltwater crocs, too—are much more likely to attack."

Fee drew in her breath. "Should we tell them?" she asked.

Poppy thought it unlikely that the boys would listen to them. "I think we should go and wake Mr. Rigger," she said. "It's for their own good. They're in real danger."

Fee knew that Poppy was right. Nobody liked to tattle, but there were times when telling somebody in authority about something was exactly the right thing to do. This, she thought, was one of them.

Because of the real danger that Hardtack and his friends were exposing themselves to, the girls lost no time in making their way down the companionway and then running along the corridor toward the section of the boat where the staff cabins were. Poppy had brought her small flashlight with her, and now she switched it on to guide them to the door bearing the notice MR. RIGGER, FIRST OFFICER. Not caring now what noise she made, she knocked loudly.

It took another couple of knocks before Mr. Rigger appeared at the door, wearing a dark dressing gown with small pictures of anchors on it.

He still looked sleepy. "What is it?" he asked drowsily. "Is something wrong?"

Poppy did the talking. "Three of the boys are swimming, Mr. Rigger. They can't know how dangerous it is. We thought we should tell you."

This quickly woke Mr. Rigger. "Oh no!" he said. "That's extremely dangerous. Where are they?"

Fee explained that they had set off to swim all the way round the ship. This brought another exclamation of alarm from Mr. Rigger, who had now retrieved a large and powerful flashlight from a shelf near his door. Then he strode out along the corridor, followed by the two girls.

"You did the right thing to tell me," he said. "Well done, girls."

Once out on the deck, Mr. Rigger made his way toward the bow. Then, leaning over the railings, he shined his flashlight down toward the sea below. The beam made a circle on the water, and when this moved forward it soon picked up a shape in the water. Then it picked up another, and another after that.

"Hardtack!" shouted Mr. Rigger. "Shark! Flubber! Get out of the water this instant!"

Caught in the beam of light, Hardtack looked up at the figures on the deck. "But we were only going for a swim, sir," he shouted back. "It was really hot. We needed to cool down."

This only served to make Mr. Rigger even angrier. "I said this instant," he called out. "You're in extreme danger."

The mention of danger seemed to have an effect, as all three boys started to swim back toward their rope ladder as fast as they could. Soon they were all clambering up onto the deck, their hair disheveled, water dripping from their swimming trunks.

"We weren't doing any harm," muttered Hardtack, scowling at the two girls as he spoke.

Mr. Rigger lined the three boys up and gave them a dressing down. "I don't think you realize the risk you were taking," he said severely. "Swimming in these waters was forbidden for a reason. And swimming at night even more so."

"There wasn't anything in the water, sir," offered Flubber in an attempt at an excuse. "We didn't see anything."

"Didn't *see* anything?" exploded Mr. Rigger. "That's exactly the point, Flubber. You don't see what's below you in the water. But it sees you, all right! Oh yes, it sees you."

Hardtack said nothing, nor did Shark and Flubber. They had all shot hostile glances toward Poppy and Fee, though, and Mr. Rigger had noticed this.

"These girls probably saved you, you know," Mr. Rigger said. "I think you should thank them. If they hadn't come to fetch me, you could be inside the stomach of a great white shark by now. Or inside a large saltwater crocodile, for that matter."

Hardtack smirked. "Oh, surely not, sir—"

Mr. Rigger did not let him continue. "So, I suggest you thank them," he said.

The boys said nothing.

"Go on," said Mr. Rigger, sounding firmer now. "Thank them." And then he added, "And that's an order."

Reluctantly, the boys mumbled their thanks, though neither Poppy nor Fee felt they meant a word of it, of course. Then, having been ordered below, they made their way back to their cabins.

Mr. Rigger turned to the girls. "You two should go back to bed," he said. "And if those boys cause you any trouble, you come straight to me."

Poppy and Fee returned to their cabin and climbed into their hammocks. Poppy was tired now and had no difficulty dropping off to sleep. Fee lay awake for a bit longer, and then she too dozed off, lulled by the slight movement of the ship. This was like a gentle nurse who rocked your cradle, backwards and forwards, until the waves of sleep washed over you like surf on the sand of a beach.

Mr. Rigger did nothing further about the swimming incident. Poppy and Fee wondered whether Hardtack and the others would be called out for Captain's Parade, and were secretly relieved when this did not happen. They were already on the wrong side of Hardtack for having called Mr. Rigger, and he would have been very much nastier had he and his friends been punished. At breakfast Shark gave a scowl in Poppy's direction, but she stared right back at him and he soon looked away. Afterward, though, when they were filing up onto the deck for the prerace briefing,

Flubber sidled up to Fee and addressed her out of the side of his mouth.

"About last night," he muttered.

Fee braced herself for a threat.

"I want you to know," Flubber went on, "that I'm glad you called Mr. Rigger."

Fee could not contain her surprise. She stared at Flubber in astonishment as he continued.

"It wasn't my idea," Flubber said, glancing about him as he spoke. "Bill suggested it."

*Bill?* It took Fee a moment or two before she realized that Flubber was talking about William Edward Hardtack. Somehow, the shortening of his name made him seem a much less threatening character than he was in reality. Of course you would go swimming with somebody called Bill—if he asked you! But then she thought: no, names tell you nothing about what the person is like inside.

"William Edward Hardtack?" Fee asked. "Are you talking about him?"

Flubber nodded. "Bill—or Tacky, as I sometimes call him—said he was feeling hot and wanted to cool down. I reminded him that we had been told not to swim, but he said that was nonsense. He said he had seen people swimming off the beach earlier on, and if they could, then why couldn't we?"

"Maybe it's safer close to the shore," said Fee. "If the water's shallow, you can see the crocodiles."

"Maybe," said Flubber. "Anyway, Geoff wanted to go too, and so I felt I couldn't say anything. They'd think I was a coward if I refused to go."

He looked at her inquiringly, as if he wanted her support, and for a few moments Fee thought of what it must be like to be Flubber and to worry about what Hardtack and Shark thought of you. She looked at Flubber and found that she felt sorry for him. Nobody was completely bad—even William Edward Hardtack, she told herself, must have some good points, and Flubber, certainly, was nowhere near as unpleasant as he was.

"You must have felt very scared down there in the water," she said.

Flubber looked at her with gratitude. He seemed relieved that here was somebody who understood.

"I was petrified," he confided. "All the time while Bill and Sharky were splashing around, I was thinking of what might be swimming around in the water directly beneath me. I tried to keep my legs up as much as possible, so that whatever was there would get to their legs before mine." He paused before he continued, "I know that makes me sound bad, but that's the way it was."

Fee made it clear that she would have done the same— after all, they were the ones who wanted to go swimming. If anything bit anybody, it was only fair that it should be them rather than the person who did not want to swim. "You don't need to feel bad," she said. "They were the ones

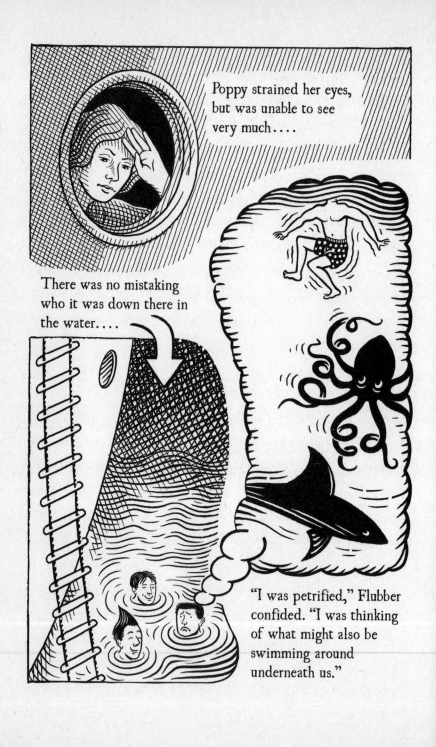

who wanted to go. You were . . . You were . . ." She searched for the right words. She wanted to say, *You were the one who was easily led,* but she realized this would not be all that tactful. Poor Flubber! Why could he not get away from the other two? Why couldn't he simply have nothing to do with them?

Flubber found the words for her. "I was the weak one," he said miserably. "I know that I shouldn't do everything they tell me to do, but it's hard, you know."

Fee felt even more sorry for him now.

"And what I wanted to say to you," Flubber continued, "is that I'm very grateful to you for calling Mr. Rigger. I think we really were in danger, and I want to say a proper thank-you."

Fee was about to tell him she was glad that she and Poppy were able to help, but before she said this, Geoffrey Shark suddenly appeared and muttered something to Flubber. Fee did not catch what it was, but she saw its effect: Flubber immediately turned away and went off with the other boy.

Poppy had seen Flubber talking to Fee and now she came over to ask her what it was.

"So what did Flubber have to say?" she inquired.

"He wanted to say thank you," Fee answered. "He was really scared in the water."

Poppy thought about this. Of the three boys, Flubber was definitely the least obnoxious. Was it possible, she wondered, that he would somehow detach himself from the other two and start behaving more reasonably? He had a reputation for lying, but for all anybody knew, he might be changing. She had known people who had taken a good hard look at their faults and done something about them. Perhaps Flubber was beginning to do just that.

"Maybe we should try to be friendly to Flubber," Poppy said.

Fee made a face.

"Yes, I know," said Poppy. "But maybe we should give him a chance."

Fee realized that Poppy was right. Friendship with somebody you didn't like could be hard, but she knew that it was sometimes what you had to do. "We could try," she said.

"Let's do that," said Poppy. "And then we could see if Shark could be persuaded to show his good side."

Fee raised her eyebrows. "Some things are very, very unlikely," she said.

"It might be worth trying," Poppy mused. "And if you don't try something, then how will you ever know whether it's possible?"

Fee had to agree to that, but she wondered what Ben and Badger would think.

"Well," said Poppy, "it's exactly the same thing: if you don't ask them, you won't find out."

Their conversation ended on that note. The Captain

had come up on deck and they needed to pay attention to what he had to say.

"In just thirty minutes," the Captain announced, "the tall-ships race will begin. We've come a long way for this. I've looked at the weather forecasts for the next week or so, and I'm happy to say that the wind is in a favorable direction—and is fairly strong. That means we have some exciting sailing ahead of us, everyone."

He unrolled a large chart on which he pointed out the route from the starting point of the race to the final destination. The voyage would take them up to the easterly tip of Australia, the Cape York Peninsula, and then across a wide gulf to a bay that was guarded by Kangaroo Cliff.

"The first ship to reach Kangaroo Cliff," he said, "wins the race."

Poppy and Fee exchanged excited glances. Ben, who was standing nearby, smiled. He asked them whether they thought the *Tobermory* might be the winner. Poppy laughed. "Of course," she said.

Fee was more cautious. "I hope so," she said.

The Captain gave detailed instructions. Ben and Badger were on helming duty for the first two hours, while Poppy and Fee were charged with handling some of the sheets— the ropes that controlled the sails. Thomas Seagrape was to help with navigation, as were Tanya Herring and Angela Singh. Others were detailed to raise the anchor, keep the mainsail in trim, and climb up the mast to keep a lookout.

Everybody had duties and was determined to do them to the best of his or her ability, even if it was something as simple as helping Cook peel potatoes for lunch.

Lunch, though, was a long time away and nobody was thinking of it just yet. They had a race to begin, and a deep ocean to sail off on. That was quite enough.

## CHAPTER 11

*Boy on the beach*

The next few days were something of a blur. A fully rigged sailing ship, moving at its top speed in a strong wind, can be like a galloping horse. It must be watched every moment—held in check at one time while being allowed to shoot ahead at another. Not only must the sails be coaxed into just the right shape—so that they make use of every breath of wind—but a sharp eye must be kept on what the sea itself is doing. Where are the waves coming from? How big are they? Will they help the ship along by allowing her to surf, or will they hinder her by making her wallow in the troughs between their crests?

It was demanding work, and while they were racing along there was no time for lessons. This meant that the normal routine of a school ship was suspended, just as it was during the official school holidays. But this was no holiday for the students on the *Tobermory:* the day was divided into watches of a few hours each, and every minute of every watch involved hard work—tugging at ropes, keeping the deck clear, struggling with the helm as the ship fought with the action of wind and wave. At the end of their watch most people were utterly exhausted, and would go down to their cabins and collapse into their hammocks for some sorely needed rest.

And at night the pace continued, as this was open sea and there was no place to drop anchor and spend the hours of darkness getting your breath back. Like the day, the night was divided into watches, and if your watch started in the small hours of the morning, you would have to wake from your sleep, get dressed, and report on deck—no matter how tired you felt.

When he and Badger were on a night watch, Ben would set his alarm for ten minutes before they were due to start their duties. Then, when the buzzer sounded and he had rolled himself out of his hammock, he would cross to Badger's side of the cabin to wake his still-sleeping friend.

Badger was a sound sleeper and was sometimes difficult to rouse. You cannot actually turn over in a hammock—or not very easily—but he would try to do that, just as you might try to turn over in a bed and bury your head under a pillow when somebody came to wake you up.

"Come on, Badge," Ben would say. "Time to go on watch."

Reluctantly Badger would open his eyes and unwind himself from the comfortable embrace of the hammock. And so the watch would begin, with a number of still-half-asleep people silently going about their duties under a wide and empty sky. But as they woke fully, they would all be caught up in sheer wonder at what they were doing. There they were, sailing across a wide expanse of sea, with only the sound of the wind and the waves to accompany them; there they were in the darkness, under the great velvet canopy of the night sky, with the stars swinging high above them, tiny specks of light that went on and on and on in uncountable numbers.

Even during the day, when the sky was filled with light and the sun played on the waves, the sea was still a lonely place. They sometimes saw a ship in the distance, making its way to one of the ports farther south; occasionally they saw a lone yacht on the horizon. But for most of the time there was nothing but ocean in every direction. Of the other three tall ships—their competitors in the race—there was no sign, although every so often somebody would imagine they could make out the shape of a mast and sails in the far distance. These sightings, though, were always unconfirmed, and when others looked they tended to see nothing.

"How do you think we're doing?" Ben asked Mr. Rigger one morning. "Do you think we're in the lead?"

Mr. Rigger smiled and shrugged. "I have no idea, Ben," he replied. "All I know is that we could be first, second, third, or fourth. Does that answer your question?"

Ben laughed. "I suppose it does, sir," he said.

The Captain spoke to the whole school each morning and showed them where they were on the chart. He could be quite sure of this from his instruments—GPS will show you exactly where you are anywhere on the surface of the earth—but Captain Macbeth still liked to use the old methods of finding this out. By plotting how long they had been sailing and at what speed, he was able to estimate how many nautical miles they had covered, and from that he could work out where they were.

Looked at on the chart, their progress seemed painfully slow. But that was because Australia was so big and their route so long. Gradually, though, they inched their way up the chart and the tip of the continent came closer and closer.

They had arrived in Australia, but had seen little of the country so far. People had talked about crocodiles and snakes, in the way that people love to frighten one another with stories, but up to that point, nobody had seen any.

It was a bright, warm day and the *Tobermory* was sailing close to the shore. Their route had taken them far out to sea, but now that they were nearing Cape York, they were much closer in, getting ready to find their way round the tip of Australia.

It was a remote and lonely part of the country. There were a few towns and harbors, but these were separated from one another by long distances and by rough and impenetrable land. In these parts, you could drive a car for hours along one of the rough tracks and not see a single other person. And you had to be careful: if you strayed off the track into the bush, then you could very quickly lose your way and never be seen again. It was not the sort of place for people who did not know what they were doing.

The coast was just as deserted. There were long miles of empty beaches backed with dense forest. There were cliffs and outcrops of jagged rocks that fingered their way out into the sea; there were river mouths that gave a glimpse of thick vegetation along the banks beyond. There were distant, mysterious hills, shimmering in the heat. If you ever wanted to imagine the very end of the world, then this was what you might see in your mind's eye.

That morning, Ben and Badger were on lookout duty. This involved climbing up the mainmast to the small platform known as the crow's nest. Not everybody liked going up there—and if you told Mr. Rigger that you did not have a head for heights, he would always excuse you and give you some other duty. But this was unnecessary for Ben and Badger, both of whom liked being that high and getting the view that the crow's nest afforded.

Their job as lookouts was to see if there were any hidden reefs in the sea ahead. The water here was shallow, and although the charts marked the main rocks, there were always obstacles that the chart-makers might have missed. It was possible, too, that there could be small boats—used by local fishermen—that the people on the helm might miss and yet would be visible from up high. These boats belonged to local fishermen from the small groups of people who lived in this lonely place. They were not many in number, and you could easily not see their settlements along the coast, but they had been there for thousands of years and they knew every inch of this vast territory.

It was Ben who saw something first. They were sailing past the mouth of a wide bay, and he was looking out at the land along the bay's edge. In the middle of the bay he noticed there was a small island—not much bigger than the deck of the ship—and it was on this that he saw the movement. At first he thought it might be an animal, but then, as he squinted against the glare, he saw that it was the figure of a person. And the person, he realized, was waving his arms to attract attention.

"Look over there," said Ben. "There's somebody on that little island, Badger."

Badger had a pair of binoculars slung around his neck and he now raised these to get a better view. "I think you're right," he said. "And he's waving."

"What's he doing there?" asked Ben.

Badger looked again. With the motion of the ship, it was difficult to focus well, but after a moment he slipped the strap over his head and handed the binoculars to Ben. "See what you think, Ben," he said. "I'd say he's calling for help."

Ben looked at the island and the small figure on the sand at its edge. "Yes," he said. "I think you're right, Badge."

It was the confirmation that Badger needed before he called out to the officers below. "Mr. Rigger!" he shouted. "Mr. Rigger!"

Down on the deck below, Mr. Rigger looked up to the crow's nest. He had been teaching a small group of students how to take compass bearings, but a warning from the lookouts took priority over everything else.

Mr. Rigger cupped his hands around his mouth and shouted back, "What is it?"

"Somebody on an island," replied Badger at the top of his voice. "He's signaling to us."

Mr. Rigger went to the side of the deck and looked ahead. He could see the island in the distance, but from where he was standing he could not see anybody on it.

"Are you sure?" he shouted up to Badger.

"Yes," yelled Badger. "We're pretty sure."

Now Mr. Rigger did not hesitate. "Alter course twenty degrees to port," he called to the people on the helm.

On helm duty were Angela Singh and Thomas Seagrape. "Altering course," they responded in unison. "Twenty degrees to port."

The great ship's bow swung round obediently, and soon the *Tobermory* was heading directly for the small island in the middle of the bay, cutting through the shallow green water at a speed that would bring them to their destination within fifteen minutes or so. Aware that something was happening, those people who were not on duty massed up at the bow of the boat, interested in seeing what exactly it was that had caused the change in course.

Mr. Rigger had called Captain Macbeth from his cabin down below. The Captain went to the helm and stood beside Angela and Thomas, ready to take over in an emergency, but content to leave them at the wheel for the time being. As he stood there, he gave orders for some of the sails to be rolled up so that the *Tobermory* would be slowed down by the time they neared the island. He also ordered the engine to be started so that once they had stopped sailing, the ship could be easily maneuvered.

"Lookouts down from the crow's nest," the Captain shouted to Ben and Badger. "And well done for spotting this."

Ben and Badger both felt proud, as a compliment from the Captain was much sought after on the *Tobermory*.

"I hope he wasn't just waving to say hello," muttered Badger. "We'll look a bit silly if he was."

Ben shook his head. "I think he really does need help," he said.

As the *Tobermory* drew closer to the island, Ben and Badger were able to see that they were right. It was now clear that the figure on the island was a boy, and that he was very pleased they were there. Although he had stopped waving his arms, the way that he paced about the beach made it obvious that he was eager for somebody to come ashore. And when they lowered one of the boats, he immediately beckoned again, pointing out a safe place for a small boat to beach on the island.

Because they were the ones who had spotted the boy, Ben and Badger were told they could row the boat that would take Mr. Rigger and Matron ashore. Matron brought her first-aid kit, just in case any immediate medical treatment was needed, and Mr. Rigger took a large bottle of water in case the castaway was desperately thirsty. And he was a castaway, they thought, as there was no sign on the island of a boat or indeed of any other way of getting back to the mainland.

As their small boat approached the beach, the boy waded into the surf to help them. They saw that he was a local boy, probably a member of one of the groups whose land this was. These were Aboriginal people—the people who had lived in Australia for many thousands of years and who still spoke the first languages that had been used in this place. They were hardy people, with the skills and knowledge to survive in conditions that would have defeated many others.

The boy greeted them in English.

"Thank you for coming," he said as he helped haul the boat onto the sand.

The coast is deserted, with long miles of empty beaches backed by dense forest....

"Look over there," said Ben. "There's somebody on that little island."

The boy waded into the surf to help guide their boat ashore.

Mr. Rigger introduced them. "My name is Rigger," he said. "This is Matron, and these two here are Ben and Badger. They're the ones who saw you waving."

The boy looked at Ben and Badger and grinned. "I'm glad you did," he said. "And my name is ... Well, I won't give you my full name because you won't be able to say it easily. A lot of people call me Will, and you can do that if you like."

Ben looked at Will. He was about the same age as him and Badger, he thought.

"So what's the trouble?" asked Mr. Rigger. "How did you get stranded out here?"

Will pointed out to sea. "My boat drifted off," he said. "I tied it to a rock at the edge of the beach and when the tide came in, it drifted. I didn't see it until it was too late."

Mr. Rigger nodded. He had seen that happen before, although not in such isolated and dangerous conditions. "I imagine it's gone for good," he said.

Will nodded. He had been smiling, but now his face fell. "It's my own fault," he said.

Mr. Rigger tried to make him feel better. "Every one of us has made a mistake," he said. "There won't be a single person at sea who hasn't done something stupid in his time."

Will seemed grateful for this, and brightened up. "It was an old boat," he said. "It used to belong to my grandfather, but he doesn't need it anymore. It's not the end of the world."

Mr. Rigger now asked Will why he had come out to the island.

"To meet the plane," Will replied.

Mr. Rigger looked blank. "The plane?"

"Yes," said Will. "There's a seaplane that comes here every other month. It brings medical supplies for my people."

They waited for him to continue.

"You see," Will said, "our people live over there." He pointed to some hills beyond the mainland shore. "It's very far from everywhere, and there are no roads going in. There's a landing strip, but in the wet, that's just a field of mud."

Matron looked puzzled. "In the wet?" she asked.

Will smiled. "The rainy season," he said. "We call it the wet. Most of the roads and tracks are blocked by mud."

Badger remembered that Poppy had said something about this. She had told him how heavy rains could turn a dry plain into a lake overnight.

Will now continued his story. "I usually come out to the island to pick up the supplies," he explained. "But a couple of days ago, when I came out here, due to the weather, I was late. So when I arrived I saw the seaplane taking off again. They must have thought I'd forgotten to come."

"Will it come again?" asked Ben.

Will shook his head. "Not until next time," he said. "And that will be two months from now." He paused. "Unless we can get in touch with them."

Will looked expectantly at Mr. Rigger, who immediately understood the unspoken question.

"We have a radio," said Mr. Rigger. "Would you like—"

Will did not let him finish. "Oh, thanks," he said. "That's just what we need. If I could get in touch with the Flying Doctor people by radio, they can send the seaplane. It could be here by tomorrow."

Matron smiled. She knew all about the Flying Doctor Service—the organization that sends doctors by plane to the remotest parts of Australia to deal with emergencies. "I'm sure we'll be able to do that," she said. "Won't we, Mr. Rigger?"

Mr. Rigger nodded. "No problem," he said. "Let's get back to the ship straightaway." He turned to Will. "You can come with us, Will, so that you can speak to them. Then you can stay with us on board until the plane arrives."

Ben was thinking of something. They were meant to be in a race, and yet here was Mr. Rigger saying that they could spend the night here—and probably quite a bit of the following day too. How could they possibly do that if they were to win the race? He wondered whether he should ask Mr. Rigger about this, but something told him that it would be tactless. Will needed help, and it was one of the firmest rules of the sea that you never refused help to somebody in need, even if you were in a hurry to get to your destination. That was one of the first things a sailor learned, and somebody like Mr. Rigger, who had been brought up on the rules of the sea, would know that as well as he knew the alphabet.

When they arrived back at the *Tobermory* there was a large crowd on deck to welcome them. Badger thought that Will might have been nervous about meeting so many new people, but Will did not seem in the least bit concerned. With a broad smile on his face, he climbed up the rope ladder onto the deck of the *Tobermory* and shook hands with the Captain, who was waiting to greet him.

Poppy was keen to find out what happened. "Was he shipwrecked?" she asked Badger.

Badger told her about Will's boat drifting away. Then he went on to explain that Will was hoping to get the seaplane to come the next day and that they would be staying where they were until then.

"But what about the race?" asked Thomas Seagrape, who had been listening to their conversation.

Badger shrugged. "We'll just have to try to catch up later on," he said.

Thomas looked astonished. "But we can't do that," he said. "We've come all this way. . . ."

He did not finish. Captain Macbeth was clapping his hands together, a sign for everybody to gather round him.

"As you will have noticed," he announced, "we have

carried out a rescue. According to the law of the sea, it is your duty—as I hope you all know—it is our duty to help anybody in peril at sea." He paused, looking out over the expectant faces of the crew. "Not only that," Captain Macbeth continued, "but in this case we are offering some additional help. We shall be staying here to receive some important medical supplies. We shall be here until at least tomorrow afternoon."

This brought a groundswell of surprised—and disappointed—murmuring, but the Captain simply raised a finger and continued, "I know many of you will be upset that we shall be losing our position in the race, but we are doing this because it is the right thing to do. Does anybody think otherwise?"

There was complete silence. William Edward Hardtack looked angry and Geoffrey Shark went so far as to sneer—but only behind a raised hand. Then Poppy spoke.

"I think it's exactly the right thing to do," she said. "We understand, Captain."

Captain Macbeth smiled at her. "I'm glad you said that, Poppy. You're an Australian, and I think you understand how important it is to help people when you're in a remote spot."

Geoffrey Shark looked at Poppy and gave a half-concealed snigger. "Is he your boyfriend?" he asked under his breath, just loud enough for Poppy to hear. "This guy we picked up—is he your boyfriend?"

Poppy pretended not to hear. She had decided that this was the best tactic with somebody like Shark; if you pretended not to hear, he would be denied the pleasure of learning you were upset by what he said.

After the Captain's announcement Mr. Rigger took Will down to the radio room, where a call was put through to the Flying Doctor Service. After they had been told what had happened, they agreed that the seaplane would arrive the next morning with the medical supplies.

Will was relieved that the arrangement had been made. He said he did not need to let his family know, as the boat trip back sometimes took two days and he would not yet be considered missing. He was reassured by Mr. Rigger that they would make a boat available to take him ashore with the supplies and that they could provide him with food and water for his journey back to his people.

"And now," said Mr. Rigger, "you have a bit of time to look about our boat. You can join us for dinner and we'll find a hammock somewhere for you to sleep in tonight."

Will enjoyed his dinner as he sat between Poppy and Badger. When the time came to go to bed, a spare hammock was found for him and hung up in the cabin occupied by Ben and Badger. Lights-out seemed to come far too soon, and the three boys talked well into the night, telling one another about the lives they led at home. Will was fascinated to hear what Badger said about his home just outside New York; it was about as different as could be from the remote spot where his own people lived. They had no electricity and no high buildings, but as Badger listened to Will tell them about his hunting dogs and his canoe, he found himself thinking about how he would happily exchange everything he had for the sort of life that Will led. You could not keep hunting dogs in New York, nor could you throw a boomerang, or fish from the beach, or ride on the back of a turtle in the waters of a bay. Ben, listening with equal fascination to Will's stories, found himself in complete agreement. And he still thought that as he drifted off to sleep.

## CHAPTER 12

### *Where's Henry?*

The seaplane arrived shortly after breakfast the next morning. At first it was no more than a distant drone and a speck in the sky to the south, but a few minutes later everybody had a good view of it as it dropped down onto the bay, bounced about a bit as its floats engaged with the surface of the water, and then taxied to a halt beside the *Tobermory*.

Mr. Rigger supervised the lowering of the boat that would collect the precious cargo of medical supplies. Will was to use this boat, he said, and he could take Ben and Badger to give him a hand. Poppy could go too, if she wished.

The friends set off, along with Will. A short row brought them to the side of the seaplane, where they tied the boat to a ring on one of the plane's floats. The pilot greeted them cheerfully, laughing as Will apologized for the failure to meet him on the previous occasion.

"Easily done, Will," he said, and then added, "sorry to hear about that boat of yours."

It did not take long to unload the supplies. Once that was done, the pilot helped them untie their boat, and he stood on one of the floats to wave to them as they made their way back to the *Tobermory*. Then, joining the others on the deck, they watched as the plane took off, bumping at speed across the bay before the floats shook themselves free of the water. Once aloft, the pilot circled the *Tobermory* at low altitude, dipping his wings in salute before the plane climbed up into the sky and was lost to sight.

Will had brought an empty backpack with him from the island, and it was in this that the supply of medicines was now carefully packed.

"We'll take you ashore now, Will," Mr. Rigger said. "Would you like anybody to come with you to say good-bye?"

Will said, "I'd like Ben and Badger, and Fee and Poppy too."

Mr. Rigger nodded. "That's fine," he said.

"And one more," Will suddenly added, and pointed.

Mr. Rigger smiled. "No problem with that," he said.

Will had been introduced to Henry earlier on. "The dog," he said simply. "Can the dog come for the ride?"

It seemed that Henry sensed he was being talked about, as he began to wag his tail enthusiastically.

Mr. Rigger smiled. "I don't see why not," he replied.

Ben said, "Oh, that's terrific! Henry loves going in the rowing boats."

"Right," said Mr. Rigger in a businesslike manner. "Let's get going."

All six of them—and Henry—stepped aboard the rowing boat. Ben and Badger took their place at the oars—they were both experienced rowers—while Mr. Rigger took the tiller. Will, who was familiar with the waters of the bay, made for the bow so that he could guide Mr. Rigger through the shoals of rocks near the beach. Poppy sat amidships, with Henry beside her; she held his collar just in case he became too excited and tried to jump into the water. He had been known to do that, and they did not want him trying any such thing.

The tide was with them, and it took no more than half an hour to get to the beach. When they arrived, Will jumped out into the surf and pulled the boat ashore. Then the rest of them disembarked, including Henry, who dashed around on the beach chasing his tail and barking with delight at being on dry land again.

There was a thick forest of trees lining the edge of the beach. Will pointed to this and explained that although this looked like an impossible barrier, there was a path through it that he knew well. If he followed that, he would arrive home, although it would take about ten hours.

"Are you sure you're going to be all right?" asked Mr. Rigger.

Will nodded. "I've done this hundreds of times," he said. "I know this coast well."

As he spoke, a flock of large white birds rose from the trees with a raucous squawking.

"Galahs," said Poppy, pointing to the birds as they rose up in the sky.

"Noisy fellows," said Will.

Ben had never seen birds like that before, and he watched in fascination. Everything about Australia was so colorful, it seemed to him—and so unusual. And there seemed to be constant birdsong filling the air and echoing up against the empty sky. *I like this country,* he said to himself.

Mr. Rigger suggested that they walk with Will as far as the beginning of his path. Then they could say goodbye to him and make their way back to the *Tobermory.* Badger felt sad about this, but that was part and parcel of living on a boat; you met all sorts of people in the places you stopped in, but you had to move on and say goodbye. It sometimes seemed to him that life was one goodbye after another.

Badger was thinking about this when suddenly Poppy asked, "Anybody seen Henry?"

Ben looked about them. "He was here a moment ago," he said.

"I saw him too," said Badger. "But ..."

Mr. Rigger reached into his pocket and took out his bosun's whistle. Raising it to his lips, he blew three shrill blasts and then looked out across the beach. "Henry's

The seaplane taxied to a halt beside the *Tobermory*.

SCHOOL SHIP TOBERMORY

As Will spoke, a flock of colorful birds rose from the trees with a raucous squawking.

"I think we should look and see what the sand has to tell us," Will said.

always come to that," he said. "I reward him with a dog biscuit. It never fails."

They waited for several minutes, and when there was still no sign of Henry, Mr. Rigger blew the whistle again. Once again, nothing happened.

Will had an idea. "I think I might see what the sand has to tell us," he said. "It'll have a clear enough story."

They all walked behind Will as he began to track the dog's paw prints across the beach.

"He headed toward our track," said Will. "Maybe he saw something over there—a kangaroo or a wallaby. He might have gone after it."

They reached the point where the track came down to the beach. Sure enough, there were Henry's telltale paw prints following the path into the forest. Will pointed them out to Mr. Rigger and then asked him what he thought they should do.

Mr. Rigger frowned. "I suppose we could wait and see if he comes back," he suggested.

"But he might not," said Poppy. "And he might get lost. If he's chasing a roo or something, he could easily get lost. We saved a penguin and a boy. We must do the same for Henry."

They all agreed. "Even our own dogs sometimes get lost in this heavy bush," Will said, pointing to the thick vegetation. "And a dog who doesn't know this place is even more likely to lose his way."

Mr. Rigger rubbed his chin thoughtfully. "But we can't all wander off into the forest," he said. "They're expecting us back at the ship within the hour. If we don't turn up, they'll send out a search party and . . ."

"And the search party itself could get lost," said Poppy. "That happened once at Alice Springs. They had to send out a search party to find the search party."

"Why don't you go back to the boat, sir?" Badger said to Mr. Rigger. "You can tell the Captain that we've gone to look for Henry. Then you can bring a boat back here in, say, three hours or so—by which time we should have found Henry."

Mr. Rigger looked doubtful. "But I don't want you getting lost," he said. "You don't know this bit of land."

"But I do," said Will. "I was born here. I learned to walk on these paths. I've walked them every day of my life."

Poppy was nodding her head in agreement. "I know a bit about the bush too," she said. "Remember, I come from Alice Springs."

"You've got a lot of bush out there," said Will.

Mr. Rigger appeared to be won over. "All right," he agreed. He looked at his watch. "How long do you need?"

They all looked at Will, who looked up at the sun and then scratched his head. "It depends on how far he's gone. I'll have to set off for our place in about four hours so that I get back by dark. If you come back in four hours, we should be here with Henry—with any luck."

Mr. Rigger agreed to this and they all began to push the boat back into the water. Then, seating himself amidships, he prepared the oars and started to row. "Good luck," he called out as the boat nosed into the surf and began to pull away from the shore. "See you again as planned."

"Right," said Will, taking command of the situation. "Everyone follow me."

They fell into line behind him. Poppy, being the most experienced bushwalker after Will, took her place at the end of the line, where she would be able to keep an eye open for any dangers behind them. One of the rules, whether you were at sea or on dry land, was "look behind you." Everything may be all right in the front, but what was going on behind you could be a different matter altogether. For all you knew, something could be stalking you, and unless you turned around from time to time you would never know that it was there.

They walked for about twenty minutes before Will suddenly held up a hand and brought them to a halt.

"Hold on, everybody," he called out. "Henry left the track here."

They crowded round as Will pointed to the place where the dog's prints veered off the narrow sandy track.

"What happened?" asked Ben.

Will shrugged. "I suppose that something distracted him," he suggested. "Or maybe he was following something that went off in another direction."

They waited for him to say more, but Will was shading his eyes from the sun, scanning the horizon for any sign of Henry.

"What should we do now, Will?" asked Poppy.

Will sighed. "We've got two choices," he said at last. "One is to say that Henry is lost altogether and we can't do anything more about it. The other is to keep looking for him."

"We can't leave him out here," Fee said as she glanced around for support. She saw that Ben and Badger were both nodding their heads in agreement.

"If we do that, we'll have to go off the track," Poppy pointed out. "And you should never do that when you're walking in the deep bush. It's the quickest way to get lost."

"But Will knows his way round here," argued Badger. He turned to Will. "You know where you are, don't you, Will?"

Will hesitated. "Usually," he said. "I've never been lost before. I take the route I know."

Poppy looked anxious. "But there's always a first time."

"I vote we carry on looking," said Ben. "Will can follow his prints, won't you, Will, just like you've been doing?"

Will said it was easy enough to do on sand, but if it became muddy, then it could be a different matter. It also depended on whether there had been many other animals around—a troop of kangaroos could quickly make tracking impossible because of the sheer number of prints on the ground.

Although Poppy had her doubts, the others were all agreed that they should continue to look for Henry. With Will at their head, they began to make their way slowly across a wide stretch of grassland that was punctuated here and there by clumps of tall trees. It was difficult going, as the land was rough and there were many holes and places where the ground fell away into ancient watercourses. Taking turns, each called out for Henry, their voices sounding small and insignificant in the middle of this wild and empty place.

"I wish we could go back," muttered Fee under her breath.

"Are you all right?" asked Ben, who was walking beside her.

"Not really," she whispered. "But don't tell the others."

Poppy, though, had overheard, and she thought it was time to make herself heard. "Listen, Will," she said. "Some of us have changed our minds and think we should get back to the beach. Once we're there, we can ask Mr. Rigger what to do."

"And Henry might find his way back by himself," said Ben. "Dogs often do that, you know."

Will did not have to think for long. "If that's what you want," he said.

"I think it is," said Poppy. "We've been calling and calling, and there's still no sign of Henry."

Will did not argue. "All right," he said. "We can turn around."

And it was at that moment that Badger spotted something that made his heart miss a beat.

"What's that?" he said, pointing to a dark shape in the distance.

Will looked where Badger was pointing. "Oh no," he muttered. And then, once again, "Oh no."

It was very clear to everybody that Will was worried. Up until then, he had been confident, but now they saw something else in his expression. This was fear, and it was unmistakable.

## CHAPTER 13

*Crocodiles*

The shape that Badger had seen was something that was lying in the grass. It was long and dark, and it had now moved slightly. Beyond it, also largely obscured by tufts of grass, was a similar shape. It, too, suddenly moved, advancing slightly before becoming immobile again.

"What are they?" asked Badger. "It's hard to see from this distance."

"Crocs," said Will. "There's a creek somewhere over there, and they've come out of it."

The others all peered at the distant shapes. They might easily be missed, or might be mistaken for a fallen tree trunk, but now that Will had identified them, it was easier to see what they really were.

"They're a long way off," said Ben. "And they don't seem to be going anywhere."

Will shook his head. "They know we're here," he said. "We're upwind of them and crocodiles have a very good sense of smell."

"What do we do?" asked Poppy.

"We move away as fast as we can," said Will.

"Should we run?" asked Ben.

Will nodded. "Just follow me," he said. "We'll have to get back to the track by a different route—those crocs are blocking our way."

They set off with Will in the lead. The rough ground stopped them from going too fast, but they still seemed to be making good progress. When they stopped, though, to see what the crocodiles were doing, they saw that the distance between them and the two large creatures had shrunk considerably.

"Those fellows move fast, even on dry land," said Will. "They don't look as if they can run very quickly, but you'd be surprised." He paused. "Okay, everybody, let's get going again."

He took a few steps and then stopped, calling out to everybody to stand still.

"What's wrong now?" asked Poppy.

Will's voice was low. "There's another croc," he said. "Just ahead of us. Look."

They all stared at the shape in the grass ahead of them. Will was right: an extremely large crocodile—the length of at least three people—had appeared from a ditch and was staring back at them.

Will looked about him frantically. "All right, everybody,"

he said, pointing off to his right. "You see those two trees over there?"

They were not far from two large trees that were growing out of a small hump in the ground.

"Yes," said Poppy. "Should we climb them?"

"Yes," said Will. "We've got no choice. We're surrounded, I think. But don't run. Just walk very quietly and very slowly. We don't want to disturb that big fellow ahead of us. He's watching."

The chilling words struck fear into each and every one of them. Ben said to himself, *Please don't let me die, please don't let me die.* Poppy thought, *We shouldn't have come out here—I should have known better.* And the others, in their terror, all thought similar things, but they did as Will ordered. Everyone moved as carefully and as unobtrusively as they could. At one point the large crocodile closest to them slithered forward, but for the most part he seemed to be simply eyeing them, sizing up his prey.

When they reached the first of the trees, Will said, "Climb up as high as you safely can," he said. "Poppy and Fee, you take this tree. We can't all fit on this one, but there's a bit more room in the other tree. Ben, Badger, and I will climb up there."

Ben and Badger were good at climbing as they liked the crow's nest. Will helped the girls up before clambering into the branches himself.

They were just in time. As they found themselves suitable places on the upper branches of the trees, two of the crocodiles reached the bottom of the trunks and raised their great heads to look up into the foliage above. As they did so, they emitted the most spine-tingling, blood-curdling hissing sound—a sort of high-pitched clearing of the throat that expressed a mixture of anger and delight at the eventual prospect of a meal. It sounded rather like this: *Gghhharrreugh!*

Poppy was sitting next to Fee on a branch that was just out of reach of the crocodile below. The tree that the two girls were sharing was not quite as big as the one in which the others were perched, and it had fewer branches. The higher branches, which would have been farther away from the crocodile, were not strong enough to bear the weight of a person, and so they had to stay on the lower ones. This meant being nearer to the jaws of the hungry crocodile below them.

They were high enough—but only just. When the crocodiles first reached the base of the trees, one of them gave a lunge upward, its great jaws opened to reveal a set of vicious, razor-sharp teeth. Both Poppy and Fee curled their legs up, hugging the branch they were sitting upon, hoping that it would not bend under their weight and deliver them to the predator below. Fortunately, it was firm enough, and the crocodile dropped back, disappointed at having so narrowly missed its prey. But it knew there would be time: it had chased prey up a tree before and was aware that all it had to do was wait until exhaustion caused the prey to lose its grip. Crocodiles are patient creatures; they think nothing of lurking immobile in the water for hours on end, only the tip of their snouts giving away their presence, waiting for some unfortunate creature not to notice they are there.

Will called out from the neighboring tree. "Are you two all right?"

Poppy replied that they were fine. "We've got a good branch," she shouted. "It's just high enough."

Then Fee asked at the top of her voice, "How long will we have to stay here, Will? When will the crocs go away?"

Like so many awkward questions, this one hung in the air unanswered. At last Will replied, "It could be some time."

"Just hang on," shouted Badger. "Help will be on its way."

"Did you hear that?" whispered Fee to Poppy. "Badger says help is on its way."

When everything looks hopeless, it is tempting not to think positively. "I can't imagine how he knows that," Poppy said to Fee. "We're miles from anywhere and even if Mr. Rigger came to look for us, how would he know where we are? We're quite a long way off the track."

"We could try shouting," suggested Fee.

Poppy looked doubtful. "There's nobody to hear us," she said. "We could shout until our lungs collapsed and it would make no difference."

Fee was silent. Then she said, "What if we took some sticks from the tree and put them in the crocodiles' jaws—to keep them from closing them and biting us?"

Poppy smiled. "I don't think so, Fee," she said. "If we got anywhere near those creatures, they would snap their jaws—and that would be it!"

Although Poppy and Fee did not know it, a similar conversation was taking place in the next-door tree. There Badger had come up with an idea that he was trying out on Will and Ben.

"You see the grass round here," he said, pointing at the expanse of grass and reeds that surrounded the trees.

Will looked at him wearily. "Yes, I see the grass. It's just grass, you know. There's lots of it."

"It's very dry," said Badger.

"Yes, it's dry," Will agreed. "But so what?"

"Dry grass can catch fire," said Badger.

Will said nothing at first, but then he realized what Badger was driving at.

"So the burning grass would drive them away.... Yes, I see what you mean." But almost immediately he shook his head. "We can't start a bushfire, Badger. It's ... well, it's just one of the worst things you can do."

"I know that," said Badger. "But this would just be a small fire. We're surrounded by rivers and creeks, and then there's the sea. There's not much room for a fire like this to travel."

"What is it?" asked Badger.
"A croc!" said Will. "There's a creek full of them over there."

"Just hang on!"
Badger shouted across.
"Help will be on its way."

"You can never be sure," objected Will. "Bushfires can jump over water—everybody knows that."

"But surely it's all right if you do it to save your life." Badger defended his plan. "If that's the only way we can save ourselves."

"Has anybody even got any matches?" Ben asked suddenly. "It's all very well to talk about starting a fire, but has anybody got any matches?"

There was silence.

"I haven't," said Will.

"Neither do I," said Badger.

"So, I don't see how we could start a fire anyway," said Ben.

Badger had seen a video of how to make a fire without matches. You could rub two sticks together, using a small string bow to turn one of them; this could generate enough heat to set tinder alight. Or you could concentrate the sun's rays by using a magnifying glass. This could then be focused on dry leaves and eventually set them alight. But that required a magnifying glass—and if nobody had matches, then they most definitely would not have a magnifying glass.

Even as he was reaching this conclusion, he noticed that Ben had a pair of small binoculars strung around his neck.

"Ben," he said quietly. "Could you let me look at your binoculars?"

Ben wondered why Badger should want to look through

his binoculars at a stressful and dangerous time like this, but he passed them over without comment. Badger took them and immediately began to unscrew one of the lenses.

"Careful," said Ben. "Be careful not to drop them. . . ."

He did not finish. As he was issuing the warning, Badger somehow fumbled his grip of the binoculars. One second they were firmly in his grip; the next they were dropping through the air, falling with a thud right next to the large crocodile down below. The crocodile appeared not to notice, and after a minute or two he moved his tail slightly, bringing it directly over the binoculars, which were now almost lost to sight.

When he saw the binoculars fall, Ben gasped out loud. His gaze dropped and he stared aghast at what he could see of the fallen instrument below. He looked at Badger.

"Oh no," cried Badger. "I'm sorry, Ben. I'll try to get them back—"

"No, you won't," Will cut in firmly. "You wouldn't last a second down there."

The three boys became silent. The sheer awfulness of their situation was beginning to sink in: they were trapped by two of the most dangerous creatures and night would fall soon. They would have to stay awake or risk falling out of the tree. How would they manage that?

It was now midday. Overhead, the sun had reached its highest point, its zenith, and had begun its slow journey back down to the horizon. Will knew that they had about six hours of daylight left before a dangerous night would begin. Looking down toward the crocodile at the bottom of the tree, he wondered what was going on in the creature's brain. He had been told that crocodiles did not have a large brain at all—that the crocodile skull was mostly bone and armor. That might be true, he thought, but they were still capable of showing exceptional cunning in the way they hunted their prey. This crocodile probably knew very well that whatever climbed a tree was bound, sooner or later, to come down—driven by the desperation of thirst or the pangs of hunger—or simply brought down by gravity when the task of holding on to a branch became too much. So the crocodile would not be anxious, but would know that he would eventually win if he simply sat it out. And why should he not do that? He had nowhere to go and not much else to do. Sitting at the bottom of a tree and waiting for your next meal was a perfectly good way of spending your time if you were a crocodile.

Will wondered whether he might be able to divert the crocodiles' attention in some way. When he had run for the sanctuary of the tree, he had been wearing the backpack containing the medicines. He still had that with him, and he wondered whether he could throw it into the grass near the crocodiles. If they saw a large object falling from the tree, the crocodiles might think it was something edible and slither off to investigate. That could give Will the chance to slip down the tree and run off for help. There was always a risk that the crocodiles might pursue him, but if they were busy investigating the backpack, then he might just have the head start needed to get away.

He explained his plan to Badger and Ben.

"But what if they don't pay any attention to the backpack?" asked Badger. "What then?"

Will shrugged. "No harm will be done," he said. "If they pay no attention, then we stay here."

"And that means we die," said Ben.

The other two boys looked at him. "Don't give up, Ben," said Badger.

Ben struggled with himself. He wanted to be brave; he wanted to act as if he were not afraid, but it was difficult. He knew, though, that he had to try. Mr. Rigger had once said to him that in a tight spot, if people started to go to pieces, then it only made matters worse. "I'm sorry," he said. "I haven't given up. We'll get out of this—I'm sure we will."

His positive tone almost convinced him, but there was still a cold knot of fear in his stomach. But he said nothing about that and struggled to manage a smile.

Will noticed the smile and grinned in return. "Just think of the story we'll be able to tell everybody," he said. "Not many people can tell a story of being trapped up a tree by a salty."

"Salty?" echoed Badger.

"It's what we call them," said Will. "Saltwater crocodiles are salties."

It was while Will was explaining this that Ben noticed something. He saw it from the corner of his eye, and he had to crane his neck to see it properly. But when he did, and saw just what it was, he almost fell out of the tree with surprise.

"Look!" he shouted. *"Henry!"*

## CHAPTER 14

*Henry in peril*

Henry appeared out at the edge of the expanse of grass surrounding the trees. The dog was walking slowly, as if he was not quite sure where he was going. His tail, though, was wagging quickly, a little black aerial sticking up confidently behind him.

Will and Badger spotted him the moment Ben alerted them. Badger was excited at first, as the arrival of Henry could mean that rescuers were not far behind. But then he reminded himself that Henry was officially lost, and that there would be nobody with him. Ben's first thought, though, was concern for the dog. He was wondering what would happen when Henry realized that everybody was up the trees. Like all dogs, Henry had a powerful sense of smell, and it would not be long before he caught their scent and worked out where they were. And once that happened, Henry would be in as much—if not more— danger as they themselves were.

"Are crocodiles afraid of dogs?" Ben asked Will.

Will shook his head. "No, I'm afraid not," he said. "Crocodiles love dogs." He quickly corrected himself. "I mean, crocodiles love *eating* dogs."

Ben looked back at Henry. The dog was now looking directly toward the trees. "He knows we're here," he said. "Oh no, look . . ."

Henry's walk had become a trot. He was now running directly toward the trees, his tail wagging even faster as he came to the conclusion that he was no longer lost. At long last he was reunited with his people!

He stopped. By now everybody had seen him, including Poppy and Fee in the tree next door.

"Have you seen Henry over there?" Poppy called out.

"Yes," shouted Will. "Can you tell him to be careful? Those crocs will be after him once they smell him."

Poppy tried to warn Henry. "Henry!" she called out. "Henry! Stop!"

Henry suddenly stopped in his tracks. This was not because he had heard Poppy's warning, but because his nose now told him of the presence of the crocodiles. For a few moments he stood stock-still, even his tail now immobile. Then, like a lion stalking its prey, he lowered himself in the grass and began to creep up toward the crocodiles.

"What's he doing?" asked Fee.

"I think he's stalking them," answered Poppy.

"But they're much bigger than he is," said Fee. "And their jaws are much more powerful than his."

"I know," said Poppy. "But what can we do?"

There was nothing that anybody could do. They all watched with bated breath. Nobody said anything until Will muttered, "I don't believe it—I just don't believe it."

The thing that Will did not believe was now happening right under their eyes. As Henry approached his quarry, the crocodiles suddenly stirred. They could not see very well through the thick grass, but when they eventually spotted Henry the effect was immediate. Slowly they rose, pulling their heavy bellies and tails off the ground as their small, clawed feet extended for movement. Then they began to slither toward him, their bodies making a strange swishing sound in the grass.

Up in his tree, Ben caught his breath. He could hardly bring himself to watch what was happening down below. Henry stood no chance, he thought. There would be a dreadful moment when the first of the crocodiles caught him, and then the whole thing would be over in a second or two.

Henry was not a foolish dog—he knew very well that crocodiles were deadly dangerous. He understood, too, that if he attracted their attention, then these great scaly creatures would be unable to resist the temptation to snatch a ready meal—of delicious dog—rather than wait for a less tasty person-snack to drop from the tree. As well as being intelligent, Henry was brave, and like any brave dog he was ready to take any risk if he felt his people were in danger.

Henry inched forward, the hair on the back of his neck raised in a tight, prickly ridge. As he moved, he growled, baring his teeth in defiance. Of course his teeth were nothing when compared with the exposed teeth in the jaws of the crocodiles. These teeth were great, yellowing fangs, each one capable of inflicting a terrible wound on whatever unfortunate creature came into contact with them.

As Henry moved forward, so did the crocodiles, and now there was barely any distance between them. Poppy held her breath; she could hardly bear to look at what she thought would be the inevitable result of this mismatched encounter.

Suddenly one of the crocodiles lunged forward, snapping its jaws in the air as it sought to cover the ground between him and the crouching figure of Henry. Had Henry been slow, that would have been the end of him; but he was not. Leaping up with a yelp, Henry turned tail and ran, pursued by the two angry crocodiles. He was much faster than they were, and so he was soon able to stop, look back at his pursuers, and then run off again, all the while drawing the crocodiles farther and farther away from the trees in which their hostages were taking refuge.

Will knew what they had to do. "This is our chance!" he shouted. "Everybody climb down and follow me."

He did not need to repeat this invitation. Shaking with a mixture of excitement and sheer relief, Poppy slid down the trunk of the tree in which she had been trapped. She was soon joined on the ground by Fee, Badger, and Ben. Then, following Will, they all ran as fast as they could in the opposite direction from that in which Henry had drawn the crocodiles.

"What about Henry?" panted Fee, glancing over her shoulder to see what was happening to the dog.

"He's smarter than those crocs. They won't catch him," Poppy answered.

Will led them back to the path he knew. It was getting late, and he decided that there would not be time to get back to the beach by darkness. It would be safer, he explained, to make their way to his village. They could go back to the beach the following day, when it would be safer.

"We can have something to eat and you can meet my family," said Will.

Badger reflected on how he was now thinking of something to eat when, only a few minutes ago, there had been something that was thinking of eating *him*.

There was a warm welcome waiting for them in Will's village. As well as being received by Will's parents, the visitors were taken to meet the head of the village, an old man with a deep voice and a pair of bright, searching eyes. He listened as Will told him what had happened with the crocodiles. "You have to watch," he said, shaking his head. "They don't give you any second chances if they catch you." Fee thought of Henry but said nothing yet.

Will's mother prepared a meal. Afterward Will showed the *Tobermory* people round, introducing them to his friends, who listened in horror to the story of their narrow escape. Then, as the sun slipped below the horizon and darkness embraced the land, Will led them to the house where they would be spending the night. This belonged to the teacher at the settlement's school, a kind woman who handed everyone a blanket and pillow and found a spot for them to sleep. Poppy and Fee shared a floor in the teacher's storeroom, made comfortable by the spreading out of cushions from her living room chairs. Ben and Badger slept on the veranda, on a couple of old sofas. From where they lay, they could look up at the night sky—a great field of stars stretching from one edge of the horizon to the other. Ben saw the Southern Cross, a constellation in the shape of an inclined cross that guided sailors. Badger saw a shooting star, a meteorite, tracing a line of silver across the sky. He wanted to draw Ben's attention to this, but tiredness was overtaking him and he managed no more than a few mumbled words before his eyes closed and he slipped off to sleep.

Poppy did not go to sleep that easily. She was worried about Henry, whom nobody had seen since he had saved all their lives earlier that day. When Will had led them off to safety, they had been unable to go in search of Henry, as that would have exposed them once more to the crocodiles. So they had no alternative but to leave him behind, hoping that the brave and resourceful dog would be able to look after himself.

"Don't worry too much about Henry," Will had said. "Dogs are smart."

"But what if he gets lost again?" Poppy had asked. "He could be lost in the bush forever."

Will had assured her that this was unlikely. "A dog's best weapon is its nose," he had said. "A dog's nose is better than a compass any day of the week. He'll be able to make his way back to the beach by sniffing."

Poppy hoped that Will was right, but that did not stop her from worrying about Henry. At long last she fell asleep, only to have dreams in which Henry was in some sort of danger. These dreams were vivid, and were made all the worse by the appearance in them of not only William Edward Hardtack, but also of Geoffrey Shark. In her dream the two boys seemed to be riding on crocodiles, having rigged up saddles and reins to make it possible for them to chase after Henry on the backs of the scaly monsters. It was a bad dream by any standards, and when she awoke, just as dawn was coming, it was with a feeling of relief.

They did not linger over breakfast, but accepted bowls of fruit and some bread that Will's father had baked. Then they set off to get back to the beach, avoiding the area where they had seen the crocodiles the previous day. But although they all felt relieved that they were going back to the *Tobermory*, they were worried about what would

As Henry moved forward, so did the crocodiles, and now there was barely any distance between them.

Ben saw the Southern Cross, a constellation that has guided sailors for hundreds of years.

Hardtack and Shark were riding on crocodiles, having rigged up saddles and reins....

happen on their return. Would they get into trouble for having gotten lost in the first place? Would they be blamed for the fact that the Captain would have had to send out search parties? These were some of the questions they asked themselves as they made their way back to the beach.

When they finally got there, they were relieved to see that Henry was waiting for them. But then they saw the boat with Mr. Rigger and Miss Worsfold standing beside it, looking far from pleased.

"What on earth have you been doing?" asked Miss Worsfold. "Do you realize that Mr. Rigger and I have been worried stiff?"

For a few moments there was silence. Then Poppy explained. "It wasn't our fault," she said. "We were trapped by crocodiles."

Miss Worsfold let out a gasp. "Crocodiles? You were in the water?"

"In a tree," said Badger.

Mr. Rigger frowned. "Crocodiles in a tree?"

"No, sir, we were in the trees and the crocodiles—"

"—were at the bottom of the tree," said Ben. "And then Henry came along and the crocodiles saw him and so we were able to—"

Fee took up the story. "We were able to climb down the tree and run. Then we went to Will's village, and by then it was too late to come back here—"

"Because of the crocodiles," Badger chipped in.

"Hold on," said Mr. Rigger. "Will somebody please start from the beginning?" He turned to look at Poppy and she recited the full story, incident by incident. And as she did so, Mr. Rigger and Miss Worsfold began to understand that nobody had been at fault and that, in fact, everybody had behaved in exactly the way they should have behaved.

"What a frightening situation, but it ended well," said Mr. Rigger at the end. "And now I suggest that we get back on board. We've lost enough time as it is."

They said goodbye to Will, who was heading back to his village. Then they climbed into the liberty boat and began the short row back to the *Tobermory*, with Henry standing up at the prow of the boat, sniffing the air and barking as loudly as he could to let everybody on the ship know that all was well.

Once back on board, they were all summoned to the Captain's cabin, where the whole story was told once again. The Captain listened intently, and then, just as Mr. Rigger had done, he congratulated everybody on keeping a cool head and doing the right thing.

"It's Henry who deserves congratulations," said Badger. "He's the real hero."

Captain Macbeth leaned down to pat Henry on the head. "Extra dog treats for you tonight, Henry," he said.

Henry wagged his tail. He recognized few words, but

he certainly seemed to know what *treats* meant. And the Captain, knowing this, reached into the drawer of his desk and extracted a packet of Good Dog Extra Meaty Treats. Taking a handful of these from the bag, he tossed them toward Henry, who leapt up into the air to catch them in his mouth. Everybody clapped. Badger was right: Henry had been a hero, and had he not done what he had done, then ... It was too awful to think about what might have happened, and so nobody said anything more about it.

That evening the Captain addressed the whole school in the mess hall after dinner.

"We shall set sail in an hour or two," he said. "We shall try to make up for lost time." He paused. "Are there any questions?"

For a minute or two nobody said anything. Then a hand went up. It was Bartholomew Fitzhardy. "Are we still in the race, Captain?"

Captain Macbeth answered without hesitation. "Of course we are, Fitzhardy," he said.

There was a murmur of dissent from the table occupied by William Edward Hardtack and his friends.

"But, sir," said Geoffrey Shark, "we've lost so much time. What point is there in going on when the other boats will be miles ahead of us?"

"Yes," echoed Hardtack. "What's the point?"

Badger turned around in his chair and glared at Shark.

"We don't *have* to win, Shark," he said. "Somebody's got to come in last. And I don't mind losing because we saved a life."

William Edward Hardtack did not like this at all. "Speak for yourself, Striped One," he hissed. "Not everybody's a loser like you."

Mr. Rigger, who had overheard this, clapped his hands sharply. "No arguing, no negative comments, please!" he shouted. "Any other questions for the Captain?"

When there were none, they were told who would be on first watch and who would be on the later watches through the night. Ben and Badger were on a watch that would start in the small hours of the morning. Poppy and Fee were on the watch that ended at dawn.

With a great clanking and creaking, the *Tobermory*'s anchor was raised and they set sail in the darkness. From the ship, the coast was just a dark shape, devoid of detail. Poppy watched it as it slipped past, thinking about how somewhere in those shadows were the crocodiles that had nearly gotten hold of them. She felt grateful that she was still alive, and not in the dark caverns of a crocodile's stomach. This was proving to be an eventful voyage—and a perilous one too.

## CHAPTER 15

*An anonymous note*

The following morning, when the *Tobermory* was well out to sea and was racing up toward the tip of Australia, news came through of the other ships in the race. It was Mr. Rigger who received this, listening in on the radio, and he lost no time in passing it on to the Captain. The Captain told Matron, and Matron told Miss Worsfold, who in turn told Poppy, who told Fee, who told . . . and so it passed around the ship until, within minutes, everybody knew.

Up on deck, Badger and Thomas were on helm duty with Amalia, a girl who had joined the ship for this voyage. Amalia went to school in St. Petersburg, Russia, but had been given permission to spend a term on the *Tobermory*. She knew some English and worked hard to learn more. Badger had been teaching her about steering a sailing ship, and how to keep it at just the right angle to the wind to make sure that the sails worked efficiently. It was part of the *Tobermory*'s tradition that the more experienced sailors helped those with less experience.

Mr. Rigger came up from below deck to check up on the helm.

"We're still in the race," he said, "so see if you can get a few extra knots out of her." Speed on a ship is measured in knots, which could make all the difference if they added a few extra. It might help regain some time when they reached the finishing point at Kangaroo Cliff.

Badger explained to Amalia how the sails would be adjusted, and then Thomas called out the instructions to the members of the crew who were tugging on the various ropes that would bring the sails into the right trim.

In spite of the fact that the *Tobermory* was in a race, some classes were held for those who were not on sailing duty. Poppy and Fee were both in a biology class being held by a popular teacher who taught both biology and general science. Miss Hedges had been explaining how green leaves trapped carbon dioxide and released oxygen. Poppy was writing this down in her notebook when she noticed Amanda Birtwhistle staring at her from the other side of the classroom. At first she tried to ignore her; ever since the incident with the giant clam, when Amanda had lied to get herself out of trouble, the two girls had not spoken. Amanda seemed to be avoiding her. Now, though, Amanda was looking at Poppy in a way that Poppy found quite disconcerting.

"Amanda's staring at me," Poppy whispered to Fee. "Look over there. See? She's staring."

Fee glanced over at Amanda. "Yes," she whispered back to Poppy. "It's creepy."

"She's trying to make me feel bad," said Poppy, "but *she's* the one who should feel bad. She's the one who lied."

At the end of the class, Poppy waited until Amanda had gone before she herself left the classroom with Fee. There was no sign of Amanda up on deck, and Poppy did not think much more about the matter. If Amanda wanted to ignore her, then there was nothing she could do about it and it did not really matter anyway. Poppy had plenty of friends and it would not be the end of the world if Amanda Birtwhistle chose not to speak to her. At the same time, nobody likes it if there is hostility in the air, and Poppy was no exception to that rule.

Every student on the *Tobermory* had a pigeonhole where mail or messages could be put for them to collect. This small box nested along with a lot of other small boxes, and it was here, too, that the teachers put exercise books for students after they had been corrected.

Poppy went to her box that afternoon to see if there was anything for her. There was an essay she had written for Miss Worsfold, corrected in the red pencil that the teacher always used, and there was a note from Matron reminding her that she should collect a fresh bottle of the sunblock that everybody was obliged to use on sunny voyages. But then there was something else—an envelope with her name written on it and, inside, a single page of notepaper. On the notepaper was written the simple message *I'm sorry.* There was no signature and no other means of telling who had written this brief message.

Poppy was perplexed. Could it have been Amanda? Later that afternoon, when everybody had free time to sit on deck to read or to practice their knots for the knot-tying test that was coming up, Poppy found herself sitting up near the bow of the ship with Badger, Ben, and Fee. It was a favorite place for the friends to sit, as there was always a fresh breeze accompanied by the swishing sound made by the *Tobermory*'s bow wave as the great ship made its way through the water.

Poppy showed her friends the note.

"Who's sorry about what?" asked Badger, handing the note back after he had examined it.

Poppy explained that the person who *should* be sorry didn't seem sorry at all.

"Perhaps it's a mistake," suggested Fee. "Perhaps somebody meant to put it in the box next to yours."

Poppy shook her head. "There was an envelope," she said. "It had my name written on it."

Ben looked thoughtful. "What about the handwriting?" he asked.

They all turned to look at him. "What about it?" replied Poppy.

"Perhaps somebody will recognize it," he said. "After all, everybody's writing is different, isn't it? Even if the differences are small—the way you dot an *i* or cross a *t,* you can tell." He paused for this to sink in before continuing, "I can always tell if something's been written by Fee. She puts a bit of a squiggle at the end of every *w.* Don't ask me why she does it, but she does."

"My writing's neater than yours," Fee defended herself.

"I wasn't criticizing you," protested Ben. "I was just saying that's the way you write."

"There's no need to argue," Poppy said. "I think Ben's on to something. If we can find out whose writing it is . . ." She stopped. "Amanda Birtwhistle. It must be her."

They all knew the story of Amanda Birtwhistle and her lies about the great clam incident.

"But why doesn't she just come to you and say sorry?" asked Badger. "If she's sorry, then why not say sorry—like any normal person."

Poppy thought for a moment. "She feels ashamed."

"You mean scared?" Badger said.

Poppy shook her head. "No, there's a difference between feeling ashamed and feeling scared."

Fee thought she knew exactly what Poppy was talking about. "I remember once when I was really mean to somebody. I felt bad about it afterward, but I couldn't say sorry because I was too ashamed of myself."

Ben agreed. "Same here," he said. "Maybe it's because it seems somehow to make it worse. You feel bad about yourself because of what you've done and you think you'll

Poppy went to her pigeonhole that afternoon to see if there was anything for her.

On the notepaper was written the simple message:

*I'm sorry*

Poppy shook her head. "No, there's a difference between feeling ashamed ... and feeling scared."

feel even worse if you say sorry. So you ..." He shrugged. "So you don't do anything and just hope it'll all go away."

Poppy looked at the note once more. "What do you think I should do?" she asked.

"Speak to her," said Ben. "Say: did you write this note?"

Poppy seemed unwilling. "But she may not have written it," she said. "And if she didn't, I'd look really stupid."

Badger thought that if that was the way Poppy felt, then it would be best to be certain it was Amanda who had written the note. "Once you've checked up on that," he said, "you can go and tell her that if she feels sorry, then she should say so to you—not leave anonymous notes in your box."

Poppy was beginning to feel sorry for Amanda; it must be hard to feel bad about yourself and not be able to face up to it. If she found out it was definitely Amanda who had written the note, then she decided that rather than go and criticize her for writing it, she would go and tell her it didn't matter. She thought for a moment. A voice within her said, *Really?* One way was the right thing to do, and the other was the wrong thing. She closed her eyes.

"What are you thinking of, Poppy?" Fee asked.

Poppy opened her eyes. "Nothing," she replied.

Poppy now asked Fee a question. "Who sits next to Amanda in class?"

Fee hesitated. "I'm not sure.... No, hold on, yes, it's Amalia, I think."

"So she would know what Amanda's handwriting is like?"

Fee nodded. "I guess so."

Poppy handed Fee the note.

"Could you show her this note? Could you ask her who wrote it?"

Fee took the note and tucked it into her pocket. A short while later as they were going into the mess hall for lunch, she saw Amalia and showed her the note.

"Whose writing is this?" Fee asked.

Amalia answered straightaway. "Amanda writes like that," she said. "Why do you ask?"

"To confirm something," said Fee. And then she added, "Thanks."

# CHAPTER 16

## *Kangaroo Cliff at last*

Later that afternoon Mr. Rigger received a warning on the radio that a major storm was approaching. Although the forecast could not be firm about exactly when it would arrive, it was clear that the *Tobermory* would be right in its path. The Captain looked carefully at the charts and consulted with Mr. Rigger. They were standing near the helm when they did this, and Thomas Seagrape, who was on helming duty at the time, was able to be involved in their decision.

"Well, Seagrape," said the Captain. "What would you do if a storm were approaching?"

Thomas had been brought up on an island in the Caribbean and knew all about storms. "I'd look for shelter, sir—if I were close enough to land."

The Captain nodded his approval. "And if you were too far out?" he asked. "What then?"

"I'd get most of the sails in, Captain," he said. "Then

I would leave just a very small amount of sail, well reefed, to keep us steady."

"Well done," said the Captain. "What do you say, Mr. Rigger?"

"I'd say that this boy knows his sailing," said Mr. Rigger with a smile.

The Captain pointed to the shore. It was not too far away. "It won't take us more than an hour to reach shore," he said. "And according to this chart, there's a bay there that'll give us shelter from the northeast, which is where they say the wind's going to come from."

The Captain showed Thomas a place marked on the chart, Fig Tree Bay. "Steer for this place, Seagrape," he said.

In less than an hour, the *Tobermory* nosed her way between two headlands into a wide, deserted bay. The Captain was now at the wheel, and all along one side of the ship a class on how to sound depths was being conducted by Mr. Rigger. Each person had a long line with a lump of lead tied on at the end. This line was knotted at various points to mark the fathoms, and this made it possible to tell just how much water there was beneath the ship. The last thing any sailor wants is to run aground, and so the navigator always has to be careful not to guide the ship into water that is too shallow. Of course the *Tobermory* had an electronic depth-sounder, but a good sailor has to know how to use simpler, older methods—just in case.

In twenty meters of water they let out eighty meters

of chain, at the end of which the great heavy anchor dug deep into the sand on the seabed. Putting the ship's engines astern, the Captain made the ship pull for a few moments against the weight of the chain and anchor until it was clear that the *Tobermory* was no longer moving.

"That's it," announced Captain Macbeth. "We should be safe here when the storm hits tonight."

Because of the danger of sharks, nobody was allowed to swim, and so people had free time, right up until it was time to go into the mess hall for dinner.

As they went in for their meal, Poppy found herself standing in line close to Amanda. This was her moment, and she seized it.

"Amanda," she whispered. "I found your note."

Amanda looked about. When she saw that nobody could overhear them, she turned to Poppy and whispered back, "I meant it."

Poppy nodded. "That's all right," she said. "I was going to accept your apology."

Amanda looked immediately relieved. "Thanks," she said.

But Poppy had more to say. "But that's not enough, you know."

Amanda frowned. "What else do you want me to say?"

"I want you to go to the Captain and tell him you lied. I want you to make sure he knows that it was not my fault," Poppy said.

Amanda's face registered shock. "I c-c-can't," she stuttered. "I can't just go in there and tell him."

"Why not?"

"Because . . . because . . ." Amanda's voice faltered.

"Then it's no good saying you're sorry," said Poppy. "It's meaningless."

Amanda stared down at the ground. "I've felt so bad," she said. "I was just too scared to tell him what really happened."

Poppy spoke firmly. The line of people was beginning to move, and she knew that they did not have much time to finish their conversation. "Then you're going to end up feeling bad for a lot longer," said Poppy. "It's your choice, Amanda—get it over and done with, or feel bad about it for as long as you're at school on the *Tobermory*. You choose."

After dinner, Mr. Rigger announced the rota of watches. There had to be at least six people on deck throughout the night, keeping a lookout for signs of rising wind and ready, at a moment's notice, to take the ship out of the bay if the wind shifted and made their situation dangerous. Procedures were set out: at the first sign of rain and wind, one of those on watch would have to go down below and wake Mr. Rigger and the Captain, who would come up on deck and take charge.

"Be vigilant," warned Mr. Rigger. "Storms can blow up

in no time at all, and if you don't act quickly, they can be upon you. Once that happens, there can be winds of over one hundred miles an hour."

Ben and Badger were on an early watch, while Poppy, Fee, and Amanda were on a watch that started just after midnight. They were to be on duty with Bartholomew Fitzhardy and Maximilian Flubber.

"Oh no," groaned Poppy. "I'm on with Flubber." She did not mention the fact that Amanda Birtwhistle was on the same watch. That, she thought, could be awkward, but at least she and Amanda had spoken to each other.

Badger laughed. "Have fun," he said cheerfully. "We've got Shark. I'd much prefer to be on watch with Flubber rather than Shark."

Because they would have to get up just before midnight, Poppy and Fee went to bed early. Poppy had a bit of difficulty falling asleep, knowing that a night watch was ahead of her, while Fee, who was tired, did not stay awake long. All too soon their turn came to go up on deck. Poppy had set her alarm to wake them, and they both climbed out of their hammocks, drowsy and disheveled, ready for duty.

Since the ship was at anchor, there was not much for the watch to do, other than be ready to report anything unusual. In particular, if the wind speed suddenly rose, they would have to make sure that the anchor held securely.

Fee and Bartholomew took up their position at the bow

of the ship. Poppy, Flubber, and Amanda were at the stern, where the helm was. Together they decided which direction they would cover: Poppy would look out for anything to stern, Amanda would be in charge of starboard, and Flubber would look after the port side.

Separated from Hardtack and Shark, Flubber proved to be surprisingly interested. He asked Poppy about their adventure with Will, and he listened wide-mouthed as she told him about being up in the tree. "I would have been really scared," he said. "I don't know how you did it. I think I would have shaken so much that I would have dropped out of the tree."

Poppy was surprised to hear Flubber say that. She did not think she would ever hear Hardtack or Shark admit to being frightened—they were always trying to impress others with their bravery.

"I think you would have been fine," Poppy said.

Flubber seemed pleased. "Still," he said, "I'm glad that you were all right."

He then offered Poppy and Amanda a piece of chocolate from a bar he had in his pocket. They both accepted, and this made Flubber smile.

Nothing much happened for the first forty minutes of the watch. Then, with no warning, a wind arose, arriving with a suddenness that was blowing hard and cold, howling loudly as it whipped across the surface of the sea. Then there was rain—a white sheet of water racing across the deck like a suddenly drawn curtain.

Poppy, who was standing near the helm, was joined by Amanda and Flubber, both of whom struggled to avoid being swept off their feet by the force of the blast.

"What are we going to do?" shouted Flubber.

"We need to wake the Captain," Poppy shouted back. "I'll go . . ."

She did not finish what she was saying. The force of the wind had suddenly increased, and she had to grab hold of the wheel to keep from being blown away. Flubber and Amanda had to do the same, all three of them hanging on for dear life, their clothes being ripped and torn by the sheer force of the squall. In such conditions there was no chance of being able to cross the deck safely to go below to wake the Captain.

"We'll have to hang on!" yelled Poppy. "Whatever you do, don't let go!"

Up at the prow, Fee and Bartholomew had ducked beneath the gunwales—the high sides of the ship—and were getting shelter. They could not move, though, and would simply have to stay where they were until the storm subsided.

Poppy wondered whether the Captain would be woken up by the movement of the boat under the wind. He was, but as the Captain came up the companionway and opened the door, he was pushed back by the sheer power of the wind. Like those on deck, he would be unable to cross it without being blown over; he was helpless, stuck where he was until the wind dropped and the wild lashing of the rain and whipped-up seawater stopped.

They might have been able to ride out the storm had something not happened that every sailor dreads. The anchor was now taking the full strain. With each gust of wind the *Tobermory* pulled more and more fiercely against the restraining chain, yanking it back like a great metal whip. Although the anchor had been embedded in the sand at the seabed, the pull of the ship was now just too great for it to remain where it was. With a great heave the anchor freed itself of the sand and began to drag across the seabed. The *Tobermory* was now moving, even if held back a bit by the weight of the chain and anchor.

Poppy saw immediately that the situation was extremely dangerous. The wind had shifted, and was now pushing them slowly but surely toward the rocks at the edge of the bay. Unless they could bring in the chain and manage to move the boat out to sea, they were facing certain shipwreck.

Poppy thought quickly. The anchor chain was controlled from up at the bow. If she could signal to Bartholomew and Fee, they would be able to operate the windlass that brought the chain in. But would they be able to see her through the sheets of rain that were restricting visibility to not much more than a few arm's lengths?

She made her frantic signals and fortunately they saw her. Crawling to the windlass, Fee and Bartholomew began to wind in the chain. At the same time, Flubber had turned on the engine, and he and the two girls began to struggle with the ship's wheel.

It was hard to control the wheel as the boat was tossed about by the storm. Poppy would never have been able to do it by herself, but together they managed to swing the wheel sufficiently to point the nose of the *Tobermory* out of the bay so that it was now facing the open sea. It was hard going, but with the three of them to bring off the maneuver, they succeeded. Soon the chain was in and the *Tobermory* was making her way into deeper, safer water. And as that happened, they noticed that the storm began to abate. The wind dropped and stopped howling quite so loudly. As that happened, the rain began to ease off. Having been a violent storm, it was now just an ordinary one, if a bit badly behaved.

As the wind dropped, the Captain was able to come out on deck. As he joined the three bedraggled students, he shouted out his praise. "Well done, all of you! Quick thinking!"

Now Mr. Rigger came up on deck, and he and the Captain took control of the ship.

"You go down below," said the Captain. "Change into

dry clothing and ask Matron to give you each a mug of hot chocolate. I imagine she'll be wide awake with all this movement."

As they made their way down the companionway, Poppy reached out and touched Amanda on the arm and then turned to Flubber. "You were pretty brave up there," she said.

Flubber thanked her, but said that in his opinion it was Poppy who had really saved the day. "I was only following orders," he said. "And you gave me the courage to do what we did."

Amanda looked at Poppy. "I made up my mind when we were out there battling the storm. I'm going to talk to the Captain tomorrow."

Poppy smiled and thought, *I knew you'd do the right thing.* She said, "Thank you, Amanda."

The Captain listened carefully to what Amanda had to say, and at the end of it he accepted that she was sorry and had learned a lesson about telling the truth. But he did more than that. Calling Poppy in, he told her he was sorry for having misjudged her so quickly and that he was glad she was shown to have been blameless. "I think we've all learned something," he said. "Myself included."

As is often the case, the final stage of the race was the most exciting part. As they sped toward Kangaroo Cliff, they began to see more of the other ships. There was the

*Prince of Hamburg,* her sails tightly and expertly trimmed, her crew ready to pull the ropes that would give the canvas whatever tug it needed to get the most out of the wind. She seemed to be in the lead, although there was not much between her and the next two ships in the race—one of which was the *Melbourne,* the other being the *Tobermory.*

Ben could hardly believe his eyes when he saw they were one of the first three. "I thought we lost any chance we had once we stopped to help Will," he said to Badger.

Badger was as surprised as Ben, but he had been speaking to Mr. Rigger, who had explained to him what happened. "Apparently, all the other ships had some sort of incident as well," Mr. Rigger told him. "Most of them were caught up in the storm last night. We were lucky—it didn't set us back too much, but others weren't that fortunate and were blown badly off course."

There had been medical emergencies on two of the other ships. One was a case of appendicitis, which had required the ship to stop altogether while a surgeon carried out an operation. But there had been complications and the ship had had to divert to a port to drop a patient off at a hospital. That had cost them several days. Sickness had broken out on board another ship, requiring it to remain at anchor for two days while the crew recovered.

Mr. Rigger had heard over the radio that the New Zealand ship, the *Spirit of Hokianga,* had sprung a serious leak and had spent a few days in a river delta while her hull was patched up. The Russian ship had lost her rudder and had to make and fit a temporary one before she could continue. All these misfortunes meant that in the final leg of the race, the *Tobermory* now stood as good a chance as any of winning.

The first sighting of Kangaroo Cliff was made by Tanya, who was on watch with Amanda up in the crow's next. When she shouted the news to the others, a great cheer arose from everybody on deck.

"We'll be there in no time at all," shouted Ben.

"And we've got a good chance of winning," shouted Badger. "Look—we're right with the front-runners."

"I told you never to give up," said Mr. Rigger proudly. "A race isn't over . . ."

Badger knew what was coming: ". . . until it's over," he added.

"That's right, young Tomkins!" exclaimed Mr. Rigger. "You seem to know in advance what I'm going to say, but remember, if you have something worth saying, then . . ."

". . . then you should always say it," Badger said with a smile.

"Exactly," said Mr. Rigger. "That's exactly what I was going to say!"

With just a very short distance to cover, the race had become touch-and-go. The three leading ships, the *Tober-*

*mory,* the *Melbourne,* and the *Prince of Hamburg,* were neck and neck, spread out in a wide line.

"Do you think it's going to be a dead heat?" Angela asked as she stood at the railing with Fee, Ben, and Badger.

Fee shook her head. "Somebody will pull ahead at the last moment," she said. "It's going to be close, all right, but there'll definitely be a clear winner."

"I hope it's us," Angela said. "Oh, I do hope it's going to be us."

It was impossible to say which of the ships would manage to put on that extra burst of speed needed to win. As she looked across at the other two ships, though, Fee noticed there were signs that the *Melbourne* was speeding up. But then, a moment later, the wind shifted a little and the Australian ship slowed down again.

Poppy and Thomas were at the helm for this final stage, with Captain Macbeth and Mr. Rigger standing immediately behind them, calling out orders. Suddenly the Captain seemed to notice something and turned to speak to Mr. Rigger. Both of them looked over to starboard, toward the *Prince of Hamburg.* There was no mistaking the look of shock on both their faces.

"Poppy and Thomas, Mr. Rigger will take the helm now," said Captain Macbeth urgently as he unfurled a chart and examined it closely, the paper flapping wildly in the wind. Once again he conferred with Mr. Rigger. Nodding to confirm the order the Captain had given him, Mr. Rigger swung the wheel over to starboard, making the ship turn sharply, right into the path of the German boat.

Fee was astonished. "Why is he doing that?" she asked.

Her question was directed at nobody in particular, and for a moment it hung in the air before being answered by Badger.

"I think he's trying to get the *Prince of Hamburg* to swerve," he said. "And look—that's exactly what's happening!"

Faced with the prospect of the *Tobermory* straying into its path, the German ship had no choice but to turn as well. This change of direction took it slightly farther out to sea, ending its chances of winning. But the *Tobermory*'s maneuver also put paid to any hope of victory for that ship. With her two rivals out of the running now, the *Melbourne* cruised decisively into the lead to win first place. *The Prince of Hamburg* was second and the *Tobermory* was third.

There was no hiding the disappointment Captain Macbeth's crew felt. It had been so close, and had it not been for the Captain's odd change of course at the last minute, there was a perfectly good chance that they would have won.

That thought was uppermost in the minds of all the students as they waited to be addressed by the Captain. They had now dropped anchor in the bay in front of Kangaroo

The great heavy anchor dug deep into the sand on the seabed.

Then there was rain—a white sheet of water racing across the deck like a suddenly drawn curtain.

SCHOOL SHIP TOBERMORY

Mr. Rigger swung the wheel over to starboard, making the ship turn sharply, right into the course of the German boat.

Cliff and were waiting to have the debriefing that every crew has at the end of a race.

"The first thing I'd like to say," Captain Macbeth began, "is well done! Coming third in a race like this is a very good result, and I think you can all be proud of yourselves."

His words were greeted in silence. It might be true that third place was not a bad result, but how much better it would have been to be first, or even second—and both those results had been within their grasp.

The Captain looked out over the heads of the students. Under his breath, he muttered to Mr. Rigger, "I know how they feel." Then he cleared his throat. "You'll be wondering about what happened toward the end," he continued. "Well, I've just been on the radio to the captain of the *Prince of Hamburg,* and I've explained to him why I forced them to change course."

The whole ship's company was listening attentively. There was not a sound to be heard other than the noise of the wind in the rigging.

"I'm glad to say that the German captain completely understands," continued Captain Macbeth. "And more than that—he thanked me for doing what we did."

Badger looked inquiringly at Ben. "Have you got any idea what this is about?" he asked.

Ben shook his head. "None at all," he replied. "Let's see what he says."

"Just before I ordered Mr. Rigger to turn to starboard," said the Captain, "I realized the *Hamburg* seemed unaware of some submerged rocks directly ahead of her. Had she hit them, she would have been seriously damaged and probably would have sunk."

Ben held his breath. "So that explains it," he whispered to Badger.

"They were so busy racing that I don't think they had consulted their charts. We could have tried to contact them on the radio to warn them, but we didn't have time. And there might have been nobody in their radio room anyway."

Mr. Rigger, who had been standing next to the Captain, now took over. "The Captain did the right thing," he said. "We had to save them from disaster, even if it meant losing our chance to win the race. And the only way we could do that was by forcing them to turn."

"I know it's disappointing," continued the Captain. "I'm disappointed; Mr. Rigger's disappointed; the whole ship's disappointed. But . . ." He paused, looking directly at the students standing before him. "But if there's a choice between doing the right thing and winning a race, then I have no doubt whatsoever which you might choose." He paused again. "Does everybody agree with me on that?"

They did.

"In that case," said the Captain, "time to celebrate

coming in third. Cook has prepared some special ice cream, and I don't want to keep you from that any longer."

A cheer went up for the Captain from the entire crew, who shouted at the top of their voices. They were proud that their ship had a captain like Captain Macbeth and that they had the honor of serving under him.

## Home Port

The race was over, but not the trip. There was still the long voyage home. The ship sailed across the Pacific, through the Panama Canal, and back across the Atlantic. All the while they were sailing, the students had their school ship lessons; all the way across the long miles of empty ocean they learned how to sail, how to cope with every sort of sea condition. They also found themselves understanding more clearly how to get on with people, how to make friends, and how to become braver, stronger, and more confident.

At last they sailed into Scottish waters and started the final leg of their journey—up through the Sound of Mull toward the colorful harbor of Tobermory itself. As the ship dropped its sails and came into harbor, a ferry that was taking on passengers sounded its horn in their honor. On the shore there were people waving, and a Scottish piper wearing a kilt greeted them with a bagpipe

tune that had been used for many years to welcome sailors home.

Now it was time for school holidays, and the crew of the *Tobermory* would all be making their way back to their parents or relatives for a month's break.

"I'm going to miss you, Badge," said Ben as they packed their kit bags.

"Me too," said Badger. "But it won't be for long. We're back after the holiday."

Badger was right. Before they knew it, they would be back together, ready for the next adventure on board the School Ship *Tobermory*. Nobody knew what that adventure would be, but they felt it was almost better that way. An adventure you're not expecting is usually much better than one you know about. And when shared with a friend—or even better, with a crew of friends—then that is the best adventure of all.

*Historic tall ships at Cádiz, Spain, during the Tall Ships Race 2016*

# DID YOU KNOW?

## The Tall Ships Races

The first Tall Ships Race, held in 1956, was meant to be a one-time event to celebrate the great sailing ships that had been replaced by steam-powered vessels. The overwhelming interest and the huge number of spectators encouraged organizers to form an association to continue the races on a yearly basis beginning in 1958. The Tall Ships Races are still held on European waters today. Each ship's crew must comprise at least 50 percent young people (between ages fifteen and twenty-five). The races foster international friendship and continue to introduce young people to the art of sailing.

## Weather and Wind

All sailors must be concerned with the weather when guiding a tall ship or a modern vessel. There are a number of ways to anticipate changing weather patterns to help ensure safe passage.

Sailors are always worried about **squalls,** passing thunderstorms that come upon a vessel suddenly. Squalls can bring high winds and torrential rain. If you're unlucky enough to find yourself in a squall, or sudden high seas, your captain may shout **"Batten down the hatches!"** This sailing term means to quickly close all portholes and hatches and tighten lines (or ropes) to keep sails in place in the coming weather.

**Barometers** are essential weather tools. They measure atmospheric pressure, or the weight of the air. Sailors use barometers to predict changes in the weather in the hours to come. This is the barometer on the tall ship *Amerigo Vespucci*.

## Clouds

One way to observe changing weather patterns is to look at the clouds. Cloud formations can often give you an idea of the weather to come. Some cloud formations include:

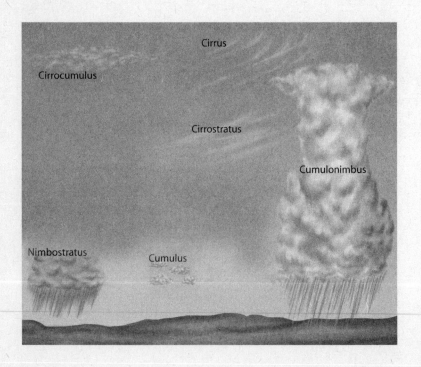

**Cirrocumulus:** High altitude, these puffy clouds typically have a rippled appearance and may form ahead of a frontal system.

**Cirrostratus:** High-altitude, sheetlike, and nearly transparent, these clouds usually signify rain or snow within twelve to twenty-four hours.

**Cirrus:** Thin, wispy, featherlike high-altitude clouds. These clouds signal fair weather for the moment but a change within twenty-four hours. By watching the movement of these clouds, you can tell which way a weather event is approaching.

**Cumulonimbus:** Tall and dense, often flat at the top and bottom, these are the classic storm and shower clouds—with possible thunder and lightning.

**Cumulus:** Low-altitude, puffy single clouds; a typical indication of fair weather.

**Nimbostratus:** Dark and low in appearance, with a seeming illumination from within, this formation indicates persistent light to moderate rainfall or snow that could last several days.

### Wind

Reading the wind is essential to a sailor's travels. There are many tools and instruments that sailors use to determine the speed and direction of the wind, including electronic wind instruments. Many larger sailboats, especially those that race or travel long distances, use electronic wind instruments.

**True wind** is the wind that blows across the surface of the water or land. If you're standing outside and your body is at rest, the wind you feel is the true wind.

**Apparent wind,** on the other hand, is the wind you experience while you are in motion.

The **point of sail** is a vessel's direction of travel in relationship to the wind when under sail.

When there is no wind, a vessel is considered **becalmed.** This is a term used by sailors to mean the wind has fallen off, or stopped, and the boat is no longer moving forward through the water. There is even a part of the world, known as the doldrums, that is infamous for its light wind. The doldrums are a beltlike region around the Earth near the equator, known by sailors worldwide because wind conditions there are so light that sailing vessels can be stalled for days or weeks at a time.

*Special thanks to Katelyn Hales and Zachary Walker*

# ABOUT THE AUTHOR

ALEXANDER McCALL SMITH is the author of the best-selling No. 1 Ladies' Detective Agency series. He has also written over thirty books for younger readers, including a series featuring the young Precious Ramotswe—one of the world's most famous fictional private detectives. McCall Smith is also the author of *School Ship Tobermory* and *The Sands of Shark Island,* companion novels to *The Race to Kangaroo Cliff.* Visit him online at alexandermccall smith.com and on Facebook, and follow him on Twitter at @McCallSmith.

# ABOUT THE ILLUSTRATOR

IAIN McINTOSH's illustrations have won awards in the worlds of advertising, design, and publishing. He has illustrated many of Alexander McCall Smith's books.

# For more rip-roaring adventure, don't miss . . .

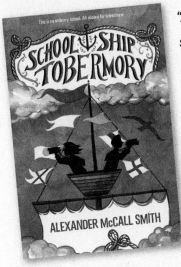

"A schooner that serves as a boarding school is an inviting setting for this breezy series opener."
—*Publishers Weekly*

"Quirky fun." —*The Bulletin of the Center for Children's Books*

"An accessible, unpretentious story full of timeless values and goodness." —*Kirkus Reviews*

"Readers will love the fast-paced tale and fascinating locations."
—*School Library Journal*

"Plenty of action and adventure . . . sure to be a hit with fans of sea stories. A fun, enjoyable read." —*Booklist*

"Instilled with wholesome values, intelligence, and action. A comfortable, wise tale that is more than anything a story of friendship."
—*Kirkus Reviews*

## FOR YOUNG READERS, INTRODUCING PRECIOUS AS A YOUNG GIRL

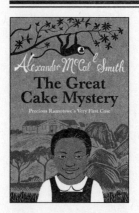

### THE GREAT CAKE MYSTERY

In her first case as a young girl, Precious sets out to find the real thief of a piece of cake. Along the way she learns that your first guess isn't always right. She also learns how to be a detective.

**Volume 1**

### THE MYSTERY OF MEERKAT HILL

Precious has a new mystery to solve! When her friend's family's most valuable cow vanishes, Precious must devise a plan to find the missing animal! But she needs the help of another to solve the case. Will she succeed and what obstacles will she face on her path?

**Volume 2**

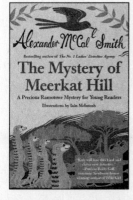

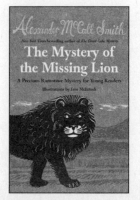

### THE MYSTERY OF THE MISSING LION

Precious gets a very special treat: a trip to visit her aunty Bee at a safari camp. On her first day there, a new lion arrives. But this is no average lion: Teddy is an actor-lion who came with a film crew. When Teddy escapes, Precious and her resourceful new friend Khumo decide to use their detective skills to help track down the lion and find out where he has gone.

**Volume 3**

Illustration © Iain McIntosh

# KILLING FEAR

# KILLING FEAR

A NOVEL OF SUSPENSE

ALLISON BRENNAN

**THORNDIKE**
**WINDSOR**
**PARAGON**

This Large Print edition is published by Thorndike Press, Waterville, Maine, USA and by BBC Audiobooks Ltd, Bath, England.
Thorndike Press, a part of Gale, Cengage Learning.
Copyright © 2008 by Allison Brennan.
The moral right of the author has been asserted.
The Prison Break Trilogy.

The text of this Large Print edition is unabridged.
Other aspects of the book may vary from the original edition.
Set in 16 pt. Plantin.
Printed on permanent paper.

| LIBRARY OF CONGRESS CATALOGING-IN-PUBLICATION DATA |
| --- |

Brennan, Allison.
  Killing fear : a novel of suspense / by Allison Brennan.
    p. cm. — (The prison break trilogy) (Thorndike Press large print basic)
  ISBN-13: 978-1-4104-0547-0 (hardcover : alk. paper)
  ISBN-10: 1-4104-0547-8 (hardcover : alk. paper)
  1. Serial murderers — Fiction. 2. Large type books. I. Title.
PS3602.R4495K56 2008
813'.6—dc22                                2008001120

BRITISH LIBRARY CATALOGUING-IN-PUBLICATION DATA AVAILABLE

Published in 2008 in the U.S. by arrangement with The Ballantine Publishing Group, a division of Random House, Inc.
Published in 2008 in the U.K. by arrangement with Little, Brown Book Group.

U.K. Hardcover: 978 1 405 64941 4 (Windsor Large Print)
U.K. Softcover: 978 1 405 64942 1 (Paragon Large Print)

Printed in the United States of America
1 2 3 4 5 6 7 12 11 10 09 08

For my grandmother,
Florence Riley Hoffman,
who loved me unconditionally
and always told me
I could do anything.
I miss you, Grandma.

# ACKNOWLEDGMENTS

As always, many people helped make this story as real as possible. If there are any factual errors, they are solely my responsibility.

First and foremost, Joe Edwards, former California State corrections officer who worked on death row at San Quentin, was invaluable in providing information about the prison and answering questions as they arose. His wife, Elizabeth Edwards, who not only served as a liaison but provided her own insight and experience. Thank you both!

Forensic psychologist and author Mary Kennedy once again answered numerous questions about my villain to help keep him both real and chilling. Seth Unger with the California Department of Corrections helped with information about the prison system; Jabie Gray, general manager of Discount Gun Mart and Indoor Range, was instrumental in helping me understand the changing gun laws, gun safety, and how the range operates; and Marty Fink with the San Diego County Sheriff's Department promptly answered questions about criminalists.

The fabulous writers in the Kiss of Death chapter of Romance Writers of America answered a myriad of questions, a huge help when I was on deadline.

I often find myself writing outside of the house, so a special thanks to Elk Grove businesses who let me claim a table for hours at a time, including: Starbucks, BJ's Restaurant, Chili's, and the Elk Grove Brewery.

To everyone at Ballantine, especially Charlotte and Dana: we make a great team. To everyone at Trident Media Group, especially Kim Whalen: thanks for believing in me from the start.

Thanks, Mom, for your constant help and support. And to Dan and our kids: I really appreciate all of you tolerating my many writing eccentricities and deadlines. I love you all.

# PROLOGUE

*Seven years earlier*

Theodore Glenn sat at the defense table alone, hands loosely folded in front of him, watching the jury foreman hand the bailiff his fate written on a folded white card. The bailiff in turn handed the paper to the judge, who looked at it without comment or expression.

Theodore wasn't concerned, confident that he'd won the jury over. He was a lawyer, after all, and not just any lawyer: a rich, successful one. So of course there was no one better to represent Theodore Glenn than himself. The fact that it took them four full days to deliberate told him there were several jurors who had reasonable doubt. If the verdict didn't come back *not guilty,* the jury would be hung.

He looked at the jurors, keeping the contempt off his face.

*Pathetic people, all of them. Barely living,*

*meandering through boring, mediocre lives, obeying authority, doing whatever Big Brother orders them to do. A jury of his peers? Hardly. The IQ of all twelve combined didn't match his.*

The old blue-haired woman in the front stared at him. Didn't they have an age requirement? If she was a day under eighty . . . but he was certain she didn't think he was guilty. No woman would look at him if she believed he was a killer.

The young chick in the back with pitiful little breasts; Juror Number Eight. *She* thought he did it. She kept her eyes firmly on the judge.

*I'll kill you, bitch. You think you can cast judgment on me?*

The queer in the front, with his earrings and prim shirt and tight pants, stared at him. Theodore remembered him from jury selection. When asked by the prosecutor if he could be impartial knowing that the victims were exotic dancers — stripping off their clothes for money — he'd said in that nasal tone, "*I* will never judge anyone by their personal lifestyle choices."

Had he voted guilty or innocent? It wouldn't matter. All it took was one dissenting juror, and he had Grandma up front.

He'd been right all along. Only the innocent testify in their own defense, he reasoned. So to be seen as innocent, he had to take the stand.

He'd lied, he'd told the truth — both with equal sincerity.

He'd explained that he had previous relationships with three of the four victims. They had ended amicably. He harbored no ill will, nor did they. He'd brought witnesses forward to corroborate.

The most exciting part of the entire trial was when he had gorgeous Robin McKenna on the stand, forced to answer his questions. She'd been a witness for the prosecution, and testified about how she identified him from a police sketch. The sketch however had been drawn from the recollections of a near-blind alleged eyewitness after Brandi's murder. Robin also told the court who he slept with and when. Women were the biggest gossips on the planet. But he'd made her eat her lying words.

*"Any questions, Mr. Glenn?" the judge asked after the stunning prosecutor, a prickly bitch named Julia Chandler, finished questioning Robin. She'd used kid gloves. Theodore didn't have to wonder why. Robin looked ready to bolt. Her dark red hair looked darker, her pale skin whiter, and her vivid hazel eyes greener against the bloodshot whites.*

11

*As he approached, he watched her tense. Suppressing his grin, he did not take his eyes from her face. So beautiful, so perfectly exquisite in every physical detail — from her soft hair to her lush red lips to her perky breasts to her long legs.*

*A perfect female for his perfect male. But the bitch thought she was better than him. That she was above him. Laughable, to be sure, but her attitude irritated him. She spoke ill of him. She looked at him as if she were smarter. No one was smarter than him.*

*What he hadn't said to Robin McKenna:* Do you know they died because of you? I will fondly remember the sweet horror on your pretty face for the rest of my life, long after I kill you, too.

*"Robin —" he began.*

*"Objection," the D.D.A. snarled. "Please direct counsel to reference the witness as Ms. McKenna."*

*"Sustained. You know the rules, Mr. Glenn."*

*"I apologize, Your Honor." Theodore chafed under the rebuke. How dare these inferior attorneys dictate how he should question a witness!*

*"Ms. McKenna," he said, noting that she had slid as far back in the chair as possible. As far from him as possible. She was terrified. She might suspect the truth about him, but she*

12

couldn't possibly know what he was truly capable of. Someday she would, and then she would have something to be scared about.

"You testified that I dated Bethany Coleman."

Robin nodded.

The judge said, "Please state your answer out loud for the record."

"Yes." Robin tucked a loose strand of hair behind her ear. She'd attempted to make herself look wholesome by wearing minimal makeup and brushing her thick, curly red hair up into a loose bun. But Theodore knew she was anything but wholesome. She revealed her body to men for money. She danced with the grace of a prima ballerina, and the seduction of a call girl. She was the best dancer on-stage at RJ's, bar none, but the only one who wouldn't give him the time of day.

The bitch.

"Mr. Glenn, question?" the judge asked.

Theodore suppressed his frustration with Robin. It wasn't anger. His policy was, "Don't get mad, get even." But the strange sensations he'd felt whenever he thought about Robin McKenna, whenever he'd watched her dance or shun him — they were new and made him uneasy.

He'd spent his entire life searching for emotion. To have feelings — something internal he couldn't define — whenever he thought

13

about Robin McKenna seemed extraordinary and was surprisingly unwanted.

Those feelings would disappear when he killed her.

He asked, "Bethany and I broke up eight months before she was killed. Is that your recollection?"

"Yes," Robin said, jaw clenched.

"Did she ever tell you that she was scared of me?"

Robin didn't answer.

"Answer the question," Theodore demanded.

"No."

"And when Brandi and I broke up, did she tell you she was scared of me?"

"No."

"And Jessica?"

"No."

"So none of the women I dated were fearful for their lives?"

"I can't say."

"But none of them told you they were fearful for their lives."

She bit her lip. "No."

"Why did you tell the police that I was the person in the vague sketch that circulated after Brandi's murder?"

"Because you were."

Theodore crossed over to his desk and picked up a copy of the sketch. He glanced at the back of the chamber and caught Detective William Hooper staring. Theodore winked at him, taking pleasure in bringing rage to the cop's face.

*I know all about you,* Theodore thought.

He held up the sketch for the jury. "Is this the sketch you identified me from?"

"Yes."

"This could be any man between the ages of thirty and fifty in this room. Me, the district attorney, the two jurors in the front here." He waved toward the jury box. "Even the detective who arrested me."

He watched as Robin looked directly at Will, then averted her eyes. Some emotion Theodore wasn't familiar with flitted across her face. Had something happened between Romeo and Juliet? Had their torrid love affair gone south?

*This pleased him.*

"Ms. McKenna, do you like me?"

She startled, glared at him, showing a taste of her inner passion. Passion that should have been directed toward him, not William Hooper.

"No, I don't like you. You killed my friends."

"We'll leave that to the jury to decide, but you just made my point. You never liked me, did you?"

"No."

"Why?"

15

"Excuse me?"

"Objection!" The prosecutor jumped up.

"Overruled."

Theodore repeated to Robin, "Why have you never liked me?"

She frowned. "I don't know."

"It's like ice cream, right? Some people don't like chocolate. They don't know why, it just doesn't taste good."

"I didn't like the way you looked at me," Robin said quietly.

"You remove your clothes onstage in front of a hundred men every night and you don't like the way they look at you?"

"I don't like the way you look at me when you think I can't see you watching," she said, her voice gathering strength.

"Ms. McKenna, isn't it true that you identified me off this vague sketch simply because you don't like me? You wanted someone to blame for the murders of your friends, and I was convenient."

The prosecutor exclaimed, "Objection!" while Robin leaned forward and said, "I know you killed them. I saw you in the picture because it is you. I told the police exactly what they asked, that the only person I recognized that looks like the sketch is Theodore Glenn —"

"Order!" The judge pounded his gavel.

"You killed them and you gloated!" Robin

*shouted.*

*"Order, Ms. McKenna," the judge said.*

*Theodore smiled. He looked right at William Hooper, the detective's face tight with suppressed anger. Rage directed at him for bringing up the truth.*

*The district attorney himself, pompous ass Bryce Descario, asked the judge for a ten-minute recess to confer with the witness. Right, Julia Chandler does all the work and Descario comes in for the glory.*

*But Theodore had gotten what he wanted: a reaction from Robin McKenna. The best reaction yet, but he wasn't done with her.*

*Not by a long shot.*

While Theodore waited for the verdict to be read, he looked to the media section. That hot little reporter Trinity Lange was writing furiously in her notebook. Now *there* was one smart cookie. He'd watched her on the news every night, reporting on his case. She had picked up on some of his accusations and run with them. He didn't care if she did it for the sensationalism or ratings, she brought up the hard questions. Like the one last night:

*"The key evidence in the Glenn trial is DNA found at the murder scene of Anna Louisa Clark, a twenty-three-year-old nursing student and exotic dancer who was discovered dead*

17

*by her roommate early on the morning of April 10. Glenn admitted to having an affair with three of the four victims, but denied an affair with Ms. Clark."*

The evidence against him was all circumstantial. He wasn't stupid, he wouldn't leave traces of himself behind. Luckily, the evidence from the first crime scene had been thrown out, thanks to the police screwing up. And he'd known immediately after killing Bethany that he'd made a mistake.

Theodore Glenn never made the same mistake twice.

Ergo, someone had framed him.

The bailiff said, "Will the defendant please rise?"

He rose. Julia Chandler and the asshole D.A. also stood.

"Has the jury reached a verdict?" the judge asked.

"We have, Your Honor," the foreman replied.

The judge handed the bailiff the findings, who in turn handed it over to the clerk. "The clerk will read the verdict."

The clerk began. "In count one of the indictment, willful murder in the first degree of Bethany Coleman on February 20, 2001, we the jury find the defendant, Theodore Alan Glenn, guilty. In count two of the indictment . . ."

Theodore's ears rang. The clerk's voice came from a great distance, deeper, quieter, with each pronouncement of *guilt* booming in his head.

They said he was guilty. The jury convicted him of murder. Four murders.

*Fools.*

"In count four of the indictment, willful murder in the first degree of Anna Louisa Clark on April 10, 2001, we the jury find the defendant guilty."

Theodore stood behind his table. Alone. His fury rose. He let the emotion fill him. Because he rarely had emotions, when anger rushed in, he seized it.

He would not go to prison forever. He had the appeals court. He had the system itself! He would use it and twist it around and in the end he would be free once more. And he would kill everyone — every pathetic human being — who had crossed him.

He whirled around, stared at William Hooper. Cocky cop. A real ladies' man. Hooper saw the truth on Theodore's face — that Theodore *knew* his dirty secret and would make him pay. Hooper's face tightened and he stared back, chin out.

*I know your secret,* Theodore mouthed, the edges of his lips curving up.

The gavel fell. "Mr. Glenn, please face the bench."

Theodore pivoted and faced Robin McKenna. During the entire trial, he had kept track of where she had been sitting. In the far corner. Trying to hide. Especially after his cross-examination. He gave her credit for returning to the courtroom after that grueling day.

She couldn't hide from him. Not now, not later.

He raised his hand, pointed his index finger at her, and fired a mock gun.

The gavel pounded again. "Bailiff!"

William Hooper jumped to his feet and ran down the aisle. "You fucking bastard! Don't you so much as look —"

The gavel pounded again and again. "Detective! Meet me in my chambers immediately. Thirty-minute recess. Bailiff, take Mr. Glenn to holding."

Theodore put that thirty minutes to good use. He memorized the names of everyone who needed to die.

# ONE

Dear Robin:
I think of you every day, dream of you every night. So clear are my visions of your perfect naked body dancing just for me that when I wake each morning I see you at the foot of my bed in this godforsaken prison you sent me to.
I will come for you, but you won't know the day or the hour. I long for the wonderful moment when I watch your face next to mine, the truth in your eyes as you surrender to me.

Theodore folded the letter and stuffed it back down his pants as he leaned against the fence of San Quentin's East Block exercise yard. Exercise? Most of the men stood in groups talking or arguing or hiding an illegal smoke, easier in the cold when

21

smoke could be mistaken for breath.

*Defeated.* That was the expression on most faces. Fated to spend the rest of their miserable lives in a crumbling, foul-smelling prison. Urine, fungi, and the stench Theodore could only describe as "wet dog" — but worse — permeated the interior. But here, in the pathetically small exercise yard, he tasted salt in the air, heard seagulls call, and remembered freedom.

Freedom that had been stolen from him by a stripper whore and the cop she was screwing.

The fog hung like a wet blanket over the exercise yard. Depressing and unnatural — Theodore despised the entire area. He missed the sun of San Diego, its warm beaches and hot days.

His appeal was only two months away, and he wouldn't be returning to prison no matter what happened in court.

He pulled out the letter to Robin and tore it into tiny pieces. *Fucking lying bitch, you will pay for what you did to me!*

As Theodore watched the paper float to the ground, the earth began to shake violently, back and forth. It threw him to the ground. What he would remember most about those thirty-two seconds was the overwhelming sound. He'd never realized an earthquake could be so loud.

It wasn't just the quake that caused the ear-splitting noise, but the collapse of the twenty-foot-high concrete wall separating the condemned inmates from the San Francisco Bay.

There were six guards posted on the catwalk outside the East Block wall, with .223 caliber mini rifles trained on the yard. But if Glenn couldn't stay upright, they certainly wouldn't be able to. He was banking on it.

Dust hung heavy in the air, burning his lungs, but Theodore Glenn jumped up and got moving. He'd felt more than seen the collapse of the concrete walls. Right in the middle they'd tumbled down, the weight of the crumbling rock yanking more of the wall to the ground, including at least one of the guards.

He ignored the sirens vibrating through the complex. Freedom was only a dozen yards away — over the concrete rubble. Theodore couldn't see the guard tower outside the fence. Had that collapsed as well? He could hope. If not, he would hope that enough of the condemned ran and he would not be shot.

Barely heard over the squeal of the alarms, there was erratic gunfire. Shouts from the catwalk caught Theodore's attention. He looked up, barely able to see the guard at the far south of the walk. The man was limping, but functional. Where were the others? Had they fallen to the other side? Twenty feet probably wouldn't kill them, but they'd likely be immobile.

Theodore carefully started up the slope that had been the wall. Razor wire, embedded in the destroyed wall, was now everywhere. While his sturdy shoes protected his feet, he couldn't use his hands for fear of slicing them. If he made it over the debris, he didn't want open cuts because there was only one way out:

*The San Francisco Bay.*

He sensed other inmates following him, and two were ahead. He saw the crooked arm of a guard, his green uniform covered in dust. Trapped by the concrete when it fell. Dead? Very likely. Theodore scanned the area for a rifle as he continued moving forward, up the concrete mountain. The weapon must be buried with the dead guard.

A voice from the far side of the catwalk ordered Theodore to stop. He didn't hesitate, but continued climbing the collapsed wall. He spied another guard near the top of the rubble, this one not dead but injured, blood pouring from a head wound. He kept shaking his head as if to clear it, but held fast to his rifle, which swung erratically to and fro. It didn't look like the guard could see much of anything, blood covering one eye. His expression was panicked. Fearful.

Theodore realized then that the guard who had ordered him to stop was trapped on the far side of the catwalk, which had partially collapsed, pulled down by the weight of the falling wall. Where were the other guards? The air was thick with dust and fog, Theodore wasn't sure what he was seeing.

"Stop!" the guard called again, but he was aiming his gun behind Theodore. How many were following him? Why wasn't the guard shooting? Afraid to hit a fallen officer?

Over the loudspeaker, a voice commanded, "Down! Lay facedown, hands behind your head or you will be shot."

Theodore ignored the warning. A guard was pursuing him, but the yard guards had nonfatal rubber bullets. Behind him were shouts and screams.

Reaching the wounded guard, without hesitation Theodore ripped the rifle from his shaking hands. The bastard should have shot first, he thought with a tight grin. With the stock of the rifle, Theodore hit the fallen guard twice — *wham! wham!* — on the head.

He collapsed, unconscious and more likely dead. Gun in hand, Theodore rolled down the far side of the wall.

"You bastard! You didn't need to kill him!"

Theodore turned to fire the rifle, thinking it was a pursuing guard. Instead, he saw convict Thomas O'Brien, another condemned man recently transferred from North Seg, the country club of death row. O'Brien rolled down behind him, cutting his hand on razor wire.

Theodore aimed the rifle at the traitorous prisoner. He'd had a suspicion about O'Brien ever since he walked into East Block last week.

A bullet whizzed past Theodore. He wished he'd had time to retrieve the guard's sidearm, but it was buried along with the dead guard's legs. Instead of killing his fellow prisoner, Theodore turned and returned fire. Enough to give him cover.

The earth rolled beneath him. Aftershock.

He didn't fall, but O'Brien did. The guard pursuing them also stumbled.

Gunfire echoed around him and he zigzagged through the short open space. He spared a glance toward where the main guard tower should be.

It wasn't there.

Sirens, shouts, gunfire sounded all around. Theodore ran. The two convicts in front of him jumped into the bay. He followed.

He swam northeast, away from San Francisco and the violence of the bay; toward the Richmond–San Rafael Bridge. If he could reach the bridge, he'd have a better chance of escaping.

The cold water burned his hands. He realized he had cuts all over them, small nicks that the saltwater turned to searing pain.

He slung the gun over his shoulder. It would be worthless in the water, but he could dry it out, use it again, if he was lucky.

He swam. Heard splashes behind him, others following suit. His active, rigorous lifestyle before prison had given him physical strength, which he'd maintained over the last seven years. If anyone could survive the San Francisco Bay, it was him. He was certain of it.

The more convicts on the run, the greater chance he had to escape. They would be slower than him. Already he had passed the two convicts who'd jumped ahead of him.

The water froze and burned, it was early February, light was fading, all he needed was the cover of dark and stamina, and he would be free. He'd been waiting for this opportunity, the first chance to be free. To think he'd wasted the last seven years on appeals when all he'd had to do was relax and wait for an act of God!

He almost laughed. Instead, he gritted his teeth against the pain and cold of the San Francisco Bay, found his rhythm, and swam hard through the choppy water.

Adrenaline surged through his blood, triggering every cell in his body. He'd never felt so alive.

# Two

Robin McKenna lingered in the Back Room — her VIP lounge — one ear tuned to the plasma-screen television in the corner. It usually aired whatever major sporting event was being telecast. While The Eighth Sin wasn't a sports bar, she allowed the TV in deference to her long-time regulars. Today they were irritated with her that she switched from ESPN to a local station which was airing reports on the earthquake that had hit near San Quentin.

Early reports stated the possibility of prisoners having escaped. Out of the hundreds of death row inmates housed in the East Block, surely Theodore Glenn wasn't one of the handful who had managed to flee, Robin tried to convince herself. *If* any prisoners had in fact escaped. There were still people trapped in the rubble. Head counts needed to be done, bodies recovered.

But Theodore Glenn wasn't just any inmate. If anyone had the will and stamina to escape, it would be Glenn. Robin couldn't dismiss her nagging fears. So she kept coming back to the bar even though it was Saturday night — her busiest — and she should be in the main hall where the music pulsed and people danced and drank, saw and were seen.

She couldn't walk away from the news. She had to know.

Then it happened. Her worst fear.

"Unconfirmed reports from authorities at the Department of Corrections state that up to twelve prisoners may have escaped during the earthquake that rocked San Quentin ninety minutes ago. No confirmation on who, but an earlier report stated that mass murderer Vincent Paul Porter was apprehended when he emerged from the bay a mile north of the prison. An anonymous citizen captured and restrained him until authorities arrived. And Theodore Alan Glenn, who murdered four prostitutes in San Diego, is at large after allegedly killing an injured prison guard."

*No, no, no!*

She watched as the mug shot of Theodore filled the screen, along with his vital statistics. Hair: Brown. Eyes: Blue. Height: 6'2". Weight: 190. Tattoos: None.

Theodore Glenn was handsome. Everyone had thought so, or at least all the other dancers at RJ's had. Why was it that only Robin had seen his dark side? Every time he looked at her all those years ago she'd felt icy cold. Brandi thought Robin's fears of Theodore were groundless, that she'd simply been an overprotective friend. She laughed and teased Robin, "You're the only stripper I've ever met who's a prude."

She wasn't a prude, but she didn't like when dancers dated patrons. It erased the line between customer and dancer, created an intimacy where there should only be business and mystery. Stripping was her job, not her life. She did it for the money, not the attention.

Glenn's description seemed vague, and the photo flashed on television seemed to show an ordinary, yet handsome fortyish man. It didn't show the ice blue of his eyes, nor the cold emptiness where his soul should be. Robin could hear people now, "He doesn't look like he could hurt anyone. Maybe he was telling the truth during the

30

trial. Innocent people go to prison. Remember that case . . . ?"

He was not innocent. Robin *knew* it and she wouldn't be at peace until he was back in prison. He had killed four of her friends. And he'd have kept killing until he got to her.

"They weren't prostitutes!" Robin said through clenched teeth, focusing on her anger instead of her fear. *They were exotic dancers, strippers, whatever you wanted to call them. But they didn't have sex for money.*

Theodore Glenn had escaped. There was no doubt in Robin's mind that he was capable of any vicious act, like killing an injured guard in cold blood.

Robin didn't realize she'd dropped the two martini glasses she'd been holding until the pungent smell of gin rose in the air. She glanced down at the rubber mat. One glass had bounced, the other had a broken stem. She bent down, picked up the pieces, and tossed them in the trash.

*Theodore would run to Mexico. Or Canada. Somewhere else. Anywhere but here, right?*

Even as she thought it Robin recognized her wishful thinking. Theodore Glenn would be coming back to San Diego to make good on his courthouse threats.

She remembered the letters she used to

get from him. She'd mistakenly opened and read the first one. Then she burned them, unopened and unread.

But she knew he wouldn't forget his promise to kill her.

"Hey, sugar, my drink."

Kip, one of her regulars, frowned at the spilled drinks and broken glass.

"Sorry, Kip." She smiled widely, putting back on her show face. She was good at that.

"Never seen you with slippery fingers. Used to slide up and down a pole like nobody's business, though." He winked at her. Kip was one of the few who had stayed after she bought RJ's and converted it from a strip club to an urban dance club. He had just celebrated his seventieth birthday.

She gave him a warm smile and poured another extra-dry martini.

"You're not worried about that guy coming back, are you?"

She shook her head, but her smile faltered.

"Sugar, they're going to catch him. Or he'll disappear down in Mexico. Sun it up on the beach somewhere. If he comes here, I'll take care of him, don't you worry. I wouldn't let him hurt you."

Robin kissed Kip on his thin, leathery cheek as she placed his drink on a coaster in front of him. "My white knight."

She turned, glanced back at the television. Someone from the U.S. Geological Survey in Menlo Park was talking about the heretofore unknown fault that had apparently been triggered by some shift deep in the earth. "The temblor, which occurred at four thirty-one earlier this evening, had a magnitude of seven point nine and was centered within the boundaries of San Quentin State Prison."

Because San Quentin prison was so old, it didn't surprise the expert that some structures collapsed.

She turned ESPN back on, done with the news. But it was halftime for whatever game was being aired and they were cutting into a national feed about the earthquake.

She shut off the television and motioned to Ginger, her best cocktail waitress and backup bartender. Robin asked her to take over the bar. "I need to go home."

"Is something wrong?"

Not everyone knew what had happened seven years ago. Not everyone had a killer walk into their lives. "I just need to do something. If I'm not back by closing, can you stay?"

"Sure, but —"

"Thanks, Ginger. I really appreciate it." She ducked under the bar pass-through and scurried to her office before Ginger asked any more questions. She'd figure it out before too long. As soon as word got out about Glenn, the press would run another story, her name and picture would be plastered in the papers, she'd have to suck it up. She had a successful business to run, and she wasn't going to let the murderous bastard ruin that for her.

She would give herself tonight to pull herself together. She had to. For her business, for her sanity.

It wasn't just Glenn who would be walking back into her life.

She grabbed her purse from her office and exited via the alley. The former "gaslight district," now known by the less scandalized "gaslamp district," had been cleaned up and renovated with redevelopment funds — which she had used to change RJ's from a low-class strip joint to a chic, urban dance club and gentleman's bar. Whereas ten years ago she'd never have walked through this alley alone, now the police presence kept the drugs off the main streets and criminals had been pushed out.

She walked two blocks, turned onto Fifth Street and walked two more blocks to the loft she had bought three years ago. All the warehouses on this street had been bought by a developer who converted the bottom floors to businesses, and the upper floors to lofts. She was one of the first to buy, and the space was one huge room on the top floor. It had twenty-foot ceilings and lots of tall windows. She'd put up partial walls and designed the space to maximize the sunlight so she could paint in the mornings. She'd been making a name for herself in the art community and had her first big art show coming up next weekend. She'd started painting as a hobby and discovered she loved it. She created bold, colorful, vibrant pictures, taking familiar scenes and making them special.

Her lights blazed behind the tall narrow windows of her loft. A timer turned them on before sunset. She would never walk into a dark room.

Seven years ago she'd walked into a dark nightmare that had been revived tonight with Glenn's escape.

She locked and bolted the door behind her, heart pounding.

"There's no way he can get to San Diego that fast," Robin said out loud. Her cat, Pickles, the fluffy gray and white tabby who used to belong to Anna, wound around her feet, purring. Robin picked him up and held him to her face. His purr grew louder.

"Yeah, I know, I'm not supposed to be home this early."

She fed Pickles, saw the blinking light on her answering machine. She pressed PLAY.

The machine intoned, "Message one, seven p.m. Saturday."

Then her mother's voice. "Robin, it's your mom. I'm sitting on the beach right now drinking a piña colada. Maui is so beautiful! I wish you were here with me. You work too hard, sweetheart. You need to have fun. I love you! 'Bye!"

Robin smiled, in spite of her mixed feelings. Didi McKenna had no idea of what anything cost. Her spontaneous trip to Hawaii drained her savings account and while there she would probably max out her credit cards. Robin wouldn't have cared so much except that she had bailed her mother out of financial messes more than once.

"Ms. Robin McKenna, this is Officer Diaz from the San Diego Police Department."

Robin froze as the answering machine continued with the message.

"I'm sorry to be calling so late, but this afternoon there was an earthquake near San Quentin State Prison and Theodore Glenn escaped when a wall collapsed in the prison exercise yard. We are taking precautions and notifying everyone who was involved in his

36

prosecution that Glenn is missing and presumed at large. If you have any questions, please call me at 619-555-1100."

Robin pounded the erase button, as if it could make tonight disappear. Like she didn't know Theodore had escaped! What good would it do to notify her? What good would it do anyone? If Theodore wanted to get to someone, he'd find a way.

Petting her cat, she walked through the loft to her bedroom. Her sleeping area was separated from the rest of the loft by three antique black silk screens. She put Pickles on the bed and sat, staring at her night-stand. Her fear was palatable: she tasted it, her pores oozed it, her hair tingled.

*Why me?*

Robin rarely indulged in self-pity. Seven years ago she'd had to shore herself up against it as well. It would have been easy to hide forever, to move back home with her mother, to disappear. But she hadn't. She'd faced the press, faced the court, helped put Theodore Glenn behind bars.

*"Why don't you like me, Ms. McKenna?"* he'd asked.

How to answer a question like that? She'd *felt* his evil. Deep down, she knew it. The way he looked at her. The way he made her feel: cold and petrified.

He'd never said anything cruel to her. He'd never done anything *to* her. He simply watched her, but she had grown terrified. Irrational. At least she'd thought so at the time.

When Bethany was killed, she just *knew* he was responsible. After, he looked at Robin as if they shared a secret. The way he tried to hold her, to console her, when she found out. It was — odd. Different and strange. How could she explain something she didn't understand?

Robin had put her gun away last year when Glenn's first appeal had been denied. It had been time to put the past behind her, once and for all, and the weight of the gun had reminded her constantly of why she had a concealed carry permit in the first place.

When Glenn was convicted of murdering four of her friends, he vowed to the courtroom that he would kill Robin. When he stared at her that horrible day, she was certain he would do it the moment he had the opportunity.

She had to make sure he had no such opportunity. If he came back to San Diego, she had to protect herself. She would not be a victim. She would not allow him to win.

She opened her nightstand. There was

nothing in the drawer except for her gun, her belt holster, and a box of bullets. She picked up the 9mm and held it in her palms.

The fear she had repressed for the last hour overwhelmed her.

It was as if she were back in her old apartment. In the dark. She had walked in, wondered why the lamp wasn't where it was supposed to be. Pickles wound around her feet. She picked him up. He was wet. The smell. God, the metallic, wet smell! It was like she knew, but still stepped forward. Tripped over something, fell in a slick, foul-smelling mess. It was Anna's blood. Her blood was everywhere; Robin was covered in it.

Now she put her head in her hands, shaking. For seven years she had lived with fear, but she'd dealt with it. Minimized it. Robin forced herself to work, stand up to rowdy guests, defend her dancers, run her business. She would not be cowed into hiding. She'd taken self-defense classes while in college, had taken even more of them after Anna was killed. She had gotten the gun. Learned to use it.

One year ago she put the weapon away and stopped going to the range. It had been time to get on with her life. To finally conquer the cold fear that chilled her every night.

The fear was back.

She walked to her dresser and opened the top drawer, pulled out her favorite leather belt, and threaded her holster through it. She checked the ammunition, though she didn't have to. The first of every month she cleaned the gun, reloaded it, chambered a round, and flicked the safety on. She'd never grown up with guns, but she was comfortable with this one.

If Theodore Glenn walked through that door, she would shoot him without hesitation or remorse.

The thought that she could kill repulsed her. What kind of person did that make her? What had fear created?

# THREE

Detective Will Hooper came up from the basement where he'd retrieved the files on Theodore Glenn in preparation for the task-force meeting.

Chief Causey thought Will was crazy when he insisted on calling the meeting first thing Sunday morning, insisting that Glenn would head for the border. Will argued passionately, *knowing* Glenn would return to

San Diego to make good on his threat.

Though unconvinced, Causey ordered everyone threatened by Glenn to be notified. He also agreed to put together the task force as a precautionary measure.

Chief Causey's opinion aside, there was no doubt in Will's mind that Theodore Glenn would try to kill those who had put him in prison. The only question: *Who would he target first?*

Carina Kincaid, Will's partner, entered the bull pen and made a beeline toward the coffeepot, her dark hair still damp. "Bastard," she mumbled when she saw Will. "You called me at *four in the morning.*"

"Wimp."

"I'd tell you to fuck off, but I'm too tired."

"Late night?"

Carina blinked. "Why do I feel we've had some version of this conversation before?"

"Because you have someone to share your bed and I don't."

"Your dry spell will be the death of me," Carina said. "What happened to Monica?"

"That was over months ago."

"Nicole?"

"I'm surprised you even know about her. That was before we were partners. We split amicably."

"What about that cute girl who works for

41

Jim? Maybe you should ask her out."

"Diana? *Cute girl?* Last I checked, she was older than you."

Carina waved her hand in dismissal. "Whatever. I think she likes you."

"Diana and I had a thing years ago."

"Hmm. She still has it bad for you. Why, I can't imagine."

Will shook his head. "I doubt that. It didn't work out with Diana. Not all of us get as lucky as you."

"You'll get no argument here, but I'm not sharing Nick with you no matter how much you beg."

Will rolled his eyes and pulled open the cardboard box.

"What's in there?" Carina asked, pulling her hair back with a metal clip.

"Everything related to the Glenn case. Except the evidence, which is at archives."

"Why isn't this in archives? The case was closed seven years ago."

"I needed it during that appeals court hearing last year. Plus, I expected Glenn to file another appeal, and I wanted to stay fresh."

"You're obsessed with that case. Remember? We got the guy."

It was a generic "we" because Carina had still been a beat cop when Will and his former partner, Frank Sturgeon, had investigated the homicides that led to the arrest of wealthy corporate trial lawyer Theodore Glenn.

"I'm not obsessed."

He wouldn't admit it to Carina, but he still dreamed about the murders. He supposed they'd be called *nightmares* if anyone was going to get technical about it.

Theodore Glenn had enjoyed playing with his victims. Seeing the bodies, knowing what he did to those four women, interviewing Glenn after he'd been locked up — Will continually replayed the investigation in his mind.

It wasn't just the brutal slayings, or the blood, or Glenn's sick humor — it was Glenn himself during interrogation.

From petty thieves to hardened murderers, most criminals lied or cast blame elsewhere: "It's not my fault," "She wanted it," or "I didn't mean to kill her, it got out of hand, it was an accident."

Theodore Glenn had not one ounce of remorse. Not one grain of empathy. He'd looked at the crime scene photos with the interest of a bored scientist. He had even criticized the way the crime scene technician had photographed the scene.

*"The lighting is awful. Had she only in-*

*creased the aperture, you'd be able to see the definition of the blood against the rug. You call this evidence?"*

Will had faced many brutal killers. He'd faced psychopaths. He'd faced gang leaders who would just as soon shoot a cop as talk to one.

But Theodore Glenn was no typical killer. He had a picture-perfect background. Upper middle class upbringing. No hint of violence in his childhood. After interviewing his parents, Will couldn't even imagine them so much as spanking their beloved son. Was that the problem: lack of discipline? Too much and it's abuse, too little and your bratty kid runs wild.

It was human nature to cast blame, to search for a specific reason why someone like Theodore Glenn killed. But the truth was simple: He had no conscience. Will saw it in his face, in his tone, in his arrogance. This bastard killed because he enjoyed it, because he enjoyed getting away with deviant acts. Was it just for the thrill? Maybe. Will wasn't a shrink, but he knew Glenn wasn't like most killers.

Something else about the Glenn murders haunted him.

*Robin.*

Out of self-preservation, Will didn't like to

44

think about Robin McKenna. Even bringing her to mind now brought conflicting feelings of love and lust, anger and remorse, fear and need. He had made huge mistakes with her — on the case, in his life.

Now he had to warn her. He'd never wanted to see her again, and at the same time he desperately wanted to make love to her. Hold her. Be with her.

He ran a hand through his short-cropped brown hair.

"What's wrong?" Carina asked as she efficiently separated the files.

"Nothing."

"Hooper, I've known you for how long?"

"Seriously, just the past creeping up on me."

"We're going to catch Glenn. Every cop in the state is looking for him."

"How many people will die first?" Will tensed. Glenn would go after Robin. Will had to protect her. The thought that she might suffer at Glenn's hands caused sweat to break out on his forehead.

Protect her? He'd be lucky if she let him through her door. Robin had made it perfectly clear she wanted nothing to do with him. Not that he blamed her, not after what he'd said and done.

Chief Causey walked in, poured a cup of

coffee. "You're on, Hooper. Now make it fast. I got the press breathing down my throat, Descario screaming about protection, and the Feds calling."

"The Feds?"

"The California Highway Patrol are working with the FBI's San Francisco regional office. They have huge issues up north — a severely damaged bridge, power outages, looting. The usual loonies running amok after a major natural disaster. They've offered to loan a Suit to us to facilitate communication and share resources."

"Whatever you think best," Will responded. "It might be helpful to have an insider, as long as we don't get the shaft."

"I'll feel them out, see what's happening, and let you know."

Carrying his box of photos and information, Will led the way into the interview room he'd turned into the task-force command center. He wanted to make sure that everyone working the case knew exactly what Theodore Glenn had done to those women.

There were four cops in the room who Causey had dedicated to Will for the time being. In an hour, Will would be speaking at shift change, but for now these were the three men and one woman who, apart from himself and Carina, would be working exclusively on the Theodore Glenn case.

"We have a lot of work to do in the next twenty-four hours," Will began. He glanced at Officer Diaz. "You've contacted everyone involved with the Glenn prosecution? Witnesses?"

"Still working on the list, sir. I reached about half of them last night."

Will wanted to ask if he'd talked to Robin, but refrained, trusting that Diaz would do a thorough job.

"Keep going. Give me a list of everyone you haven't spoken to personally before end of shift."

"Yes, sir."

Will looked around the room. Other than Diaz and Carina, no one else had been on the force seven years ago when Glenn was at large.

"A little background on Theodore Glenn. Seven years ago he killed four strippers who worked at RJ's in the gaslight district. The club is no longer there. It was bought out and renovated during the big redevelopment push a few years back. Glenn had been a regular at RJ's for about a year. He had dated at least three of the victims."

Will took out crime scene photographs and placed them on the whiteboard with magnets. First an enlarged snapshot of a gorgeous young woman. She was twenty, blonde, and had a dazzling smile.

"Bethany Coleman was Glenn's first victim. She dated Glenn for three months before, according to witnesses, they parted friends." He put up a picture of her dead body. Glenn had cut her skin more than forty times, feet to face, one- to two-inch-long shallow cuts that would have scarred and defaced her. Painful, but not fatal. When he'd finally tired of torturing Bethany, he'd slit her throat.

"Was Glenn a suspect from the beginning?"

"Way down on the list. Bethany had seven former boyfriends the year before she was murdered, and Glenn hadn't been the most recent. There was some evidence at the scene and it was being processed by the crime lab when Brandi Bell was murdered fourteen days after Bethany."

Will put up Brandi's photograph. She was an unnatural platinum blonde with another winning smile and huge brown eyes. "There was a witness in Brandi's homicide. An elderly woman across the street gave a description of a man leaving Brandi's duplex to canvassing officers. From that, Robin McKenna, a friend and colleague of the victim, identified Theodore Glenn, a regular patron of the club who had dated both Bethany and Brandi."

"The wounds on the bodies look different," Carina interjected. "The cuts on Bethany's body are a mess, blood smeared. On Brandi they look like they were cleaned. Did he wash the victims after killing them?"

"Good guess, but no," Will said. His jaw tensed as he imagined what Brandi had suffered in the final minutes before Glenn slit her throat. "He poured bleach over her body."

"To destroy evidence?"

"Possibly." He paused. "The bleach was poured over the wounds while his victims were still alive."

Carina shivered as if she'd heard nails scratch on a chalkboard. It would have felt like being burned alive to the victims. It had the added benefit of destroying potential evidence.

Will continued. "We pulled Glenn in for an interview and court-ordered DNA test, based on Robin McKenna's identification. The killer had left DNA at the scene of the first murder — three strands of hair, pulled from Glenn's scalp as Bethany struggled." He took a deep breath. This was the part that was totally fucked. "We had him. We

49

had him in custody and we had the DNA test. We handed the case to the D.A.'s office. Immediately, the case was thrown out."

"Why?" one of the newer cops asked.

"The criminalists had come directly from another homicide. The DNA collected at the scene was contaminated: the hair samples got mixed with hair samples from the other crime. Descario tossed out both cases. Without the DNA, we had nothing to tie Theodore Glenn to the murders."

"What about the witness?" Carina asked.

"The D.A. didn't feel she was reliable." Will shook his head. "And as much as I hate to admit it, Descario was right on that point. The woman was eighty and in a lineup she couldn't pick out Glenn. Going from a secondhand identification off the sketch — no jury would have convicted him. We had to let him go." That had been one of the worst days of Will's life: knowing he had a killer behind bars and having to let him out. He'd never forget the smug expression of victory on that bastard's face.

"How did you connect the two killings? If you couldn't use the DNA from the first murder, and bleach was used in the second, how did you make the connection?" Carina asked, curious.

"A similar M.O. The multitude of small,

painful cuts with the same type of knife. The way the hands and feet were bound. The slit throat with a double-edged blade. And the victims were dancers at the same club." Will paused. "Glenn must have realized he'd screwed up with Bethany Coleman, and that's why he used the bleach at Brandi Bell's crime scene. Even if he left trace evidence there, the bleach would have corrupted any DNA samples."

One of the cops in the back shook his head and lamented, "Because of all those forensics shows, killers are becoming smarter."

Will shrugged. "Perhaps, but remember this was seven years ago. Those shows didn't have the impact on criminals and jurors that they might have today."

Will put up Jessica's picture. A brunette. "You can see that Glenn has no preference as to type: Bethany and Brandi were Caucasian, Jessica a Latina. What they had in common were their good looks, and all were strippers at RJ's."

"And hadn't each victim dated Glenn at some point?" Carina asked.

"All but his last, Anna Clark."

"If you knew Glenn was the killer, why didn't we follow him?" she asked.

"We did, but —" Will didn't want to get

51

into it. He wasn't about to publicly criticize his former partner. Water under the bridge. Frank was no longer a cop. He could do no more damage.

"Anyway," Will continued as if the question wasn't asked, "Glenn had a loose alibi for Jessica's murder, which was one month after Brandi was killed. We were all over him at the time, pulled him into interview, but again had no hard evidence. A week after Jessica, he killed Anna Clark. He shook our tail."

He put Anna's picture up. Black hair, blue eyes, and porcelain skin. Sweet. And in death? He put up the crime scene photo. In death she was another mangled body, another crime victim in a police file.

He took a deep breath. *It could have been Robin.* And in his heart, he believed Glenn had meant to kill Robin all along.

"The crime scene is a mess," Carina said. "What happened?"

"Anna's roommate came home and tripped over the body in the dark." Will's stomach lurched, picturing Robin in the dark, slipping and falling in Anna's blood. When he'd arrived at the scene only minutes later she had been huddled and shaking outside her apartment door, holding a cat drenched in his owner's blood. "In fact, the

52

entire scene was compromised. But Glenn was careless this time: though he bleached Anna's body, several of his hairs were found in Anna's fist."

"What about sexual assault?" Carina asked. She'd been flipping through the files, reading the reports.

"None," Will said. "He didn't rape or have sex with his victims immediately prior to their murders. He did have consensual sex with all the victims, with the possible exception of Anna Clark, weeks or months before their deaths. Anna Clark was a lesbian. She wouldn't have had consensual sex with Glenn."

"He doesn't sound like your garden variety serial killer," Carina said.

"He isn't," Will said. "He's smart. Very smart. Do not underestimate Theodore Glenn."

"Next step?" Carina asked.

Will turned to Diaz. "You finish the warning calls to witnesses. I want the rest of you to split the city and start canvassing motels, hotels, and dive apartments that rent by the week. Flash Glenn's picture around to anyone and everyone. If everyone is looking for him, he can't hide for long."

"You really think he's going to come here and not try to leave the country?"

"I know it."

Trinity Lange listened intently to Chief Causey's bland, perfunctory report to the press on Theodore Glenn's escape and the subsequent response of the San Diego Police Department.

She had better information off CNN and Fox News. She glanced behind Causey to where Detective Will Hooper stood, deceptively casual. He was watching the crowd. Looking for Glenn? Feeling out the audience?

What did the cops know that they weren't telling?

Trinity had made a name for herself as a crime reporter, starting as a freelancer and working her way up to a star reporter with her own monthly show. She'd had every major law enforcement officer from the Attorney General down to the smallest police chief on her television program, and her ratings continued to grow. It was just a matter of time before she had New York knocking at her door.

She didn't honestly believe that Theodore Glenn would show his face in San Diego. She'd followed the trial closely, listened to him, even interviewed him in lockup. He wasn't a dumb criminal. But on the off chance that he did show up, Trinity wanted to be there. Reporting the news before anyone else.

That meant knowing what the cops knew. And they always knew more than they told the press.

Her hand shot up. Causey called on another reporter.

"Jerk," she mumbled, keeping her hand in the air.

"Chief Causey," the reporter asked, "are you alerting prostitutes to be cautious now that Glenn has escaped?"

*Idiot.* Glenn hadn't gone after prostitutes. The novice certainly hadn't done his homework.

Causey seemed at a loss. He said, "Glenn targeted women with whom he'd had a previous relationship. Our primary concern is for individuals he specifically threatened at his trial. We are contacting everyone involved in the trial, and going from there. All units are on alert, and we're working closely with the California Highway Patrol and federal authorities to track the known movements of Theodore Glenn. As I said at the beginning, Glenn was spotted in Fresno late last night and is suspected of stealing a 2004 white Honda Accord."

*Yeah, yeah, yeah.* Trinity rolled her eyes.

Stupid question, leading to repetition. She waved her hand again.

Causey picked someone else. What was with him? She looked at Will, tried to catch his eye. He looked over at her, gave her a half grin, then turned his attention back to Causey.

Had Will Hooper told the chief not to call on her?

Finally, Causey pointed at her. Trinity asked, "Chief Causey, who is in charge of the task force and what are they planning on doing to protect the citizens of San Diego?"

Causey turned to Will. "Detective William Hooper, a twenty-year veteran of San Diego PD, is heading up the task force. He was involved in the original investigation and was instrumental in capturing Glenn seven years ago."

Before Causey could call on anyone else, Trinity spoke up. "Do you have any actual indication that Glenn is headed for San Diego?"

"None," Causey said emphatically, but glanced at Will. Why?

Will took the microphone and said, "The smart thing for Glenn to do would be to attempt to leave the country. Every cop in San Diego County — every cop in the state

56

— is looking for him. He killed an injured guard in cold blood during his escape.

"But Glenn is not that smart," Will continued. "Glenn only sees one thing, and that is he was convicted. Now he wants revenge. And that's why he'll come to San Diego. Watch for him. He may alter his appearance. But if everyone in San Diego is looking, we can catch him before he hurts anyone else, and put him back on death row."

Theodore despised Will Hooper. And listening to the press conference on the news, sitting safe in an old, worn La-Z-Boy, and having that asshole cop call him *stupid* pained him.

Hooper knew damn well he was a genius. It was only bad luck that a witness caught sight of him coming out of Brandi's duplex. He should have gone in and killed that old biddy when he saw the curtains move. But he honestly hadn't believed she could see that far away. How was he to know she regularly used binoculars to watch the comings and goings from all her neighbors' houses?

He'd *seen* the sketch on the news. It didn't look enough like him to have him concerned. It could have been *anybody*.

Then to have that high-and-mighty hypocrite Robin McKenna tell the cops that *he* was the man in the sketch. Bad luck. It should never have happened. How that slut was able to make the connection unnerved him, and pissed him off. It was a guess on her part, simply because she didn't like him. She'd made *that* perfectly clear right from the beginning.

Robin. He closed his eyes and saw her perfect form take shape. The way she moved onstage. Liquid energy. Smooth, perfect, music in motion. He'd wanted her something fierce. He saw in her eyes something he'd never seen before. An intelligence and *knowledge* that mirrored his. She was better than this, better than a stripper, and she knew it. Her self-confidence rivaled his. Her poise and elegance. Everything about Robin McKenna was a dream dance, an act, an image she wanted to show. Just like him. All he wanted was for her to touch him. Why didn't she see that they were the same?

But instead of joining him, she'd turned against him. Long before she identified his sketch for the police, she turned on him. Told Bethany he was dangerous. A year before he killed the girl, Robin was warning her.

Smart, cold bitch.

He'd been set up. He hadn't killed Robin's pathetic roommate, yet he'd been convicted for that murder as well.

How did he know the bitch herself hadn't knocked off her roommate to frame him? She'd wanted him out of the picture so badly. And she was cold and heartless enough to kill, of that Theodore was certain. They were two of a kind, and before he was done with Robin McKenna, she would recognize that fact.

He had his list, and he would take care of each person on it in due time. Blood was thicker than water, and he had a score to settle.

His sister should never have testified against him. She would suffer for her betrayal. Robin could wait. Watch him take his revenge on others first. She'd know he was coming for her. She'd know and that fear would fester deliciously under her flawless skin.

He smiled at the thought of Robin cowering in the corner. Waiting for him to come and put her out of her misery. Because he would. And he would not be merciful.

Jenny Olsen slouched into the living room with a tray of food. She was a fat bitch, might have been pretty if she didn't look like a cow. But she'd been faithfully writing to him in prison these last seven years and she'd told him she'd do anything for him.

He'd called her on it when he showed up on her porch early Sunday morning.

"I hope you like it," Jenny said, beaming.

*Stupid wench.*

He tasted the meal. Chicken, rice, carrots, and broccoli. The best meal he'd had in years. Simple, flavorful, home-cooked.

"Delicious," he said honestly, favoring her with a smile.

She beamed brighter, rubbing her chubby hands together. "Can I get you anything else? A beer maybe?"

"Do you have red wine?" Theodore detested beer, and he dreaded what sort of wine this white-trash female would have on hand, but he hadn't had a drink in seven years.

Jenny looked worried. "N-no. But I have some Scotch, I think. It was my father's, before he died."

"Let's see it."

She walked over to the hutch in the dining room. Her small fifties cinderblock house was clean but full of clutter. Knick-knacks. Glass figures. Her life, on show for everyone who walked through the door.

Pathetic.

She bent down, fumbled through bottles.

She came up with something that actually looked good. "Is this okay?"

"Pour it," he said.

She did, he sipped. "Not bad."

He ate and drank, not caring that Jenny watched his every move. She *adored* him. He could see it in her doe eyes, in her obsequious manner. Wasn't she the least bit scared? Wasn't she the least bit concerned that he might kill her?

Theodore wasn't surprised he'd gotten away yesterday. The only truly hazardous part of the escape was the hour he'd spent in the frigid water of the San Francisco Bay. He'd been victorious partly from luck, partly from intelligence. He'd immediately slipped away from the pack because those other fools were going to get themselves killed or captured. When he finally made it to shore, he'd lucked out that he emerged only yards from a convenience store. Before going to prison, he'd never known how to hot-wire a vehicle, but he'd learned a lot behind bars and it only took him two tries before he successfully stole a truck. He once again felt that familiar jolt of adrenaline, the high from being smart and on the edge.

More good luck was that there was a suitcase in the stolen truck. He pulled out a white T-shirt and windbreaker. Enough to get rid of his prison duds and look like ordinary Joe Citizen.

Glenn had headed north, then east around the bay, then south down highway 99, because there were more places to stop and hide off the road if necessary. He swapped cars in Fresno, suspecting that the owner of this pickup he had stolen would have reported it missing by that time. Three hours later, he merged onto I-5 near the Grapevine and went over the hill toward L.A. There was no abnormal police presence that he noticed. He stayed just a few miles over the speed limit, drove through the night, and was now only an hour away from his hometown, in the home of Jenny Olsen, one of the many women who had written him in prison. Jenny had said she would do anything for him.

So far, she wasn't lying.

# FOUR

Monday morning Robin arrived at the gun range she'd frequented twice a week for nearly six years. Ten minutes before they opened, she sat in the parking lot, unloaded her weapon, and secured the ammo and gun in a carrying case. For so long, the range had practically been a second home to her.

The owner, an ex-cop named Hank Solano, had taught her everything she now knew about guns.

Authorities had recaptured one of the convicts, one had drowned in the San Francisco Bay, but more were still at large. Including Theodore Glenn.

Seven years ago her life exploded. No longer was she anonymous. Her name, photograph, and entire life history had been splashed across the local papers after the murders and during the trial. Two years later she'd bought a building in the gaslamp district — the business owners had worked to change the image by also changing the name from "gaslight" to "gaslamp," which she didn't completely understand but went along with it anyway. When she opened The Eighth Sin, the press had done a feature on her.

"FORMER STRIPPER OPENS SEXY NIGHTCLUB."

It didn't matter that her girls didn't strip. It didn't matter that she had just as many beautiful men on staff as women, or that she was trying something new and innovative, or that she'd gone into the black after two years. All the press cared about was the past. That Robin had been a stripper, that the notorious Theodore Alan Glenn had killed four exotic dancers — her friends, women she cared about — and was given the death penalty.

Glenn's M.O. was that he had consensual sex with his victims, then later, months after the relationship was over, broke into their homes, tortured, and killed them. Anna had never slept with Glenn, but he killed her anyway.

Justice was too slow, too painful. But in the end, justice had been served, hadn't it? Bethany and Brandi, Jessica and Anna avenged. Glenn would be dead sooner or later. In prison, he couldn't hurt her. In prison, she could almost forget he existed.

At least until forty hours ago when she learned he'd escaped from prison during an earthquake.

"God," Robin muttered, glancing up at the roof of her car. "What did I do to deserve this?"

She rubbed her face with her hands, taking a deep breath. Why would Glenn risk returning to San Diego? Everyone was looking for him here. Did he think Robin wouldn't shoot him on sight?

But that didn't mean she wasn't afraid now. For years, she had been living in fear. Sleeping with the lights on. Waking with nightmares nearly every damn night. Waking with the iron scent of Anna's bloody death on her hands. She hadn't had a full day of peace since that terrible night.

The past would come full circle. Already the media was talking about the murders of her four friends. It was only a matter of time before Robin's name and photograph were again plastered all over the papers and television. Before the press tantalized the public with unproven rumors that the old club called RJ's had been a haven for prostitutes.

Shaking her head, she looked across the parking lot and watched as Hank unlocked the doors from the inside. He saw her car, watched her through the glass. Did he recognize Robin? Of course he did. Once a cop always a cop, he'd told her. *"If it wasn't for that gang initiation stunt, I'd still be a cop."*

A beat cop in L.A., Hank had been shot as a test of gang loyalty. He'd nearly died on the street. He now walked with a limp and was missing three fingers on his left hand, but he could still load a magazine faster than she could with all ten fingers.

He stared as she stepped out of her car. She tried to keep her pace light, her face calm, but the truth was she could hardly wait to hit the range and see if she'd lost her eye.

Hank opened the door for her. "It's been awhile."

She nodded, her smile genuine. For all the crap that had happened back then, she'd made a few good friends. A silver lining on a very dark cloud. "You're looking good, Hank."

He pulled her into a hug, slapped her on the back, then stood back and looked at her critically. "You sure you're good?"

"I'm ready."

"Think shooting a gun is like riding a bike?"

She smirked. "Sure do."

"Twenty bucks says you miss a perfect score."

"You're on."

Hank pulled several boxes of ammo out of the cabinet and went with her into the range, leaving his assistant to man the front. Robin ran through all the safety checks, forgetting nothing.

"When was the last time you cleaned your gun?" Hank asked.

"The first Saturday of the month. I've never forgotten."

"Hmm."

"You heard?" she asked.

"Who the hell didn't?"

Robin set up the target, and pushed the

button to send it back. Fired. Again. Rapidly.

She missed one.

"Shit," she mumbled, handing Hank a twenty.

"You done good, girl. I didn't think you'd still have it in you."

"I scored perfect last time."

"You're still a great shot."

"Because you taught me. I owe you."

"You owe me nothing. I have some work to do. Why don't you work on your technique?"

"There's nothing wrong with my technique," she teased.

He grinned, his brown eyes twinkling. "I know. I just like watching pretty women shoot guns. Stay as long as you like."

When Will learned Diaz had left a message on Robin's machine but hadn't spoken with her personally, he couldn't help but worry. Will should have gone to her immediately, face-to-face. She deserved to hear about the investigation and what they knew — no matter how minimal — from him, not from someone he assigned to the task.

He couldn't find Robin at her new loft so he went to her club. It was closed, but when Will showed his identification, the assistant manager who was setting up for a retirement lunch told him that she was at the Solano Gun Mart. The girl scrunched up her nose in distaste, and Will wondered if she had a problem with Robin, a problem with guns, or both.

Will glanced around the modern dance club. Minimalist with lots of sleek metal and high-end acrylic, lots of black, white, and silver. The recessed lighting appeared colorful — which would add dimension to the place when it was on. The only splashes of color were large murals hanging here and there, scenes hinting at the vibrancy of nature — bolder greens and blues in a mountain stream; vivid reds and oranges of a sunset. Deceptively simple paintings that drew the eye and the imagination.

Robin had done well for herself. He'd followed her career from the periphery, both her business and her art. He couldn't help himself, he wanted to make sure she was doing all right. And she was. She was living her dream: owning her own business, and next week she had her first major art show.

Last year he had bought one of her paintings. At first glance it looked like the ocean on a hot summer day. Simple but vibrant. The few people populating the beach were like an afterthought. But he saw the detail

68

from a distance, and realized she'd painted them, holding hands, watching a dolphin leap in the distance.

He'd hung the painting in his living room. Every time he looked at the picture he saw something different, felt something more. And remembered his failings.

The Solano Gun Mart was only a few minutes from downtown. When Will stepped through the doors, the scent of gunpowder and cleaning solvent mixed with metal was pervasive. Turning to the right, he looked through the windows and saw Robin at the far end of the range, her back to him. An older man — trim, six foot, graying dark hair — was also watching her. She was running through a standard target — near, close, and far — and doing a damn fine job of hitting the bull's-eye.

His chest tightened, but he didn't want to examine his feelings too closely. To say Robin was a good-looking woman was an understatement. Tall, curvy, with legs that went up and up, she could dress in a burlap sack and still stop traffic. She'd pulled her long, thick, dark red hair into a wavy ponytail, her high cheekbones cut sharply across her face. Long, elegant nose; full, lush lips; a slender, delicate neck.

But Robin McKenna was not delicate. She

had a core of steel and an attitude to match. Everything she did, she did with passion. She loved passionately and hated passionately.

Will knew. He'd been on the receiving end of both.

Seeing her now, he knew he wasn't ready to talk. His mouth was dry and all he wanted to do was drop to his knees and apologize for how much he'd hurt her.

There was no going back.

Dear Lord, how he wanted to. He wanted to hold her, to take her back to his bed, to make love to her and be made love to. Seeing her brought back every memory and emotion and hope and fear.

The door opened and the rangemaster stepped out. "Can I help you?"

Will needed time to stamp out this reaction and put some distance between his feelings and his job. Just a few minutes. The assistant manager at her club had told Will that Robin would be back there at noon, he'd see her then.

"Just checking out this place. I haven't been here before."

The owner looked him up and down. "A lot of cops shoot here. I run a clean place. I had twelve years on the job before I went out on disability."

His limp was slight but evident as he walked around the counter.

"I'm sure you do." Will extended his hand. "Detective William Hooper, SDPD."

"Hank Solano. Rampart Precinct, L.A."

"What happened?"

"Six bullets in a gang shooting. Fortunately the kid was a lousy shot and missed all major organs. But my left knee's all plastic and metal now."

"Who's the girl?"

Hank didn't take his eyes off Will. "You tell me." His casual stance as he eased onto a stool belied his probing stare.

Will gave a half smile. "I heard she was here. I need to give her some bad news."

"You think she doesn't know that bastard escaped from prison?"

"Good point." He especially didn't want to talk to Robin with an audience. He needed to regroup, to harden his heart.

"Has he been spotted in town?" Hank asked. He didn't have to say Glenn's name for Will to know who he meant.

"Not yet."

"I trained her myself. She's a good shot."

"I can see that." And that saddened Will on many levels.

"Why don't I introduce you to her? Might make any other news — or lack thereof —

71

easier on the girl. She's been through hell."

"I know." He stared at the man. "I arrested Theodore Glenn."

Suddenly, Hank's face hardened. What had Robin told him? Was Robin involved with this guy? Emotionally? Physically? A streak of jealousy ran through Will, and he squelched it. He had no claims on Robin. Not anymore. Maybe not even seven years ago.

"Why don't we just pretend you never stopped by?" Hank Solano said, his voice low and vibrating with a restrained anger.

"Good idea." Will started for the door.

Hank had the last word.

"Find that bastard, then stay the hell out of her life."

# FIVE

"Mom, please be careful," Sherry said to her mother over the phone as she nervously glanced at the clock. It was one fifty. At two o'clock every afternoon, Sherry walked four blocks to her daughter's school. The bell rang at two fifteen and Sherry never wanted six-year-old Ashley to have to wait, to wonder if her mother forgot.

Especially today.

"Sherry, sweetheart, Theodore would

72

never hurt us. He couldn't hurt anyone. It was just a big mistake."

For nearly seven years, Carl and Dorothy Glenn had been saying the same thing. *There was a mistake. Theodore wouldn't hurt a fly. It was all just a big misunderstanding.*

And for nearly seven years, Sherry had tried to convince them that yes, in fact, their son and her brother *had* killed four women, that the police had been right to arrest him, and she had been right to testify against him.

Her brother had shown a far darker side to her than to anyone else in their family.

"Mom, you don't know what he's capable of. Don't let him in the house. Promise me you'll call the police if he shows up."

"The police have already been here. They have a police car down the street. What will the neighbors think?"

It was useless trying to convince her mother that Theodore was anything but an angel. "I need to pick up Ashley. I'll call you tonight. Please don't let him in the house."

"I'm sure he'll turn himself in. He just wants to set the record straight," Dorothy Glenn said.

Sherry couldn't take any more of this conversation. " 'Bye, Mom." She hung up, angry and sad. She just wanted her parents to see who Theodore was — the person he *really* was. It wasn't their fault they only saw good in their son. Carl and Dorothy were loving parents. Gave their children everything they could without spoiling them. A nice house, good neighborhood, a top school. Paid for two college educations and Theodore's law school.

Why couldn't they *see* the monster in Theodore? Sherry did. Her entire life she'd walked on eggshells around her brother. Testifying for the prosecution had been cathartic. Telling the world that she'd always known he was bad. He'd hurt Sherry for the sole purpose of hurting her. Because he could.

Most of her testimony had been thrown out. The most difficult thing she'd ever done in her life — harder even than getting clean after years of drug use — was facing Theodore in that court and telling the jury how he had tormented her when they were younger. About the time he'd broken her kitten's neck in front of her.

Crying, he'd told their parents it was an accident.

But Sherry had watched him squeeze the life out of Muffin. She'd heard the snap of breaking bones. She'd buried the poor creature's little body in the backyard and cried. Sherry had cried not only for the helpless dead animal, but because no one would believe her.

*It was an accident,* Theodore sobbed.

*He did it on purpose!* Sherry screamed.

He'd played everyone so well. Everyone but her. And he relished that only she had seen his true nature. Played with her, tormenting her until she ran away from home just to get away from *him.* She'd been branded a problem child and was in and out of juvenile homes. None of it was fun, but it was better than living with her brother.

At his trial, Theodore had objected. Nothing she said had any relevance to the murders. And the judge agreed with him. Did she have firsthand information about the murders? No, she didn't. The nice woman from the District Attorney's office insisted that Sherry's testimony was important because it went to Theodore's character. The judge didn't agree.

Theodore had called their parents to the stand. They told the court what a wonderful child Theodore had been. A straight-A student. Graduated top in his law school. Kind, thoughtful, a good son.

"He never gave us any trouble," her father

had said to the jury.

The D.A. refused to cross-examine, and Ms. Chandler told her later that it would do more damage to their case if they went after two elderly parents than if they simply let the testimony stand. "They're not lying," Ms. Chandler said. "They believe every word they said, and anything I do or ask will only make us seem heartless to the jury."

At the time, Sherry had never been so scared in her life. She'd been so certain the jury would acquit. Who wouldn't believe Carl and Dorothy Glenn? They were good people. So good they couldn't see the bad in anyone. Until Theodore was convicted, Sherry had planned to change her name and flee California. Go somewhere her brother couldn't find her.

Because Sherry knew Theodore would kill her.

Two-oh-two. She had to go. It seemed ridiculous to drive four blocks to the school. A waste of gas. She'd always loved her walk, the time alone with Ashley listening to her talk nonstop about her day and her teacher and friends.

But she was scared. Her car seemed so much safer than walking. If she saw her brother, she'd run him down.

Sherry grabbed her purse and went out to the garage. Her hand automatically went to the garage door opener and pressed it.

Nothing happened. She heard the mewling of a kitten. Sherry didn't have a cat. She'd never been able to have another pet, not after what Theodore did.

The neighbors next door had a cat.

"Hello, Sherry." In the dim light, Theodore smiled. He was wedged between two boxes. He'd probably overheard Sherry's entire conversation with their mother.

Her face froze, then her bottom lip trembled. He watched her face closely as he broke the neck of the animal with a quick movement of his hands, the *snap* surprisingly sharp.

Eyes wide, terrified, Sherry's scream came out too high-pitched to be heard by anyone outside the garage. She stepped toward the kitchen door.

Theodore acted fast. He probably shouldn't have played with his sister, but it had been fun. He took no pleasure in killing the animal, but he enjoyed the reaction he caused. When he'd killed Sherry's furry little pet all those years ago, he'd laughed at her anguish. But what was truly the most fun was digging up the dead cat and putting it in her bed. Her scream then was even

77

better than the pathetic yelp today.

Before she could even reach the doorknob, he grabbed her from behind. She kicked and bit at his hand. Feisty bitch. Too little, too late. He'd always been stronger, and prison made him more so. Be strong or be killed.

Sherry had been such fun for him to torment over the years. Then she'd betrayed him in the worst way. Shared their private games with the world. Told everyone he was *sick*. Thought she'd have the last laugh. Wrong.

He wasn't sick. He acknowledged that he was probably evil, but doing whatever he damn well pleased was so much fun. But sick? Hell no. That accusation had grated on him for years, as if something were *wrong* with him.

He'd pay her back for turning against him.

He whispered in her ear, "You thought you were going to get away with talking? Sis, I told you I'd kill you. Now you're dead."

He snapped her neck, holding her close to him while she fell slack, then dropped her dying body to the concrete floor. He knelt over her, looked into her eyes as they lost focus, faded, taking satisfaction that he was the last face she'd ever see. Sherry's face was frozen in fear, her mouth open, silently moving, blood trickling from the corner.

He stood, found the cat where he'd dropped it, and tossed it on Sherry's body.

One down.

He almost left, but had an idea. Something that would fuck with William Hooper like a bitch in heat.

Theodore went into his dead sister's house as if he owned the place and quickly got to work. He had a message for William. The only thing he regretted was that he wouldn't be here to see his face.

But he couldn't hang around too long. He had places to go. First the library in downtown San Diego.

Glenn had left something there seven years ago, and couldn't wait to get his hands on it. When Hooper saw it, he would go through the roof.

Robin left the gun range an hour later with renewed confidence. She could defend herself if she had to.

Before she left, Hank said, "Robin, you should consider hiring a bodyguard."

"I don't need a bodyguard."

"What about added security for the club? What about the people who work for you? Glenn is a sadistic killer. He wants to hurt you, and the best way to do that is hurt those around you."

*Like he did last time.*

She cleared her throat. "Can you recommend anyone?"

Hank flipped through his Rolodex and came up with a card. "Take it, I have more. Tell Mario I sent you."

The card was blank except for *MEDINA SECURITY* and a phone number.

"Thanks." She pocketed the card and left.

She ran some errands, then went to the club. What else could she do? Sit home and do nothing but be scared? She certainly couldn't paint with the fear and worry consuming her.

Today there was a private lunch at the Sin. Laughter and good humor emanated from the special dining hall. That was the way the game was played at The Eighth Sin. Leave your problems at the door and have a good time.

The atmosphere was sexy, the allure was sensual, but no stripping, though she allowed it for private bachelor and bachelorette parties. It was all image. All on the outside. The public persona.

Much like her. Few saw the real Robin McKenna. That was the way she wanted it. Needed it.

Screw the men in her life. Seriously, what

did she expect from them? First her father got her mom pregnant and told her to have an abortion because he didn't want to pay for a kid. Then her first college boyfriend who, when he found out she was a stripper, brought all his friends to watch her perform. And did she give the performance of her life, before breaking up with him. The problem was that word traveled fast and just because she was a stripper, the guys on campus thought she'd be an easy lay.

She'd become a stripper in the first place to pay for her college education. Her first week on campus she'd answered a casting call for dancers in a school production. She'd gotten the part, but the rehearsals conflicted with her schedule and she reluctantly backed out. The production's dance instructor, Brandi, told Robin that she moonlighted as a stripper and thought Robin would fit in at RJ's. "And RJ pays well. You do your job, you get paid a helluva lot more than waitressing at some grease pit."

At first, Robin didn't think she could do it. But she found she had a knack for putting on a show. For creating an image that she wanted people to see. She put up necessary shields to protect her from the catcalls and the letches, and she danced so well she made great tips and RJ was happy. Or as happy as the sour old man could be.

Robin kept her two lives separate after that first boyfriend humiliated her. She never told the guys she dated what she did, and since she was in college they didn't always assume she also had a job. The lack of honesty bothered her, but her heart needed to be protected. In her childish fantasies, she believed that when she fell in love, when someone loved her, it wouldn't matter that she was a stripper working her way through college.

She'd kept the secret from Sean for over a year. They were in love. He proposed when she was a senior in college and he was a pediatric resident at a local hospital. He loved her, *said* he loved her, and wanted to marry her. So she told him the truth.

*"Slut."*

She could still hear him whisper that word with such hatred and disdain.

She pushed back the tears. What had she expected? She'd taken her clothes off in front of men for money. Money to pay for college and help support her mother, but as Sean pointed out so crudely, she could get a different job that didn't require her showing horny men her tits.

How could love turn to hate so fast?

Sean had been the last man in her life for a long, long time. Until she opened her heart just a little, just enough to make it bleed again.

She opened the club's back door and walked down the hall to the Back Room. And there he was, sitting alone at *her* bar. In *her* club.

She'd seen Will Hooper on the news, but that was nothing compared to his physical presence. She couldn't swallow, could barely move, her heart pounding loud in her ears, her eyes dry. He saw her at the same time, put down his coffee mug, and stood. He was tall, over six feet, lanky, and far too sexy. He could have been a model, with those GQ good looks, sun-bleached brown hair cut short on the sides and longer on the top, strong jaw, and dark ocean-blue eyes. But he wasn't a sex god or a model, he was a cop. A cop who hadn't trusted her, even when she thought he understood her. A cop who hadn't loved her as she had loved him.

Robin realized that her act, her public persona, was all she had. No one believed she had anything inside, anything that needed love and respect and care. All she was to men was a body, a smile, and a wink. And whose fault was that? Stripping had been her choice. She had only herself to blame.

"Hi, Robin."

She walked behind the bar, putting the solid mahogany counter between them. She pulled a water bottle out of the cooler. Opened it. Drank half of it. Tried to slow her racing heart, cool her hot blood.

He'd hurt her, betrayed her, and still she reacted to him. Still she remembered his lips on hers, felt his hands on the back of her neck. She'd once felt like she was the only person in his world, the only woman in his universe.

An act. Like her, Will Hooper was all about the attitude. The public act. Did he care about anything or anyone other than himself?

"Shouldn't you be out looking for a certain psychopathic killer?"

His jaw tensed. "I'm heading the task force —"

She cut him off. "I saw the news conference." She wanted him out of her club. Her emotions were too exposed, her fears too raw. She could picture herself falling into his arms, letting him hold her. Touch her. Kiss her. Make love to her. In Will's arms, she had felt *safe*. Real. Loved.

But she wouldn't do that to herself. She

was far too valuable a human being to allow her body to be used by a man who didn't respect her, who didn't love her, who didn't believe in her.

"Robin, please —"

"I don't want you here."

"Hear me out."

She shook her head. She couldn't listen to his excuses. She didn't want his lies. "I can take care of myself, Will. I've been doing it a long time. I did it before you came into my life, and I did it after you left. I'm ready for Theodore Glenn. I won't let him walk away."

Will's temper rose, his face deepening in color, his jaw even tighter. He leaned forward. She stood firm.

"Dammit, Robin! Listen to yourself. The Lone Ranger. Just because you have a gun and some self-defense training, you think you can protect yourself against that crazy bastard?"

She leaned forward, hands on the bar. "You investigated me?"

"Damn straight! I had to find out where you lived so I could increase patrols in your neighborhood. I ran your record and found out you managed to snag a concealed carry permit. Well, good for you. But do you think that Glenn isn't prepared?"

"Oh, and only you, the big and mighty Will Hooper can stop him?" She barked out a laugh. "A lot of good you did for Anna!"

Robin had gone too far. She saw it in Will's face. He pushed back from the bar. Hurt and angry. Just like her.

She swallowed her own guilt. She was just as much to blame for Anna's death as Will. Maybe even more so.

What Will was about to say, Robin didn't know. His cell phone rang and he turned from her, answered it. "Hooper."

A moment later he exclaimed, "What the fuck happened? Where were the —" He stopped, glanced at Robin with a mixture of anger and worry. "I'm on my way. Call Detective Kincaid and have her meet me there."

He hung up and stared at Robin with a pained expression. "Sherry Jeffries, Theodore's sister, is dead."

# SIX

Sherry Glenn Jeffries had lived in El Cajon, a suburb north of San Diego. Technically out of the jurisdiction of SDPD, Police Chief Causey had been called when the arriving officers identified the victim.

Will arrived before Carina. The Jeffries

lived in a two-story house in an upper middle class neighborhood where similar two-story homes stood close together. Judging by the size of the trees, the neighborhood was less than five years old.

Sherry and her family had a confidential address. How had Glenn found out where she lived?

"Detective Hooper?" A uniformed cop approached. "I'm Lieutenant Ken Black."

Will nodded. "Thanks for calling us so quickly."

They stood on the driveway. The garage doors were open and Will saw the corpse lying on the floor right by the inside door. Glenn had waited for her in the garage. For how long?

"What happened?" Will asked Black.

"When Mrs. Jeffries didn't pick up her daughter from school, the principal called the house and got no answer. Normally they wouldn't do that, but Mrs. Jeffries had told the school that Ashley's uncle was in town and might want to harm the girl. When Mrs. Jeffries didn't pick up on the house or cell phone, the principal phoned Dr. Jeffries at the hospital."

Sherry Jeffries's husband was a surgeon, Will recalled.

The lieutenant continued. "Dr. Jeffries

called police to check on the house, then went to pick up his daughter. He has a solid alibi. He was in surgery when the teacher called, had been since ten this morning."

It was common to immediately rule out the spouse or boyfriend whenever a woman was killed.

"Police arrived on scene and when there was no answer, they walked the perimeter of the home. Looked in through the window of the garage door and saw the body. The officers called for backup, broke in to determine whether the victim was still alive. She wasn't. When backup arrived, they searched the house and found no one. However, the killer left a message in the kitchen."

Carina drove up then and joined them. Will filled her in. He wanted to see the message, but said, "Let's check out the body first."

Sherry Jeffries had died quickly. Her neck had been broken and she lay crumpled on the smooth concrete floor next to her minivan. Her purse and keys lay next to her body. A dead cat lay on top of her. Will vividly remembered Sherry's testimony about her brother killing her kitten in front of her. This psychological torment practically screamed Theodore Glenn.

Sherry Jeffries's wallet had either fallen out of her purse, or was dropped there. "Has the body been photographed?" Will asked.

"Yes."

Will pulled on gloves and picked up the wallet. Empty. Credit cards gone, no money.

But this wasn't a robbery. Glenn might have needed the money, but he didn't kill his sister for it.

He killed her for revenge.

"Let's see the message."

They walked through the house. In the kitchen, the crime scene techs were still working, so Will and Carina stood back.

"Shit," Carina murmured.

Will stared at the message meant only for one person.

On the wall of the breakfast nook, Theodore Glenn had written in black permanent marker:

William, once again I killed right under your nose. I'm surprised they let you keep your badge seven years ago, but I suppose that professional ethics mean little to cops who plant evidence and fuck witnesses.

If you think you can save her, think again.

He was talking about Robin.

"Will, what does he mean?"

Will didn't say anything. He couldn't. His entire body filled with a fear he'd never known before, a foreboding that told him Glenn's sick games had just begun. If Will hadn't just left Robin — with a marked car outside the Sin — he would have immediately gone to her.

"Will?" Carina asked softly.

He ignored her, gave her a glance that said, *not here, not now.*

"Save who?" Carina asked, skeptical, still pushing for answers. "Who's he talking about? The daughter?"

"Robin McKenna." Will cleared his voice. "Anna Clark's roommate who testified against him. Or he could mean Julia Chandler or the old woman who saw him leaving Brandi Bell's house." But Will was just saying that. Glenn was talking about Robin, no doubt in his mind.

"You talked to them today, right?"

"I talked to Robin and Julia," Will said. "I sent patrols to talk to the other witnesses who Diaz couldn't reach on the phone." And he'd just spoken to Sherry this morning. She of course had heard about the prison break. She'd been scared.

"Connor is going to flip."

"Lieutenant, would you mind if I asked our criminalists to work with yours?"

"No problem. We contract with the Sheriff's Department for most crime scene work. Our lab is bare bones."

"Thanks. I'll have them send a team immediately."

Will would never forget when Sherry Jeffries told him and Julia the story about her cat while they prepared her for testimony.

*"No one believed me. Theodore was a perfect kid. A straight-A student. Never raised his voice. Kind and polite. But with me he was different. Jekyll and Hyde. And he broke my kitty's neck, looking at me the whole time. Watching my face, my reaction, my pain.*

*"I buried Muffin. I cried and buried him. Theodore dug him up that night and put the body in my bed. I woke up in the morning with my dead cat at my feet."*

Sherry hadn't been a good witness. She'd fallen apart on the stand and she had no firsthand information about the murders. With her history of juvenile delinquency and drug use, it didn't matter that she'd been clean for more than a decade before the trial. When on the stand, the judge sustained every one of Glenn's objections. Nothing Sherry said was on the record.

91

Only during the penalty phase did her testimony help.

Now she was dead.

"How did he get her address?" Carina asked the same question Will had been thinking. "I thought she'd moved since the trial."

Will's stomach dropped as the only plausible answer sunk in. "Call a patrol immediately and send them over to Carl and Dorothy Glenn's house."

The elder Glenns were alive and hadn't seen their son. Will believed them.

But Will's instincts told him that the only way Glenn could have found out where Sherry lived so quickly was through their parents. He called Jim Gage, head of their crime lab, who'd just arrived at the Jeffries homicide. While the Glenns hadn't *seen* their son, he could easily have walked inside, even with the unmarked unit watching the front of the house.

The Glenns were distraught over the death of their daughter, yet didn't believe their son had killed her. Will didn't push it, not wanting to add to their anguish. They'd never believed their son capable of the heinous crimes of which he'd been convicted.

Carina came back from her inspection of the house and motioned for him to follow her out. "There's a key under the mat at the back door. Want to bet the Glenns have always had a key under their back mat?" Carina had also found an address book on the top of the Glenns' neat desk. She had bagged it. "Sherry's current address and phone number are in here."

Will confirmed the information with the Glenns. They'd lived in the same house for forty-two years, since they married. For all those years, they had a key under the mat.

"We've never been robbed," Mrs. Glenn stated emphatically.

*Only robbed of your daughter.*

Will gave his condolences and received permission to take the key and address book. He went back to the Jeffries crime scene and handed the evidence off to Jim Gage, who was talking with the El Cajon technician.

"You'll find Theodore Glenn's prints on these," Will said.

"He'd probably wear gloves," Jim said.

"He doesn't care. He knows we know it's him. He's already on death row. It's a game with him, don't forget that for a minute. His parents are both borderline deaf. He could have walked into the house while they

93

sat watching television at ten thousand decibels, found Sherry's address, and left without them suspecting a thing."

"How'd he get down here so fast?" Jim asked.

"The Feds are tracking stolen cars. Glenn stole a Dodge Ram truck on Point San Pedro Road, which is on the bay north of San Quentin, dumped it in Fresno and nabbed a Honda. It was nearly out of gas in Frazier Park at the top of the Grapevine and he grabbed another truck, this time a Ford Ranger, but it was hot because the owner saw him, so he dumped it near Disneyland. The Feds aren't so sure after that. There were six cars stolen within a two-mile radius of where the Ford was found at nine a.m. this morning."

"So in the five hours after he dumps the truck in Anaheim, he arrives in San Diego, locates his sister, kills her, and is still at large."

"For the time being, that just about sums it up."

## SEVEN

"An anonymous tip has led to the capture of Robert Gregory Cortez, one of the twelve convicts who escaped from San Quentin during the San Quentin earthquake forty-eight hours ago," the newscaster said.

"Turn it up!" Will called, crossing to the stand where the break room television had been brought into the task force command center.

A cop punched the remote and the San Francisco–based newscaster said louder, ". . . and authorities have not released the identification of the caller, though a source close to the investigation spoke on condition of anonymity that it was in fact another escapee who detained the convict. Drew?"

"What?" Will leaned forward, temporarily forgetting his confrontation with Robin that afternoon, the murder of Sherry Jeffries, and the fact that Theodore Glenn was in his city.

The shot turned to a reporter standing outside of San Quentin State Prison where smoke still rose from the recent fire on the far side of the compound.

"Sources close to the investigation have stated that Robert Gregory Cortez was found tied to a lamppost in Vallejo, about seventeen miles northeast of San Quentin. An anonymous 911 call gave police the location of the suspect and when they arrived on the scene, they discovered Cortez beaten and naked."

"Drew, do the police speculate as to who the tipster was?"

"No, Joan, the police are being tight-lipped not only about the tip and the capture of Cortez, but also his condition."

"Any similarities between Cortez and the apprehension of Porter and Douglas Parks?"

"Yes, and the police refuse to comment. However, both Parks and Cortez were beaten and tied in a very public location, followed by an anonymous call to 911."

"Vigilante?"

"The police refuse to speculate at this point, but now three of the twelve escaped convicts have been recaptured and are being processed in Alameda County, across the bay from San Quentin."

The camera turned back to the studio and Joan said, "Cortez was sentenced to die by lethal injection for the 1998 kidnapping and murder of six young boys in the quiet community of Laguna Niguel in southern California . . ."

Will said, "That's two of them captured by the same guy."

"Could be coincidence." The cop shrugged.

Will shook his head. "I don't buy that."

Carina walked into the room talking on

96

her cell phone. "Connor, chill. She has the best security system money can buy." She sighed. "I gotta go."

"What's his problem?" Will asked when she hung up. Connor was Carina's brother and engaged to the deputy district attorney who had prosecuted Glenn, Julia Chandler.

"He's worried about Julia. She won't let him move in, even temporarily, until they're married, because her niece is living with her. He now wants to elope. Mama would have a fit."

"I've increased patrols in her neighborhood," Will said. "And she's getting a police escort to and from work every day. We have it covered, and Julia's smart. She's not going to do something irresponsible."

"You know how protective Connor can be." She glanced at the television. "What happened?"

"Another scumbag was caught. Tied to a lamppost."

"Same as the first guy?"

"Seems like it," Will said. "Makes you think they're turning on each other, doesn't it?"

"Stranger things have happened," Carina said, flipping open her small notepad. "I finished researching the two Glenn jurors we couldn't find this afternoon. One is now living in Arizona and one is overseas in Iraq."

"I think that guy is safe. At least from Glenn. What about family?"

"He has none in town. His juror interview stated that he was a sophomore in college when he served and was also in the Reserves at the time. The desk sergeant is going to try to contact him and the Arizona juror, just as a heads-up."

"Thanks."

"You never told me how your talk with Robin McKenna went. Did you tell her about Glenn's sister?"

Will kept his face impassive. "I was with her when I got the call."

Carina stared at him. "You're not telling me something. Does this have something to do with that message left at the Jeffries house?"

He didn't answer. "I was just about to go talk to my old partner, Frank Sturgeon. Diaz couldn't reach him yesterday, left a message."

"I'll join you."

"You don't have to. It's already after eight. Why don't you go home?"

"Now I know you're hiding something from me."

"Fine, come with me, what do I care?"

He turned to the cop manning the hotline. "Any sighting, call me on my cell."

Will drove his personal car, a black Porsche 911, over to Frank's house, just a mile from Carina's place. He'd bought the car five years ago at a government auction. It had been seized at a border drug raid and he'd had his eye on it the entire time it was in impound. Cost him a pretty penny, but far cheaper than on the retail market.

"You didn't have to come," he said to Carina.

"I know." She paused. "You've been acting weird since Glenn escaped."

"You read my case files. The guy's a sick sociopath. He had not one ounce of remorse, not one shred of guilt. He's the most arrogant criminal I ever met. The guy was so arrogant he *fired* Iris Jones."

Carina turned to him. "Have you called her?"

"His defense attorney? Why would he go —" Will stopped. "Shit. I didn't think. She wasn't on Diaz's list because she never actually went to trial with him."

"I'm sure she knows, but —"

Will pulled out his cell phone, called dispatch, and got Jones's mobile number.

"Iris Jones," she answered in her crisp, formal style.

"It's Detective Will Hooper with SDPD."

"What can I do for you, Detective?"

"You heard about what happened at San Quentin."

"Of course."

"Theodore Glenn escaped and —"

"Detective," Jones snapped, "if you think that I would harbor a fugitive, you are sorely mistaken. I can assure you that I have no ties to that man, nor would I harbor him, nor would I represent —"

"Iris," Will interrupted. "I was just calling to tell you to watch your back. We have a task force here, but we're contacting everyone involved in the case to make sure that they are taking precautions."

Pause. "Thank you," she said quietly. "I'm sorry I jumped down your throat. He fired me. I had nothing to do with his conviction."

"He may blame you for something, we don't know."

"I doubt —" She paused. "Detective, I don't scare easily, but Theodore Glenn scares me. I'll keep an eye out."

Theodore Glenn couldn't help but feel superior. He'd been sitting right outside the police department for hours and they hadn't spotted him. Either his disguise was more than adequate — he'd threaded his brown hair with gray and popped in over-the-counter contacts to change his blue eyes to brown — or the police were even dumber than he thought.

More likely, the police didn't expect him to hang out in the middle of their own territory. They'd assume he would hide out in a motel or run for the border after taking care of Sherry. Now he needed information, but he wasn't confident his disguise would pass intense scrutiny — if Hooper saw him, for example.

That made sitting here even more exciting.

Theodore craved adrenaline. He'd shoplifted as a child not because he needed anything, and certainly not for the attention, but for the punch of adrenaline when he staked out a shop, monitored the staff, avoided cameras, grabbed anything from candy to money in a change drawer. The activity bored him after a time, because no matter how many risks he took, he'd never been caught. He was that good.

Team sports held no allure for him. He'd tried, but he was better than everyone else and the idiot coaches would insist that everyone have a turn. Even the stupid fat-ass sissies who would run away from the ball instead of toward it. Theodore couldn't fathom doing that for years before finally being old enough to make a team that would truly value talent.

He went for individual sports. He ran. When he came in first in any given race, it was over. Once he'd proved he was the best, there was no other place to go. He didn't need twelve first place trophies.

He'd discovered skateboarding young, then dirt bikes, then motorbikes. His parents gave him whatever he asked for because they recognized that he was special. He could accomplish anything he set his mind to.

When he fell — and he often did at first — a rage came over him. Even when he had no injuries, his failure physically hurt, a knife twisting in his skull, telling him he *couldn't.* Only in conquering that failure could he seize on the power that gave him the high and reward he needed.

But eventually, the adrenaline from personal achievement wasn't enough. How many times could he skydive? How many times could he bungee jump off a bridge? He'd traveled all over the country seeking thrills that needed to be bigger, better, more dangerous just to get the same satisfaction.

Until he killed.

The strippers weren't the first. The first time was two years before them. Spontaneous.

Theodore was still in law school the first time he BASE jumped, over the Royal Gorge in Colorado. The first time he jumped had been the most exhilarating experience of his life. Free-falling, before he pulled the parachute cord, Glenn felt a euphoric high that lasted for weeks. No subsequent jump gave him that intense thrill. He couldn't go back to bungee jumping, which seemed so childish by that time, and instead tried a variety of other BASE jump locations. Nothing satisfied him, not the same way. The more he failed to get the rush, the more he craved it.

So he went back to the Royal Gorge one weekend, to regain the excitement that he was *the best* and jumped.

The thrill was gone. He might as well have been jumping off a two-story house. He'd done the Gorge once, he knew what it felt like, and the second time he felt nothing. *Nothing!* It was like being a kid again, watching the other kids laugh and play and smile and not know what the fuck they were finding so fun.

If Dirk Lofton, a prick he'd jumped with before, hadn't walked up just then, after

Theodore made a perfect landing in the Gorge, Lofton would still be alive.

"Nice landing," Lofton said. " 'Course you had perfect weather. No updrafts."

Lofton had always been competitive. While others might have called it "friendly," it twisted and festered in Theodore's stomach. Churning until all he wanted to do was snap the asshole's neck.

Picturing Lofton lying dead at his feet gave Theodore a rush. And an idea.

The next morning Lofton planned to jump. When Lofton went on his early morning run, Theodore broke into his hotel room and subtly rearranged his parachute. Lofton had packed it the night before and used his own, unique chute, so there was no way Theodore could swap it out. But moving the cords around, twisting one of the cables, that Theodore could easily manage without Lofton noticing anything amiss at a glance.

It might not work, but that was part of the thrill. The *unknown.* That Lofton might die, might live. Maybe he'd break his back and be paralyzed for the rest of his life. All because of Theodore.

He felt on top of the world. Anticipation fed his need for excitement.

Later that morning, Theodore watched Lofton from the bridge along with everyone

104

else, a dozen or so bystanders and jumpers. The winds were whipping up, but Lofton said he could do it. Gave Theodore that dumbass smile. "You had perfect weather yesterday, Glenn. It takes *real* balls to jump today."

Theodore grinned; pasted the *aw, shucks* look on his face. Lofton's girlfriend Sandy patted Theodore on the back. "He's just being a jerk. You were incredible yesterday."

"It's fine," Theodore said. And it was: His heart was racing and his eyesight was clear. Everything was brighter, more brilliant. Lofton climbed onto the platform. Tested the wind. Climbed down. Checked his safety harness. He climbed back up. The wind died. Lofton jumped, perfect form. Soaring down, down, down . . .

"Fucking shit!" an observer shouted, though Theodore didn't hear. He watched in ecstasy. The world stood still except for Lofton falling faster, faster, to the beat of Theodore's raging pulse.

Lofton had pulled the chute and it tangled. He veered sharply south, falling too fast.

Sandy screamed.

Dirk Lofton hit the rocks 1,053 feet below.

Theodore bit back his smile. Pasted his look of *oh my God, I can't believe what I saw* on his face. He was what he needed to be.

He turned to Sandy, who was in shock. Took her in his strong arms. "Don't look," he told her, his voice quivering — not from tears, not from fear — from intense satisfaction. The thrill!

Theodore pushed the memories back. Thinking about that first kill had satisfied him for a long, long time. But he'd known then, as he knew now, that faded memories had nothing on the here and now.

He watched William Hooper leave the police station with some hot Latina chick. A cop. Partners? When Hooper arrested Theodore, his partner was a fat slob named Frank Sturgeon. Perhaps he had retired? Been reassigned?

Theodore followed Hooper in the little Honda Acura he'd borrowed from his "friend" Jenny with the overused La-Z-Boy. She'd been more than happy to help him, and he'd kept the act up for her. "They're going to kill me. They framed me and are going to kill me. I need to leave the country."

She'd bought it, asked to go with him.

He'd looked into her idiotic eyes. "For your safety, sweetheart, you need to stay."

She had nodded solemnly. *A piece of cake.* Stealing money had been easy. His parents had always kept their emergency money in his father's desk. Two thousand dollars in cash. And Sherry was just like them. She had five hundred dollars in an envelope with her panties.

So predictable.

He only needed the cash to get by for the next few days, until he could access his own money. He had plenty of money set aside to disappear. Before he started his little game with the strippers, he'd put money in a bank account he controlled under a shell corporation. Setting it up was easy as sin, and he'd quietly put money in, pulling it out for "legal fees." Legal fees he'd paid one of his many "groupies."

The system thought he was without friends while locked in prison? On the contrary, he had hundreds of fan letters like the ones from Jenny Olsen. He had letters from Bible-thumpers insisting he had been on a religious mission to rid the world of promiscuity, and they were praying for him.

Maybe their prayers brought the earthquake that freed him. Theodore laughed out loud at the thought.

He'd gotten letters from women who watched the trial on television. Women who thought he had been wrongly convicted, or who thought he was misunderstood, or who wanted to "stand by his side." They sent pictures of themselves. Most were homely, overweight slobs, but one was quite attractive.

Sara Lorenz.

Dear Theodore:

I watched your trial and saw something in your face that told me you needed someone to listen. To listen and understand and not judge you. I am that person. I don't know if you are guilty or not, and I don't care. The system is unfair. I thought it was noble of you to represent yourself.

If you want to talk, about anything, call me. They let you make calls from prison, right? On television they do, but I don't know if I can believe that. I'm giving you my phone number and my address so write me if you can't call.

I'm a legal secretary. If you need me to do anything for you, let me know. Please. I'm happy to help.

I think they're wrong about you. You have such pretty eyes.

Sincerely,
Sara

Sara, legal secretary, became his "attorney." Theodore taught her how to forge the documents. And over the last few years they'd regularly corresponded and he had her discreetly funnel money out of his account for "legal fees," paid to a legal corporation he controlled. Most of his legit money was tied up by a trustee for restitution to his victims' families. Like they deserved his hard-earned wealth. But he was entitled to legal representation, and he used that loophole to hide cash.

He'd never planned on staying in prison forever. He had a plan for his last appeal. No matter what the judge decided, he would not be going back to prison.

The earthquake beat him to it.

He now had well over a quarter million dollars he could access easily, and even more he could extract with time and patience. Money would ensure his freedom, and after he finished taking care of those who had screwed him seven years ago, he would disappear.

He didn't trust anyone, and he wasn't going to start with some woman who contacted him in prison, regardless of how well she had been jumping through his hoops. He'd never given her control over all his resources. Just enough to get her to trust him and do what he needed. And so far, she'd performed beautifully. He might not even kill her.

He had doubts about going to Sara's house. Though all correspondence was in the name of the corporation, he didn't trust the system. If the police started digging, they could learn who Sara was and where she lived.

But he wanted to see her in person. Touch her. He hadn't had sex in years, and Jenny Olsen up in Anaheim was a pig. The fags in prison had stayed the hell away from him after he nearly bit the dick off one who tried to force him. Sex wasn't that important in the whole scheme of things. BASE jumping gave him a greater thrill than screwing. But now, after being celibate for so long, he suspected the thrill would be worth the risk.

The police probably didn't even know about Sara, not this quickly.

But he would be careful. He'd fucked up before; he wouldn't this time. He needed to dump Jenny's car, and Sara would have one for him.

He followed William Hooper to a quiet little middle-class neighborhood. He stopped in front of a weed-choked yard framing a dilapidated house. Theodore drove on by. He didn't need to know who lived there. He would find out soon enough.

He went back to the motel he was staying in. A little dive near the police station where he paid cash for a week and the fat broad behind the counter barely looked up from her soap operas except to count his money. It had taken him an hour to find the perfect place. He had done some shopping earlier, and now took the time to ready his room. The sheets on the bed had to go. He would not sleep on sheets others had used. He made the bed with new linens. Topped it with a new blanket. The sheets and filthy spread were folded and put in the closet.

Using the industrial-strength cleansers he'd purchased, he scoured every surface of the motel room. Adequate. The carpet he could do nothing about, but he would simply wear his shoes at all times, even when he slept. He sanitized the toilet and shower, then stripped and took a hot shower.

Better.

He drove back to the police station just as a news crew began to set up. It was dark and he blended in well.

Trinity Lange was talking to her cameraman. She had covered his trial and asked the tough questions. She was a sexy little thing, with blonde hair and dark eyes, a hint of Latina in her skin tone. Theodore didn't particularly like mixed-race women, but this reporter could pull it off.

He didn't plan on fucking her, anyway. He had other plans.

Suddenly, everything clicked into place. His blood flowed hot, his mind was sharp. The world glowed bright.

He pulled an envelope out of his back pocket. He'd retrieved it from under a shelf in the medieval history section of the downtown San Diego Public Library, where he'd secured it more than seven years ago. He'd made the right guess that no one would find it while he was incarcerated, and if they had, oh well. He'd put the photos there on the spur of the moment, the day after he killed Jessica.

There were two pictures. The first was that fat slob of a cop, Detective Sturgeon, sleeping in his car while supposedly staking out Theodore's house to make sure he didn't leave and kill anyone.

Theodore laughed, remembering that night. He'd been prepared to kill William Hooper, but it had been Sturgeon watching him instead. Having the cop as an alibi was more fun, but he'd taken the picture spontaneously, still unsure what he would do with it.

The other picture was of William and

Robin. Naked. Theodore had been standing right outside William's sliding glass doors, contemplating killing both of them. Or tying William up and fucking Robin in front of him. Rape held no allure for Theodore, but watching the look on William's face while he screwed Robin would have given him intense satisfaction.

Instead, he took a picture and wondered what he would do with it. Considered sending it to William's superiors, but there wasn't a crime in screwing a witness. Someday it would come in handy. He almost used it at the trial, but feared he would have given the police too much evidence — that he had been stalking Robin or some such nonsense. That he was obsessed with her, as William tried to get him to admit during that farce called an interview after Anna Clark died.

The photograph brought back other memories, though. It was that night he had left William and Robin having sex in the kitchen and gone to kill Brandi.

The memories were nothing like the surge of adrenaline during the hour he'd had Brandi under his blade. He couldn't bring back the same emotions, and he squirmed in his seat, uncomfortable and irritated.

He watched Trinity Lange talk to the cameraman while he packed up. The past brought nothing but frustration.

Focus on the future.

He waited for the pretty reporter to leave in her bright little Volkswagen Beetle.

He followed.

# EIGHT

Will hadn't been to Frank Sturgeon's house in years. The cover of darkness couldn't hide the dead lawn or trash accumulating on the small porch, and he expected no better inside. Whenever they'd gotten together for lunch, Frank met him at Bob's Burgers or another cop hangout. Occasionally, Will had seen him in the bar around the corner from the station, reliving war stories. Will didn't go to the bar often, but he'd heard Frank was still a regular.

Frank Sturgeon had been forced to retire two years ago when he turned fifty-five. He was lucky to get that. After the Jessica Suarez homicide, he'd been put on desk duty; officially because he had a bum knee, privately because he'd been drinking on the job — seven years ago, in the middle of the Theodore Glenn investigation.

Truth was, Frank should have been put on the desk years before, his weight and his drinking a huge problem after his wife left him. It only got worse with time, and Will had inherited the problem when they'd been assigned to work together.

Frank opened the door, smiled widely at Will and Carina. "Kincaid, right?" he said, gesturing for them to enter. "How's your brother doing? I heard he was laid up in the hospital."

"He's okay," Carina lied. She glanced at Will, her face and posture telling him she didn't quite know what to make of Frank. Will wasn't surprised. He'd kept Frank's problems to himself whenever he spoke to Carina about his former partner.

"Patrick's still in a coma," Will said, "but the doctors are optimistic." After eight months, Will was losing his optimism, but he knew the subject was sensitive to the Kincaids and he didn't want to talk about it in front of Carina.

Will glanced around Frank's bachelor pad, trying to keep the disgust off his face. It was the proverbial pigsty, with empty beer and whiskey bottles, overflowing ashtrays, and a layer of filth so thick Will wasn't certain what color the carpets were supposed to be. A foul odor saturated the furniture, drapes, and walls, indicating that the place hadn't been cleaned in months. A police scanner sat on a cluttered desk, its volume low, lights blinking hypnotically.

Like Will, Frank had divorced years ago. Unlike Will, Frank had two children and the divorce had been brutal.

"Do you have a minute?" Will asked.

"Must be business." Frank grabbed a half-full beer bottle from the end table. He snorted heavily, his bulbous nose twitching. He reached into his pocket for a stained handkerchief, blew his nose, and stuffed it back into his pocket without a second glance.

"Let's go into the kitchen," Frank said and led the way. He'd always been overweight but until being put on the desk he'd been in moderately good physical shape. Now, his beer belly sagged over his belt and he sported a solid double chin. He hadn't shaved in at least two days.

Frank gathered bottles and empty pizza boxes off the round table and slapped them onto the counter, unmindful of anything he knocked over. The scent of grilled onions and stale bread hung heavy in the air.

*Why didn't I just call him on the phone?* Will knew Frank had been resentful at forced retirement, but to sink this low?

*Is this how I'm going to end up in fifteen years?*

The thought angered and depressed Will.

He didn't want to be Frank, then or now. But he had no wife, no close family — his dad died of a heart attack five years ago, his mother lived in a South Florida retirement community and traveled half the year, and his brother was even more of a workaholic than he was. While he was a neat person (Carina often said bordering on obsessive), Will could picture himself sitting in a tidy version of Frank's house, drinking Scotch, listening to the police scanner, and watching twenty-four-hour news and sports, yelling at bad football calls. Existing, not living.

He sat and said, "Frank, it's about Theodore Glenn."

Frank snorted. "I watch the news, got the message from some cop who sounded younger than my son. I know he escaped. Probably halfway to Costa Rica."

"I'm taking his threats seriously. He killed his sister this afternoon."

Frank stared at him blankly, then laughed. "You mean you're thinking about what he said back then? At his trial?" He laughed again, drained his beer, coughed, and wiped his mouth with the back of his hand. "Shit, Will, I trained you better than that. Glenn's not that stupid. He's going to get out of the country as fast as he can. Staying in San Diego would be suicide. He probably had a score to settle with his sis and did her on his way out of town."

Will clenched his teeth. "I disagree, Frank. I went to his appeal hearing last year. I looked him in the eye. He wants revenge."

"Who wouldn't? We put the scumbag behind bars. Now that he's free, he's not going to waltz around town taunting us."

"Don't be so sure."

"He comes for me, I'll take him down before he blinks."

The idea of Frank with a loaded gun terrified Will. He'd probably shoot himself in the foot before he killed an intruder.

There was no getting through to Frank. It had been the Glenn investigation that soured Will's relationship with his partner, and nothing had changed since.

"Fine. If you see him, call." Will pushed back from the table. Carina followed suit.

Frank stumbled up. "Hey, you know, I can come back, help in the office. With the task force. I know this guy, you could use me."

Will stared at him. The desperation and loneliness was clear, but all Will saw was his own future. "You know the rules, Frank."

Frank reddened. "You know, I was a detective while you were a little brat living in Chicago. I know a thing or two about scumbags like Theodore Glenn."

Will turned, not wanting to listen anymore. He shouldn't have come; he should have called, but he thought Frank deserved the face-to-face.

Frank didn't like being dismissed. "If it wasn't for me, you'd never have caught that bastard!"

Will should have walked away. Instead, he stepped toward Frank. Why hadn't he seen who this man was years ago? If he had only faced the truth, he would have gone to Chief Causey earlier. Will was just as responsible for Jessica's death as Frank.

"If it weren't for you, Jessica Suarez would still be alive."

"Fuck you, Hooper. I knew it was you who fucking turned me in to Causey. Told him I was drinking on the job. Asshole." He lunged for Will, who easily sidestepped him. Frank stumbled, then braced himself against the wall.

Will said, "The only thing I regret was not trusting my instincts earlier and getting you pulled off active duty."

Frank reddened. "So, what you going to do now? Go *protect* that hot little whore you were fucking?"

Will didn't know he was going to deck Frank until his fist connected with his jaw. *Shit, that hurts.*

Frank stumbled, and Will glared furiously, hand throbbing, blood burning. He didn't lose his temper, not like that. He didn't get in fights, he didn't react with violence.

*Frank called Robin a whore.*

*So did you, buddy.*

"Hey!" Carina shouted, her hands outstretched, stepping between the two men.

"Glass houses, Hooper!" Frank pulled himself off the floor. A beer bottle fell from the table and broke. "I should have fucking told the chief that you were screwing a witness!"

Will swallowed uneasily and left, heading directly for his car.

"What the hell was that about?" Carina said as she slammed the passenger door closed behind her.

"Nothing."

"Don't lie to me. *Again.* This has to do with that Robin McKenna, doesn't it?"

"I don't want to talk about it."

"Should I arrest you for assault?"

"Leave it alone, Carina."

"Don't shut me out, Hooper. We're partners. I need to know what's going on. Did you have something going on with a witness?"

"This has nothing to do with *you!*"

"The hell it doesn't. I'm your partner,

Will. I thought I was also your friend."

"Dammit, Carina —"

"Take me home. I've had it up to here with you. Do you think I'm so stupid that I don't see that there's something more going on? You slugged Frank Sturgeon, a cop. A drunken slob, but still your former partner. If I say something to piss you off, are you going to slug me, too?"

Will tried to interrupt, but Carina was on a roll. "What's this all about, Will? I feel like I don't even *know* you."

"Carina, I —"

She put up her hand. "I don't want excuses or lies. You have until tomorrow morning at oh-eight-hundred to decide if you trust me. And frankly, if you don't trust me with this, how the hell do you trust me to cover your ass? And if I can't trust you to tell me the truth, how can I trust you to cover mine?"

He pulled the vehicle in front of her house. Carina had the door open before he put on the brake. Without another word she stormed up the front walk. Her fiancé, Nick Thomas, had the door open before she could retrieve her keys, and they kissed. Nick said something to her, she answered, and he looked at Will in the car, a frown on his face.

Will drove away. How could he tell Carina that he had screwed up seven years ago and had an affair with a witness?

Talking about it with Carina would bring it all to the surface. How hard he'd fallen for Robin, and how much he hurt her when he walked away. Because it was easier to walk away than admit his feelings.

"You're an asshole, William Lawrence Hooper."

*Four days after Bethany died, when Robin still didn't know Theodore Glenn was a killer, Robin had gone to visit Detective Hooper at the police station. She had to do something proactive. Not knowing what was going on in the investigation, or if the police even cared, gave her sleepless nights.*

*She couldn't put Bethany from her mind.*

*"You wanted to see me?"*

*Robin stared at Detective Hooper, wanting to hate him, wanting to consider him part of the problem, but she couldn't. He was a cop doing his job, trying to find out who killed her friend.*

*He slid a Diet Coke in front of her, turned around his chair, and sat across from her, arms casually draped over the back of the chair, stormy blue eyes full of compassion and intelligence. Faint laugh lines radiated along* the edges. He was handsome and all that, but more than his good looks he looked at her as if she were a valuable person, someone who commanded respect, who should be treated well.

"You okay, Robin?" he asked.

She shook her head. "Bethany is dead. I don't know what to do. I'm scared and mad and I want to quit and I want to fight all at the same time."

"That's normal," he said.

"Is it?"

He nodded.

"Be honest with me," she said. "Are you going to catch whoever killed Bethany?"

He looked at her for a long time. "I don't know," he admitted. She hated the answer, but appreciated that this man trusted her with the truth. "We have some evidence, but no solid suspect."

"But you're still working on it?"

"Absolutely. I'm not going to bury the case, Robin. That I promise you."

"It's just that — the press is talking about us like we're hookers. Almost like" — Robin forced out the words — "like Bethany deserved to be killed."

"Robin." Will's voice was firm. She looked up at him again. "The press is always looking for the sexy angle, something to sell papers or get people to watch the eleven o'clock news instead of reruns. Bethany has as much right to justice as any other victim in San Diego, and I promise you I'm not going to forget about her."

"Thank you." She stared at her Diet Coke, not knowing what to say, but not wanting to leave. Detective Hooper made her feel comfortable, safe.

He glanced at his watch. "I was supposed to clock out over an hour ago. Do you want to get a bite to eat?"

"I'd like that. Thanks."

He held her chair out for her and their hands brushed. Robin glanced at Will, found herself drawn to his incredible blue eyes, his handsome face. He squeezed her hand and she felt butterflies. So cliché, she thought, but enjoyed the sensation. It had been a long time since a man made her feel important, and by the look on Will Hooper's face, he was feeling the same thing.

He smiled. "Let's go."

Robin startled awake. The television was on, a rehash of Channel 10 reporter Trinity Lange's earlier report, but only Will Hooper was on Robin's mind.

She certainly hadn't planned on going to bed with Will that night, or any night. She didn't sleep around, and it had been a long time since she had let a man into her bed. But after a good meal, a few drinks, and hours of down-to-earth conversation, they ended up at his place.

Robin shoved the memories back where they belonged: in the past. Her relationship with Will was based on fear and safety, passion and lust. Nothing else had held it together. It certainly didn't have trust.

She wished she could convince her unconscious mind as easily as she could convince her waking mind.

On-screen, Theodore Glenn's mug shot appeared, reminding her that she had more important things to worry about than her failed love life. Hank was right: She had to protect her employees and business.

Though it was late, she called the number Hank had given her.

"Medina Security. Leave your name and phone number." *Beep.*

An edge of panic crept into her voice. "My name is Robin McKenna. Hank Solano gave me this number and said to talk to Mario. I need security. As soon as possible." She left her number and hung up.

Robin slept uneasily, lights on, gun at her side.

# NINE

A body fell on top of her, a hand over her mouth. Trinity Lange struggled to pull herself from deep sleep, flailing about.

"Don't move or I'll slice your throat."

Grogginess disappeared as Trinity recognized that voice.

"Good girl. Nice place you have here. I checked out your neighbors next door. They're on vacation, and since you back up to the golf course and there's no one on the other side of you, I don't think your screams will be heard. What do you think?" Theodore Glenn's low voice was gleeful.

Through the fear, she processed his words. He would kill her. Rape her and kill her. No, he hadn't raped the other victims. He'd tortured them, cut them repeatedly with an X-ACTO knife. Their faces. Their bodies. When he tired of the game, he had slit their throats. As described by the shrink who had testified for the prosecution, it was *a game.*

She tried to shake her head for no reason except maybe to wake herself from this nightmare, but his grip on her was firm. Theodore Glenn was over six feet of solid muscle, and prison had made him harder and stronger. She'd researched his background extensively during the trial. He'd been into extreme sports, like bungee jumping and skydiving and white-water river rafting. He was handsome and smart and rich, and had many girlfriends, some of whom had testified that he was the most considerate boyfriend they'd ever had. Others had testified that he was cruel and played mind games with them. Even one of the former strippers from RJ's had testified on his behalf.

"I'm not going to kill you, Trinity. Relax."

Right. Relax.

"I need your help," he said.

Did he actually think she would *help* him escape? But right now she would do or say anything to live one more day.

"You covered my trial. You sat in that courtroom every day. You heard the testimony. You talked to the cops. You were fair and you asked good questions."

Did he want her thanks?

"I didn't kill Anna Clark."

"Hmm!" she mumbled against his hand.

"I think you know, in the back of your mind, that there was something wrong with the trial. And you're going to find out exactly what it was. I want to know who framed me. I think I know, but I want proof."

She squirmed.

"I will let you go so you can ask me questions. We're a team, Trinity. Partners. Help me, and I will let you live. I think that's fair."

Pinning her body with his, he reached down and grabbed her right wrist and, with duct tape, taped her to the bedpost. Then he eased off her, pulling the blankets off her body.

*Oh God, he's going to rape me.*

As if reading her thoughts or body language, he chuckled. "Women give themselves to me voluntarily. Happily. If I wanted to force a woman, it wouldn't be you. I need to make sure you don't do something stupid. You're the only one who can help me, and I don't want to have to kill you. That would make me unhappy."

He crossed her ankles and wound the duct tape around them several times. She wore a long T-shirt. He pulled it down past her panties.

It was dark and she could only make out his shape, not his exact features. His hair looked dark, but was that because he dyed it or a trick of the light?

He handed her the notepad from her briefcase and a pen. He knew she was left-handed. He'd been watching her. Or had he remembered after all these years?

The only light came through the blinds.

128

Her night vision was strong, but she could barely make out the paper which seemed almost blue in the odd, filtered light. Glenn sat in the corner, in the shadows.

"What do you want to know?" he asked.

A crime reporter's wet dream. A killer willing to talk. To say anything. Though she knew she had a rare opportunity, not knowing what Glenn would do to her terrified her. How could she trust a convicted murderer? How could she trust a man who tortured his victims, then poured bleach into their open wounds?

"Trinity, I'm talking to you. I know you want to ask me questions. You're going to die if you don't."

She swallowed, sputtered. "I-I —"

"Calm down, Trinity." He paused. "What an odd name. What were your parents thinking?"

She didn't know if he wanted her to answer, but she did automatically, since she'd been asked that question so many times in her life. "I was supposed to be triplets, but my two sisters died in the womb. They thought the name was a way of paying homage to the two who didn't make it."

Why had she said that to this man? Because it was comfortable. Almost *normal*. To answer a common question with her pat answer.

"Now your turn, Trinity. Ask." He paused, and when she didn't answer, he said, *"Ask me a fucking question!"*

She nodded, cleared her throat. "F-for the record, you said you didn't kill Anna Clark?"

"Correct. I did not kill Anna Clark."

To buy time she wrote down his exact quote. *I did not kill Anna Clark.*

"Did you kill Bethany Coleman?" she asked.

"Yes."

"Brandi Bell?"

"Yes."

"Jessica Suarez?"

"Yes."

He shuffled, and Trinity flinched. He laughed. "I have a present for you. Something that should look good on the evening news, in the newspapers, and it will definitely get you some attention." He put an envelope on her bed, just out of her reach.

She stared at it, thinking, and asked, "But you didn't kill Anna."

"I'm not going to answer the same question twice."

She took a deep breath. He didn't seem as dangerous now. Maybe he was telling her the truth, that he wasn't going to kill her.

"You think someone framed you for Anna's murder?"

"Correct."

"Why?"

He laughed without humor. A chill settled in the pit of her stomach.

"Because the cops fucked up."

"You must know that virtually every convicted murderer says that they were framed. Why should I — why should the public — believe that you're telling the truth?"

"Because I don't like being made a fool of. Someone is playing with me, and I don't like it. I didn't kill Anna, and I damn well want to know who did and who planted evidence against me."

"I don't know why you think I can help with this —"

"Because you're an investigative journalist!" he exclaimed, and Trinity jumped. She saw then and there what this killer was capable of. "Wouldn't you like to know what cop framed me? Wouldn't you like a nice juicy story to propel you into the journalistic stratosphere? Don't think that I haven't followed your career while in prison. You're on the cusp, and you like to get in people's faces. Do it now. Do it for me."

"H-how?"

131

"That's what you need to figure out."

Trinity changed tactics. "But does it really matter?" In asking the question, she realized it sounded stupid. "I mean, you still would have been convicted of murder. You killed the other three women. You still would have gotten the death penalty."

In the darkness, Glenn remained silent. Trinity shifted uncomfortably on the bed, swallowed, her left hand shaking so hard she almost dropped the pen.

"Yes," he finally said, as if he had only just thought about it. "It matters. You think that we're all that different? Do you think that under the right conditions, you would not kill?"

"You didn't kill in self-defense," Trinity couldn't stop herself from saying.

"That's irrelevant."

"Why did you kill them?"

He chuckled. "Because I could. To see if I could get away with it."

*Because I could.* The cold calmness in his words terrified her almost as much as knowing what he had done to those poor women.

"But you *didn't* get away with it. Doesn't your life mean something to you? You had everything — a high-paying job, a million dollar house, a nice family — and you killed for what? A game?"

"I *would* have gotten away with it!" His anger vibrated across the room. Trinity couldn't help but think he was playing a game with her, right then, and that he would kill her if she asked the wrong questions.

"I'm s-s-sorry," she mumbled.

He spoke, his voice tight and clipped. "Don't you see? They couldn't have convicted me. Not on the first three murders. The evidence from my first kill was thrown out by the judge. The jury wasn't allowed to consider that evidence, they never even heard it! You didn't report on it, and you probably didn't even know that the cops fucked up! It was the evidence from *Anna's* murder that they used, and tied the other three to that. But I didn't kill Anna, and therefore I should never have been brought to trial! I *would* have walked away. I had only planned to kill three, unless —" He stopped.

Trinity had to ask. "Unless what?"

He didn't answer, but stood. "You have what you need. Find out who killed Anna Clark. Exonerate me."

"You'll still go back to prison when they catch you."

He laughed. "*If* they catch me." He started for the door. He was going to let her live!

*For now.*

She shivered, her mind running through everything he'd said. "Mr. Glenn," she said.

He stopped. In the faint light, she made out his shadow by her bedroom door. "More questions?" He sounded humored.

"Who? Who would frame you for Anna Clark's murder?"

"Why don't you ask William Hooper?"

"Hooper?" Will Hooper was a solid cop. Trinity couldn't see him planting evidence.

"Something didn't come out at trial, but is relevant to this case. While Anna Clark was murdered, Mr. Hooper was fucking Robin McKenna."

Robin McKenna was the stripper who had been Anna's roommate. She had testified against Glenn. Robin had since bought the strip joint where they worked, and The Eighth Sin was now one of the hottest nightclubs in San Diego. Trinity had been there a couple times. Urban, chic, with trendy music, lots of dancing, good drinks, and an attentive staff.

Robin McKenna herself was gorgeous, but Trinity sensed at the trial that she was also smart and savvy. It didn't surprise her that she could turn a fledging strip joint into a high-class nightclub. Had she been involved with Will Hooper? Hooper was a stud. He had a long list of girlfriends. His reputation was no secret among cops and reporters.

Years ago, she'd slept with Will Hooper. He was cute, funny, attentive, and smart. What woman wouldn't fall for him?

But the relationship had just . . . evaporated. That last date when he took her to a lovely restaurant on the coast outside Coronado, she thought they might be moving to the next level, then he kissed her good night on her porch and she never heard from him again. Every time she saw him he smiled and was polite, and not once had she heard from any cop that she'd slept with Hooper. He told no one. She doubted his partner Carina Kincaid knew, because Carina was an easy read and protective of Hooper. She'd have said *something,* even just a snide remark. Nothing.

Will Hooper did not kiss and tell.

She could picture how Will and Robin McKenna met over tragedy. Forging a relationship. How had it ended? Had he taken her to a nice restaurant and kissed her good night? A quiet good-bye . . .

"You *know* William, don't you?" Glenn's voice was mocking, almost a laugh.

"How do you know he was involved with Robin McKenna?" Trinity asked, gathering her thoughts.

The killer chuckled. "I followed every step of the police investigation."

"No one is going to believe you didn't kill Anna Clark."

"That is *your* job. I don't know how they did it, but I didn't kill that bitch. The truth is in the evidence, but do you think they would show me? Do you think that they'll just open their books, even when they have to? Go ask William Hooper, or the D.A., or the fucking crime scene investigator!"

He stepped away from the door and paced. She shouldn't have set him off. She couldn't see him except a darker shape in the shadows, but his movement was frantic. Fear ran over her, but she suppressed it. He said he wasn't going to kill her.

Damn, was she going to believe him? After he admitted to killing three women?

"William didn't kill her," Glenn said as if thinking out loud. He stopped at the end of her bed and stared at her, the whites of his eyes almost glowing. Chills ran down her back and she shivered. "He was screwing Robin McKenna. I watched. Robin. She was supposed to be next, but she wouldn't go out with me. All the other whores let me wine and dine them, but that bitch was cold. Liquid fire onstage, but in person . . ." his voice trailed off.

"I watched them. They were in the club. It was two in the morning. Robin sat in the bar. Crying. William Hooper walked in. 'What's wrong?' And they were on each other like animals. Couldn't even walk across the damn street to find a bed. If they had, maybe Anna would still be alive. But while they screwed, poor little Anna Louisa Clark died."

It was after midnight when Will came home. He couldn't sleep, so he lifted weights in the second bedroom, his iPod loud enough to drown out both thoughts and memories. An hour later, sore and drenched in sweat, he showered, then fell onto his bed wearing only boxers, the cold February night breeze coming in through his open windows. The last time he saw the digital clock it mockingly glowed red: 2:01.

Then he dreamed. Remembered.

*Will watched Robin from the shadows. She picked up her glass — a martini, straight up — and sipped. The stress of the investigation was getting to her. Three of her friends had died and he knew who the killer was, had interrogated him twice, but that wily bastard gave nothing up. Even three days in prison hadn't fazed Theodore Glenn.*

*Will didn't know what was going on with him.*

He didn't mess with victims. He didn't get personally involved with witnesses. But Robin McKenna was no ordinary woman. He couldn't get her out of his mind. Every morning he woke with her in his thoughts, every night he wasn't with her he was lonely, empty, incomplete.

Six weeks ago they'd acted on a mutual attraction that began when he first interviewed her after Bethany Coleman's murder. He'd have forced her to stay in his bed to keep her safe, but Robin wasn't a woman to run. She faced the fear. But he'd been watching her. Worried. They'd argued the night before. "Quit," he'd said, knowing he had no right. It wasn't that she was a stripper, it was that being a stripper put her on the killer's hit list.

Though he'd be lying to himself if he didn't admit that her job bothered him on more than one level. Because he felt more for her than he could say out loud.

She'd shaken her head. "Someone else will die. You have to find him, Will. Stop him. Only then will I — we — be safe."

Now watching her, he saw her fear and her beauty, her vulnerability and her strength. He walked over to her. "Robin, honey, what's wrong?"

His hand rested on her shoulder. She was crying without sound, her body tense and shaking, tears rolling down her pale cheeks.

"I'm scared, Will."

"Come home with me."

"I can't. I'm not going to be chased away from my home."

"Please — Anna did the sensible thing and went to visit her mom. I can't stand the thought of you being here alone. Vulnerable."

He kissed her. She was water to a dying man, all the woman he ever could want, ever need. He drank her greedily, his tongue searching for hers, finding it, pulling it in, taking everything he could.

In the back of his mind, he knew this would not last, yet he desperately prayed it would.

"Robin," he murmured against her mouth, her arms wrapped around his neck, her legs wrapped around his waist. He kissed her mouth, her throat, his tongue moving down to her breasts, easily found through the loose-fitting blouse she wore. He tasted her tears on her skin.

Her tears ate at him. He stepped back. "Please don't cry. I can't stand it." He wiped them off with his palms, trying to take away her anguish and hold it inside him.

"Hold me, Will. Hold me."

"Always."

"Nothing is forever."

"Don't say that."

*"Make love to me."*

*She reached down and unbuttoned his fly. He was hard. He always was when in her arms. He didn't want it like this, in the bar, but he couldn't let her go. He needed her, and she showed a rare vulnerability and need for him. He had to prove to her that he was real, that he loved her. Wanted her fully, not just like this.*

*But like this was heaven.*

*Entering Robin was like coming home, better each time. As they greedily took each other, he realized he didn't want to live without her. Ever.*

Will jolted awake as his cell phone rang. His cock was hard and he was on the verge of a wet dream. With Robin.

This was so screwed.

He glanced at the clock as he answered his phone. 4:14 a.m.

"Hooper."

"Sergeant Fields here. That reporter, Trinity Lange, just called. Theodore Glenn paid her a visit tonight."

# TEN

Carina beat Will to Trinity Lange's town house. She met him at the front door and, without preamble, said, "No sexual assault.

140

He tied her to her bed and from what she told responding officers let her interview him. She specifically asked to talk to you, and they told her you had already been called."

Carina's tone was cool, still ticked off over their argument the night before, but ever the professional. Will didn't know how to make it right with his partner. His strength was his people skills, yet right now he felt like he had none as far as Carina was concerned. She wouldn't be satisfied until he'd spilled his guts, and he wasn't ready to do that.

"How's she holding up?" Will asked as they walked through the foyer. Trinity was smart and sassy, with the kind of self-possession that attracted Will to a woman.

Carina rolled her eyes. "Better than I would be after being in a room with a killer who likes to carve pictures on his victims with an X-ACTO knife."

"Has the lab been called?"

"They're on their way over."

"Gage?"

"Probably, considering how high-profile this case is." Since both Chief Causey and the current District Attorney Andrew Stanton had prioritized anything to do with Theodore Glenn, the crime lab would expedite the processing of evidence. If only they'd been able to prioritize Bethany Coleman's murder seven years ago, maybe she'd have been the only one to die at the hands of Theodore Glenn. Maybe if they hadn't been overworked and understaffed there'd have been no contamination of the DNA evidence in the first place.

Trinity sat at her kitchen table, a coffee mug at her side, writing frantically in a notepad. An officer stood behind her, trying to see what she was writing, but she shielded the page. She glanced over her shoulder to give the cop a dirty look, then spotted Will and Carina. Her eyes glowed. "Detectives. Coffee?"

She flipped the notepad over and stood, walking over to the steaming carafe on the counter.

Formal. Professional. She had indeed pulled herself together quickly.

"Thanks." Carina sat down at the table. Will saw her staring at the notepad. He, too, was curious as to what Trinity was writing. More flies with honey, he thought, giving Trinity a friendly smile.

"That would be great, Trinity." He watched her. She'd dressed in jeans and a white T-shirt. Trinity was a hair over five foot three, and with her blonde hair loose she looked much younger than Will remembered her to be: thirty-two. But her eyes were sharp, intelligent, and he could practically see the gears in her head working.

"Cream? Sugar?" she asked.

"Black," Carina said.

"Cream," Will said, though he knew he didn't have to. Trinity would have remembered.

She made one too many furtive glances at the cop standing sentry in the kitchen. Will turned to him. "Officer, do you mind giving us some privacy? It may be easier for Ms. Lange to recount her ordeal without an audience. How many are on scene?"

"Four, with more units on the way."

"Great. Pick someone to help canvass the neighbors. I don't care that it's four thirty in the morning, we need to know if anyone heard or saw anything between one thirty and four, or has seen Theodore Glenn anytime in the last twenty-four hours. You have his sheet?"

They'd put together photos of Glenn at arrest along with sketches of him with altered appearances. The first thing he'd have done was purchase over-the-counter color contact lenses. Glenn's sharp blue eyes were so bright and unusual that people would remember them. According to Chief

Causey, the FBI was following that avenue by contacting businesses along the 99 corridor, which they now knew he'd driven after his escape.

"I'm on it," the cop said, and left.

Trinity carried the mugs to the table. Will sat down next to her, facing the entrance to see who came in through the door, while Carina was to his left, directly across from Trinity.

"Tell me what happened," Will said.

"I woke up with him on top of me. He clamped his hand over my mouth." She shuddered. "He told me he wouldn't kill me. Then he used duct tape to bind my feet together and my right hand to the bed."

"Just your right hand?"

"He handed me my notebook and a pen. Told me to take good notes."

"He knew you were left-handed."

She nodded. Though it was unnerving that Glenn remembered such a small detail nearly seven years later, Will wasn't surprised. Glenn was smarter than most people gave him credit for.

"What did he tell you?"

"He wanted to set the record straight. He insisted that he didn't kill Anna Clark."

Will slammed his mug down on the table, hot coffee sloshing over the sides. Trinity grabbed her notebook out of the way of the spill, and Carina jumped up to get paper towels.

"I'm sorry," he mumbled. *That bastard.*

He helped clean up the mess, placed his mug carefully in the sink. He rarely lost his temper, but look what he'd done. Here, and decking Frank. Theodore Glenn brought out his dark side. Will hated him for it.

"You remember what he did to his victims," Will said. "He tortured them with an X-ACTO knife before tiring of the game, dragging them to the front door, and slitting their throat so that the next person who walked into the room slipped in their blood. We *know* he killed those women."

Carina frowned and Trinity stared at him. He took a deep breath. "Trinity," he said through clenched teeth, "Glenn loves the game. He's using you. He will kill you when you don't do what he wants."

"What did he say he wanted from you?" Carina asked.

Before Will could say anything, Trinity said, "He takes credit for the first three murders. He admitted to me that he killed Bethany, Brandi, and Jessica. He wants me to prove he didn't kill Anna."

Will bit his tongue. Hands clenched, his heart rang in his ears. What was his angle?

Why would he admit to killing the first three victims, but not Anna? It didn't make sense. Just another one of his many games. Did he just want to torment Robin? Knowing that if Anna's murder was discussed in the media it would hurt Robin?

Will would do anything to spare her the pain.

But — why? Why would Glenn admit to three murders and not the fourth? There were some minor discrepancies in the murders, but Bethany was different as well. He hadn't used bleach on Bethany, but had on the other three. Yet Anna had fewer marks on her. Will and the crime scene analysts had determined at the time that Glenn was rushed. There had also been the theory that Anna hadn't been the intended victim, that Glenn planned on Robin coming home, not Anna, who was supposed to be out of town.

But the truth was the M.O. was virtually the same, the knife was identical, and the jury was unanimous in its verdict that Glenn killed all four women.

"Trinity," Will said, forcing calm. "We've known each other for what? Nine, ten years?"

She nodded, searching his eyes, her face piqued with interest but her expression unreadable.

"Glenn wants attention. He wants you to stir the pot, create dissent in the ranks." Will would look into Anna's case again, one last time, but he was confident Glenn killed her. His hair was found in her fist. She fit Glenn's profile . . . except Anna hadn't slept with him.

Will shook his head. "You'll be bringing up the past and hurting the victim's friends and family. Don't let him use you. Don't print his words. He wants that. He wants to be the focal point. The animal is a convicted murderer. During his escape, he fatally bludgeoned an injured guard. He killed his own sister yesterday because she testified against him. His intelligence and good looks disguise a sociopath. He has no remorse, and he will kill you without a second thought."

Carina cleared her throat. Will took a deep breath, the red rage that grew whenever he thought of Theodore Glenn fading but not gone. It would never be gone as long as Glenn walked free.

Carina asked Trinity, "Did he give any hint as to where he was going? What his plans are?"

Trinity shook her head. "Nothing."

"Did you get a good look at him? Has he

altered his appearance?"

"It was dark, and he stayed in the shadows. I only saw his outline. He seems bulkier than during trial. Not fat, but like he's been working out."

"The damn prisons let the convicts use a weight room," Will muttered. "Are we talking upper body muscle?"

She nodded. She opened her mouth to say something else, then closed it.

"Don't hold back, Trinity. We need to know everything."

She glanced at her notepad, which was still face-down.

"Like Will said," Carina interjected, sensing that, like Will, Trinity was holding something back, "Glenn plays games. But the truth is, forensic evidence — biological evidence — proved he did in fact kill Anna Clark. His hair was found on the victim's body. Evidence doesn't lie."

"He contends that the evidence was planted," Trinity said.

"Him and O.J.," Will spat out, standing. "Are you buying into his act?"

Trinity stood and looked up at him, hands on the table. "I'll tell you what I *know*, William Hooper. I know that he hates you. I know that he hates Robin McKenna, Anna's roommate. And I know that he would kill me in a heartbeat if he didn't think I was helpful to him.

"But I also know the police can screw up. I know that *individuals* can make mistakes. We are all human and fallible." She pulled an envelope out of her notebook and slapped it in front of Will. "Frankly, if what Theodore Glenn says is true, a killer has truly gotten away with murder. And if I can prove it, I'll have a ticket to New York City so fast I won't have time to say *thanks for the ride.*"

"Is that what this is about?" Will fumed. "Your career?"

"He picked me because I know about this case and —"

"Listen to yourself! He *picked you!* This isn't a popularity contest. He picked you and he will kill you. Don't play his game. Don't give him print."

"Last I heard this was a free country, Detective Hooper," Trinity said, her hackles raised.

"Don't be stupid."

*"I'm not."*

"You've got to watch your back." Angry, yes, but Will was concerned about Trinity's safety. He didn't want anything to happen to her.

His obvious concern diminished the anger

149

between them. He touched her hand. "I'm serious, Trinity," he said softly. "You're not safe here, not alone."

"Thank you." She swallowed, squeezed his hand. "I'll be okay." She nodded toward the envelope. "He left that for me."

"Why did you touch it?"

"I — I almost forgot he'd left it. I had to see what was inside. I only touched the corners. But I want that picture, Will."

Will frowned, slipped on latex gloves, and flipped open the flap of the envelope. Judging by the glue, it had never been sealed.

Inside was a single picture. Of Frank in the car he drove seven years ago, a large American sedan. Asleep at the wheel, his mouth open, his head back. Will could almost hear him snoring.

From the angle of the shot, Will could see a flask on the passenger seat.

He turned the picture over. In block letters:

APRIL 2 1:05 AM ASLEEP ON DUTY

Jessica Suarez had been murdered on April 2. Frank had sworn he'd watched the house all night. Will hadn't believed him. When he confronted Frank, his partner had jumped all over him. Brought up his affair with Robin. That he, Frank Sturgeon, was a cop with over twenty-four years on the force, and who was Will Hooper? Ten years and change? Walking in his daddy's footsteps?

Frank had always known how to rub Will the wrong way. And Will had no proof Frank had fallen asleep on the job.

Until now.

"I'm running with the story, Will," Trinity said softly.

"What story? That a killer paid you a visit?"

She shook her head, looked at the photo.

"Don't," he said. "This is evidence."

"I don't care. I already scanned a copy and sent it to my boss. Glenn contacted me for a reason, Will. And you know what? I believe him."

"He killed four women!"

"He killed three women. The jury's still out on whether he killed Anna Clark."

"Don't —" He caught himself. Shit, he was only going to make it worse if he made ultimatums. He was going to have to trust Trinity that she would be smart. And he'd do what he could. Increase patrols in her neighborhood. He could probably even justify to Chief Causey that she needed a tail.

"You're going to destroy Frank Sturgeon."

"That should be the least of your concerns," Trinity said. "Did you cover for him back then?"

"I didn't know —" Again he caught himself. He was not going to be trapped into an interview with a reporter. He wanted to rail against her, threaten her, but instead he said, "Be careful, okay?"

"I promise."

"You have no problem with the crime techs coming in and collecting evidence?"

She shook her head. "Anything they need. And —"

She stopped.

"What?"

She glanced at Carina. The look wasn't lost on either Carina or Will.

"I'll call you later if I remember anything else," she said pointedly.

Jim Gage stepped into the kitchen. "Carina, Will. Are we set?"

"He appeared to have spent the most time in the bedroom," Will told Gage. "He left this for Trinity. She's touched it."

Trinity said, "You can print me, no problem. I pulled off the duct tape and left it upstairs. I changed, but didn't touch anything except my dresser, and haven't been back in there."

"I'm not holding out hope that he dropped a motel receipt, but you never know," Will said, still disturbed by the photograph and trying to figure out what Glenn's game was this time.

Carina spoke up. "How did he know where Trinity lives?"

No one spoke. Then Will said, "Trinity is a public figure. She works at a television studio, he could easily look up the address, follow her home, come back whenever he wanted."

"Which means he could be following anyone and they might not know."

Jim turned around and motioned for his team to come in as he asked Will, "Do we know how he entered?"

Carina answered. "The responding officer said the door was jimmied."

"You don't have security?" Will asked Trinity.

"I didn't think I needed it."

"Maybe you should rethink that," Will admonished.

Diana Cresson and Stu Hansen stepped into the modest kitchen, crowded now with six adults standing around the four-seat table.

"You brought the A-team with you," Will said with a nod to the two crime techs Jim had with him. Diana was the assistant lab director under Gage, and Stu was a trace evidence specialist who'd done his training in New York City. Both had been in the lab for more than ten years. Will often wondered why Stu hadn't moved on — he was more than capable of running his own lab, as Gage once told him. But Stu simply said he never wanted to be in charge. Diana, however, was definitely on a career-focused path. Will wouldn't be surprised if she soon announced she was leaving for a lead position in another jurisdiction — Jim Gage wasn't yet forty and didn't look like he'd be retiring anytime soon.

"I have clearance for any overtime necessary," Gage said, "which isn't surprising. This won't take long, Ms. Lange."

Trinity rolled her eyes. "God, Jim, we've known each other for a gazillion years and you call me *Ms. Lange?*"

He shrugged. "You've never been a victim before."

"And I'm not a *victim* now," she insisted. "I'm fine. He didn't hurt me, and I'm going to be careful."

Everyone turned to stare at her.

"I promise," she said, forcing the confidence into her voice. "I'm going to be very careful."

# ELEVEN

Theodore Glenn started visiting RJ's a year before he killed Bethany.

He'd hit a low point in his life. The thrill of killing Dirk Lofton wore off after the investigators ruled that it was an accident caused by a poorly packed chute. No one even considered that someone might have messed with Lofton's equipment. Why would they? There had been no threats on his life, there was no money at stake, and Lofton had always been arrogant about his jumps. He would have laughed at anyone who wanted to double-check his equipment.

Theodore went home after that week, the elation waning, completely gone by the time his plane hit the tarmac — *his* plane, because he'd obtained his pilot's license a few years back. He still enjoyed flying, but not as much as he used to. There was no challenge in it, unless he was battling the elements, and no one cleared him for takeoff if a storm was expected.

One of the managers at the megacorporation where he served as the staff attorney had a bachelor's party at RJ's, a strip club in the gaslight district. Back then, it was still an area where hookers walked the streets and drugs could easily be bought, usually in the open. The police presence was nominal, or focused on encroaching gang activity, not streetwalkers and low-level drug dealers.

That first night, he'd watched the strippers with both fascination and disdain. What decent woman would remove her clothes, gyrate in front of horny men, all for a few bucks in tips?

But Theodore appreciated their beautiful, firm bodies and slick moves. He wondered what the women thought while onstage sending come-hither looks at the patrons. Did they get a thrill in turning men on and not giving them relief? Perhaps they were all a bunch of lesbians who got off bringing men to the brink and leaving them hot and bothered.

Theodore soon learned that some of the strippers were easier than others. Like Bethany. She latched onto bachelor boy Paul for the night, accepting his money in her teeth, with her toes, between her legs. Paul didn't drink enough to cheat on his fiancée, and suggested Bethany move on to Theodore. They both tipped her *very* well.

That night Theodore went home with Bethany. He almost killed her then. He pictured himself wrapping his hands around her neck, squeezing, watching her face as she died. Watching her eyes lose focus. Would she be scared? Would she know what he was doing? What was the fun in killing her if she didn't know she was going to die?

Instead, he just fucked her. Too many people had seen him leave with Bethany. It would be stupid to kill her now as he would most certainly be caught.

But the *idea* of killing her appealed to him. More, the idea of her knowing she was going to die appealed to him. Unlike Dirk Lofton at the Royal Gorge, who didn't suspect he was going to die when he jumped, Theodore figured it would be much more thrilling to kill someone who knew he was going to steal their last breath. And better, know that he would enjoy every minute of their anguish.

The following week he drove to Los Angeles, picked a woman at random. Followed her home. Watched the house. Her husband came home at six. An hour later he left.

Theodore put on gloves, entered the house, and shot the stranger in the back while she stood over the stove.

Then he walked out and didn't look back.

He'd listened to the news reports of the murder with growing fascination. Bought copies of the *L.A. Times* to make sure he didn't miss anything. He even called the public information officer for LAPD and pretended he was a college criminology student doing a project on crimes of passion. The husband had been the primary suspect, but he had an alibi and there was no evidence that he'd killed his wife. No gun, no biological evidence on the husband, nothing.

While Theodore received a thrill from the initial kill — aiming the gun, pulling the trigger, watching the body fall and the blood spread — it was short-lived. He had more fun watching the investigation and knowing that the cops would never in a million years connect him with the crime. *That* was a heady experience.

But what if he had told the woman she would die? What would she have done? Would she have stared at him, disbelieving? Screamed? Tried to run?

He would never know.

Tonight, he did the same thing as he had with that housewife in Los Angeles. Only this victim was no stranger, he wasn't cooking in the kitchen, and Theodore wasn't killing for the thrill. Frank Sturgeon was passed out at the kitchen table, and killing him was too easy to be fun.

■ ■ ■ ■

Will and Carina parked in the lot at the same time and walked toward the police station. Dawn barely crept over the eastern skyline.

Carina's mouth was in a tight line and she stopped walking. Will turned. "What?"

"Did you have an affair with Trinity Lange?"

Will shifted. "We went out for a few weeks."

"Dammit, Will, why didn't you tell me?"

"When? When we became partners? Was I supposed to give you a list of all the women I've slept with?" Will didn't like his ethics being questioned.

Even though perhaps they should have been seven years ago.

"You know that's not —"

"Carina, I don't announce to the world who I'm involved with. It's nobody's business. For what it's worth, Trinity and I dated after the Kessler trial three years ago. We split amicably. I like her. She's smart and fun. But it didn't work out, okay? And that's that."

"You know I don't care about your love life, but —"

"You don't? You constantly make snide comments about my dating. I've let it go because we're partners and friends."

Carina frowned. "I didn't realize it bothered you."

Will shrugged. "Water under the bridge." He paused. He considered telling Carina about his relationship with Robin, but right now it wouldn't matter. She already knew what was important. The records reflected that he'd been across the street in the bar with Robin after hours when Anna was killed. He just never told anyone that they were in there having sex.

"Let's focus on Glenn," Will said, pushing back the encroaching emotion. "He had a purpose in seeking out Trinity."

"She said he wants her to prove he didn't kill Anna Clark."

"And the evidence — the biological evidence — points to him. It was a righteous conviction. Theodore Glenn is a cold, ruthless killer. I don't know what his game is, but I'm sure he has one."

But even as he said it, Will couldn't figure out Glenn's angle. Why admit to a reporter that he killed three of four women?

"You don't think that there's something just a little — weird in this?"

He sighed. "Yes, something is off. When

Gage has a few minutes, maybe the three of us can look at the evidence again. But I still think Glenn is trying to divert our attention to this instead of focusing on his recapture."

"Maybe you're right."

"We can work through the facts after we get him back into custody. He's dangerous, Carina. And he will continue to kill until we lock him up."

"What do you think if we give my brother Dillon a call?"

"Dillon knows about Glenn," Will said. Carina's brother was a forensic psychiatrist who had consulted with the police department and served as an expert witness for the district attorney until he moved to Washington, D.C., last year. "He didn't work the case, but he knows enough and we can bring him up to speed quickly." He glanced at his watch. "It's eight thirty on the East Coast. Why don't you call him?"

Carina asked what Will had been thinking since leaving Trinity's. "What if Glenn is telling the truth about Anna Clark? What if he didn't kill her?"

"Then we have two killers at large." He still believed Glenn was the only one who could have killed Anna, but at the same time he couldn't figure out his game.

Carina was dialing Dillon's number when

Will's cell phone rang. "Hooper," he said as they entered the building.

"Shots fired at 1010 North Highland. Neighbor phoned it in, officers en route. But the address is flagged."

"Frank." Will slammed his phone shut and turned to Carina. "Tell your brother we'll call him back. Shots fired at Frank's house."

## TWELVE

Once Jim Gage and his two assistants left, Trinity felt alone and restless, even with a police car parked out front. She didn't want to stay around the house, and finally showered — with the bathroom door locked and a chair propped against the knob — dressed, and went down to the television station. She'd put on an act around Will and the others. Truth was, she *was* scared. And she would be very, *very* careful. She didn't want to end up dead.

But there was a story here, a potentially big story, and she didn't want to get scooped. Theodore Glenn had given her *something* — she just had to figure out exactly what it was and how to use it.

As soon as she walked into the main offices of the television station where she'd worked for eight years, her direct supervi-

162

sor, Charlie Boyd, rushed to her side. "Where's the photo?"

"The police took it."

"Damn, I told you not to give it to them."

"I couldn't withhold evidence, Charlie. You know that."

He sighed, ran a hand through his thick hair. "I know, I know, but damn, I wish we had it as backup."

"They're not going to lie about it," she said. "They may claim 'no comment,' but Will Hooper isn't going to deny the picture exists. I scanned it high res, it should withstand scrutiny."

"What else did he say?"

Trinity motioned for Charlie to follow her into her office. She had a small closet with a tiny window, just enough for a chair, desk, and computer, but it was all hers — she had earned the door.

Charlie put his hands up on either side of his head. " 'Award-winning reporter held captive by escaped convict,' " he said, dropping his hands. "How does that sound?"

"It would be bigger news if I were dead," she said, trying to laugh it off, but her heart wasn't in it. She kept replaying the conversation between her and Theodore over and over in her head.

"We have to get this on the air. ASAP."

"The police don't want to give him air-time. Detective Hooper thinks that will only encourage him. Charlie, he killed his own sister."

Though Trinity pushed envelopes whenever and wherever she could, she also prided herself on maintaining a good working relationship with the police department since she specialized in reporting on crime and punishment. She'd covered every major trial, interviewed both killers and cops, and had an exclusive program with the district attorney himself, Andrew Stanton, which aired pre–prime time the first Wednesday of every month. That show alone had brought the attention of bigwigs in L.A., who'd offered her a show and more money if she'd sign a five-year contract. But she didn't want to go to L.A. for five years, and they wouldn't agree to a year-by-year, so she stayed put in a position where she could leave whenever an opportunity arose. And she was looking for one.

She wouldn't go against Hooper's orders to lay low on this, but that didn't mean she wasn't going to do *something.* She had reams of paperwork on this case, access to the files, and interviews she'd conducted with detectives Hooper and Sturgeon, the victims' families, and the strippers who had worked with the dead women. Then there was the trial transcript itself.

The only thing she *didn't* have were the sealed records of what had happened in the judge's chambers. She couldn't simply trust Theodore Glenn's word that evidence was tossed out because of police or lab error. But there might be someone else she could go to.

"You sent me that photo — a cop sleeping on the job when he was supposed to be watching a suspect? That's news. I'm not sitting on it."

"Charlie, I need a few days to pursue this story."

"Then why did you send me the picture?"

"Because I knew I had to turn it over and I'd never see it again. This way, we have it for when we go big."

"This is television, baby. We go big now, and make it bigger."

"Yes, there's a story, but the cops aren't going to talk about one of their own. You know that. We have to dig deeper and then hit them all hard." She ran a hand through her hair. "I should never have sent it to you."

"Don't clam up on me now, Trinity."

"I'm not. I need to do some research, some more interviews. No one else has this,

Charlie. No one is going to scoop me." She hoped.

"You're not going to try and contact Glenn, are you? The man is insane."

"He's not insane. Dangerous, yes. A sociopath, probably. But he knows exactly what he's doing. I'm going to be careful. The police are watching my place, and Glenn isn't going to try anything in broad daylight. Not with the Feds, the CHP, and the San Diego Police Department all looking for him. He'll probably lay low during the day. He's smart."

Charlie raised a brow. "Smart, yes, in that he's having you do his work for him."

"But what if he's telling the truth? What if he didn't kill Anna Clark? It doesn't make him any less a murderer, but it *does* mean that someone else got away with murder. And that doesn't sit well with me."

"Not to mention it would be the story of the year if you uncovered it," Charlie said quietly.

"There's that," she agreed. She loved San Diego, but Charlie knew she wanted a national gig. She was good enough. Smart enough. Pretty enough.

She just needed something to make her stand out. And this story would do it. She was as certain of that as anything.

"All right," Charlie agreed, "but you check in with me twice a day, do not attempt to contact Glenn, and do *not* do anything stupid. If he contacts you again, call the police. Watch your back, kid."

"I've already gotten the lecture from the detective in charge," Trinity said. "I don't have a death wish. I'm not going to antagonize Glenn, and I definitely don't want to see him again, but I can't get this out of my head. There's no reason for him to admit to killing three women, and not the fourth. It doesn't make sense."

"Maybe he wants to have the conviction overturned. If he was wrongfully convicted, that could happen."

"But he *admitted* to me that he killed those three women."

"I doubt it would hold up in court. Beyond that, you need to be doubly careful. You're the only one he confessed to."

Robin wanted to stay in bed all day, door bolted, gun under her pillow. Loaded. Or better yet, in her hand, with the safety off.

Fear ate at her. A real, physical, gnawing presence that started in her mind, slithered along her nerves, until she was nearly paralyzed.

Staying in bed felt safe, but it was also

wrong. She couldn't let Theodore Glenn destroy her independence. She couldn't lock herself away until he was caught. What if the police didn't catch him? What if he taunted them for years? Or he came to town for a few high-profile murders, and then went down to Mexico? He could be next door . . . or a thousand miles away.

For a year, she had danced for a killer, served him drinks, smiled and flirted, because it was her job. When she'd realized he'd killed her friends, she'd been physically sick. When she'd learned what he did to them, when she'd slipped in Anna's blood and fallen on her body, she'd nearly lost her sanity.

One minute she had been safe in Will's arms, the next minute she had walked into a waking nightmare.

*Will had kissed her in the foyer of her apartment building. It was nearly three in the morning and they'd spent the last hour in the bar. She wanted him to come up, but at the same time she knew he had a job to do.*

*"I don't want to leave you alone," he said.*

*"I have an alarm. I'm okay."*

*He frowned, touched her chin. "Robin —"*

*The dim yellow light made his eyes darker. He looked at her as if he really cared. As if, maybe, he loved her. The thought lifted her* up. He knew she was a stripper, yet he treated her with respect and affection and intelligence.

He tucked her hair behind her ears and kissed her lightly, but with more intimacy than their frantic coupling in the bar earlier. She melted against him. "Good night."

She felt him watching her walk up the stairs. She waved at him from the landing at the top, and he left, double-checking that the door that led in to the common entry was secure.

Maybe they had a future. There was something different about their relationship, something that Robin hadn't had before. Powerful. Passionate. Special.

She unlocked the door, reached for the alarm to put in the code and reset it. The keypad was lit in faint green, so she didn't need lights to see, but she wished she had left the kitchen light on or something. It was pitch-black with all the drapes pulled.

"Meow, meow, meow."

Anna's cat brushed against her legs. "I fed you early because I had to work, you just forgot, silly cat." She picked him up.

Pickles was wet. Sticky. "Now what did you get into?"

She smelled bleach, and while her mind started to send her a warning, her first thought was for the cat, that he was going to get sick if he knocked over the bleach and inhaled too *many fumes.*

*She took two steps forward feeling for the lamp she couldn't see but knew was on the end table right there on the left of the door, but she tripped. The cat jumped from her arms as she fell, her hands falling into something sticky and wet. The smell. Why hadn't she noticed the smell? It was foul, sickly sweet. Metallic — and bleach. Her chest tightened and she couldn't breathe. She reached back to push herself up and touched a person. A hand.*

*Her stomach heaved as she fumbled standing in the dark. Someone was here, on the floor. A person. Blood and bleach. Blood and bleach. No, no, no!*

*She found the lamp, shaking so hard that she knocked it over. She ran to the door, feeling the wall for the light switch. Turned it on.*

*Anna. Her blood pooled on the hardwood floor. Her eyes were wide open, staring at Robin. Duct tape over Anna's mouth. She was naked, red cut marks all over her body. One deep bloody slash across her throat. She was dead.*

*Robin flung open the door and screamed. She ran down the stairs, hoping Will was still there. In the back of her mind, through the pounding in her head, she heard the shrill shriek of her alarm.*

*The street was empty. Will was gone.*

*Robin ran to the bar and called 911. That's where she remained, covered in Anna's blood, until the police arrived.*

*"He killed her," Robin told the first officer on scene. "Theodore Glenn killed Anna and you couldn't stop him!"*

*But in the back of her mind, Robin couldn't help but think that this was all her fault.*

The phone rang and Robin shook herself out of her nightmare. They had finally built a case against Theodore Glenn and put him in prison. The police would catch him again. She held on to that hope.

"Hello," she said.

"Hello, Robin."

*Theodore.*

She slammed down the phone, acting on instinct and not common sense. She stared at the receiver. Damn, damn, damn! The police might have been able to trace the call. Maybe she could have learned something about where he was or what he planned to do.

"Call back, you bastard!"

Damn him. What had she done? Let her fear take control again.

Robin had met Theodore soon after he started visiting the club regularly. Back when it was still RJ's, back when they

171

stripped and danced and paid the house half their tips. But even then, she'd made enough money to put herself through state college and keep her mother from losing the small house that had been her grandparents', but which her mother had taken a new mortgage on to pay for whatever she thought she needed.

Robin had just graduated from college, with honors in commercial art and art history, and she could have quit stripping. But there were two things that she valued, both of which cost money. Her dream to own her own house — a real home — and to be an artist. Paint supplies weren't cheap, and she needed time and daylight to paint what she loved. She didn't want to be miserable at a desk job or creating ad campaigns to sell more useless stuff, like all the junk her mother was continually suckered into buying.

But she couldn't say she was happy stripping, either. Robin didn't know what she could do to realize her dreams, and she felt trapped. Uncertain. And lonely. Especially after Sean left her.

That first night Theodore came into RJ's, Robin knew something was different about him. Not a good different. She couldn't put her finger on what it was that disturbed her, even when Bethany rushed up to her, flushed and excited.

*Bethany was energized when her dance was over. She ran into the dressing room, her thong concealing little. Robin tossed her a silk robe and Bethany absentmindedly put it on, chattering, "He's here again! Oh my God, Robin, he's so gorgeous. And he tips so good."*

*Robin frowned. "Are you talking about the guy you slept with last week?" Robin didn't condone Bethany's laissez-faire attitude about sex. At twenty-three, Robin was one of the oldest dancers, and she'd been working here for five years. She was the one who stood up to RJ when he was an asshole, she was the one who got raises for the girls and fought to reduce the house percentage of tips from fifty to a third. And she was the one to keep a watchful eye that the girls weren't selling more than their dances.*

*Bethany was nineteen, beautiful, and had next to no common sense. She'd run away from Tulsa, Oklahoma, to L.A. when she was seventeen to be a star, got sidetracked to San Diego because of a jerk she met, and was practically homeless when she applied for a job at RJ's. Robin had a soft spot for her.*

*"Bethany, I told you to be careful with the men you go home with. Most of these guys are okay, but you never know."*

"You have to meet him."

RJ, a tall, skinny sixty-year-old man who looked eighty and had owned the club for thirtysome years, came in without knocking. "Robin, babe, you're up and late."

"I'm coming."

"Move your ass!" He closed the door, unmindful of the women in various stages of undress.

Robin finished with her makeup as Bethany said, "He's at table six. He's over six feet tall — I love tall men — and really cute. Brown hair and the most incredible blue eyes you ever saw."

Robin blocked Bethany's voice, running through her routine in her mind. She was a dancer, an actress. She put on her public face: makeup accentuating her cat eyes, glitter adding sparkle to her dark red hair that she pinned up in what appeared to be loose curls, but which were held tight in place so as not to come undone during her vigorous, sexy dance.

Robin wasn't the star — that was Brandi, who did extensive lap dances and played up to the audience. But Robin was technically the best dancer. She used her strength — her talent.

She couldn't see the audience under the bright lights, which was more than fine with

174

her. She danced her heart out, then left the stage. From the wings, she glanced at table six.

He stared directly at her. She couldn't make out his features clearly, but he was attractive and well groomed. "An attorney," Bethany had gushed, and Robin could see that.

She shivered. Even at this distance, his piercing blue eyes chilled her. He saw her looking at him, nodded his head. She turned away.

As soon as she had her cocktail costume on — that had been her last dance and she would wait tables for the rest of the night — Bethany pulled Robin onto the floor. Right to table six.

"Theodore," Bethany said breathlessly, "this is my friend Robin. I just wanted her to meet you because she's such a mother hen."

Robin gave a reserved smile. Theodore extended his hand, and she accepted the gesture. His hand was solid and calloused, as if he worked or played outdoors. He was larger than she'd originally thought, solid upper body muscles, flat stomach, fancy clothes.

"Nice to meet you, Robin."

"Likewise," she mumbled, unable to tear her eyes from his. They unnerved her and she forced herself to keep the polite smile plastered on her face.

*She didn't like him. She couldn't explain it, couldn't find any flaw in his appearance or attitude, but she felt as if an entire army rippled under his perfect skin. The way he looked at Robin — with a familiarity even her few lovers hadn't shown — deeply disturbed her.*

*"You're an exceptional dancer," he continued, a slight frown on his mouth telling Robin that he noticed her aloofness and did not approve.*

*"Thank you." She bowed her head slightly, pasted on a brighter smile, and looked him in the eye. "I need to get to work. You understand. Have fun." Robin hurried off.*

*Bethany left that night again with the creepy Theodore. Robin didn't sleep well, and called her first thing in the morning. "Just want to make sure you got home all right," Robin said, relieved.*

*"Of course, silly. Shhh."*

*"What?"*

*"I have company. Whoops!" Bethany giggled. "Gotta go."*

*Robin hung up, cold fear turning her stomach. She didn't know why, she didn't believe in premonitions or any of that nonsense, but something was wrong.*

*Over time, Robin's fear dissipated. Theodore Glenn became a regular, always Wednesdays and Fridays. He dated a few of the girls, even Brandi, who was discerning about the men she slept with. Theodore Glenn was polite, smart, and attractive. He was a stripper groupie, and the girls all liked him. And even when he started going home with other women, Bethany never thought ill of him. By that time she had her sights set on another regular, an older man who Robin was certain was married. Bethany laughed that off as well.*

*Except for Robin, everyone liked Theodore Glenn. When he looked her way, she turned cold. Even if she couldn't see him, she sensed his presence. Watching. Waiting — for what, she had no idea. She kept her distance and did her job and didn't think too much about her initial reaction to Glenn until RJ called her in the middle of the night a year later and told her Bethany had been murdered.*

Robin stared at the phone. "Dammit! It's just another game to you, isn't it? Call, you bastard."

And even though she asked for it, when the phone rang Robin jumped.

# Thirteen

Theodore heard the click when Robin picked up the phone. He smiled, picturing her. Maybe sitting in her bed, as it was still early and she was a night owl. What would she wear to bed? Sexy lingerie? Sweatpants? Nothing at all? Her hair would be mussed from sleep, though he doubted she'd slept much since the earthquake freed him.

That he was on her mind pleased him. It put him in control.

"I knew you would answer."

"What do you want from me?"

Hanging up on him had been her fear, and he relished those two words — his voice speaking, "Hello, Robin" — had set her off. What power he had over her. Robin hadn't changed. All kinetic action. He'd seen her energy when she danced, saw it in her paintings. Bold, brilliant art that seemed to move. She'd improved from when he'd known her seven years ago. During his time at the library yesterday he'd done some online research. Found out a lot about Robin Mc-Kenna and her achievements.

But she still feared him, and he would use that to his advantage.

"Did you miss me?"

"Go to hell."

He laughed. Her verbal abuse certainly wouldn't faze him. He expected it. Enjoyed it. "Hell would suppose that there is also a heaven, which I do not believe. You can't have one without the other, though I find religious philosophy tedious. Life is what we make it, isn't it? You've certainly made something out of *your* life."

"What do you *want?*"

Her voice rose, as she lost what little patience she had. "You know what I want, Robin."

"I can't read minds, and if I could I certainly wouldn't choose yours. You're sick and twisted and the cops are going to find you. You can't hide forever."

"Neither can you. Which one of us can hide longer? My money's on me."

"I'll kill you, Theodore. You killed my friends —"

"You picked them, Robin."

She didn't say a word, and he knew he had her.

He smiled and leaned back in his car. The cell phone belonged to Jenny Olsen. He'd be dumping both the car and the phone soon because he imagined that Jenny wouldn't be able to keep her big mouth shut when the police came knocking at her door.

"You're out of your fucking mind," she finally said, her voice barely audible.

"Bethany told me that you treated her like an overprotective big sister. You cared about her, didn't you?" Theodore continued without giving Robin time to answer. "And

Brandi — she told me she's the one who got you the job at RJ's in the first place. She was jealous of you, did you know? She recognized that you were the better dancer. But she also respected you because you didn't try to take her job. Why didn't you, Robin? You were the leader of those sluts, why didn't you just take over?"

She didn't answer. He tapped his fingers on the steering wheel, wondering what she was doing. Pacing, most likely. She couldn't sit still for this long. She never had before. Even when she'd been on break at RJ's, she'd been moving. She might put her feet up in the Back Room, but her hands would be doing something, sketching on notepads, and her toes would be tapping to the music.

He'd watched Robin far more than she suspected.

"And Jessica. Now there was one hot little minx. It was a shame I had to kill her, really. She was the best fuck I'd had in a long, long time.

"I can only imagine what you'd be like in bed, Robin. Or on the floor. Or the kitchen table."

"Why did you kill Anna?"

He knew she'd ask. "I didn't."

"You fucking liar! You're playing your

pathetic games again, doing this to torment me."

"You don't know what torment is, Robin." His voice grew hard. "You put me in prison. San Quentin is a hellhole. The food is barely edible. The men on death row are borderline retards. Stupid fools. I would never have been convicted if it weren't for you. I meant what I said at the trial. You identified me off that sketch and that's how the cops got my DNA. That's how they framed me —"

"Framed you?"

"For Anna's murder. And believe me, I will find out who did it and cut their heart out.

"But first," he said, his anger building, "I have a special treat just for you."

"You're psycho," she said. "If I don't shoot you myself I'll be there when the state kills you."

"That's not how this game plays out. I will kill you, Robin, slowly. And the last thing you see before you die will be my smile."

"Fuck you!"

"How's William?"

He hung up, heart pounding. Shit, he'd planned out the conversation perfectly, then something snapped and now he was angry.

She should have been cowering in fear.

She should have been begging for mercy. Instead *she* threatened *him.*

He would kill her. He would make her suffer, but first he would make her fear him.

Trinity found Deputy District Attorney Julia Chandler in her office later that morning. As soon as Julia saw her, she said, "You'll have to talk to Stanton. I have no comment."

Trinity couldn't help but grin. "Off the record, Julia. Five minutes."

The pretty attorney eyed her suspiciously. "Five minutes."

Trinity closed the door behind her. "Thank you."

"Five minutes and counting."

"Seven years ago there was a private meeting in the judge's chambers where evidence that proved Theodore Glenn killed Bethany Coleman was thrown out on a technicality."

Julia's eyes narrowed. "Where did you hear that?" she asked, her voice deceptively calm.

"Theodore Glenn paid me a visit early this morning."

Julia processed that information, blinking rapidly. "You saw him?"

"More or less. It was dark, I didn't see much of anything, but it was him. He confessed to killing Bethany, Brandi, and Jessica. He denies killing Anna Clark."

"He denied killing Anna?" Julia repeated.

"He wants me to prove it."

"What the hell are you doing?" Julia asked. "Helping him? Why didn't you call the police? I need to —"

Trinity interjected, "I called the police. Told them everything." *Almost.* "And believe me, I'm not too keen on meeting up with him again even if he thinks I'm on his side. But he said a couple things that I'm curious about, and I'm compelled to follow up on them."

"Did he threaten you? Harm you in any way?"

"Julia, he told me about the evidence that was dismissed. I was at the trial, but obviously not privy to sealed information. The only physical evidence that connected Theodore Glenn to those four murders was DNA evidence found on Anna Clark's body. Without that, all you had was Robin McKenna's testimony on his sexual relationships with the first three victims and the old woman who saw him coming out of Brandi's duplex the night of her murder. An old woman with bad eyesight. No weapon was ever found, and no evidence discovered in Glenn's house."

"His house was immaculate," Julia said. "He is obsessively neat and ordered. He's also very intelligent, with a borderline genius IQ. This creep knows how to clean up after a crime."

"But there *was* evidence that was thrown out, correct?"

Julia stared at her, then nodded. "That should tell you that he's guilty as sin. I watched his interrogation. After Brandi Bell died, Will Hooper interrogated him for hours. What Glenn *didn't* say was more important than what he *did* say. But the truth is, that man is a psychopath. We *know* he killed Bethany Coleman, as sure as I'm breathing. But we couldn't use the evidence because of a screwup in the field. The DNA was contaminated. It happens, as much as we hate it — we are all human, mistakes happen. But that doesn't make it hurt any less, knowing that because of that screwup we had nothing to hold him on after Brandi's murder."

"Why didn't you arrest him after Bethany's murder if you had the evidence, even if it was contaminated? At least interview him?"

"Brandi Bell was murdered two weeks after Bethany. The evidence hadn't been processed until the eyewitness identification, and that was when the contamination was discovered." Julia sighed. "We have one of the best labs in the country, but they still can't process evidence immediately. There's still a two- to four-week turnaround on most evidence, longer if there's a big case pending that takes more staff time. You know how it is."

"Now that's a story I can run with."

"What? Attack the people who work their asses off to catch killers?"

"No, about how the government spends billions of dollars on pork and next to nothing on basic services."

"More power to you if you can get some attention to this problem."

"So the evidence was thrown out and Will Hooper had to let Glenn go."

"I've worked with Will since I became a D.D.A. and I've never seen him so angry or frustrated with the system. But we had physical evidence linking Glenn to the Anna Clark homicide. Irrefutable evidence, as you remember from the trial. His hair in her fist. The bleach he poured over her body didn't touch her hand, and the evidence was preserved. With the same M.O., Robin McKenna's testimony, and the known sexual relationships with the first three victims, we had enough evidence to tie

Glenn to all four murders. Enough that a jury of twelve people had no reasonable doubt that he was guilty."

"If the police suspected Glenn after Brandi was murdered, why didn't they put a tail on him? Jessica was killed four weeks later."

"You'll have to ask Will Hooper about what the police did and did not do." Julia averted her eyes.

"I know what happened, Julia. I just wanted to know what you knew."

Julia was about to respond when her door burst open and both women jumped. Trinity turned to see Connor Kincaid, a local P.I. who'd been a cop years ago. She'd heard he and Julia were involved.

Right now, Connor looked like he wanted to hit something.

"Frank Sturgeon is dead." He faced Julia. "No arguments. I'm taking you to a safe house. Far from San Diego."

## FOURTEEN

Will had first sat face-to-face with Theodore Glenn after Brandi Bell's murder. His partner Frank Sturgeon leaned against the interrogation room wall, glowering.

They'd thought they had a solid case and

could keep this twisted killer in prison. Will had also thought he was dealing with the typical, arrogant killer who would talk himself into a confession if Will played him just right.

By the end of the interrogation, Will knew he had a different breed of sociopath on his hands.

*Two women were dead and Will faced their killer.*

*They'd kept Theodore Glenn in lockup overnight. The day before, a witness during the canvass had come forward with a description of a man who had left Brandi Bell's house early that morning. According to Robin Mc-Kenna, the description matched a regular patron of RJ's, a man who had dated both victims.*

*Theodore Glenn.*

*They'd arrested Glenn at his home without incident. In fact, he almost seemed to enjoy it. "I'm sure we'll get this all straightened out soon enough," he'd told Will.*

*Now, the bastard was looking at him with idle curiosity. He didn't fidget. He didn't talk nervously. He didn't fume. He looked as crisp and neat as when they'd brought him in the day before.*

*"What can I do for you?" Glenn asked, a faint smile on his lips.*

"You're a regular at RJ's, a club in the gaslight district, correct?" Will asked.

He nodded.

"Please speak your answers out loud for the recording, Mr. Glenn."

"Yes, I go to RJ's once or twice a week."

"How long have you been a regular customer?"

"About a year, maybe a little longer."

"Why?"

"Why do I enjoy going to a strip club?" Glenn raised an eyebrow, smiling.

"When did you first go to RJ's?" Will asked.

"A colleague of mine had his bachelor party there last year. I thought the dancers were quite talented. And very attractive. Not like some of the clubs in town showing only old, tired women with sagging breasts and no attitude.

"I particularly enjoyed Brandi. She was the head dancer, very gifted. I'm sorry something happened to her."

Will watched carefully as Glenn put a frown on his face and shook his head back and forth. There was a falseness to Glenn's actions, as if he were an actor following a script.

"I also enjoy watching Robin McKenna."

Will kept his expression in check. Why would Glenn mention Robin specifically? To play with him? A tickle of fear crept up his spine. What if this bastard was watching Robin? What if she was his next target?

Had Will been so wrapped up in Robin that his instincts went south?

"Where were you last night?" Will asked.

"With a lady friend of mine."

"A dancer at RJ's?"

"No, not last night. A colleague. Ingrid Vanderson."

"How long?"

"All night."

"Where?"

"At my home."

"Do you have contact information for Ms. Vanderson?"

"Of course. It would be in my address book. I believe you took that from my house."

Too cocky, overly confident. Most innocent men would be protesting. Upset. Especially at having been kept in jail overnight.

"When was the last time you were at RJ's?"

"I don't think I need to answer any more questions, do I? I've given you my whereabouts last night, and the woman I was sleeping with."

Frank suddenly slammed his fist on the table, always the one to play bad cop. "We have a witness who places you at the crime scene at the time Brandi Bell was tortured and killed."

Glenn didn't even blink. He showed no reaction to Frank's temper, and in fact didn't even look at him, responding instead to Will. "Your witness is mistaken."

Will knew from Robin that both Bethany and Brandi had had a sexual relationship with Theodore Glenn. "Did you know Brandi Bell outside of her employment?"

"Do you mean did I see her outside of the club?"

Will nodded.

"Yes."

"Did you have an intimate relationship with her?"

Glenn nodded with a sly smirk. "Yes, I had sex with her."

Will tried, but knew he failed, to contain his surprise at the admission. Killers with personal ties to the victim often denied it until confronted with solid evidence. Even then, they often continued with the lie or made excuses. "When was the last time you had sex with Ms. Bell?"

"Hmmm, about a month ago. Let's see. February second. Yes. There was a rerun of that movie Groundhog Day on one of the cable stations. They play it every year now, don't they? It gets tiresome, but Brandi enjoyed it. We had sex once during the movie, on the floor of her living room. Then afterward, *we had a late dinner. Sex on the kitchen table — have you ever done that, William? Sex on the kitchen table?"*

*Will gritted his teeth. Glenn was toying with him. There was no way he could have seen him and Robin. No way. They had been in his town house. The blinds were closed . . .*

*"When was the last time you saw Brandi?" Will asked Glenn.*

*"Last week. At the club. Friday. I'm there every Friday, and most Wednesdays. Ask Robin. She always makes a point to come by my table and say hello. Now there is a beautiful woman. I've often wondered, as I watch her remove her clothes, why such an attractive, smart woman would take the job of a slut?"*

Will's fist hit the steering wheel.

Carina was in the passenger seat. She turned and frowned at him, but said nothing.

He drove directly from Frank's house — where his former partner had been gunned down sitting at his kitchen table — to The Eighth Sin. He'd had a call from dispatch that Robin McKenna had left a message for him, but when he tried her number no one answered. He called the unit watching her loft and learned the uniform had driven her to the Sin for a meeting.

"I'm sorry, Will." Carina thought he was thinking about Frank and how his former partner died. But Will had been remembering that first interrogation. Glenn had controlled it from beginning to end. Will took another shot at him later that day, but the damage was done.

Glenn had sabotaged his relationship with Robin. Planted seeds of doubt in his head about her. After Anna's murder, Will had been too ready to believe that Robin had been the intended victim, that she had slept with Glenn, just like the first three victims. Because it was Glenn's M.O., and Anna didn't sleep with men. She was a lesbian.

"I'll kill him," Will muttered.

"Stop."

Will swallowed, pushed Robin from his mind and focused on what Glenn had done to his retired partner.

"You saw the scene. Frank was drunk. Likely passed out. And Glenn walked in and shot him in the face."

"You don't know —" Carina began.

"Hell yes I do! It was Glenn. You know it, I know it."

The cocky bastard was sly as a fox, slippery as a snake. And Theodore Glenn wanted Robin. He'd always wanted Robin. Because she had refused him. Had said no, not interested.

A man like Theodore Glenn would never tolerate rejection.

Yet Will had doubted Robin after Anna was killed. Doubted her because he knew the M.O. The facts. The damn evidence. Glenn had relationships with all the victims. Anna wasn't supposed to be in the apartment that night — she was supposed to be at her mother's house in Big Bear. According to Robin, Anna hadn't told anyone else that she was gay. She feared she'd be fired if anyone knew. So that night, Robin would have been home, alone, if she and Will hadn't been having sex in the bar.

"Fuck."

Carina stared at him. "You don't swear."

"Leave me alone."

"Screw that," she said, angry. "We're partners. What's mine is yours and all that crap. At least how it relates to the job. Got it?"

Carina was right. Will had been letting the past get to him. Remembering not only the success of Glenn's conviction, but their failures — including Frank's drinking during the stakeout and especially seeing Robin again. When he wasn't working specifically on Glenn's escape, he was thinking about her.

"Got it. I'm sorry."

"You haven't slept much, I can cut you a little slack. But not forever, pal."

He pulled into a parallel parking place in front of The Eighth Sin. Robin would automatically have been at the top of Glenn's target list: She was instrumental in his conviction, and credible to the jury even after his odd cross-examination. Will's greatest fear was that Glenn would finally kill Robin. Why had she called? It had to be serious if she wanted to talk to him.

"You had something going on with her?" Carina said softly.

"What do you mean?"

"We've been partners for over two years, but I've known you it seems forever. You're worried about this Robin McKenna, over and above what you would normally feel for a potential victim."

"She's not a victim."

Carina stared at him without comment.

Will's body tensed. He couldn't flat-out lie to Carina, not after everything they'd been through together, the trust they'd built. He reluctantly said, "We were involved for a while. During the investigation. It didn't work out. That's my M.O., right?"

"Right," Carina said, making no move to get out.

"What? You know now, leave it alone."

"Thing is, I *do* know you. You're hung up on her. You don't act like this. The only time you ever get all funky about a woman is when Wendy comes to town and you agree to go to dinner with her."

"She's my ex-wife."

"Yeah, but you loved her, didn't you?"

Will shrugged, but it was the truth. Of course he'd loved Wendy. He wouldn't have married her otherwise. But love wasn't enough. Not then, with Wendy and wedding vows, and certainly not seven years ago with Robin and their insatiable lust.

"Let's go inside," Carina said, getting out of the car.

Damn. Her anger was gone and somehow that made Will even more uncomfortable. His partner was half Cuban, she didn't just drop things.

Carina was ringing the bell before Will closed his door. "Swanky place. I remember walking the beat down here when I was first a cop, before redevelopment. I'm glad the city cleaned it up."

Will was proud of what Robin had accomplished. Even though they'd only been together for a few weeks, he knew she'd wanted to own her own business. And she'd done it, in style.

No thanks to him, and without him at her side, but what could he do about that now?

The intercom buzzed. "May I help you?"

"Detectives Kincaid and Hooper, San Diego Police Department, to speak with Robin McKenna, please," Carina said.

"Please come in." The door buzzed.

Will frowned, thinking anyone could lie and be admitted, then he saw a discreet security camera angled above the door. Of course Robin would have security. She was a smart woman.

An attractive, petite blonde woman met them in the entrance. "I'm Gina Clover, assistant manager. Robin is in a meeting, but she'll be done momentarily. Please follow me."

She led them through the club — metal and hollow in its emptiness — to the Back Room which was far more welcoming and comfortable with rich, earthy tones, plush dark green carpet, and a warm atmosphere.

"Can I get either of you something to drink? We have soft drinks as well as bottled water, flavored water, or perhaps some Tazo tea? It's fresh-brewed."

"We're fine," Will said, answering for

both of them.

"Water would be great," Carina said, frowning at Will. "Thank you."

Gina nodded with a smile and motioned for them to sit wherever they liked.

The Eighth Sin was much larger than the former RJ's, and Will realized that Robin had bought the adjoining business and expanded. He couldn't remember what had been in this space, but Robin must have been doing much better than he thought to be able to afford this. Maybe she had an investor. Maybe she had a lover . . .

What was it to him? He'd tossed her aside, told her that he didn't believe her. Worse, she hadn't defended herself.

Yet had he been in her shoes, would he have denied the accusations, pleaded his case? Hell no. He would have walked, furious and upset that the person he loved had no faith in him.

If he couldn't forgive himself, how could he expect Robin to forgive him?

After the assistant manager delivered Carina's water, Carina said, "First Sherry, then Frank. Connor has good reason to be worried about Julia, and I'm glad he took her out of town. Maybe you should be watching your back as well."

"He'll kill me last," Will replied.

"What?"

"He wants me to see everyone else die before he comes for me," Will said with certainty.

"I thought Robin McKenna was his primary target."

"You have to understand how his mind works. He plays off people's fears. I'm a cop. I protect people, or like to think I can. With every person he kills, he's showing me I'm a failure — I can't even protect the innocent. It's Glenn's way of twisting the screws. But with Robin —"

"Does Glenn know about your relationship with Robin?" Carina asked quietly.

Will almost said no. "I don't know," he admitted. "I didn't think so, but — he said some things during the interview after Brandi was murdered that made me think he'd been following Robin."

"Stalking her?"

"Yes, but not in the traditional way we think of stalkers. I think he wanted to see how she reacted to the other girls being killed."

"Then why wouldn't Glenn want to see Robin's reaction to *you* being killed?"

"Because Robin doesn't care about what happens to me," Will said. "We haven't been involved in seven years."

"He doesn't know that."

"Maybe. Maybe not." But that gave Will something more to chew on. What, exactly, did Theodore Glenn know about his life? Or Robin's? Had he found a way to track her while in prison? Did he have help? Will couldn't imagine Glenn confiding in anyone, but he was charismatic and manipulative. Maybe he did have someone working with him. A subservient.

He said as much to Carina.

"You're beginning to sound like Dillon," Carina said, talking about her brother.

"I'm sure Dillon would agree with me. I arrested Glenn. He's smart, shrewd. For example, he knew Frank was a drunk. I remember that first interrogation, Frank playing bad cop, me playing good cop."

"You always play the good cop," Carina interjected.

"Thing was, I *wanted* to go for his throat. And Glenn knew that. He understood the game. He had both of us pegged the minute we arrested him. And for the last seven years he's been planning revenge. He knows how to get under my skin."

"You know, and that's half the battle, Will. You're expecting it, you can stop it. Don't let him in. Don't make it personal."

*It's always personal.* While he could dis-

199

tance himself from the suffering of victims and the violence of criminals, when it came right down to it, it was always personal — he was the cop, it was his job to serve and to protect. When he couldn't, he took it personally.

A door, flush against the wall when closed, opened. Soundproofing had prevented any noise from escaping and Will hadn't noticed it. A tall, muscular, dark-skinned Cuban exited, followed by Robin. She was smiling, looked stunning in jeans and a soft dark purple sweater. Her hair was pulled back into a ponytail, but wisps had escaped. She looked both young and wise at the same time.

Damn, he missed her.

A tightness crossed his chest when she shook hands with the man. Jealousy? What right did he have to be jealous?

"Thanks, Mario. My business is in good hands." She glanced at Will. "Let me introduce you to the detective in charge of the task force."

Mario nodded, turned to face Will. Will didn't recognize him, but Carina did. "Hey, Mario!" She walked over and slapped his hand in a complex handshake usually reserved for use between men. "Good to see you."

200

"Cara, how's it going? Patrick hanging in there?"

Sadness crossed her face. "Hanging in," she said.

"Ma has a prayer group meeting weekly for him."

"I know it's helping."

Will cleared his throat. Carina made the introductions. "Mario, my partner Will Hooper. Will, Mario Medina is an old — very old" — she hit him in the ribs — "family friend. We went to school together. After a few years in the military, he opened up a private security company."

"You don't keep in touch," Mario said. "My sister tells me you're getting married."

Carina grinned sheepishly. "Yeah, I am. Three weeks. I'm sure you're on the invite list. My mom is inviting the world. They won't fit in the backyard, I keep telling her."

"We'll manage." He clapped her on the back. "I'll be there if I'm not working. I'm happy for you." He looked at Will. "I'm putting a team together to cover the Sin. As long as my men are watching, no one will be hurt."

Great. Cocky *and* a friend of the Kincaids.

"I'm glad you hired security," Will said to Robin.

She stared at him blankly, but her eyes

201

clouded. What was she thinking? Why couldn't he read her?

"Mario's the best," Carina said confidently, smiling at Robin. "Hi, Robin. I'm Detective Carina Kincaid, Will's partner. Nice to meet you."

Robin smiled and shook Carina's hand, her eyes darting between Carina and Mario. Not looking at *him.*

"What about you?" Will asked, turning to Mario. "What's your plan for security on Ms. McKenna?"

Mario said carefully, "As long as she's here, she will be covered."

"What about her residence? Her free time?"

"One of my team will escort her from the Sin every evening. We'll make sure she arrives home safe."

Will frowned. "Robin, what about your loft —"

"You have the cops sitting out front. As long as no one falls asleep, I'll be safe."

The jab hit as hard as Robin intended. She hadn't heard about Frank's death yet, and Will didn't say anything.

Will asked through a clenched jaw, "You called the station and said you need to talk to me."

She reached behind the bar and tossed

him a CD encased in a thin plastic case. "Glenn called me. I recorded the conversation."

Will hid his surprise. "You expected him to call?"

"Yes," she said, chin up. She glanced at Carina and her confidence wavered a fraction. "He called earlier," she admitted softly. "I hung up on him. Then I hit myself for being so stupid. It took him fifteen minutes to call back. I had enough time to get it together."

Will barely noticed Mario and Carina exchange a glance. "Robin, he's not going to stop until he goes after you."

"Then I'll kill him." Robin turned and lifted up her sweater, revealing a holstered gun in the small of her back. Will didn't know why it bothered him that Robin was packing, but he was frustrated. Private citizens shouldn't have to carry weapons to feel safe, but Robin obviously had cause for a CCP.

Will asked, "Do you have a death wish, Robin?"

"What do you want? You came here yesterday, did your duty. Warned me only eighteen hours after I heard about his escape on the TV news."

Will bit back an argument. "Do you have

a CD player?"

Robin held out her hand and he tossed back the CD.

She played it through the bar's speaker system. Hearing Glenn's voice coming from all around gave Will the chills. He looked at Robin, saw that she was having a difficult time listening to it again. He marveled that she had the wherewithal to set up the recording in the first place. It took brains and courage. She caught him staring at her, averted her eyes.

*Glenn said, "I will kill you, Robin, slowly. And the last thing you see before you die will be my smile."*

*"Fuck you!"*

*"How's William?"*

Will's jaw clenched tight. Glenn would kill Robin if he had the opportunity, and Will vowed never to give him that chance. Between her private security and San Diego PD, Robin would be safe.

"He's going to kill you," Robin said, her voice cracking at the last moment. She cleared her throat. "He killed my friends to hurt me. He thinks killing you will hurt me, too."

Will's head spun. Robin was concerned about his safety? Glenn had baited Will by dropping Robin's name during interrogation, and was now baiting Robin by dropping Will's name. Theodore Glenn was playing on their personal fears, and doing it damn effectively. Will couldn't let him in.

*Don't make it personal.*

Right.

"What phone did he call you on?"

"My house phone," Robin said.

"Is it listed?"

"No."

Mario said, "But that doesn't mean anything. Unlisted numbers are easy to get if you know what you're doing."

"Or he could have help. Someone who's been keeping an eye on Robin while he's been in prison."

Robin sat heavily on a bar stool and Mario took her arm. "Are you okay?" the security expert asked, his voice concerned. Will felt a pang of jealousy. He should be the one consoling Robin.

"Why? Why would anyone want to help a killer?"

"You'd be surprised," Carina said. "Sometimes they don't even recognize that they're aiding and abetting."

"He's not going to get to you," Will told Robin. "I won't let him."

Carina reached behind the bar and popped out the CD. "I'm going to call this in, get our people working on tracking down the number he called from. It might take a little time to get the information out of the phone company, but we should have it by the end of the day." She nodded at Mario. "Let's check out the security system while I make the call."

"I already — um, right. Let's do that."

They left. Will was alone with Robin. Her chin tilted defiantly up, jaw clenched. "Robin, please. You never let me apologize."

She blinked rapidly. "You never tried."

"Hell yes I did!"

Her jaw dropped. "Your idea of a fucking apology was pathetic! You accused me of bringing it on myself, that what I did naturally made you doubt me."

"I never said that!"

"I guess you didn't have to." She turned from him. He went to her, put his hands on her shoulders.

"You read things into that night that weren't there," he said.

"Did I?"

"Dammit, Robin! I was wrong. I should never have — but I admitted that. Right then and there."

"Some things you can't take back." She sounded so lost, so lonely. Will hated hearing her anguish.

"I —" What could he say? That he was sorry? Again? How many times could he apologize? As many times as it took for Robin to forgive him. It pained him that he hurt her, and he'd do anything to take it all back, but that was in the past. And right now, nothing he could say would take away the pain and anger that stood like a brick wall between them.

He turned her to face him. She was so close. So beautiful. Her eyes, damn, her eyes highlighted her kind and generous soul. How had he ever doubted her? How had he questioned her loyalty? Her honesty? Her love? He touched her jaw, her skin so smooth and flawless she could have been eighteen as easily as the thirty-one he knew she was.

His thumb skimmed her lips. A faint cry escaped her throat. Will remembered holding her that first time, when he'd taken her home after she came to him at the police station to ask what the police were doing about her friend's murder. They'd gone to dinner, and had a few drinks, and she told him everything about RJ's and her friend Bethany Coleman. She'd been drained, and he'd never felt so protective of a witness.

Now, he needed to touch her again. He bent, touched his lips to hers.

A hint of a kiss wasn't enough. It would never be enough. He sank into her like a dying man, thirsting. His hands found the nape of her neck, rubbed, held her, devoured her lips.

He'd get on his knees and beg her forgiveness if it would help, but maybe, just maybe, his kiss would be enough. His kiss would show her how sorry he was. His kiss would prove Will had never stopped loving Robin.

She gasped, not expecting him to touch her. To put his lips on hers. She wanted to give into him, to hold on and let him take her away to the moon as he'd done before. After Sean, it had taken her years to let a man into her heart. The one man she'd opened up to was this one, this cop, and he'd sliced her to the bone with one question.

*"Did you sleep with Theodore Glenn? Are you next on his kill list?"*

She put her hands up. Her heart wanted Will back, her heart wanted to forgive him, but her head knew the truth. That there would always be doubt in his mind. He hadn't believed her then, when he'd claimed to love her. Why would he believe her now when they had nothing but regret and bitterness between them?

She'd done nothing wrong and he hadn't

believed her. She'd seen it in his eyes. Heard it in his voice. She couldn't live with that shadow of doubt between them.

Using all her emotional strength, Robin pushed him away. There was nothing more that she wanted except to bring Will Hooper home with her. To have him protect her. Save her, not only from a killer, but from deep, numbing loneliness. Even with her business, her painting, with all that she did, she went home alone every night. The hollowness grew, and she was drowning in her empty life.

But Will Hooper was not the man she could allow into her world. Not again. No matter how scared she was, how lonely she was, she wouldn't, couldn't, let him get close.

He stared at her, his smoky blue eyes pained. They mirrored her heart. She swallowed. "You have the CD. I hired a bodyguard. You don't need to come by anymore."

He stayed silent for a long moment. The tension between them was palpable. She wanted to touch him. She wanted him to hold her. She wouldn't allow herself to flinch, to show even one iota of interest toward Will Hooper. He'd never know how much he'd hurt her, deeply, inside, where who she was mattered.

And she'd never show him.

"Glenn killed Frank Sturgeon. Early this morning."

She sucked in her breath. She wasn't surprised, but the reality stung. There was no love lost between her and Frank — she had never liked that man — but she'd never wanted him to die.

She nodded. What could she say?

"That's it?" Will asked, his hands on her shoulders. She forced herself to be a stone.

He dropped his hands and said curtly, "You know the danger. You hired security. You won't have to see me."

He turned, walked away, and Robin held her breath. *Just go, Will. Please go.*

He stopped, turned, and looked at her from the doorway. "I messed up with you, Robin. And no one is sorrier about that than me."

Then he was gone.

# FIFTEEN

Will agreed to meet Trinity late that evening at Bob's Burger across from the police station. She'd spoken cryptically, essentially telling him she had additional information about her meeting with Theodore Glenn the night before. To say he was angry was an understatement — had she kept important information from the police?

He sat in the bar section of the bar and grill and ordered a double Scotch while he waited. He didn't normally drink when working a complex case, but if he was going to sleep even a couple hours tonight, he was going to need something.

Chief Causey had called him earlier to tell him the Feds were on their way. Specifically, one agent by the name of Hans Vigo who had some familiarity with the case and was a criminal profiler. Causey had cleared it, and now Will had another partner.

Not that he minded, as long as Vigo was one of the good guys. The truth was, the FBI was hit or miss, depending on who they sent. Sometimes they screwed with the locals, sometimes they helped. At this point, Will could use an objective eye, someone who might be able to figure out where Glenn was hiding or who might be helping him — if anyone.

That Theodore Glenn seemed to have just disappeared irritated Will to no end. They had hundreds of cops in both the city and county on full alert for Glenn. His picture was plastered in all media outlets — television and newspaper. His parents' house was staked out 24/7. The bulk of Glenn's assets were in a trust administered by the court, but he still had enough resources available to him. By law, the court could only retain the amount necessary for restitution. The bastard was worth over ten million dollars plus whatever interest had accumulated. When he was put to death, the remaining assets after legal expenses and restitution would be given to his surviving family, in this case his parents.

Not that they would take much consolation in receiving the money. Not with both their children dead. Nor would Glenn's money help their little granddaughter Ashley accept or understand the brutal murder of her mother. Her mother who had done the right thing and was now dead.

Where was Theodore Glenn right now? They'd sent officers to hotels and motels in the area, both cheap dives and upscale establishments. Glenn was a neat freak, Will couldn't see him in a dive, yet his self-preservation was paramount and therefore maybe he *would* tolerate the filth. Maybe he'd learned to, being in San Quentin — one of the most decrepit prisons in California. They were talking about selling it, over four hundred thirty acres of prime California real estate right there on the San Francisco Bay.

There were nearly one thousand hotels, motels, and weekly apartments in San Diego County. Glenn didn't have any friends left, the trial had killed most of the loyalties anyone may have had with him. But he was charismatic and Will didn't doubt Glenn could talk his way into or out of virtually anything.

Look at Trinity. She was nearly convinced that Glenn hadn't killed Anna. To what end? Will wanted justice, he wouldn't want a killer to get away with murder, but he honestly didn't believe that had happened in this case. The evidence was clear, but more than that, Will had faced Glenn and *knew* in his gut that Glenn had murdered those women. He was vicious, cruel, sadistic, and had absolutely no remorse for his crimes. He enjoyed the game, and playing with Trinity was just another game to him. A thrill. He'd pled not guilty to all four counts of murder, yet told Trinity he'd killed three of the four women. What was his angle?

What if he was telling the truth? The trouble with sociopaths is that you never knew when they were telling the truth and when they were lying.

The Feds were going through Theodore Glenn's possessions and communications from the prison. If he had someone on the outside, the Feds would know about it soon enough.

*I hope.*

Will had no problem trusting the Feds in this matter. They were just as concerned about the escaped convicts as every jurisdiction in California and the rest of the country. Twelve killers — nine now, after the latest report — on the loose. To haunt their old hangouts, or to disappear?

The fact remained that most convicts were recaptured within thirty days. Glenn was now a cop killer and that put the chances of his arrest that much higher — only a small handful of cop killers were never caught.

Trinity was late. Will would be irritated if he wasn't so worried about her. He pulled out his cell phone to call the cops watching her place — to make sure she was safe — when she walked in. She looked as tired as he felt, and made a beeline to the bar, sliding onto the stool next to him while kissing his cheek at the same time.

"Thanks for meeting me."

"I didn't have a choice."

"A choice? You always have a choice."

"You told me over the phone that you lied to me this morning. I could have you arrested."

"You wouldn't."

"Don't test me. I'm not in a good mood. You didn't tell me everything this morning."

"I couldn't. Not then."

The bartender came over and Trinity ordered a Diet Coke. After she was served, Will said, "What's going on? I want the truth."

"You brought Theodore Glenn into custody two days after Brandi Bell was killed. According to the arrest report, he'd been identified by an elderly woman who lived across the street from Brandi, and by Robin McKenna."

"Are we going to rehash the case? All that is in the transcripts."

"Bear with me, okay? This is important, Will."

Her sharp brown eyes were serious.

"Go on."

"So this Mrs. Tchtivski gives a relatively vague description of a suspect, and Robin McKenna pegs him as Theodore Glenn, a regular customer."

"It wasn't that vague."

Trinity read from the report. " 'Over six feet tall with brown hair, maybe dark brown, and not fat or skinny.' That's pretty bare bones."

"Robin had mentioned Theodore Glenn after Bethany's murder. Glenn had been involved with Bethany and Robin felt something was off about him from the moment they first met. I didn't hold much weight to that — a lot of those guys are creeps — but I quietly looked into Glenn's background. Just to check him out. Corporate attorney, wealthy, owned a plane, a stunt junkie. He didn't seem to fit. But —"

"Go on."

"After Brandi was killed Robin told me about his relationship with Brandi, and how he came in the night after the murder and asked about Brandi. Something about the way he asked disturbed Robin. I showed her the sketch and she identified him. Even though the eyewitness *was* vague, with Robin's identification I could petition the court for a mandatory DNA sample from Glenn. I couldn't hold him past the seventy-two hours, but the lab was working on the DNA and we were watching Glenn. If I had a suspect in custody, the lab would push the DNA tests to the forefront."

"But the evidence was thrown out."

"Don't fucking remind me. All the evidence from Bethany's crime scene was contaminated. We could use nothing from it. When I had to let Glenn go it just about

216

killed me. I *knew* he was guilty. But until Brandi was killed, we didn't even know we had contaminated evidence."

"What I need to know is how Glenn got away with killing Jessica Suarez."

"You know that, Trinity. You saw the picture."

"But what I don't understand is why you didn't know Frank Sturgeon had a drinking problem?"

Will closed his eyes and drained his Scotch. The bartender came over and nodded toward the glass. Will shook his head. He would not end up like his dead partner.

"What are you doing, Trinity?" he asked quietly.

"I'm trying to figure out what happened seven years ago."

"Theodore Glenn killed four women, was convicted, sent to death row, and has since escaped from prison. What more do you want to know? What more can *help* anyone?"

"He said —"

"Theodore Glenn is a sociopath, Trinity. He's a liar. You can't believe everything he says."

"But what if he's telling the truth?"

"Off the record?"

"Of course."

"We're quietly looking into Anna Clark's

homicide. I can't reopen it, not based on the word of the man who was convicted of her murder — a man who has now admitted to killing at least three other women — but I'm listening to you, Trinity.

"But," Will continued, "digging into the past isn't going to do either of us any good."

"Finding the truth will —"

"Buy you a ticket to New York City. I get that."

"You make my career sound evil, Will. That's not fair."

"I'm doing this on the QT, Trinity. I don't want this on the front page until Chief Causey gives his press conference. Got it?"

She nodded. "All right. Off the record, Will. What did you know about Frank Sturgeon seven years ago?"

"Off the record?"

"Have I ever lied to you, Will? In the ten years I've known you — during the weeks that we dated — did I ever lie to you?"

"Well, there's this morning."

"I didn't lie."

"You didn't tell me everything."

"I couldn't."

"And now you can?"

"Are you going to tell me about Frank?" she asked.

Will wanted to haul Trinity's pretty little

ass to prison and make her tell him the truth. He didn't like these kinds of games.

"If you spill any of this — a word — I swear no cop will ever speak to you again, on or off the record."

"I give you my word, Will. As you said, though, I have the photograph."

"We had Glenn under surveillance after we were forced to release him. But there were only the two of us on the case, Frank and me. No one cared that two strippers were dead. Priorities, you know? And the politicians put strippers right down there with hookers. In fact, the D.A. at the time, that prick Bryce Descario, told me when I went to him with the evidence after Brandi's murder that he had more important cases. 'Lie down with dogs, Detective,' he told me with that condescending grin of his. He didn't care that many of those girls had been abused as kids, that some of them were working their way through college or grad school."

Will took a deep breath, motioned for the bartender to pour another Scotch. To take the sting out of the past. When she left, he continued, talking to himself as much as to Trinity.

"I couldn't get more personnel. Now that Glenn is an escaped convict going after mothers and retired cops, I have every man I need. But then, I had no one. Just me and Frank. And Frank —" He took a deep breath. "Frank wasn't all right back then. He had some personal problems, had a couple DUIs that no cop ticketed him for. He swore up one side and down the other that Theodore Glenn never left his house the night Jessica was killed. We were taking turns, you know. I did one night, Frank did the other. We were doing this off the clock. We still had to cover our shift."

"But you didn't believe Frank," Trinity said quietly. "If Frank swore Glenn didn't leave his house, how did Chandler get a conviction?"

"If you remember, Frank didn't testify."

Trinity thought back and nodded. "You were the arresting officer."

"If Glenn had called him to the stand, he was instructed by the chief to admit that he had fallen asleep. If Frank lied on the stand, Causey was willing to send him up for perjury if necessary. We didn't put any of this in the final report. Only Causey, Frank, and I know what really happened that night. Was that right? No, but would it have been more right to drag the department through a scandal? It wouldn't matter that we were on our own time. Frank's drinking and other problems would have been exposed, the department put under a public microscope. Causey put Frank on a desk to keep his pension — we handled it internally. Glenn couldn't have brought Frank to the stand because it would have proven he had the opportunity to kill Jessica, and we had nothing in writing that indicated Frank was watching Glenn."

Will continued, heated, remembering how he'd felt when he realized his own partner — a man he should have been able to trust with his life — had let not only him down, but the victims. "If you let Glenn get close enough, he'll identify your weakness with little effort. He waited until Frank had passed out and left his house. Probably whistling 'Dixie' right past Frank's unmarked car. Snapped the picture for kicks. He killed Jessica, returned, and Frank hadn't moved."

"So even though there was no direct evidence pointing to Glenn as killing Jessica Suarez, because of the M.O. you got the conviction."

"It was touch and go whether the D.A. was going to charge him for all four murders. We only had hard evidence on Anna Clark. But because forensics proved, and the coroner backed up, that the same knife was used in all four murders, Descario decided to go for it." Will paused, swirled his Scotch around the glass. "Remember, we all knew he'd killed Bethany Coleman. We had hard DNA evidence that we couldn't use in court, but we knew he was guilty. It was only a matter of time before he slipped up again. You don't know how sorry I am that I let Frank surveil alone that night."

"What were you supposed to do? Go without sleep 24/7? You may have fallen asleep without the aid of alcohol sitting in front of Glenn's house."

He shook his head. Frank had insisted, and Will didn't argue even though he damn well knew about Frank's drinking problem. Frank was the senior detective, after all. And Will wanted time with Robin.

Trinity's voice was low. "Last night when Glenn told me he didn't kill Anna Clark, he said to ask you."

"What the hell is that supposed to mean?"

"He saw you and Robin. In the bar."

Will clenched his glass, jaw tight, and said nothing.

"He said that you and Robin were, um, involved. It was two o'clock in the morning."

"Fucking *bastard!*" He punched the bar,

stood, and tossed money next to his empty glass. Glenn had watched them have sex. It put all his other cryptic comments into context. The kitchen table. Will's entire relationship with Robin felt tainted and exploited, now that he knew that Theodore Glenn had watched their most passionate moments.

"Don't you see what this means?" Will said. "He just put himself at the scene of the crime. RJ's was across the street from Robin and Anna's old apartment."

"Why would he admit to killing three women, and not Anna? It doesn't make sense."

Glenn could have been watching him and Robin in the bar. Stalking them. Left them alone, went to Robin's apartment to wait for her. Anna was home, surprised him, and he killed her instead. It fit.

But would he have had enough time to kill Anna and disappear? The wounds inflicted would have taken quite some time — they were methodical, cautious, not a frenzied attack. The cuts were to maximize her pain and suffering, both physical and emotional. If Glenn had in fact seen Will and Robin having sex in the bar, he'd only have had fifteen or twenty minutes to cross the street, break in, and kill Anna.

But there had been no break-in. Anna had either opened her door to the attacker, or the killer had a key. All the evidence pointed to the killer already being in the apartment when Anna arrived — her packed suitcase next to the door, for example.

Should he reopen Anna's case? All on the word of an escaped convict to a glory-hungry reporter?

He pulled out his cell phone and dialed dispatch. "I need a car to pick up Ms. Trinity Lange from Bob's Burgers and take her home. And sit on her. I'll get the overtime authorized." He slammed the phone shut.

"Do not move from this stool until a uniformed cop walks through that door and follows you home. Glenn is playing with you, and when he's done he will kill you. That's what cats do to mice, and Glenn has sharp teeth."

Theodore staked out Sara Lorenz's house in Rancho Santa Margarita.

*His* house, he should say. He'd bought it. In fact, he'd insisted that Sara buy a house in the corporation's name and live there.

Ironically, he'd never seriously considered escaping from San Quentin. The prison was secure, and he didn't like the idea of being shot in the back. He'd planned on finding another opportunity to escape — such as during one of his appeals. At the time of the earthquake, he still had one more appeal pending. Sara had planned to join him at the courthouse, fully prepared. He had the money to buy people and equipment. He'd been preparing her for this. She had been excited.

There was always the risk that she'd turn on him. That the police had figured out who she was and where she lived. He'd buried the money trail, but letters were still opened and read in prison. He was confident the corporation *itself* was protected, they'd worked out a code for all corporate business, but what if the cops had somehow traced Sara? What if after his escape she'd had second thoughts? She might think that as long as he was in prison, he was "safe." On the outside, the stakes changed.

There was only one way to find out where Sara Lorenz stood. Confrontation.

Theodore was good at confrontation.

He watched the house he'd bought. He circled the neighborhood. All quiet. He parked behind the development and walked in, through the hills, into the backyard. He had told Sara no security on the perimeter of the house, but that the password to the security system must be *robin.* And the doors must open on a security code, not a key.

"After the bird?" she asked with humor during one of their weekly phone conversations. She knew all about Robin. She'd been keeping track of her for years.

"Of course. I've always liked robins," he said.

"Not me. I'm always thrilled when my cat catches one."

He watched from the slope in the backyard. Dark and silent. A night-light in one of the rooms glowed dimly.

He walked to the back door. The security panel was there, the numbers glowing faintly green.

76246.

*Robin.*

The red light turned green. He smiled and let himself in. Listened.

Nothing but the faint tick of a grandfather clock somewhere downstairs.

Sara hadn't betrayed him, which was good because he'd been prepared to slit her throat.

He climbed upstairs without a sound. The double doors directly ahead at the top of the stairs were framed by recessed alcoves which held urns of fake flowers. That must be the master bedroom.

He crossed the upstairs foyer, the carpet plush against his ill-fitting shoes. Sara was supposed to have purchased a closet full of clothes for him.

He opened the doors.

There she was, sleeping. A thick white comforter covered her slim body. Six or more pillows piled around the head of the bed. Everywhere, white. Everywhere, clean. Neat. Orderly.

Just the way he liked it.

He crossed over to the bed, sat next to her.

"Sara," he said.

Her eyes opened, confused. "Who —" She blinked, her eyes adjusting to the dark. "Teddy."

Sara was the only one he allowed to call him by a nickname. It seemed to be important to her, though he never allowed anyone else to use anything but his full legal name.

She wrapped her arms around his neck and for a moment he felt strange. At a loss as to what to say or do.

"I was so worried about you," she said, hugging him tightly.

"Everything is fine." He swallowed heavily.

"You must be hungry. Tired."

"I'm hungry for you, Sara."

She pulled back, stared at him. "Oh." She

227

started unbuttoning the prim little night-gown she wore.

"Stop," he said. "Let me."

Instead, he kissed her. She responded fully, as if they had kissed before when the most they had done was touch fingers through the bars of the prison.

That Sara was so eager for him, neither flinching nor complaining when he touched her, turned him on. It had been a long time since he had a woman, and a rush filled him. He didn't expect it to last — sex was predictable, especially with the same woman — but this was a first for him with Sara. He pulled off her nightgown, but hid her face.

"Tell me you want it," he whispered in his ear. "Tell me you want me."

"I want you, Teddy. I want you so bad. I've been waiting for this night for years."

Sara had a nice body. Not long and lithe with big tits like Robin, but nice and tight and firm.

He pictured Robin beneath him, Robin wanting him. Robin asking him to screw her, Robin begging him for more.

He slammed into Sara and closed his eyes. His dick swelled and he exploded.

"Yes!" Sara cried, and Theodore didn't care if she was faking. All he heard was one

woman screaming for him.
*Robin.*

# Sixteen

The knocking on the door persisted.

*Theodore Glenn wouldn't knock,* Robin thought. *He'd break down your door, come through the window, grab you in the parking lot.*

She hadn't been sleeping well, but before she was fully awake, her gun was in her hand. She didn't need to check to see if there was a round chambered; she knew there was. It was nearly two in the morning. She'd slept for all of forty minutes.

She crossed her open loft. Before she looked through the peephole she heard the man on the other side.

"Robin, please let me in. I have to talk to you."

*Will.*

She looked through the peephole. Will's head was low, his hands on both sides of her door. He looked rumpled in his slacks and button-down shirt. He wore no jacket, his shoulder holster exposed.

He pounded on the side of the door. "Robin!"

She didn't want to talk to him. She didn't

want to see him. Today at her club it had been all she could do not to give in to his kiss. Not to let herself be held. Be loved.

Love hurts.

"Please let me in."

She punched numbers into her alarm system. Disarmed. Slid open one bolt. Turned the second. Pushed back the chain. Opened the door.

They stared at each other. Will's blue-gray eyes, the Pacific Ocean before a storm, stared at her.

He asked, "Can I come in?"

She stepped back without comment. He closed the door behind him. "Robin —"

She walked around him and bolted the door. She couldn't leave it unlocked. She felt almost obsessive-compulsive, but in the seven years since Theodore Glenn had killed her friends she couldn't help herself. She was terrified. Even in her own home.

She skirted Will and went into the kitchen, keeping the counter between her and the man she used to love.

"Who did he kill now?"

Will blinked. "No one. That we know about."

"Then why are you here?"

"I'm worried about you."

She held up her gun and gestured toward

the door. "I'm fine. You can leave."

"Dammit, Robin! You're not fine."

"I'll be fine when he's behind bars. Or dead. Better dead, I think."

"He knows about us," Will said quietly.

Her stomach flipped. "What do you mean?"

"He saw us. Together."

"You mean *together*?"

"Yes. Having sex. That night, in the bar."

"Oh God." She dry-heaved into the sink, her head spinning. She put her gun on the counter because she could no longer hold it, her hands shaking, reaching for the edge of the sink to hold herself up. The thought that Theodore Glenn had not only watched one of the most intimate moments of her life, but that he'd then gone across the street and killed her roommate, undid her rocky composure she'd been barely holding together since his escape.

Will was at her side, pulling her into his arms. She clung to him, dragging them both down to the hardwood floor. He gathered her into his lap and leaned against the wall.

What was happening? How could that coldhearted killer have watched her having sex? Killed Anna? Why had he spared her? Suffering as a survivor was almost worse than death. Maybe she should have died.

Because she certainly hadn't been living these past years.

She'd lost four friends. Then she'd lost Will. When she needed him most, he'd turned his back. She'd never grown close to anyone since, either a boyfriend or a girl-friend. It had been all business, no personal relationships, for seven years.

*"You see why I don't believe you?"*

The words Will spoke back then clouded her mind as if he'd whispered them just now in her ear. She stifled a sob, Will's arms around her tightened.

"Robin, I am so sorry. I know you don't believe me, I broke your trust. I can't tell you how I feel about that. My life has been on hold. When I saw you yesterday it was like time had stopped. There you were, even more beautiful than I remembered, than I've dreamed about. All I wanted to do was hold you. Make love to you. Never leave you. I blew it, Robin, big-time. And I don't see how you can forgive me. Still, I need you to forgive me. I need you."

"I needed you, Will."

*Needed.*

Will heard exactly what Robin said, and it hurt. "I know."

She shook her head into his chest. "No. You don't."

"Please, Robin. Don't —"

"I can't. I can't do it. Please don't ask me to put my heart on the line again. I don't have anything left to give."

He wanted to scream. How could he convince her he wasn't the man she'd first met?

He kissed her hair, her forehead. She let him hold her. Until he heard the phone conversation between Glenn and Robin, followed by Trinity's revelation that Glenn had watched them having sex, Will hadn't realized the depth of Glenn's obsession with Robin. Seven years ago he'd known Robin was possibly a catalyst, that Glenn was fixated on her for some reason, to hurt people in her life but not her specifically.

Now, the truth started to fall in place. It had all been about Robin. They simply didn't have enough information back then to see it. And now Glenn had had years to plot his revenge, to obsess on Robin. Will had feared for Robin's life since he'd first heard of Glenn's escape, now he knew she was the reason he'd returned to San Diego. Everyone else Glenn wanted to kill was extraneous to him, no one compared to Robin.

"I won't let him get to you," he whispered, rocking her in his lap.

"I'll kill him, Will."

The coldness in her voice disturbed him. He suspected for the first time that yes, in fact, Robin McKenna could kill Theodore Glenn. She'd had seven years to practice. Seven years to hate. He'd stolen so much from her — her security, her safety, her friends.

And Will. Had Glenn not planted those seeds of doubt — if Will hadn't let him — he'd never have doubted Robin. Or would he have? Was he that shallow? Except that he was a cop first. He had to ask the hard questions. And based on Glenn's M.O., he had to ask Robin if she'd had a sexual relationship with him.

Maybe he'd just been so close to her that he was scared of his own emotions. Pushed her away the only way he could. Accusing her of lying to him. Accusing her of sleeping with a killer.

He'd take it all back if he could. She wouldn't listen to him, maybe she would let him touch her.

He kissed her. Firmly. Closely. Intimately. To show her that he loved her. Believed in her. Her lips opened. He tasted the salt of her tears on her tongue. She moaned and he held her head tightly, his hands tangled in her long, curly auburn hair. He kissed her again and again, almost disbelieving that she was kissing him back, her hands around his neck, her mouth seeking his as much as he sought hers.

She shook her head, turned her lips from his. "Will, no."

"God, Robin, I love you."

She shook her head over and over. "Don't. Don't do this to me. You can't walk into my life like this because it won't last. Without trust, love means nothing."

"I was wrong. Dammit, Robin! I was wrong!"

"I know that. And you do, too. But what about next time? What about the way you looked at Mario Medina today?"

"The bodyguard?"

"Like I had walked out of my office after screwing him on the desk."

"I didn't. I —" He had been jealous. He'd taken one look at the good-looking, muscular bodyguard and instantly thought something had to be going on between him and Robin. Because she was a beautiful, sexy woman.

"You're not like that anymore —" He bit his tongue. "I mean —"

"I'm not a stripper anymore. So when I was a stripper, you expected me to spread my legs for every halfway decent looking man who walked into RJ's? I did it fast enough for you, didn't I?" She pulled herself up.

"Don't, Robin. You know it was never like that between us. I didn't mean it the way it sounded —"

"Go away, Will. I'm not going to do this to myself. I can't."

He stood, held her arms. "Robin, I love you."

She shook her head. "You only think you do. You don't know what love is. And I don't, either. I let my heart be broken twice, and I'm done."

Will sat in his car outside Robin's loft. He was sick about their conversation — that he'd hurt her so deeply she couldn't trust him — but he planned to spend the rest of the night watching her loft. If Glenn was going after her, it would be when he thought she was asleep and unprotected. He'd put in a couple hours sleep once dawn broke.

His cell phone vibrated in his pocket. "What?"

"Good morning to you, too," Carina said.

"It's two a.m."

"And you're not home."

"What do you want?"

"The Feds just called Chief Causey. They

want to meet at oh-eight-hundred. They have some information about Glenn's activities in prison."

"Causey called me earlier."

"You didn't tell me?"

"You were already planning on being in at eight." The truth was, after talking to Trinity he'd forgotten to clue Carina in. Chalk one up to lack of sleep.

Will was about to hang up when he saw Robin in the window of the loft. All the lights were on as she looked directly down at his car. He wasn't exactly inconspicuous in the Porsche, even if it was black.

"I need a favor."

"Sure, I'll give you a wake-up call."

"I need your friend's home address."

"I have a lot of friends."

"Mario Medina. The bodyguard."

"Why?"

"I have a job for him."

"Last I checked he had a job."

"Dammit, Carina, are you going to make this difficult?"

"Yes." She paused. "You're sitting outside her place, aren't you?"

No use lying to her. "And?"

She sighed. "I hear you. Hold on."

Will looked at the window again, wanting another glimpse of the last woman in the world he'd ever wanted to hurt.

She was gone, but the lights blazed. In the days after Robin found Anna dead, she had been terrified of the dark.

Time didn't heal all wounds. Or fears.

"It's after three in the morning."

Mario Medina was not happy about being woken up in the middle of the night.

"Thanks," Will mumbled. Mario lived in a condo right on the beach. Not too large, but with the view and beach access off the sliding glass doors, Will knew it cost a small fortune. It was neat, clean, and sparsely furnished. Will suspected he didn't spend a lot of time here other than sleeping. He had a similar place a little farther south. The Naval base at Coronado could be seen to the southwest in daylight, now only a faint smattering of light.

As if reading his mind, Mario said, "Six years, Marines not Navy."

"MP, Army."

"I figured you're from a long line of cops."

"I need a favor."

Mario laughed. "You want a favor? Why should I do anything for you?"

"Why shouldn't you?"

"Want a beer?"

Will nodded. They walked out on the

patio, each with a Dos Equis in hand. It was freezing as far as Will was concerned — under fifty degrees. Not why he moved to San Diego. But Mario, in a black T-shirt and shorts, didn't seem to notice. He drained half his beer. "What?"

"I want to hire you to keep an eye on Robin McKenna."

Mario showed no expression. "The woman who hired me to watch out for her?"

"She hired you to watch the club and her employees, correct?"

He nodded.

"And not her, specifically."

Mario shook his head.

"She needs someone watching her back and I can't do it. This investigation is going 24/7 and I can't justify spending the time on her. I have increased patrols in her neighborhood. We have a cop on-site at the club during regular business hours. But Theodore Glenn is going to look for that. Surveillance. He's going to find a hole and exploit it. He's been planning revenge for too long."

"I can't do it."

"Fuck, Medina, what's your game?"

"I can't do it because I committed most of my staff to her to protect her employees. I have two pairs rotating twelve-hour shifts

239

on the club, open or closed. I don't have a large operation. My guys are all independent contractors. And one of my best is otherwise occupied."

"Who? I'll pay him."

"Doubt it. Connor Kincaid is watching his fianceé 24/7 and nothing's going to buy him off that one. Can't say I blame him, she's a spunky little number."

"You have no one else?"

"I'll make some calls."

"Dammit, that's not good enough!" Will clenched his fists. How could he protect Robin while he had a job to do?

Mario looked out at the ocean. "I'll keep my eye on her. You have a car on her tonight?"

"Yes. I just checked and he's solid."

"I'll attach myself to her starting tomorrow morning. But I have to have your assurance that I will be clued in to every step of the investigation. What you know, I know. I will not be surprised, got it?"

Will nodded, relieved. He'd have much preferred to stay with Robin himself, but he couldn't watch her 24/7 and work the case.

"Anything I should know?"

"We have the Feds coming to town in a few hours. They apparently have something from San Quentin to share."

"Wonderful." He sounded less than enthused.

"I'll check in with you tomorrow after the meeting."

"I'm counting on it, Hooper."

# SEVENTEEN

Will slept like shit for three hours before dragging himself into the shower and heading over to the station for whatever the Fed was going to report. He arrived before the FBI and debriefed Chief Causey on everything, including his previous relationship with Robin McKenna.

He waited for an admonishment. Instead, Causey said, "Did your relationship with Ms. McKenna affect your duty as a cop?"

"Not at all, sir. Except —" He stopped.

"Except?"

"I let Frank run with the investigation. If I had been more concerned about the investigation than with Robin, I would have been sitting outside Glenn's house the night Jessica Suarez was murdered."

Causey didn't say anything, and Will worried his honesty may have cost him the head position of the task force. "Will," Causey said quietly, "I should have pulled Frank long before the Glenn case. If anyone is culpable for that girl being murdered, it's me."

"With all due respect, sir, I disagree —"

"I knew Frank had a drinking problem and I relied on you to carry him through retirement. The last thing I wanted to do was pull a once-fantastic cop and destroy his reputation. I've known Frank for a long time. We were in the Academy together." Causey sighed, rubbed a hand over his face. "We also had politics to deal with seven years ago. Between Descario and the perceived reputation of the victims, we didn't have the man power to devote to the case. And if the crime scene techs hadn't fucked up the DNA evidence, who knows what would have happened?

"We'd like every case to run smoothly. To do our job, interview witnesses, process evidence, arrest a suspect, earn a conviction. But you know as well as I do that textbook perfect cases are just that — in textbooks. You're a good cop, Will. Mistakes happen and, unfortunately, sometimes with fatal results. But it's not all on you, or Frank, or me, or the crime lab. It's on an imperfect system and the imperfect humans within it."

"Thank you, sir," Will said quietly. He'd rarely heard the chief utter more than two sentences together.

"The Feds will be here any minute. Prepare to brief them."

Putting the conversation with Causey aside, Will reviewed the reports that had come in from the field. Nothing from Theodore Glenn himself in twenty-four hours, since he'd phoned Robin at her loft. No dead bodies, no sightings, nothing. Every patrol that came in at shift change reported to Will where they'd been, who they'd talked to, and all with the same conclusion: No one had seen the escaped convict.

They had two patrols following up full-time on tips from the hotline, which was ringing nonstop with "sightings" of the escaped convict. So far, none were credible, but they had to follow up on each and every call.

"Carina, anything come in from the patrol outside Glenn's parents' house?"

"No activity," she said. "Mrs. Glenn brought them coffee and donuts this morning."

"He's not going home. He has no beef with his parents, and he already got what he needed from them: his sister's address."

The main bull pen doors swung open and Chief Causey walked in with a Suit, male, in his mid-to-late forties. The Fed was under

243

six feet tall, with the face of a character — the kind of cop who in the movies always played the wise old mentor or sidekick. Someone you'd have fun shooting the breeze with over beers at the bar.

Causey walked over to Will's desk and introduced the Fed as Special Agent Hans Vigo out of Quantico.

"Quantico?" Will asked. "You're a long way from home."

"I go where I'm needed," Vigo said with a half smile that reminded Will of a leaner Columbo.

Causey said, "Hooper is heading the task force. He worked the case seven years ago, has a good grasp on Glenn."

Vigo nodded. "Good you're still here. I'm ready when you are."

"You in town for a while?"

"However long I can be of help."

Will pulled in Officer Diaz, who was coordinating the patrols, Chief Causey, and Carina. They met in the makeshift task-force command center.

"To save some time," Vigo said, "I read the past case files. Your chief was kind enough to fax them to me yesterday so I could review them on the plane, as well as the current reports."

"Then there's nothing you don't know,"

Will said. "Glenn has been quiet for the last twenty-four hours. You're a profiler, right?"

"Correct."

"What I want to know is what he plans on doing next."

"I'm a criminal profiler, not a psychic. If you don't mind, I'd like to listen to the conversation from yesterday —" Vigo glanced at the file in front of him. "The conversation between Theodore Glenn and Robin McKenna."

Will put the CD in a player and they all listened. Hearing Robin's strained voice again, and Glenn's taunting, angered him and made him doubly glad he'd gone to Mario Medina the night before. Robin didn't have a death wish, but she was far more concerned about everyone else's safety than she was about her own.

"We've warned everyone we can," Will said, "but that doesn't mean they'll be on guard 24/7. The crime lab, the cops working the case, the prosecution, are all on high alert. We've contacted the jurors and everyone else who testified. He's already taken out two people close to the investigation, his own sister, who testified against him, and my former partner." Will paused. "The prosecution's primary witness, Robin Mc-Kenna, has hired additional security for her business, and we've increased patrols in that neighborhood. We're still tracking down other witnesses."

Will glanced at Vigo. "You have something new?"

The Fed nodded. "You've gone above and beyond. If all jurisdictions were as organized as this one, maybe more than three convicts would be back in custody."

"Wasn't that the work of some vigilante?" Diaz asked.

Vigo said, "We think one of the other escapees has been tracking the men and restraining them."

Causey asked, "A convict is beating up the others? I thought that was media grandstanding. We didn't hear anything formal about it."

"It's not something we're advertising. Because when we get the guy back behind bars, we don't want the prison population knowing that he was once a cop. As it is, we'll probably have to move him and put him in isolation when he's found, or send him to a federal penitentiary."

The news sunk in, that one of their own had turned. Yet hadn't turned so far that he condoned the escape of convicted murderers.

"What do you have on Glenn?" Will asked.

"We've been working with the prison authority on seizing all personal property of the escaped convicts," Vigo said. "We have their journals, their books, their letters. We have sent in a computer expert to pull down all e-mail communication. Prisoners are not allowed e-mail communication, but we know they find ways to access the Internet. We can get everything except privileged communication with their attorneys, but we have a legal team working on that with a federal judge."

Vigo tilted one side of his mouth up. "We may get in a little hot water for that one, but at this point these men have already given up their rights. Theodore Glenn is not the only one who has killed since the escape. A gang of four are on a robbery spree in San Francisco. Two clerks are dead. You'd think in a city that geographically small we could get a handle on them —" Vigo stopped himself. "But right now we have info on Glenn that can benefit you and I'll help in any way I can."

Will appreciated that Vigo didn't force himself into the case. At this point, he would ask for all the help he could get.

"Give it to me," he said.

"I work in the Investigative Support Unit, which basically means that I think like the bad guy. I try to figure out his next move. To do that, I look at his past. If you understand why a killer did something, you can predict what he will do in the future.

"I don't need to tell you all who Theodore Glenn is. You know he's a borderline genius corporate attorney who, before he turned to murder, received intense thrills through extreme sports — things like skydiving and BASE jumping. I've read his transcripts, and concur with what Detective Hooper said on the stand: Glenn is a sociopath with no ability to feel remorse for his actions. He will kill again if it gets him what he wants.

"Most serial killers kill to live out a fantasy. They gain satisfaction in either the hunt or the kill or both. They relive that fantasy as long as they can. When the memory or souvenirs from the kill no longer gives them the physical and emotional satisfaction as the act itself did, they kill again. They are constantly perfecting their crime, making the fantasy better, more complete, in their minds.

"This is why Glenn changed his M.O. almost immediately."

"The bleach," Will said. "We guessed he did that because he'd left evidence behind at the first crime scene."

"Exactly. He knew it as soon as he left.

He has finely developed instincts, which is why he's been so elusive since his escape.

"Theodore Glenn is not a textbook serial killer," Vigo continued. "But if you've studied them as long as I have, you understand that they rarely fit into a set mold. Glenn, for example, displayed only one of the early symptoms of serial killers — we know he killed one or more animals. But I read the testimony of Sherry Jeffries several times. Glenn didn't receive any sexual, physical, or emotional satisfaction in killing his sister's cat. All the pleasure he received was in his sister's reaction. If there wasn't an audience, he'd never have killed the animal."

Hans Vigo let that sink in. Will had always sensed Glenn's core need to emotionally hurt others, but hearing his thoughts validated made Glenn more of a monster, more real.

Will said, "And the phone call to Robin. It was to hear her reaction."

"Bingo. In fact, he called for two reasons. To hear her fear — to live vicariously off her heightened emotions — and to relive his crimes. He wanted to make sure that Robin McKenna knew exactly why he had killed those women, he wanted to make sure she hurt — to attempt to cast blame on her.

That she 'chose' the victims by her own actions — and inactions."

"It's always been about Robin," Will said.

Vigo nodded. "I believe he was obsessed with her from the very beginning, something triggered it. Possibly her perceived inaccessibility — she didn't date him, unlike the others. Or something about her appearance. It could be one of a thousand things, but something triggered his obsession and that is why he began to kill those around her, to watch her reaction. While in prison, his obsession grew and consumed him.

"First, Glenn is seeking revenge, as he announced he would in court. People conspired to deny him freedom. To take away his ability to do what he wants. They must be punished. His sister first, because she was easy. She scared easily. He could torment her, but because he's being cautious, he took care of her quickly. Still, he couldn't resist picking up the neighbor's cat and scaring Sherry Jeffries with it prior to killing her. It was spontaneous — he had no way of knowing there'd be a cat nearby when he came to her house."

"He saw the opportunity and seized it," Will said.

"Glenn is one of the smartest killers I've come up against, but he's a narcissist and that's the Achilles' heel of many of them. He knows he's smart, he doesn't believe he'll ever be caught."

Vigo tapped the large stack of files. "Look at the way he killed his victims. He had a physical relationship with them. Consensual. He was attractive to women, charismatic. Nonthreatening. A regular. One of the boys. None of them saw anything but what he wanted them to see."

*Except Robin.*

Vigo seemed to read Will's mind, looked right at him, but instead of mentioning Robin, he said, "He killed Bethany Coleman by restraining her in her own bed. Cutting into her skin. Not because he received any pleasure from the cutting — he can't feel that — but because he saw the reaction on her face. He felt *her* reaction.

"I know this sounds like splitting hairs, but you have to understand why he does what he does. You touched upon this in your reports, Hooper, and during the trial," Vigo said. "Theodore Glenn is incapable of feeling any real emotion, at least not the normal human emotions you and I feel. He has to watch other people to see how emotion works, how he's *supposed* to feel in the same circumstances. I suspect when we dig further into his background we will learn that he was a voyeur as a young teen. That he didn't receive the same sexual pleasure from sex as he saw others receive. He learned the right responses by watching others. His parents, maybe. Certainly his sister and her boyfriend."

"That's just gross," Carina interjected.

"For most of us, it's unheard of. We don't want to witness the sexual relations of other people, especially people we know. But Glenn had to somehow learn how *he* was supposed to react. I went through his background as carefully as I could on paper. And everything we know about him is that he grew up in a normal, average, upper middle class home. Two parents who have been in a seemingly happy marriage for more than forty years. They did not severely discipline the children. No child abuse, no sexual abuse, no emotional abuse. If anything, the Glenns were *too* conciliatory toward their children. But spoiled children do not routinely grow up to be serial killers.

"Glenn was an overachiever. In school, in work, in play. He did everything to the extreme. And something happened that triggered his killing urge. Not because he received any pleasure in the act of killing. Because he didn't. Look how he positioned the bodies where someone could find them.

See them. He wanted *their* reaction. The horror. The fear. The pain. *That* is what he thrived on. And that is what I think was missed seven years ago.

"Theodore Glenn was either still in the room when the body was discovered, or he was around when friends and family of the victim were told about the murder. He had to be. He didn't kill for the pleasure of killing. He killed to hurt the survivors."

Will clenched his fists. The evidence pointed to Glenn killing Anna Clark — notwithstanding his claims to Trinity that he hadn't. What if after watching Will and Robin in the bar, he left, got into Robin's apartment, was surprised by Anna and killed her? Then waited for Robin to come home. Had he been there when she found Anna?

"Right, Detective?"

Everyone was staring at Will. He didn't know what the Fed had said, but he nodded anyway.

"So all that is in the past — yet time didn't stop seven years ago when he was incarcerated," Vigo said.

Carina said, "But our witness saw him leaving Brandi's house. Her body wasn't discovered until the next day by the police. Glenn wasn't in the house then."

"That's an excellent observation, and it proves my point."

"Which was?" Will asked, rubbing his temple.

"He wanted to see the reaction of someone specific when told of Brandi's death."

Will had already told Chief Causey. Now he needed to clue in the Fed. "I have recently learned that Glenn had been following Robin McKenna. Stalking her, at the time of the murders."

"That makes sense. I said earlier that he was obsessed with her, which prompted his call to her yesterday. While in prison he likely fantasized about her. Based on his conversation, she was the focal point of his killing spree seven years ago. Everyone who died had a relationship with her — friends and colleagues. He wanted to hurt Robin McKenna, see how she would react."

"She was also the key witness against him during the trial."

"So his feelings are even more complex. He's obsessed with her on one level, and he blames her on another. He likely blames her for his obsession, though he wouldn't recognize it for what it is. Glenn probably doesn't understand why she's on his mind, why he's fixated on her, and he would blame her for that as well."

"What would you say if I told you that he watched Robin McKenna having sex with her boyfriend?"

"I'd say that the boyfriend is lucky to be alive."

Will hadn't been expecting that answer. "Why? Couldn't that relationship — with Robin and another man — have prompted Glenn to go after her?"

"Absolutely," Vigo said. "And what better way to hurt Robin McKenna than to kill a man she was intimately involved with? That she may have even loved?" He tapped the file folder. "During Ms. McKenna's testimony, she stated that she didn't like Theodore Glenn from the beginning. Unlike her colleagues, she never went out with him. Was never alone with him. Some people are more sensitive to sociopaths, or simply better readers of human emotion. Or, in Glenn's case, lack of emotion." Vigo paused. "And?"

Will said, "I was dating Robin at the time of the murders."

"I guessed."

Will raised an eyebrow.

"I, too, am a pretty good reader of human emotion," Vigo said with a half smile. "It's my job." He grew serious. "You need to be doubly careful, Detective."

"Robin and I aren't seeing each other anymore."

"It doesn't matter. You had a part of Robin that Theodore Glenn never had. That makes you vulnerable. Second, even if you aren't involved, Glenn knows that if he hurt you it would hurt Robin. And finally, you put him in prison. To be perfectly frank, Detective, I think your life may be in greater jeopardy than Robin McKenna's."

Will dismissed Vigo's comment. He was a cop, he wasn't overly worried about himself. "The chief said you had information that might help."

"The prison authority has copies of all incoming and outgoing correspondence, except privileged communication with his attorney. We've put together a list of nineteen women who, for lack of a better word, form a fan club of sorts."

"Fan club?" Carina interjected. "Nineteen women admire that monster?"

"That's just in San Diego County," Vigo corrected. "Over two hundred women across the country have written to him, but we determined that if he was using any of them most likely it would be someone local, considering we know that he's in town, or he was yesterday."

"He's still here," Will said. "He has a plan,

and killing Sherry Jeffries and Frank Sturgeon was only a small part of it." He looked at Vigo. "What you've said is no different than what we put together seven years ago, aside from Glenn wanting to participate somehow in the reactions of the survivors. But that makes sense, especially after his phone call to Robin yesterday."

"Like I said, this department has been on the ball. If you don't need me, I can go back to San Francisco."

Will shook his head. "No, I'd like you to stay. I didn't mean to imply otherwise. A fresh set of eyes, a clean perspective, is always good in a case this complex."

Vigo nodded. "Of those nineteen women, we ranked them in terms of most likely to harbor a fugitive. Six are considered high risk. We have their names and addresses, though some of these letters are more than a few years old. It's important to track down all nineteen women, but imperative that someone in law enforcement speaks to the six women on the high-risk list as soon as possible."

"How did they make the list?"

"They are white, single women between the ages of twenty and sixty. They all own property under their own name. They are professionals to some degree. Glenn would not be attracted to an illiterate woman. This is someone he has already tested. Someone he has probably already asked to do something illegal, who has done his bidding to his satisfaction. But since we don't know *what* test he would have put them through, we don't know what to look for in their recent activities. None have federal records, but I'll give the list to your people to check for a local rap sheet."

"Do you really think Theodore Glenn is with one of these women?" Chief Causey asked, handing a copy to Officer Diaz with the order to run the list. Diaz left.

Vigo nodded. "Without a doubt, he'll make contact with at least one of them. I wouldn't be surprised if he rotated between two or three of them, but he'll be cautious."

"How can you be so positive the woman won't contact the police as soon as she has a chance?" Carina asked.

"The type of women who contact convicted murderers usually fall into one of four categories: First, they want to express their outrage and usually tell the killer to rot in hell."

"I'm with them," Carina said.

"The second type is religious or spiritual. They want to pray for the killer, encourage him to find God and ask for forgiveness, be repentant, show remorse. The third type are celebrity hounds, those who collect mementos from famous people. They want a letter back, so they can either add the signature to their collection or sell it. They may enter into a correspondence and attempt to find out additional facts. Some of these people may also exhibit sociopathic tendencies, and live vicariously through the convict, but the women in this group are usually nonviolent."

"And the last type?" Will said.

"Often, they have been abused in the past, most likely by a male authority figure. They have justified the abuse in their minds. They deserved it, according to their reasoning, and if only they had done X, Y, and Z the man wouldn't have hurt them. It's similar to many abused wives: They think they can see the good in the abuser. They need to be needed. They are good listeners. It's interesting that some of these women are professionals — smart, on the surface someone you wouldn't expect to initiate a friendship with a killer. But they are wired different emotionally. They want to cure all the ills of the world, and they will start by being whatever the killer wants them to be. They understand him, they think. They are sympathetic. They see a side of him that others ignore. But when you talk to them, don't assume they are dumb or unmanipulative. They will say or do anything to protect the man who they believe they can save. They may even think he is innocent or misunderstood. Or that he had a good reason for doing what he did."

Carina shook her head and Will said, "Glenn is already a manipulative personality. He could convince almost anyone he was wrongly convicted."

Vigo agreed. "Coupled with the fact that he is attractive and independently wealthy, he would be appealing to these types of women on multiple levels. Many of them are physically homely or have been told so by those they trust. But physical appearance is not a major indicator. Emotional immaturity and prior abuse, either emotional or physical, is the key."

"What about greed?" Will asked. "We both agree that Glenn hid money. What if he's paying them to help him?"

"Not that simple, but it's part of the big picture. The woman might see that she can get something for what she thinks is a low price. Glenn has been moving money for the last few years."

Will sat straight up. "His money is in a trust."

Chief Causey spoke. "Some, not all. Only the funds needed for court-ordered restitution are held in a trust. He had plenty of property and stocks to manipulate."

Vigo interjected, "Our finance experts are working on tracking his money trail. He's paid over a quarter million dollars to his legal firm."

"But he represented himself," Will said.

"He hired a firm to do research and prepare reports. It's not unheard of," Vigo said. "And someone of his ego might be thinking he'd rather give his money to attorneys than to the victims or the state or his parents when he dies. Because right now, when he's executed, any funds minus restitution will be given to his parents."

"Small consolation for having two dead kids," Carina said.

A knock on the door interrupted their conversation, and Officer Diaz reentered. "Detective, here's the reports on those six women you needed sheets for."

"And?"

"Only one person has a record. Jane Plummer. She was arrested ten years ago for possession, given probation. Then nine years ago she was arrested for possession with intent. Again, probation. I talked to the arresting officer and he said her boyfriend was the bad guy, not her, but she was scared of him and wouldn't talk. They threw the guy in prison for six months, gave her probation."

"What was his name?"

"Javier Rodriguez."

"And where is he?"

"Dead. Overdosed six years ago."

"What do you think?" Will asked, glancing at Jane's record. Fairly innocuous, and she'd been clean since Rodriguez OD'd.

"I think she's a good bet," Vigo said. "She's already been in one possibly abusive relationship. Definitely check her out, and I'll see if we can dig deeper on our end."

"Excuse me," Carina said. "I get that these women could be cowed by Glenn. But what I don't understand is how he could have prepared for this. I mean, he didn't *cause* the earthquake. He took advantage of an opportunity. What you're saying is that he's had something planned for a long time."

Hans nodded. "Good observation, Detective Kincaid. I suspect that he has been planning an escape, though not from San Quentin. He has requested three transfers through his law firm that have all been denied. But two months ago he was severely beaten by a prison gang. He filed again, and the plea was pending in front of a sympathetic judge. I suspect that if he were going to escape, it would have been during a transfer, with help from the outside. A long shot, but definitely more plausible than planning an escape from San Quentin.

"I'm sure you haven't forgotten that Theodore Glenn is a wealthy man. While his finances have been watched carefully, he's an attorney and most of the people working in the court system are only looking for big red flags. I believe he made financial provisions in case he was arrested. He would have hidden a substantial amount of money. And my guess is that one of these women is the key to that money pool."

"I'll call Doug up in e-crimes and see if he can track down the finances of Glenn's law firm," Will said, making a note.

Carina asked, "But why didn't he run after Brandi Bell was killed? Why take the risk of killing Jessica and Anna?"

Will answered. "For the thrill. He wanted to get away with it, he wanted to rub our noses in our own mistakes. Taking the picture of Frank sleeping — that was arrogance. His intelligence trumping the cops'."

"Then why didn't he use the photo during trial?" Diaz asked.

"And blow his own alibi?" Will shook his

head. "Seven years ago he was a step ahead of us. He picked victims who wouldn't elicit a lot of public sympathy. The public equates strippers with hookers. Then when he made a mistake, luck was on his side. The crime techs contaminated the evidence. But he knew he'd screwed up, and started using bleach. Not only to torture his victims, but to destroy any evidence he inadvertently left behind. I think he took the picture of Frank more for himself than for anyone else."

"You're right," Vigo said, "except for the last point. He'd always planned on using that photograph, and I imagine he has more hidden. You simply stopped him before he had an opportunity."

Carina spoke up. "We know that he dumped a stolen vehicle in Anaheim. Do you have any women from Orange County who wrote to Glenn?"

Vigo nodded and looked at his file. "Three."

"Maybe we should check them out as well," Carina said.

"Good call, Detective," Agent Vigo said. "I'll call the Orange County field office and they'll get on it today."

"And we'll start on the nineteen in San Diego," Will said.

"There's something else you need to

consider." Vigo paused.

Will nodded. "I already have."

Vigo raised an eyebrow.

"You were going to ask if I believed Theodore Glenn didn't kill Anna Clark, as he told the reporter and Robin."

Vigo nodded.

"I've been looking at the case files," Will said. "If there's another killer out there, I want to find him. But honestly, I think this is one of his tricks. It was never released to the media that Glenn used bleach on his victims. That didn't come out until the actual trial."

"You understand if Glenn is telling the truth, then whoever killed Anna had inside knowledge of the investigation."

"I know," Will said, shifting uncomfortably.

*If Glenn is in fact innocent of Anna's murder, someone I know — possibly someone I trust — killed her.*

"But why?"

"That," Vigo said quietly, "I haven't figured out yet. I'd like to talk to Robin McKenna and everyone else involved in Glenn's prosecution."

"Fine," Will said, "as long as I can ride along with you."

"I insist, Detective. In fact, you're the only

one I'm confident didn't kill Anna Clark."

## EIGHTEEN

Robin spent Wednesday morning at the gun range, then went to the club. She nodded to Mario Medina's man who was monitoring the entrance. She didn't remember his name, but he was bigger than her largest bouncer and if she could afford him, she'd have hired him in a heartbeat. Just one look, and anyone with a nefarious intention would run away. Fast.

"Where's your partner?" she asked, knowing Mario had two men on the club at all times.

"Around," the hulking man said.

That would have to be good enough.

Having the added security made her feel better. Proactive. Not a victim any longer, but the strong, independent woman everyone thought she was.

She went back to her office to focus on work, but after kissing Will the night before, she couldn't get him — or the day she left him — out of her mind.

*It was the day after she found Anna dead. The club was closed, she couldn't get into her apartment — not that she wanted to ever go back after what happened to Anna inside. She*

266

had nowhere to go. No one to talk to. Will was her lifeline, her strength.

He brought her to his town house on the beach after she gave a statement to the police. Though she had washed in the police bathroom, she hadn't showered. She still felt Anna's blood all over her, even if she couldn't see it. Like she'd never rid the smell from her nose, the taste from her mouth, the slippery feeling from her hands.

"Shower," he told her.

"Don't leave me," she begged, feeling pathetic and needy. And fearful. She didn't like being scared.

He caressed her hair. "Never. If I could take away what you saw I would. I wish I could change everything. I'm so sorry about what happened." He kissed her lips. So light. Loving.

"Come with me," she said to him.

He hesitated. Just a fraction and she felt like a stupid, clinging woman. "I know you have work to do. I'll be fine."

"No, it's not that. I just — are you sure?"

She nodded.

He took the ill-fitting clothes off her body. She'd had to give up her own clothing as evidence. Because she had fallen into Anna's blood. Blood coating her body. Her hands. Her face. She hadn't known what she had fallen on, not until she scrambled up and turned on the lights.

Then she saw . . .

She began to cry. "No, Robin, please don't cry." Will brushed away the tears with his palms, then took off his own clothes, and helped her into his shower. She sobbed and he scrubbed her body. "Harder," she said. "Her blood is all over me."

"It's gone."

"Please."

Will scrubbed until her skin was raw and the water painful. He washed her hair three times, used his soap on her body. She now smelled like him, and that gave her some peace. To be wrapped up in Will Hooper, she could live with that. She'd been thinking a lot about what they had and what they didn't have. Will knew she was a stripper. He still showed her more care and compassion than any man in her life. There was something there, something more than there had ever been in her life.

They went to bed. Slow and passionate, two people brought together by tragedy forging something beautiful out of the evil surrounding them. And she slept, awaking only when she didn't feel Will's arms around her.

"Where are you going?"

"I have to go in. The lab found evidence that links Anna to Theodore Glenn. The D.A. is already working on the warrant, and I need to be there to haul him in."

She sat up, pulling Will's sheet around her naked body. "Take me with you."

"You know I can't."

"I can't help but think I could have done something to save her." No tears came, she was drained.

"You didn't know."

"Didn't know what?"

Will slipped on his slacks. "That Anna had sex with Glenn. She wasn't on the target list we put together after Brandi was killed. He must have been watching her, knew she'd returned from Big Bear early."

She blinked, watching Will button up his shirt. "Anna didn't have a relationship with him."

"Why would he change his M.O.?" Will shook his head. "I interrogated that bastard. I know his game. He thinks it's part of the fun to kill women he had sex with. Sort of a reverse obsession. Usually rejection prompts a man of Glenn's ego to act, the stressor to get him into a killing frame of mind. But with him, he gets the thrill of killing those who trust him. It's not just about the victim. It's about who finds the victim. He wanted you to find Anna."

She shook her head. "No. Anna never had

sex with him."

"How can you be so sure?"

"I am."

"How?"

"Anna is a lesbian, okay?" she said, angry. "She was raped by her own father when she turned thirteen. That was her birthday present. He sexually abused her for two years before she ran away. Then the police brought her home and because she was too scared to talk about what her father did to her, she went through the same thing for six more months."

"I'm sorry." Will's voice showed he did care about the girl Anna had been, the trauma she had suffered. It was one of the many reasons Robin had fallen in love with Will. His compassion was boundless, but didn't border on pity.

"Anna ran away again, smarter this time, lied about her age, got a fake ID, and started working at RJ's. I knew she was underage when he hired her, but RJ wouldn't listen to me. He didn't care about that, as long as he could justify his ignorance if he was ever caught." She closed her eyes. "Anna was so scared. But she put herself out there. She told me once that stripping gave her power over men that she'd never had before with her father. One of the other girls was a lesbian; she befriended Anna, and Anna told me when she moved into my apartment that she was gay and asked if that bothered me. I said it didn't."

"Maybe she was bisexual. She was young, maybe —"

"She wasn't."

Will stared at her. "Are you sure?"

"I am. She had the same reaction to Theodore Glenn as I did when I first met him. She wouldn't have slept with any man, and she certainly wouldn't have slept with him."

Robin watched the expression on Will's face harden. What was he thinking? "What? Does this mean something important?"

"Robin, I want the truth. Did you ever sleep with Theodore Glenn?"

She felt sucker-punched. "I told you I didn't. You know how I feel about him."

"Maybe it was a long time ago. Maybe you were in denial that he was targeting his former lovers. Maybe he expected you to be home, not Anna. Everyone knew she was going to Big Bear. And when she opened the door, he panicked, killed her instead."

"I never had sex with him."

Will stared at her and his eyes told her he didn't believe her.

She rose from the bed, her nudity embarrassing her for the first time in her life. She'd given her heart to Will Hooper and he'd shredded it.

271

*"You can see why I'm finding it hard to believe you," he said quietly.*

*She pulled on the jeans that were too big and the top that was too small. Tears burned behind her eyes, but she would not cry in front of this man. Never again.*

*"Because I'm a stripper?"*

*"No, because of the M.O. He wouldn't —"*

*"Fuck you, Will Hooper."*

*She ran out of his town house.*

"Ms. McKenna?" A deep, male voice came over her intercom. The security guard.

"Yes?" she said.

"There's a Trinity Lange here to see you. She doesn't have an appointment."

Robin frowned. She didn't like talking to reporters, but Trinity Lange had been fair during the trial. Unlike the print media, she hadn't harped on the fact that the victims were strippers, and seemed to honestly believe they deserved justice just as much as any other victim.

But why did the reporter want to see her? She was wary, especially now. "What does she want?"

A moment later, the voice said, "She says it's completely off-the-record."

Off-the-record. She didn't know if she could trust Trinity, but Robin was curious. "All right, bring her back. Thank you."

272

Robin shut her emotions in her office and met Trinity at the Back Room bar. Trinity smiled and thanked the bodyguard. "You have the most *gorgeous* staff," she said.

"We want our customers to enjoy all five senses."

"Thanks for agreeing to talk to me."

"I haven't yet."

Trinity opened then closed her mouth and nodded. "I guess I deserved that."

"You don't deserve anything, good or bad. You were the only major reporter who didn't talk about my friends like they were hookers. That kindness bought you this time. But I do not talk to the press, and I will not be quoted."

Trinity took a deep breath. "Theodore Glenn paid me a visit the other night."

Robin sat down before she fell over. Will hadn't told her. "What happened?"

"He broke into my apartment and tied me to my bed. I was scared out of my mind."

"Rightfully. He's a killer. You sat through the trial. You know what he did to my friends."

Trinity nodded. "He admitted to me that he killed Bethany, Brandi, and Jessica."

Robin blinked. Her world tilted and everything seemed brighter. "And Anna?"

Trinity shook her head. "He said he didn't

kill Anna Clark. He was emphatic about it."

"Don't believe him." Her voice was low, quivering. She swallowed bile.

"Normally I wouldn't, but . . ."

Robin stared at the reporter. "I don't believe you're not doing a story on this."

"Not on you. Not on the victims. But put yourself in my shoes. A convicted murderer admits to you that he's killed three women, but not the fourth? How does it benefit him?"

"It gets him press. Gives him a platform. Buys him time to do whatever it is he's planning on doing!"

"But —"

"And you're buying it?" Robin fumed. "I never pegged you for a stupid woman, Trinity."

The reporter bristled. "I'm not being stupid, Robin. I know what I'm doing."

"Do you?"

"I think he's after Will Hooper."

"I'll alert the media," Robin said sarcastically, a pang of fear in her chest. She didn't want Will dead. "That's no big revelation. He killed Detective Sturgeon, the other cop who arrested him. It makes sense that he'll go after Will, too."

"It's personal with him."

"Isn't murder always personal?"

"Why are you asking me the questions?"

"Why are you buying Theodore Glenn's act? I knew the man. He's the biggest manipulator on the planet. He thrives on these twisted games."

"He knew about you and Will," Trinity said quietly.

*He saw us. Watched us, that night in the bar.*

Will's words from last night came back to her.

He'd told her Glenn had watched them, but she hadn't asked how he'd come by that information. Now it made sense; a sick, twisted, obscene sense.

Robin said, "You told Will about this?"

Trinity nodded.

"Who else?"

"No one."

"Really?" She stood to pour herself a shot of her favorite Reposado tequila and slammed it back; the smooth, flavorful liquor coating her senses.

"I told Will in private," Trinity said. "I didn't put it into the official record. I probably made a big mistake, but I like Will. I don't want him to be hurt by this."

"What does he want?"

"Will?"

"Glenn."

"He wants to find out who killed Anna Clark," Trinity said.

Robin slammed her fist on the counter. *"He killed Anna!"* she shouted.

She turned, head down, and put her hands on her knees. Took deep breaths. What was going on with her? Theodore Glenn was succeeding in breaking her. God, what if he really was after Will to hurt her? Why? Because she refused his advances? Because she never played his little games at RJ's? Because she *knew* exactly who and what he was and steered clear of him?

*You never thought he would kill.*

Not until it happened, then she couldn't imagine how she hadn't seen it sooner. Found a way to stop him.

"I think he wanted you," Trinity said quietly. "He said something to me that only makes sense now that I know he wasn't lying about you and Will Hooper."

She stared at Trinity, lips drawn tight.

"I didn't tell Will. I meant to, but after I told him about Glenn watching you and Will being intimate, Will got all weirded out."

"What didn't you tell him?"

"You were supposed to be next, but you refused to go out with him. And he was furious."

The words sunk in. Robin sat down heavily on a bar stool, unable to stand.

"I think Glenn got jealous," Trinity said quietly.

"Jealous?"

"Of Will. That you chose Will over him. And he wants to make someone pay for it. You? Will? I don't know, to be honest, I'm not a shrink. But he's obsessing over both of you, I saw that when he talked to me. I need your help, Robin."

"My help? What can I do? Believe me, I will shoot Theodore Glenn before I talk to him."

"I don't think he killed Anna Clark."

Robin pleaded with Trinity. "Don't believe a word he says! He's a killer. You can't listen to him."

"I've been going over the court transcripts and all the evidence. Anna doesn't fit the profile. She never had a relationship with Glenn."

"Serial killers change M.O. all the time," Robin said. She'd read too much about serial killers in the last few years; trying to understand why Anna died and she didn't, why Theodore Glenn wanted to kill her friends in the first place. Nothing made sense to her, maybe because she couldn't think like a killer.

"In your testimony, you said that Anna was supposed to be in Big Bear visiting her mother."

"Yes."

"And you thought she'd be gone for a week."

"Yes."

"But she came back after only two days. Why was she back in the apartment that night? Why didn't you know?"

Robin had wondered the same thing for a long, long time.

"I don't know why she didn't call me, but Anna didn't like being alone. Since her mother was late, she might have decided to just come home and drive back at the end of the week. They had a complex relationship, I didn't really understand it at the time."

"But you stated that everyone at RJ's thought Anna would be gone all week, right? It was no secret."

"I don't understand what you're saying."

"Anna was not the intended victim."

Robin stared at the reporter.

"I think you were. And I don't think it was Theodore Glenn who wanted you dead. I believed him when he told me he didn't kill Anna. What other enemies did you have, Robin? Who else would want you dead?"

# NINETEEN

Their meeting with the Fed had just broken up when Will's cell phone rang. He was at first surprised to see Robin's business number on his cell phone, then worried that something might have happened.

"Hooper."

"Why didn't you tell me that Theodore attacked a reporter?" Robin demanded.

"Trinity? I —"

She interrupted. "You didn't tell me Glenn told Trinity about our relationship! Or that he's telling everyone he didn't kill Anna. I can't believe you'd keep that from me!"

"Robin, calm down. I'll come over and we can talk about this —"

"What's there to talk about? You don't *believe* him, do you?"

Will swallowed. He wasn't certain what he believed, but he had to look at the facts and right now, Glenn just didn't look good for Anna's murder. Will wasn't ready to declare him innocent of that death, but Causey had okayed him to quietly look into the case with Agent Vigo. Vigo was willing to take the heat if something went south on the case — including putting himself up to the media as the whipping boy — which placed him way up there on the good guy list for Will.

"You do. You believe him. How could you, Will?"

"We need to talk, Robin —"

She hung up.

Hans Vigo approached. "Everything okay?"

"That was Robin McKenna. She's not ready to accept that Glenn might not have killed her roommate. Shit, why did Trinity go talk to her in the first place?"

"She's searching for answers. Maybe she thinks Robin knows something important."

"She doesn't. She's been traumatized enough."

"We're going to need to talk to Robin later. She might know something she doesn't realize is important. If Glenn is truly not guilty of killing Anna Clark, we have a lot of work to do."

"On the QT," Will added.

"Absolutely." Vigo paused. "What do you know about Jim Gage?"

"You don't think —"

"If Glenn isn't guilty, we need to look at people who have the access and knowledge of evidence collection —"

"I vouch for Jim. He dated my partner for three years. I just can't see him as being capable of murder — he's one of the most even-tempered people I know."

"We'll probably need to bring him in on this, but he can't talk about it with anyone else. And you need to have a talk with that reporter," Vigo added. "If she keeps flapping her mouth, she could be putting herself in the middle of a train wreck."

"No argument there," Will concurred. "But don't discount that Glenn could just be playing with us."

"I haven't. But I don't see what benefit he gets from it. You're going to have to accept the fact that someone else might have killed Anna Clark, and the only person who would have known each detail of the crime would have been someone who worked at least one of the previous three crime scenes."

Sara made Theodore breakfast. It was the best meal he'd had since being sent to San Quentin. She both looked and cooked better than the unappealing Jenny. He could get used to this.

He wondered if he could get Sara to dye her blonde hair red. Dark red.

"I'm going to lay low for the next day or so," he told her.

"When are we leaving?"

"Why?"

"I just want to know. I have to pack —"

"I'll tell you when you need to know. Right now we need my money."

"It's all taken care of."

"Passports?"

She nodded. "They're in a safe-deposit box along with the foreign account numbers you gave me."

"Get the passports and account information. You have a computer, correct?"

"Yes, in the den downstairs."

"While you're doing that, I'll start moving some money around and hide the trail. By the time the cops figure it out, we'll be in South America."

"But what if they find you down there?"

He bit back the urge to yell at her. Stupid woman. With forced calmness, he said, "Money buys a lot of freedom. I will take care of it."

"Of course."

"After you get the passports and account numbers, bring them to me, then I have another job for you. It's important. I want you to deliver a letter. You can't allow yourself to be captured on any security camera. Can you do that?"

She nodded without hesitation. "When and where?"

He stood, grinning, the anger at her earlier

foolish question gone.

"Come here."

She walked right into his arms.

He hadn't decided whether to kill Sara or not. He had no compelling urge to slit her throat. If he killed her, it would simply be a means to an end. But he might let her live. He could read in the papers about her plight once the cops caught her aiding and abetting a convict. Might help pass the time while he traveled throughout South America, living comfortably on his wealth.

He most certainly wouldn't take her with him, an albatross around his neck.

Theodore kissed her, hard, his hands on her breasts. He closed his eyes and pictured Robin with him. The smell of breakfast reminded him of the first time he saw Robin McKenna with William Hooper. In Hooper's kitchen. His fist clenched, his breathing quickened.

Sara gasped beneath him, but he didn't pay her any attention. It wasn't Sara, it should never have been Sara here.

He pushed her onto the table, in the same position Robin had been in all those years ago. He took the role of her lover, and did exactly what William had done.

*He watched from the beach, his binoculars trained on the open window. They were all*

*over each other, their clothes only half re-
moved but neither noticed. Robin pulled the
cop down on top of her, falling back onto the
table, a glass crashing to the floor.*

Theodore knocked his coffee mug off the
table, the ceramic shattering.

*The cop went down on Robin, his mouth on
her cunt, and she arched her back, her long
hair spilling over the edge of the table.*

Theodore lifted Sara's dress, covering her
face. He didn't want to look at her, couldn't
look at her. It was Robin here for him,
Robin who arched her back and begged him
to send her over the edge.

*Robin pulled him back up and guided him
into her. Hard, fast, frantic. The table moved
beneath them with each thrust.*

Theodore guided the woman's hands to
his throbbing cock. She figured it out and
pushed him in.

*"Teddy!" Robin cried out.*

He shook his head, looked down at the
table. The dress had shifted and Robin's
face morphed into Sara's. He closed his
eyes, opened them, remembered where he
was and who he was with. He withered
inside.

"Oh, Teddy, I love you." She climaxed
around his limp dick.

He wanted to kill her. She'd destroyed his

fantasy. He was antsy and unsatisfied.

He pushed off of her and walked to the doorway.

"Go do your job. And next time, keep your mouth shut while I fuck you."

## TWENTY

Robin went back to the gun range that afternoon. Hank was surprised, but didn't say anything. Good. She didn't want to have to explain. Not now.

*Who else would want you dead?*

Who?

She fired her entire clip into the target. One large hole filled the paper silhouette. In the chest.

"Let me show you something."

Mario Medina came up behind her. He held his hand out for her gun, which she handed to him, grip first. He reloaded it and said, "You're a good shot, Robin. But there's a rule of three."

He set up another paper target.

"See, every shot will jerk the gun up almost imperceptibly. Use the natural momentum to your advantage. Your shots are good, but you assume an unmoving target. Aim low and let the momentum of the gun work with you, keeping your eye on the target's eyes so you know which way he's going to move."

He fired three shots in succession. They hit in the groin, chest, and center of the head.

"My way he's still dead."

Mario grunted his agreement. "But you used up all your ammo. This is a fifteen-round clip. You can guarantee five kills."

"I only need one."

"Point taken." He handed her back her gun, butt first. "You left the club."

"Obviously."

"Do you have a death wish?"

"What's that supposed to mean?"

"You left the club without letting me know."

She just stared at him, her jaw tight, feeling like a child.

"If you have a death wish, that means my men are in danger. I won't have that."

"I don't have a death wish. Why do you think I'm here, practicing? Why do you think I have a concealed carry permit? Why do you think I can't sleep —" she stopped. "Why are you here?"

"Because you are being stupid, and I don't like to protect stupid people. I'm going to keep my eye on you."

"I hired you to keep your eye on my employees."

"I have enough men to handle the club."

Mario took a step closer and said in a low voice, "What I won't tolerate is you slipping out without a word. A call to your assistant that you're heading to the gun range is insufficient."

She was shaking and hoped Mario couldn't see. "Okay."

"So we have an understanding?"

She nodded. "It was stupid of me to leave alone. I get that. I'm done here." She emptied her weapon for the rangemaster to check. "I have work to do, anyway. I'll follow your rules, Mario. That's fair. But you don't have to be with me 24/7. I'll call when I'm leaving the loft or the club and wait for you. But I value my privacy." *I need it.*

"What is your life worth?"

Robin turned away. "That's not the point."

Mario forced her to look at him. "Humor me. I'm discreet."

"Why are you doing this?"

Mario grinned. "Everyone is entitled to secrets."

"That's not good enough, Mario."

He looked at her, his lips pulling into a tight line. "It'll have to be."

Will and Carina split the list of six women

with two other detectives. They started with Jane Plummer, the twenty-nine-year-old bank teller who had received probation for two drug offenses nearly ten years ago. She worked within walking distance from her downtown apartment. "Maybe that's how Glenn plans on getting his money," Carina commented.

"I think he already has it," Will said. "But having someone inside a bank would be a benefit to him, perhaps to cover up a money trail? I hope the Feds can track it down, they have far more resources on that end than we do."

"If Patrick were around, he'd be able to find the link," Carina said sadly.

Will nodded, squeezed her arm. After eight months, Will thought Patrick's coma would have been easier for the Kincaid family to deal with. Instead, it put them in a sort of emotional limbo. But Carina was right; Patrick would have been all over Glenn's financials. Though the SDPD had other good e-crimes cops, Patrick had been the best.

Jane was just leaving for her lunch break when Will and Carina walked into the bank. "Ms. Plummer," he said, showing his badge. "We'd like a minute of your time."

She frowned. Jane was a large girl with

stringy brown hair pulled back into a limp ponytail. Her skin was smooth and blemish free, but her three chins detracted from her pretty face. A simple gold cross necklace was her only jewelry. "Why?"

"We just have a couple questions."

They had already attracted attention from the other bank tellers, and the manager was stepping out from his office. Will smiled at Jane, put a hand on her shoulder. "Why don't we go for coffee? There's a Starbucks on the corner."

She nodded, flustered. "Sure." She went with them.

Will sprang for three coffees and they found a table outside, out of earshot from the other customers. "Jane, we have the letters you wrote to Theodore Glenn at San Quentin State Prison."

She frowned. "Is that a crime? Are you going to arrest me?"

"No, it's not a crime to write to convicted murderers. Did you know that he escaped from prison?"

"I watch the news."

"Has he tried to contact you since Saturday night?"

She shook her head, looking confused. "We haven't been pen pals in a long time."

*Pen pals.* Will kept the disdain off his face.

"Do you have many pen pals at San Quentin?"

"A few. I wrote to Scott Peterson. And Cary Stayner. And Erik Menendez, in Coalinga. They all wrote back. I write letters every month. Some people never talk to them after they go to prison. I feel sorry for them."

Will sent a warning glance at Carina, who looked like she wanted to shake sense into the girl. He put on his best game face and asked, "And when was the last time you heard from Theodore?"

"A year ago. He wrote me a lovely letter. He has beautiful penmanship, you know. He said he was preparing for his appeal and that he didn't have time to write anymore, but asked me to keep him in my thoughts and prayers."

"And he hasn't tried to contact you?"

"I'm not lying, Detective."

"I didn't say that you were, Jane. Did Theodore Glenn ask you to do anything illegal? Perhaps in the bank?"

"Absolutely not! Why are you talking to me? Is it because I was arrested for drugs years and years ago? I'm clean, you know. I haven't touched drugs since I found the Lord."

"Did Glenn discuss his crimes with you?

Did he —"

"I know what you think he did," Jane interrupted. "And maybe he is guilty. But he deserves forgiveness just as much as anyone else. It's not our place to decide who lives and who dies. Judgment is reserved for God alone."

Will's jaw tightened. "Jane, your pen pal has already killed three people since he escaped. A prison guard, his own sister, and a retired police detective. Glenn has no conscience, and he will continue to kill until he is stopped."

Jane sighed. "That's the problem with you people. All you see is the bad in others. Don't you think it's possible for someone to try to make amends for their sins?"

"Absolutely," Will said. "Starting with giving their life for those they stole."

"I haven't seen or talked to Theodore," Jane snapped. "Can I go now?"

"If you see him — if he contacts you in any way — call me." Will handed her his card as he stood.

As he and Carina walked to their car, she said, "You told me to go easy on her, then you jumped down her throat. Since when do you lose your temper with a potential witness? I thought I always got to play bad cop." She was trying to make light of Will's reaction, but he was still angry.

"I just couldn't take it, Carina. I'm all for forgiveness, but killers like Theodore Glenn don't deserve to keep their life. It's the only thing he values and dammit, I hope to be there when they fry him."

"They stopped using the electric chair years ago," Carina reminded him. "Cruel and unusual punishment."

They drove ten minutes to a quiet community outside of downtown. The next name on the list was Sara Lorenz. Her well-maintained house was in a middle-class neighborhood.

Carina looked at her notes. "Sara Lorenz, thirty, bought the house five years ago. Nothing on her. No record, not even a parking ticket. She has a late-model Honda Civic registered to her name at this address."

"Doesn't look like anyone's home," Will said as they walked up the brick pathway.

They knocked, heard a small dog barking, but no one came to the door. Walking around the house they peered into the single-car garage; no vehicle.

"Where does she work?"

"The Feds didn't have that information. It just says 'pending.' " Will called Agent Hans Vigo on his cell phone. Voice mail picked up. "It's Will Hooper. We're at Sara Lorenz's last known address. No one's here, and there's no place of employment. Can you look into that for us?" When he hung up, he asked Carina, "Who's next on the list?"

"Dora Halverson. Lemon Grove. Time for a drive."

Dora Halverson was a fifty-nine-year-old grandmother of seven whose primary hobby was collecting signatures from famous people — actors, politicians, killers.

"That was a waste of time," Will mumbled as they drove back to San Diego. "Swing back by Sara Lorenz's house. Maybe she's home."

Traffic was miserable, and it was after six when they pulled up in front of the Lorenz house. A ten-year-old Toyota was parked in the driveway. "All right," said Carina. "Let's put this wild-goose chase to rest and get back to real police work."

"You're in a foul mood," Will said. "Besides, Lorenz drives a Civic."

"I've been a cop for twelve years, a homicide detective for the last two, and never before have I confronted so many women with such a sick fascination with homicidal maniacs."

"Grandma Halverson sure seemed pleased with her collection," Will said, ribbing Carina. "Manson, Bundy, Schwarzenegger —"

"You're not helping."

They walked up the pathway and Will knocked on the door, then stepped back. The dog barked. It was a little dog, one that his former partner Frank used to call a dust mop.

The woman who opened the door was forty, trim, and wearing a business suit, minus shoes. She bent down to pick up the little yapper — a black-and-white long-haired something.

"Can I help you?"

Will identified himself and Carina. "Are you Sara Lorenz?"

She shook her head. "Stephanie Barr. Sara owns the house."

"Is she here?"

"No."

"You're a friend?"

"No. Not really. I'm her tenant."

"How long have you been renting from Ms. Lorenz?"

"A little over a year."

"Do you have a way to contact her?"

Ms. Barr frowned, looked from Carina to Will. "What's this about?"

"I'm sorry, I can't tell you that, but she's

not in any trouble. We just want to talk to her about someone she used to know."

The tenant looked skeptical. "Just a minute," she said and closed the door.

"Not very cooperative," Carina said. "Why don't the records have this house listed as a rental? If Sara Lorenz was living elsewhere, there should be another house with her name on it."

"Unless she's renting."

"Why would she rent when she owns a house?"

"Maybe she moved out of the area," Will suggested. "The Feds only pulled local records, and there's no statewide database of property records."

The door opened and Ms. Barr pushed open the screen far enough to slide over a card. "This is the address I send rent checks to, and the number she gave me for emergencies."

The address was a P.O. box in downtown San Diego, the phone number a 619 area code. Also San Diego. Will recognized the prefix as a cellular carrier.

"Thank you, Ms. Barr," Carina said.

"Do you know what she does for a living?" Will asked.

Ms. Barr shook her head. "I never asked. Sorry."

"How did you learn about the rental in the first place?"

"An ad in the *Tribune,* nearly a year ago."

"Thank you for your time."

In the car, Will said, "So Sara Lorenz wrote to Theodore Glenn using an address of a house she no longer lived in. Why?"

"I hope Diaz and White had better luck with their three," Carina mumbled.

Will dialed Sara Lorenz's phone number from the car while Carina drove back to the station. "Voice mail," he said, then right as he was about to speak, he hung up.

"What?" Carina asked.

"I don't know. A feeling. Let's try to find a physical address for Ms. Lorenz. We may be able to get one off the number."

"Unless it's a pay-as-you-go plan," Carina said.

"Maybe she used a credit card. We need a break somewhere. And if she didn't use a credit card, why? Why would she need a cash phone?"

"Got me there."

"If she's the one Glenn's using," Will said, "I don't want to give her a warning that we're coming. Let's get this info to the Feds, see what Diaz learned, and regroup. No sign of Glenn for thirty-six hours. I'm getting antsy. He probably is, too."

"So who's next?"

"I wish I knew, but I'm sure as hell glad Julia Chandler is out of town. No doubt she'd be high up on Mr. Charming's list."

Theodore Glenn had parked down the hill from Julia Chandler's pricey house on a cliff near the coast and walked, keeping to the shadows. He didn't see a patrol car, nor any added security.

Something wasn't right.

He approached her house from the back. The sun was setting, but the beauty of the moment was lost on him. No lights were on inside, the only illumination a porch light.

When he was confident no one was patrolling the grounds, he approached the house casually, in case anyone was watching. From a distance, his disguise would work, but close up D.D.A. Chandler would ID him.

The gun fit comfortably in his hand.

He walked up the porch steps, then around the outside of the house, looking in windows that were only partially draped. The blink of an alarm panel caught him off guard, but he watched it closely and it didn't appear to change. Probably the doors and windows were wired.

It quickly became evident that no one was home. Had she run, scared he would come to kill her?

Smart woman, that was exactly what he'd planned to do. But *why* he wanted to kill her was completely different than she might think. As if her doing her job would have ranked her high on his list.

Sherry deserved to die because she betrayed him in court. The cop deserved to die because he was a fool, and Theodore despised fools. Theodore would have killed the judge who allowed Robin's testimony to stand, except that he was already dead. Heart attack, he'd read in the online newspaper archives.

Theodore had considered blowing up the crime lab where those idiots who had gathered evidence *claimed* they had found his DNA on Anna's body. They very well may have, but someone had planted it, and if they were so stupid not to see that, then they too deserved to die. Especially that arrogant director Jim Gage.

Blowing up the crime lab meant getting too close to the police department, since the buildings were attached. Glenn wasn't confident he'd be able to pull it off, but he was thinking about it. He would most certainly be able to make the bomb, it was access he questioned.

William Hooper would die. For arresting

him. For looking at him as if he were dog shit on his new Nikes. For screwing Robin.

And Robin let him. Robin had let that asshole cop touch her perfect body. Intimately. She stripped for him, came for him, let him fuck her.

The box in Theodore's hand crunched and he looked down, blinking at the depth of his rage. He didn't have emotions like this. He was always in control of them, because they were so few, so rare. But Robin brought them out, Robin brought out this passionate, allconsuming need to just *see her.*

He'd been thinking a lot about how to punish Robin for hating him. For testifying against him, for not liking him, for not letting him touch her. She was a fucking stripper! Yet she looked down her nose at *him!*

William and Robin may no longer be screwing each other, but there was still something there. Theodore read people very well. In the courtroom, William had definitely been protective of her. And he was a cop, someone who took pride in his job to "protect and serve." Honorable. Dutiful.

William, William, William . . . Shakespeare.

Theodore smiled. *Romeo and Juliet.* Starcrossed lovers. Romeo believed Juliet was dead and killed himself. Juliet awoke, saw Romeo dead, then stabbed herself.

If William thought Robin was dead, he would act irrationally. Perhaps recklessly.

Or maybe if Robin thought William were dead, or injured, Theodore could more easily get to her.

Oh, the possibilities! It made his present to William all that much more sweet.

Theodore kicked Julia Chandler's door. He'd planned on shooting her and leaving the box on her body, but this would have to suffice. Her life didn't hold much allure for him, she had never personally slighted him.

The alarm panel started blinking rapidly. A phone rang.

Someone would be here soon.

Theodore put the box on the kitchen table, then left, jogging down the winding hill, sticking to the ravine, watchful of cars on the road. He was nearly to his car when he heard sirens.

He stayed hidden until the police car passed, then sprinted the last two hundred yards and left the scene, the adrenaline rush making him smile.

He slammed his hand on the steering wheel and bounced in the driver's seat, grinning, forcing himself to keep to the speed limit.

300

He wished he could see the look on William Hooper's face when he saw the contents of that box.

## TWENTY-ONE

Will and Carina arrived at Julia Chandler's house less than twenty minutes after the first officers arrived on scene. Will was walking up the porch steps when Agent Hans Vigo drove up. Impatiently, he waited for the Fed to catch up with them.

As soon as he'd heard there was a box inside with his name on it, Will knew Theodore Glenn had broken into Julia's house.

"Did you say that the D.D.A. left town?" Hans asked Will.

"Her boyfriend, an ex-cop, took her and her niece somewhere," Will said.

"Montana," Carina said. "My fiancé owns property in Bozeman and they left yesterday morning." She looked a little unnerved, and Will didn't blame her. Julia was her future sister-in-law, and her brother Connor could easily have been here when Glenn showed up. The thought gave her chills. Glenn would have no qualms about killing "innocent" people — those innocent to his twisted mind — to make his point.

"The box is on the kitchen table," the

responding officer said. "Chief Causey said no one could touch it until the bomb squad checked it out. They're in there now."

"Bomb? Doesn't seem like Glenn's style," Will said.

"I agree," Hans concurred, "unless it was a bigger target, something that would cause mass devastation. Where he'd get a thrill out of being bold. By the way, we found Jenny Olsen's Acura, abandoned, at the San Diego Public Library downtown. It had been left in the lot overnight and the security guard called for it to be towed. The impound lot ran the tags. Olsen admitted she let Glenn borrow the car."

Will glanced at his watch. "If we leave now, we can make it to Anaheim by midnight."

"I talked to Chief Causey and he agreed to allow an agent from the FBI's Orange County field office interview her. Personally, I think he used her and left with her car — one that we wouldn't be alerted to. And he dumped it when he picked up a safer ride."

"He wouldn't have told her anything important," Will said. "He doesn't trust women, and he's too smart to trust a woman who struck up a letter-writing campaign with him in prison." He frowned. "Unless

302

there was something the woman could do for him, something he couldn't do himself . . . Any word on Sara Lorenz? Where she works?"

Hans shook his head. "Between our two offices something is bound to break sooner rather than later. But she's definitely a red flag. She's the only one of the nineteen women in San Diego County we haven't made contact with."

"Did you get the phone number I left on your voice mail earlier?"

"Cash phone, pay-as-you-go. We did learn it was bought at Wal-Mart, and the merchandising manager is looking at which specific store it was purchased at, though I don't think that's going to do us any good."

"Why?"

"It was bought eighteen months ago."

"Where does she refill it?"

"She doesn't."

"If she uses it she'd have to put minutes on it."

"She bought one thousand minutes. Only four hundred and seventeen have been used."

"And the phone numbers?"

"Impossible to trace. There are no records kept."

"All clear," the bomb squad reported,

coming out to the porch. "We opened the box, but didn't touch anything inside."

"Thanks, guys," Will said, striding into the house.

He stared at the box, his heart rising in his throat.

It was a small, generic pink donut box. Inside was a bird. A robin.

Dead.

"Interesting," Hans said.

Will spun around. "*Interesting?* This is a threat against Robin McKenna."

"What I find interesting is that he came up here to deliver it. And he didn't seem to be overly irritated that Ms. Chandler wasn't around. But even more interesting is that I doubt it was easy to find a robin in February. A simple examination should determine if the bird has been frozen."

That sunk in. "Which means someone kept a dead robin for him since last spring?"

Carina frowned. "What I don't get is how could he have planned all this? Like Will and I talked about before, he couldn't have planned for the earthquake. And even if he planned an escape during his next appeal, there was no guarantee he'd be successful."

Vigo nodded. "I think it's Glenn's way of making his time in prison bearable. San Quentin is filled with men of low to average intelligence. Someone with Glenn's IQ and background would have a difficult time of it, at least mentally. And even though loss of freedom is a huge problem in the psyche of the average prisoner, for someone like Glenn it would be devastating. He fixated on Robin to keep his mind focused. While he may have had an obsession with her before, it intensified while he was away."

Will's gut twisted. "Then why hasn't he just gone after her?"

"Because he's shrewd. He knows you have cops on her house and business. He may even suspect that she would hire a bodyguard. He's going to wait until he's confident he can get to her. He doesn't want to go back to prison, but I think that his ego would demand that he take her out even if that means he dies, too."

"He has nothing to lose." Will realized for the first time. "He's having fun with this."

"That he is," Hans agreed.

"There's a letter here," Carina reminded him. "Addressed to you, Will."

Will put on gloves and picked up the #10 white envelope.

WILLIAM

Will carefully opened the envelope and

305

unfolded the single sheet of paper.

It began: *William:*

The first two sentences had been crossed out. They were: *I'm truly sorry I had to kill Julia Chandler. She really was just a puppet of the prosecution, hardly more to blame than an enlisted soldier during war.*

After scratching them out, Theodore had scrawled on the side: *You win this one. Julia is a smart woman, I hope she's enjoying her vacation. I'm sure her door can be fixed.*

The letter continued. He'd obviously written it before he arrived at Julia's house.

Julia Chandler was never the problem. It was the asshole she worked for. I will admit I enjoyed seeing Bryce Descario skewered in the media during his failed reelection. But public embarrassment isn't quite the same thing as death, is it?

I am tiring of the game, William. I may leave for a while. Or not. Does that scare you? I doubt it. You don't scare easily. The only time you were really scared was when you thought Robin was dead. Those were the days.

Do you really think that the bodyguard, the police, you, or Robin's pathetic attempt to protect herself with a gun will keep me from her? Lock her up

306

tight. You can't keep her from me forever.

Sooner or later I will kill her. And I promise you, William, it will hurt.

Maybe I'll even let you watch.

Carina carefully extracted the paper from his hands as Will's fists clenched, wrinkling the evidence. "He's doing this to get to you."

"He got to me, dammit." He breathed deeply. It would do Robin no good if he lost his focus. The anger was still there, but contained.

"Descario," he said.

"What about him?" Carina asked.

"Chief Causey called him after Glenn's escape, then again after he made that big spectacle in front of the press. He's retired, but still has a confidential address."

"Glenn couldn't get it."

"He shouldn't have been able to get Julia's, either, but he did. And how did he find Frank Sturgeon? What about Trinity Lange?"

"Followed her," Carina guessed.

"That's the only thing that makes sense." Will glanced at Hans. "Theodore Glenn is making all of us look like fools."

"I think he has an accomplice," Hans said. "Someone who is helping him. Someone nondescript or nonthreatening."

Will had a patrol watching Ms. Plummer. Some of her answers had bothered him. "He must be using a woman like Jane Plummer or the elusive Sara Lorenz."

"Exactly."

Will called the crime scene techs and ordered the uniforms to stand guard until someone from Gage's staff arrived to process the scene.

"We need to talk to Descario, make sure he's covered," Will said as he, Carina, and Hans left. "Want to ride with us?" he asked the Fed.

"Thanks."

Hans got in the back and Will made a call to Mario.

"Medina Security."

"Mario, it's Will Hooper."

"Whatcha need?"

"Is she okay?"

"Locked up tight. I'm right outside her door. No other way in or out, except the fire escape, and I checked it top and bottom. No way for it to be lowered except from her loft, and it's secured. What happened?"

Will told him about the dead robin at Julia's house. "Don't tell Robin. I'll come by later. We have a stop to make first."

The hot shower burned the tension from Robin's muscles. It distracted her from the gnawing fear that was eating her alive. She might as well have been a prisoner, bolted in her loft, a guard at her door. Her home had never felt so small. But finally, she stretched and relaxed and after days of jumping at the slightest sound, Robin almost felt normal.

She heated some leftover minestrone soup and sat down at the kitchen counter for a late supper. When her grandmother had been alive, the two of them would cook together. Robin missed that time with her grandma. It had been the only real stability in her life. Robin didn't cook much anymore — why when she lived alone and had few friends? — but cooking brought her back to her roots, to her grandmother, the one person in the world who had unconditionally loved her.

Robin shook off her frustration and regret and ate more from habit than because she was hungry. She noticed the mail she'd picked up when Mario brought her home earlier. Absently she went through it, tossing the junk right into the trash can at the end of the counter. Junk, junk, junk, bill, junk, ju—

She stared at the envelope. It was blank. No return address, no stamp, no postal insignia whatsoever.

The handwriting made her hands shake. Sweat broke out on her forehead. It was Theodore Glenn, no doubt about it. She'd burned dozens of unopened letters he'd sent her from prison. But they'd all been sent to the Sin. She'd always taken some comfort that he didn't know where she lived.

Not anymore.

How had Theodore Glenn gotten past security? How had he put a letter in her box with no one seeing him?

She pushed the soup away, bile rising up her throat. In the back of her mind, she knew she should call 911 right now, not even open the letter. But what if she was wrong? What if it wasn't Theodore Glenn's handwriting? What if she was overreacting out of lack of sleep and fear?

Holding the envelope only with her fingernails, she carefully slit it open with a sharp knife from the butcher block next to the stove. Hands shaking, she extracted a single sheet of paper. In small, perfect handwriting, it read:

Robin:

You are even more beautiful now than you were removing your clothes for me at RJ's. But beauty doesn't buy you a life.

I know you're working with the police. I could threaten anyone, and you would still go to them. Your mother? Pathetic woman. But it appears she's not home. Another vacation? I know you drained your savings account to get her house out of foreclosure because she spends all her money shopping on television. You'd have been better off without her.

Maybe you still would be.

Your father? You never met him, but I did some research. It's amazing what kind of access I had in prison. But if I killed him, you wouldn't care. You have no attachment to him, he's only a name on your birth certificate.

And your friends, well, we all know what happens to people you care about, don't we? Have you considered that your affection is toxic? That perhaps your tainted love kills? No matter, really, because I have been keeping tabs on you. I know you live alone with Anna's cat. I know you have no friends. I know you still sleep with the lights on.

But we both know that you're a cold-hearted bitch. You lied to put me in prison, and for that I will never forgive you. For that I will make you pay.

I have always marveled at the word *love.* What does it mean? Truly, how can anyone care for anyone other than themselves? The pain, the betrayal, the suffering. For what? To live as a prisoner to another's emotions?

I would free you, but somehow I think your death would cause William far more anguish than his death would cause you. You lied. William was just doing his job.

It's a pity, because all you had to do was be nice to me and no one would be dead. How does it feel to know you're culpable, Robin? How does it feel to know you could have stopped all of this if you'd simply fucked me?

## TWENTY-TWO

Bryce Descario's house was dark. The calls to both his cell phone and house phone had gone unanswered for the thirty minutes Will had been trying. A patrol sat out front, having arrived before Hooper.

"Did you knock on the door?" Will asked.

"Yes, sir, and walked the perimeter. No

signs of forced entry. I don't think he's home."

Will wasn't so sure.

Perhaps Descario had left San Diego. Chief Causey had told him to inform the department if he was leaving town, but that didn't mean squat. Someone as arrogant and bitter as the former D.A. wouldn't feel he had to report into the lowly police department, especially since the police union supported his opponent over him in the election he lost. Chief Causey had been the head of that cause.

Will glanced at Carina. "I have a feeling."

"Me, too. Bad."

He nodded, pulled his gun. He rarely pulled his weapon, relying on his ability to talk his way out of virtually any situation. He'd gone through hostage negotiation training and was often called in to handle sensitive situations. But here, now, he sensed something was amiss.

Was Theodore Glenn watching? Was he waiting to see how Will would react to whatever was inside Descario's house?

Descario was either dead inside the house, or not home. The message Glenn left for Will wasn't the ravings of a lunatic, but a man with a purpose. He'd wanted Will to come here. Why?

To show his power. That he could walk free when every law enforcement agency was looking for him.

"Oh, yes, Theodore, you're very, very smart," Will whispered. "Is that what you want? Me to acknowledge your genius?"

"Excuse me?" Carina said.

"Nothing." But Will was getting a far greater sense of his prey now, much better than he had seven years ago.

They skirted the edge of the large, private house in Rancho Santa Margarita. The wealthy neighborhood was quiet, which wasn't surprising. Will rarely came to this neighborhood. Crime was minimal. In fact, the last time he'd been here was ten months ago, when a prominent psychiatrist was thought to have committed suicide. Property crimes, occasional domestics, rarely anything violent. Nothing that would come to the attention of a homicide detective.

It was when he and Carina met back up at the front that he realized exactly what was wrong.

"Security."

"What?"

"Where are the lights? Virtually every house in this neighborhood had security lights. A cat walks across the yard, and spotlights come on."

"If the power was cut, wouldn't the alarm company have called? Checked it out?"

"Depends."

"On?"

"If the security system was activated."

Will hesitated. If he was wrong and Descario had left town or was out with his girlfriend tonight, he'd be putting the department in a bad light. Cops breaking into homes. Still, an escaped convict had threatened the former district attorney. What more probable cause did he need?

"I'll go around back. Count to thirty and then we both go in."

Carina nodded. Will motioned to the uniform to back his partner up. He went around to the back, counting. Two sets of French doors opened into the backyard off the breakfast nook. He was there at count twenty-four.

Twenty-five.

Twenty-six.

Who was Glenn going after next? How could they stop him if he had help?

Twenty-nine.

Thirty.

Simultaneously, Will and Carina broke down the doors of the house.

No alarm went off.

Will searched the rear half of the house.

315

He met up with Carina in the foyer. She'd already covered the living and dining rooms. She shook her head and Will motioned to go upstairs. She nodded, covering his back.

The master bedroom doors were closed. Will held up three fingers. One. Two. Three.

They pushed open the doors.

A piercing alarm sounded. Spotlights went on all around the house.

And no one was in the bed.

"Shit," Will said. "He played us."

"Human beings are so predictable," Theodore told Sara, enjoying the spectacle down the street, a faint smile on his lips.

"You're so smart, Teddy." Sara rested her hand on his arm, her fingers tracing his bicep.

Not just humans in general, but William Hooper in particular was predictable. Theodore had, of course, imagined killing Bryce Descario. But in the end, when he had the chance, he let it go.

Watching William's reaction to the setup was far more fun than killing the pathetic former district attorney. His letter to William had done exactly what he expected — sent them to Descario's house. So predictable, and that helped him know how to handle his next few moves.

Through binoculars Theodore watched Descario drive up in his slick Mercedes. The fat little dictator started pointing fingers, yelling at William, threatening him. And the detective took it. Of course he did. He wouldn't fight back, not like that. He didn't have it in him.

William Hooper would sacrifice his life for Robin McKenna. He wouldn't fight back, he would give it. On Theodore's word? Hmm, perhaps. That would be very interesting now, wouldn't it?

*"William, allow me to kill you and I'll let Robin go."*

Would the cop agree? Would Theodore even give him the choice?

There was nothing Theodore wanted more than to have William Hooper and Robin McKenna at the opposite ends of the same rope. He wanted *both* of them to know the other was dead. If this modern-day Romeo thought Juliet was dead, what would he do?

That small feeling, a minimal emotion, which Theodore kept alive through sheer determination and constant thought about Robin McKenna, consumed him. This was no longer a simple game, where he would prove (again) that he was smarter than the police and everyone they put against him. This was bigger than winning or losing. It was destiny, as if everything he'd done, learned, tried, put him here, at this point in time, to destroy two people.

It was heady, really, something few people had the capacity to understand. It was more than the game, more than the risk, and for the first time, it was more than the thrill.

For the first time, he knew he would be sustained after everything played out. After pitting Romeo against Juliet.

"Teddy?"

Theodore faced Sara, held her face in his hands. He could snap her neck without a thought. He could slice her throat. But not now.

Not yet.

Sara had been productive during her excursion to the gaslamp district. Not only had she taken care of the letter to Robin, she'd learned that Robin was thinking about not opening the Sin tomorrow.

"I think we need to wait until her art show," Sara said.

Theodore tensed. "Since when did I ask you to plan anything? I will make all the decisions."

"I just —"

He slapped her. Not because he received any pleasure from hitting her, but because he wanted her to shut up.

"You've been valuable to me for the past year. Don't fuck with me now, Sara."

"I-I — Teddy, I love you."

He swallowed back a biting comment. He needed this woman, as much as he loathed to admit it.

But he wouldn't need her forever.

He forced himself to soften his tone. "Sara, you're the best thing that ever happened to me." He touched her face softly, remembering how William had touched Robin the night Anna was killed.

She melted into his hand, much like Robin had done to William. Was this a female response? Theodore closed his eyes, imagining Robin leaning into his caress. Parting her lips for him. Giving herself to him, only him.

"Let me kill her for you," she said.

Theodore opened his eyes, genuinely surprised for the first time in his life. Sara looked at him, an earnest expression on her face.

He hadn't expected this. He looked at Sara with a renewed respect, and a touch of suspicion. Was she trying to pull something on him?

"I have to do it myself."

Sara shook her head. "She'll be the death of you, Teddy. They're looking for you. You won't get near her. But I have an in, I can get to her —"

"You don't know me, woman. You don't know anything about me. I can and will kill Robin McKenna, right in front of that bastard cop." But he was curious. "What is your plan?"

She smiled like a schoolgirl who had the rapt attention of her favorite teacher. "If she closes the club, the only place you can get her is at her loft, or at the art gallery on Sunday. She won't cancel it. It's her first showing."

"If she'll close her business, she'll cancel the art show."

Sara shook her head. "I don't think so. You don't know how important this is. It's in all the papers. And what if she thought you'd left town?"

Something clicked. Theodore leaned forward. "I'm all ears."

Sara smiled, bit her lower lip. "This is my idea. Friday night we drive to Mexico . . ."

Theodore listened. And for the first time was impressed with the intellect of another human being.

He leaned over and kissed her. Spontaneously — an odd gesture for him.

Her plan just might work.

In fact, it was brilliant.

What a shame he would have to kill the person who came up with it.

"Can you drop me off at the hospice?" Carina asked Will. "Nick is there, he'll take me home."

Will hit the steering wheel. "It's Patrick's birthday."

"You remembered." Her smile was strained.

Will glanced at the clock. "Barely. It's ten minutes to midnight."

If Patrick were fully here, he'd have been part of their team. He would have used his extensive skills and easygoing manner to manage their overall security and track Glenn's financial potential. Patrick didn't need a committee, his mind was wired differently. He saw connections where few people saw them.

But it wasn't just his value as a cybercop, it was Patrick's good nature that Will missed most of all. They'd been friends, and Patrick was one of the few people Will talked to about stuff. They'd kick back, drink a few beers, shoot the breeze. Patrick had been his best friend. Will missed him.

Patrick's life was in limbo — it had been eight months since an explosion put him in a coma — Carina was getting married, Dillon had moved to Washington . . . everything was changing, growing, dying, and he was just walking around doing a job.

The job certainly couldn't keep him warm at night.

Will pulled up in front of the hospice. "I was thinking earlier that we could use Patrick about now."

"Well, think hard on that. Maybe it'll bring him out of never-never land." Carina gave Will a kiss on the cheek. "Thanks. You're not just a great partner, but a good friend." She started to get out of the car, then paused.

"You love her."

He didn't have to ask who Carina was talking about. "It doesn't matter."

"It certainly does."

"All that matters is that she's safe. I said things —" he shook his head. "I was wrong."

"Tell her."

He laughed bitterly. "You think I haven't tried? I've apologized so many times I sound like a broken record. I said I was sorry then, I said it now. Being sorry isn't enough. I hurt her. Deeply, irrevocably hurt her."

"Will, we've known each other for more than a decade. You've never intentionally hurt someone. You're one of the most compassionate men I've ever met. I've

322

teased you about your women, but the truth is, you never hurt them."

"My track record sucks. I never — I just didn't want to put my wife second. I couldn't put any of them in that position again, not after Wendy."

"It doesn't have to be that way."

"It was with my father."

"You're not your father."

"How do I convince her to forgive me?"

"You can't," Carina said. "But honesty usually works."

"I've been honest."

"Have you?" Carina took his hand. "If there's one thing that Patrick's coma should have taught you is that life is too unpredictable to not fight for what you want. If you love her, Will, fight for her."

He didn't say anything. Carina was more right than he wanted to admit.

He closed his eyes and saw the dead bird again on Julia's kitchen table. Heard Glenn's courthouse threats. Thought about what Hans Vigo said, that Glenn would take Robin out even if it meant getting himself killed.

If Robin died, he'd never forgive himself for not at least trying to make it work. He'd never put her out of his mind. Robin had been in his thoughts — or his dreams —

every night for the last seven years.

"Tell Patrick to get back to work. It's an order," Will said.

She smiled thinly. "Yes, sir."

Will watched Carina walk into the hospice, the night guard letting her in. It was after hours, but being a cop opened many doors.

He started for his house. He wanted to go to Robin. He wanted to see her, talk to her, touch her.

Tell her one more time that he was sorry.

He pictured Patrick in his coma. Life was too short, too unpredictable . . . he hung a U-turn at the same time his cell phone vibrated.

Damn. He was off-duty, unless it was related to Glenn.

"Hooper."

"Detective Hooper, Sergeant Fields here. There's a 911 call at 101 Fifth Avenue, number 301."

Will's heart quickened. *Robin.*

"What happened?"

"I don't know, exactly, but Robin McKenna — who's on your Glenn list — called it in. Then hung up. We tried calling back, but no one answered."

"I'm on my way." Will hung up and dialed Mario Medina's cell. "What happened?"

"What do you mean, what happened?"

"Robin just called 911! Where the hell are you?"

"Standing right outside her door. I'll call you back."

Why didn't Robin pick up the damn phone? Oh, God, what if Glenn got to her? What if he was there right now? What if the Descario prank — the allusion in the letter that he was going to go after the former D.A. — was a diversion?

"If you touch her, I'll kill you," Will said under his breath.

He screeched up to Robin's building at the same time as two patrols.

Then Mario called that she was alive.

## TWENTY-THREE

When Will burst through the door, Robin had never been so relieved to see anyone. She found herself rushing to him, then she hesitated at the last minute.

What was she doing?

Will grabbed her by the arms and pulled her the final two feet. Held her so tightly that she would have protested except that he was shaking. She breathed in his all-male scent, held on to him as if she were drowning. She never wanted to let him go. She never wanted him to let her go.

*Everyone else, go away. Just go away and let me be at peace. With Will . . .*

"You're okay. You're okay," Will whispered in her ear. She tried to speak, but couldn't.

Will gently pushed her back. In his eyes was fear. Fear, concern, and something more. Something that had been there seven years ago, something she'd ignored when she walked away. Because he'd hurt her and she didn't want to see anything else.

But he was back.

"Sit down," he said, escorting her to the couch. "Are you okay?"

She nodded.

"How about some water? Wine?"

She shook her head. "I have some tequila in the cabinet next to the refrigerator."

"I'll get it," Mario said from his perch next to the door. She'd felt like such a fool when he burst into her loft, cracking the door-jamb. She hadn't been able to answer his shout from the hall. She'd called 911, then slid down to the floor, her chest tight. The simple act of breathing had been a chore.

*You're not helpless, Robin! Why are you acting like such a stupid, weak girl?*

She swallowed, gathering her strength, her eyes on Will. "I —"

"Why didn't you call me? I got the call

from dispatch. I didn't know — you didn't even tell Mario. What's the use of having a bodyguard if you don't tell him when Glenn contacts you?"

She looked down at her hands, which were clenched in front of her, knowing she'd allowed her fear to get the best of her after she'd read the letter from Theodore.

Will knelt in front of her, took her tight fists in his hands. "Robin, I'm sorry for yelling. But listen to me. *Look* at me."

She did, her breath catching in her lungs. "Will —" She swallowed. "I just didn't expect it. I'm not as strong as you think I am."

"Like hell you aren't. You're stronger. God, Robin, you're the strongest woman I know. Down here" — he hit his chest — "where it matters. Who wouldn't crack under Glenn's scrutiny? Who wouldn't be scared when a sociopathic killer has them in their sights? If you *weren't* scared, then I'd worry."

There was a knock on the door, and Mario looked through the peephole, then let in a forty-something man Robin had never met. He was shorter than Will, a tad on the pudgy side, but with a warm, handsome face and sparkling pale blue eyes framed with crow's-feet. Attractive, in a comfortable, best friend sort of way.

Will nodded at the stranger. "Robin, this is FBI Special Agent Hans Vigo. He's out of Quantico and helping us on this."

"Pleased to meet you, Ms. McKenna," Hans said, taking her hand.

She gave him a half smile.

"I called him after speaking with Mario. He's a criminal profiler with the Feds, someone who probably understands Theodore Glenn better than anyone."

"I don't know about that," Hans said. "Will had him pegged early on. But I'll help in any way I can, and right now, we need to brainstorm and try and predict his next move."

"Which means we need your help, Robin." She blanched. "Me?"

She felt trapped like a bug caught in a spider's web, waiting, waiting, waiting for the spider to cross the web and swallow her, kicking and screaming. Devour her alive . . .

Then she looked at Will and drew in his strength. This was a man she could count on.

A man who'd also thought the worst of her.

But he'd always been there when she *really* needed him.

Except that one time.

"Ms. McKenna," Hans Vigo said, "let's sit down."

She nodded and sat on the couch. Will sat next to her, his leg touching hers. Mario put a bottle of tequila on the coffee table with a glass, but she didn't touch it. She was surprisingly calm.

Vigo sat on the love seat across from them, leaning forward. He put a letter on the table, obviously a photocopy, turned it so she could read it.

The letter looked exactly like the letter she received from Glenn. Except it was addressed to "William."

She looked at Will, panic rising. "What happened?"

"He delivered a package to me as well."

She read the letter to Will, hands shaking. She read it twice, three times. *The only time you were really scared was when you thought Robin was dead.*

*I will kill her.*

*I may leave for a while. Or not.*

Hans said, "He's trying to scare you both. Threatening Will with your death, threatening you with Will's death."

"Why?" she asked, her voice a squeak. She cleared her throat. "Dammit, why? Why does he care? Will and I are long in the past. It's over and —" she stopped. What was she saying? She glanced around the room. Two cops and Mario, discreetly trying not to look at her.

Oh, God, what was she doing?

"Robin," Will said quietly. "Robin, look at me."

She did, lips trembling. She took a deep breath, calmer.

"I told Hans about us. He's heard the conversation you recorded."

"It's not about me," she whispered, closing her eyes, knowing she was lying as the words came out.

"Robin, don't."

She breathed deeply. "God, Will, they died because of me."

"They died because of *him*."

She shook her head. "You heard him. On the phone. Th-the letter. I — why? If only —"

"Stop!" He squeezed her hands. "Robin, stop it. Glenn is a sociopath. He enjoys hurting you. Emotionally torturing you. He wants you to feel guilty. It's part of his game, to make you so scared you'll do something stupid. You're anything but stupid, Robin."

"Why me?" She glanced from Will to the FBI agent. "Why me? You're a criminal profiler, why does he want to hurt *me*? I never did anything to him."

Hans answered. "You didn't jump when he said jump. You didn't do what he expected you to do. Somehow, you saw him for exactly who he is. That both scared him and excited him. He may have thought that initially he'd found a soul mate, someone as cold and calculating as he is. Later, he realized you simply didn't like him; perhaps acted superior to him. That angered him, because he's used to getting what he wants. Manipulating people. His parents. His sister. At work, friends, colleagues. But he couldn't get to you. You didn't react to him."

"So it *is* my fault!"

"No!" Will exclaimed. "Dammit, Robin, if you think anyone other than Theodore Glenn is to blame, you're letting him win."

"He knows where I live. Why didn't he kill me earlier?"

"He couldn't get to you. You hired security, you have an alarm system, and we had cops out front," Will said. "It would have been suicide for him, and he doesn't want to die without —" He cut himself off.

"Without what?"

"Finishing everything he started."

"Exactly," Hans said, "and that may be his Achilles' heel."

"Pardon me?" Will asked.

"He's not going to be reckless, which actually plays into our favor," Hans said.

"Why send the letters?" Robin asked. "Why try to scare me?"

"Because he wants *you* to act recklessly."

"He's watching me," Robin said. She glanced at Will, almost embarrassed to tell him, but said nonetheless, "He wrote to me from prison."

Will was furious. "Why didn't you tell me? Why didn't you file a complaint?"

"I burned all the letters," she said. "After the first one, I knew they were from him. He wanted to keep me scared so I didn't read them." She glanced down. "But I had nightmares after every letter arrived."

"He sent them here?" Hans asked.

"No, to the club. It's no secret that I own it, he could have found the address online."

"But this letter" — Hans held it up — "was delivered here."

She nodded. "But there's no postal mark on it. No stamp. He brought it by, put it in my mailbox."

"Shit," Will muttered.

Hans said, "I think it's clear that you both are the primary target of this killer — you and Will. The way I see it, we have two options. Either you can go into federal protection, or you can help catch him."

"No," Will said. "Robin isn't going to be bait."

"Let's go back to the beginning."

"Read the transcripts."

"I have. Several times."

"So you know that Theodore Glenn stalked the women he killed. Manipulated them. Seduced them. Then he killed them."

"Except for possibly Anna," Hans said.

Robin jumped up. "Oh, please! Don't tell me that Trinity convinced you that Glenn didn't kill Anna? I can't *believe* you're listening to a woman who's helping a killer. An escaped convict who killed two cops." She looked to Will, feeling betrayed all over again when he avoided eye contact.

*He also thinks Glenn is innocent.*

*"Who else wants you dead?" Trinity had asked her.*

"Ms. McKenna," Hans said, "I haven't spoken with Trinity Lange yet. I simply read the report. But you said yourself that Anna Clark didn't have a sexual relationship with Glenn."

"She didn't." Robin sat down again, away from Will. She was acting like a jack-in-the-box. She'd better get herself under control or they'd think she'd lost her mind. Maybe she had. She wanted to touch Will, for support, but she had a hard time accepting that he thought Anna's murder was *unsolved*.

"You're one hundred percent certain of that."

She hesitated. Was she? After seven years, *nothing* seemed like what it had been. "Anna was a lesbian. I'm *almost* positive she wouldn't have slept with any man, and if she *did* it wouldn't have been Glenn. She didn't like him."

"I agree," Agent Vigo said. "And, for the record, you didn't have a relationship with Glenn either."

"No," she answered through clenched teeth. "Why is it all you cop-types think that just because I was a stripper I slept around?" She glanced at Will, confused and trapped. She rubbed her head. Damn, she didn't want to remember how she'd felt all those years ago. All she wanted was to remember how good it was to be held by Will, how happy she'd been when she was with him. How he showed genuine appreciation for her paintings. Like he knew she'd go right to the top in the art world, with a confidence and assurance that she didn't have about her own work.

Vigo said, "I'm just verifying the facts. It's natural that, based on the M.O., the police would believe either you or Anna had been involved with Glenn. But knowing what we know now, I think Glenn's behavior proves he has unfinished business with you." He glanced at Will, who nodded. Had they talked about this before, or were they just on the same wavelength? Robin rubbed her temple harder.

"Which leaves two possibilities," Will said. "First, let's go on the assumption that Anna wasn't supposed to be in town."

"Will — you —" She felt like Alice down the rabbit hole, nothing she saw or heard familiar or comfortable.

"Ms. McKenna, I've reviewed all the files in this matter and witness testimony states that she was supposed to be in Big Bear," Hans said. "In your statement you said you didn't expect her to be home that night."

"I didn't. I just don't know why she came back early, or why she didn't call me."

"Who else might she have called?"

"I don't know. Maybe RJ, though I doubt it. She would have more likely called me."

"Would she have called you on your cell phone? At the bar?"

"I didn't have a cell phone then. That was seven years ago. She probably would have called the bar, or maybe left a message on the answering machine. Unless . . ." She shook her head.

"What?"

"She knew about Will and me. Maybe she thought I was at his place." Robin hated that her private life was being exposed for all to see.

Hans said, "Glenn killed people you were close to in order to hurt you, to watch how you reacted. He didn't take pleasure in killing his victims. He took pleasure in watching *you* suffer. You heard that when he called you. He wanted to make sure you understood that."

"Oh God. Oh God."

Will moved to sit right next to her, wrapping his arm around her shoulders.

Will said, "I never asked you, Robin. Where were you when you found out about Bethany's murder? The testimony states that RJ told you."

She nodded. "He called me over after my dance, said Bethany hadn't shown up and he sent one of the boys — one of the bouncers — to her apartment to check on her. RJ could be a total ass wipe, but he cared about our safety. And there she was . . ." Her breath caught.

"So you were at RJ's?"

"Yes."

"Was Theodore Glenn there that night?"

Robin paled. "He came backstage and asked if everything was okay. I was in shock,

I think. Brandi burst into tears and told him about Bethany. He hugged her. God, he hugged her and stroked her hair and told her everything would be okay." She slammed her fist on the table in front of her. He'd held Brandi, but he'd been looking right at Robin with those eerie blue eyes. She didn't think anything about it then, and even after everything, that moment in time had been buried. Until now. "That bastard!"

Hans and Will exchanged looks.

"What?" she demanded. "I deserve to know what's going on, don't I? Will?"

She jumped up. Paced. She wanted to run away, but there was nowhere to go.

Will stood and grabbed her hands, forced her to look at him. She blinked back the tears. "It is *not* your fault, Robin. Glenn is a sociopath. If he didn't fixate on you, he would have fixated on someone else. What we have to deal with now are the facts."

"All right." She sat back down, hands clasped tightly in her lap.

Will remained standing. She bit back her fear, her face a mask of calmness when Will knew she was petrified. She thought she was weak? He didn't know many civilians who could keep it together in the face of an evil like Theodore Glenn. It was so hard not to touch Robin, but right now they needed information.

"The night Anna died, there was a message on my cell phone," Will began. "It was a page from your apartment."

Robin's brows furrowed, but she didn't say anything.

"I thought it was you calling. I didn't call back because I was only a few minutes away, so I came by. I was going to go up to the apartment, but I saw the bar lights still on and I remembered that you had been working that night."

Hans asked, "Did you think it was odd that she paged you with her home number?"

"I didn't. I didn't really think anything about it, or if I did it was that she must have accidentally put in her home number, or thought she'd be home in a few minutes. I don't know, I really don't remember what I thought at the time. But I went into RJ's, and that's where I found Robin."

"Anna was murdered at about the time that Will arrived at the bar," Hans said. "Give or take fifteen minutes. She may have been dead when he got the page, or she may have been killed after he arrived at the bar."

"Theodore told Trinity that he was watching us in the bar. He could have killed her, then came down and watched —" Robin stopped, her face pale.

338

"I know this is hard for you, Robin," Will said. "But it's important that you think back to that night and try to remember everything that happened."

"I gave my statement seven years ago," she said.

Hans nodded. "In your statement you said you closed up the bar, walked across the street to your apartment, and found Anna dead in the living room."

"That's true."

Will sat next to Robin. "I made a huge mistake seven years ago. When you didn't put in your statement that we had been together in the bar, I should have. I should have said something."

"That's not relevant to anything," she said.

"No, except it wasn't the complete truth. I omitted the truth."

"Had you been totally honest, would that have saved Anna?"

"No," Will said.

Hans spoke up. "What we know for certain is that Glenn was in the bar during the same time you and Will were in the bar. When could he have gotten in?"

"I thought you were watching him," Robin said. "After Jessica —"

Will nodded. "We were. I had a patrol on him. He slipped out, again. He lived in a

339

beach house. We had someone on each entrance. What we didn't have covered were his upstairs windows. He could have climbed onto the roof, then scrambled down. He has experience rock climbing; scaling a house would be nothing to him."

"In the trial you said something about that," Robin said. "That impressions had been found on the north side of the house or something."

"Exactly, that was our theory. And it gave reasonable doubt that he was in the house all night. No one saw him there, no one spoke to him. And even though we had men on the house, the evidence that he'd scaled down from the roof, out of sight, proved he could have left undetected."

Hans said, "Robin, how long were you alone in the bar?"

"It was a weeknight, we closed at midnight, locked the door." She paused. "There were three regulars still there, but they just finished their drinks and chatted while RJ and I cleaned up."

"Who let them out?"

"I don't remember. It could have been either of us. Probably RJ."

"Why wasn't RJ there when Will arrived?"

"He was tired. He had heart problems and was on medication. He'd been talking about selling out. In fact, he later sold to me. After Brandi was killed RJ lost his drive. He was already old, but he suddenly got older. I told him to go home, I would stock up and finish. He didn't want to, but — I promised him I'd be okay. He left about one. Will came in shortly after that."

"Did you see Theodore Glenn at all that night?"

She shook her head. "RJ banned him. He wasn't allowed on the property."

"Could he have snuck in?"

"I don't see how. We had a bouncer, and —" She paused. "The bouncer left after the last dance. That's eleven on weeknights."

"So there was an hour when he could have snuck in," Will said. *An hour where Glenn could have killed Robin.*

"I don't see —" She swallowed. "Yeah, he would have known our routine. But — I don't see where he'd have been."

"What about in the dressing room?" Will said. "If the shows were over, would there have been any reason for you or RJ to go back there?"

Slowly, Robin shook her head. "The last two girls left at eleven thirty that night. Together. Safety in numbers and all that."

"Why did you let RJ leave you there alone?" Will asked.

341

"I don't know. Maybe because I never seriously thought Theodore would hurt me. He was targeting women who slept with him. I never did. I didn't feel he was a personal threat to *me.* I was scared, but not that kind of scared. I don't know!"

"When did you turn on the alarm?" Hans asked.

"When I left."

"So he left before that," Hans said.

"I — I guess. It was on motion detectors, so if someone were inside the alarm would have gone off."

"Could he have had the code?"

"I doubt it," Robin said. "RJ changed it monthly and every time an employee left."

Will said, "We checked the logs per routine and it was untouched after Robin locked up at one fifty-two that morning."

"See?" Robin said. "He saw Will and me, then went over to kill Anna."

"But everyone thought Anna was out of town," Will said. "You said so yourself — she told everyone at the club."

"Then — he went there to kill me and she was there." Robin swallowed.

"I don't think so," Hans said. "Whoever killed Anna had time to restrain her, cut her, and position her body." He paused. "After reviewing the crime scene, the killer must have spent at least fifteen minutes there, and that's rushing it. If Glenn killed her before midnight — before he could have slipped into the club — the time of death would be completely different. And while time of death is not wholly accurate, when we have the body that quickly we can narrow it down better. If he killed her after watching you and Will — the time of death would have proven that. As it was, death was fixed at between one and one thirty a.m. Will received the page at twelve fifty-five. He told me he arrived at the club at one-oh-five or so. You both left at one fifty. Since Glenn knows information about that time period, he couldn't have killed Anna. He wouldn't have had enough time. Not considering what was done to the body."

Hans looked from Will to Robin. "The million dollar question is, who called Will from your apartment? Anna — or her killer?"

Will squeezed Robin's hands. "I see where you're coming from, Hans. I can't believe I overlooked that back then."

"You didn't. You assumed Robin called you."

"But I didn't ask her. If I had, we could have figured this out seven years ago."

"But the conclusion would have been the

same," Hans reminded him. "The evidence points to Glenn."

"Could Anna have called me?" Will asked, almost to himself. "If she was scared or heard something, why wouldn't she have called 911?"

"I was right across the street! Why didn't she call me?"

"We don't know, we're only speculating . . ."

"Or Glenn called Will," Robin said, grasping at straws. "You said the killer may have called him. To scare him. Didn't you say that he wanted to scare me by making me think he was after Will, and scare Will to make him think he was after me?"

"If the time line proved that, I'd say it was a damn good guess," Hans said. "I do believe that Glenn was after you that night. Then Will came into the bar. He wasn't expecting him. Maybe he wasn't prepared."

"So who killed Anna? Who would want her dead? She was harmless. Sweet."

Hans was about to say something, but Will interrupted. "We don't know, but we will find out. In the meantime, we have a more important problem. Glenn is still out there and he is playing with you. And me." He looked at Mario. "Sit on her tight. Don't let her out of your sight."

"What about you?" Robin asked, her voice wavering.

"I'm a cop. I'm surrounded by cops. I'll be okay."

She didn't look convinced.

"Glenn killed Anna," Robin said emphatically. She didn't look at either of them.

Pickles jumped in her lap. Will stared at him, looked at Hans. "This is Anna's cat," Will told him, awestruck.

"What does that have to do with anything?" Robin said, scratching the cat's ears.

"If Theodore killed Anna, he would have wanted to torment her first," Hans said.

"Remember his sister's testimony?" Will said softly. "About how he tormented her by killing her cat? And no one believed her?"

She nodded.

"It's part of his M.O.," Will said. "He plays with his victims. Cutting them. Pouring bleach over them. Killing their pets in front of them. But Anna's cat lived."

"Maybe Pickles hid from him," Robin said, her voice almost a whimper.

"This is the friendliest cat on the planet," Will said. "The cat proves it."

"Proves what?" Robin demanded.

Hans answered. "Theodore Glenn didn't kill your roommate."

# TWENTY-FOUR

Will walked outside with Hans. He instructed the patrol to be on alert, then pulled Hans away from the other cops.

"She's going to be okay," Hans told him.

"We laid a bomb on her tonight," Will said, frustrated. While last night he'd been only half convinced that Glenn *hadn't* killed Anna, tonight he was certain. "I never thought about that phone call coming from Robin's apartment," he admitted. "It just didn't enter my mind. Shit, I could have saved Anna."

"You don't know that. She could have been already dead. You could be dead now. You can't second-guess yourself in this business. It'll eat you up. We make difficult decisions instantly and then spend years thinking about every fraction of a second. What if we did this, what if we did that. I've worked hostage negotiations, and I've worked with hostage negotiators who were on the edge because they began to question themselves after an assignment went bad." Hans stared Will in the eyes. "Don't do it. You can't afford to lose your judgment now. You're going to have to make those difficult decisions, and you can't doubt your instincts and experience."

Will let out a pent-up breath. "Who? Who wanted to kill Anna?"

"Or, who wanted to kill Robin?"

Hearing it out loud unnerved Will. "Other than Glenn," he added.

"It's nearly two in the morning." Hans Vigo glanced at his watch. "She's worn out and on edge right now. We're going to have to talk to her in the morning about her life back then. But first we have to bring in Jim Gage."

"Because of the evidence on scene."

Hans said, "I've played with every scenario I could think of, but the only thing that makes sense — if we agree that Glenn didn't kill Anna Clark — is that someone involved in the case killed her and framed Glenn by planting the evidence."

Will nodded. "Hair would be easy forensic evidence to plant. It doesn't need special storage, like blood, and it doesn't degrade."

"The follicles would degrade after a short period of time," Hans said, "and I need a more detailed report as to exactly how the hair was tested and what they found."

"I don't like this."

"Neither do I."

"We do this quietly," Will said, rubbing his face. "I'll talk to Trinity again tomorrow, make sure she keeps it off the air. If Anna's killer thinks we're looking into the case again, he may get scared and do something rash."

"And we have to consider that the killer may already know. Trinity's report wasn't all that secret."

"They wouldn't know we took Glenn's comments seriously. Hell, I pretty much called Trinity a fool for even considering the possibility."

"Which gives us a break. Everyone knows how you feel about Glenn, you're running the investigation, and if you don't give credence to Glenn's claims, then no one else will."

"What if we asked Trinity to play along with us?" Will suggested, an idea popping into his head.

"How so?"

"We do an interview. Say only what we want Anna's killer to hear. Trinity can go public with the fact that Glenn contacted her, ask us about his statement, and we put it to rest."

"There's only one problem with that," Hans said.

"It'll piss Glenn off."

"Exactly."

"We'll keep watch on Trinity 24/7. And give her an out. Let her say no. We issue a formal statement through Chief Causey, get the information out there either way."

"But Trinity Lange is respected and known," Hans said. "It would give credence to our statement." He gave a quick nod. "If both she and your chief go for it, I think it'll work. It'll buy us time to find Glenn. Once he's behind bars we'll all rest easier. But until then, you're one hundred percent confident in Jim Gage?"

"Yes. No doubts."

"Then we need to meet with him out of his office tomorrow. Away from any police hangouts."

"What about here, at Robin's place?" Hans agreed.

"Let me set it up with Gage and smooth the way," Will said. "He's not going to like what we have to say."

"He doesn't have to like it. He just has to keep his mouth shut."

Robin relished her privacy. Running a popular club, always having her social face on, was draining. Having people in her home was equally draining.

She couldn't consider anyone but Theodore Glenn killing Anna. Not tonight. Her head was pounding and all she wanted to do was go to sleep.

But she feared the nightmares.

She contemplated drinking herself to sleep, but didn't want to use alcohol as a crutch. More important, what if Glenn came around? Tonight, tomorrow, the next day? She needed to be on full alert.

She walked over to her art corner, looked at the project she hadn't touched since Saturday. It was going to be a gaslamp scene, an expression of her love for this area and the people who lived and worked here. The view was of storefronts on the same street as the Sin. She'd taken a series of photographs from two corners, and had designed the piece to reflect both sides of the street, focusing on perspective and color.

She loved working with color.

Her first art show was Sunday. She didn't want to cancel, but she didn't see that she had a choice. If Glenn wasn't in jail by then, how could she put all those people in jeopardy?

She had to make the decision about opening the club tomorrow as well. They would normally open at five in the evening. They had a large after-work crowd who mostly came to drink, listen to music, and socialize. They blended into the evening dance crowd that really came on scene around nine.

She didn't want to close. Her business would suffer. Her employees counted on their wages. Could she afford to pay them without bringing in income? Not for long. Maybe for this weekend. But it wasn't just wages, they received more in tips than they did in their paychecks.

She turned away from her art, which usually brought her joy. There was no joy left tonight.

A loud rap sounded on the door. She crossed over and looked out the peephole, expecting Mario.

Will stood there again. Staring right back at her, though Robin knew he couldn't see her.

Her heart jumped. Her emotions were on overload, but she admitted she was relieved — happy — to see him.

She turned off the alarm, unbolted the door, and let him in. "I thought you'd left."

"I walked Hans out. Can I come in?"

Robin stood aside, let Will in, then re-bolted the door and reset the alarm. She put her forehead against the door. "Will, he's going to kill you." She couldn't believe that was the first thing she said, but it was her greatest fear.

"No, he's not."

Will was right behind her. His hands were

on her shoulders and he squeezed. She stifled a cry. She'd wanted him to touch her. Stay with her. Protect her from her fears and doubts. Reconnect with him, rediscover what they'd lost seven years ago. If only she had forgiven him back then, would her life have been different? Maybe she wouldn't feel so alone.

She said in a whisper, "Do you really believe that someone else killed Anna?"

"Yes," Will said, his voice tight.

She began to shake. The more she tried to control it, the worse the shaking became.

"First things first," Will said, turning her to face him. His eyes explored her, his arms wrapping around her, keeping her close, rubbing her shoulders. "We'll recapture Theodore Glenn. He's the immediate threat. Don't forget that. Whoever killed Anna thinks they got away with it. Hans and I are going to do everything we can to make them think just that. So if you hear on the news tomorrow that we don't give any credence to Glenn's statement, don't believe it."

"I — I can't think about Anna right now. It's hard for me to accept. I just —" She swallowed, unable to get her thoughts to come out right.

Will was so close, his face inches from

Robin's. "I understand," he whispered. "I hate it. That I might have made mistakes in the investigation, that I didn't think anything of that page from your home number, that I might have been able to save Anna —"

"Or be killed."

He kissed her lightly. "I can't stand the thought of anything happening to you. God, Robin, I —"

He dropped to his knees, his mouth skimming her clothing. He looked down at the floor, then up at her.

"Will —"

"I need you to forgive me, Robin." His arms wrapped around her waist and he kissed her stomach. "I was so wrong, I made a mistake, I'm sorry. I'll apologize every day for the rest of my life if that's what it takes to get you back —"

"No —" she whispered.

He cut her off. "I've missed you. I think about you every night. I've lived with this deep regret for too long. I threw you away, I didn't know what a precious gem I had in my hands."

"Oh, Will, don't —"

"I have to make you understand. I *need* you to understand."

Robin fell to her knees so that they were face-to-face. She kissed him. She didn't want to hear him say *I love you.* Not now, not like this. Not when she didn't know if she could believe him, if the words would be spoken out of guilt or regret.

She'd never stopped loving him, but forgiveness was so hard for her. The pain twisted in her heart, the love and the hurt entwined.

Robin wrapped her arms around his neck, pulled him close to her, at first taste remembering the passion and discovery they'd enjoyed when they first met. She'd missed him, missed the intimacy and intensity that she'd never had with any other man. She didn't need to lead or follow, she didn't need to direct or act. With Will she was herself, giving fully, receiving fully, her glorious potential exposed, bringing the best out of Will and he drawing the best out of her.

He moaned into her mouth and she swallowed his desire. Her hands worked on his buttons, frantic now. Not wanting to wait to remember everything they'd had. She pushed off his shirt, pulling his undershirt out of his Dockers, his chest hot to the touch. Her mouth moved from his lips to his chest, her tongue swirling around his nipples as she pushed him back to the floor.

*This* was how she remembered Will. The heat and excitement and heavy desire. No waiting, no holding back. All of him, right now. His hands were under her shirt, his fingers unsnapping her bra with a flick of his wrist. Then his hands on her breasts, kneading, pulling, pushing, making every cell in her body throb for more.

She licked him, all the way down his chest, to his navel. Her fingers popped open his button fly and freed him, but she didn't stop. She pulled his slacks off, jerking his shoes off at the same time.

"Come here, Robin." Will's voice was thick and deep.

As she trailed wet kisses up his body, his hands grabbed her arms and pulled her up so she lay on top of him. When he kissed her this time, her breath disappeared. Will rolled over, covered her body with his, his kisses going deeper, harder, more fierce as they tried to get even closer. His hands gripped her hair as their bodies moved together; her hands couldn't stop. It had been so long, too long, since they'd touched, kissed, held each other skin to skin.

"Take. Off. My shirt." Robin could barely catch her breath, Will had intoxicated her.

He leaned up just enough to pull her T-shirt over her head and she tossed her bra across the room. Then their chests touched and she moaned, grabbed Will and brought him back down to her, her long jean-clad legs wrapped around his waist, her mouth finding his, the roughness of his nighttime stubble arousing her as much as his tongue dueling with hers. His mouth moved to her neck and suckled, biting her lightly, then to her shoulder, down to her breast where he took as much into his mouth as possible, the suction causing her to gasp and arch her back. His hand found the other breast where he massaged, until he switched sides, the exquisite pleasure with a touch of pain, just enough to make it real, to make her regret walking out seven years ago. To make her yearn for the past and crave the future.

"Will." She said his name on a wisp of a breath, all her feelings and energy focused on the intensity of attention he paid to her chest. Only Will could turn her on so quickly, make her abandon all thought of patience and drawn-out lovemaking. She wanted him all, right now, and later. "God, Will."

She used all her muscles to push him off and over, rolling on top of him, moving her pelvis into his hard erection. She sat on him, his hands on her butt, squeezing, massaging her, as her hands rubbed his hard chest, trying and failing to slow her racing heart. Will's heart raced with her, she felt it under his skin, *thump thump thump,* pounding against her hand. She kissed it, drawing his nipple into her mouth and biting lightly until he groaned. His hands fumbled with her jeans and she moved to the other nipple, not being gentle anymore, his rough hands pushing down her jeans, kneading her, pulling her toward him before she could pull the jeans off. They tangled around her ankles.

"I need you, Will. Right now. Take me away. Like the first time. Like the last time."

Will rolled back on top, unmindful that they had moved halfway across the living room in their urgency. He jerked off Robin's jeans, her long dancer's legs smooth and soft under his hands. She was the most beautiful woman in the world with the finest body. He remembered every inch of her peaches and cream skin, the light covering of freckles on her shoulders, the mole on the inside of her left thigh. He kissed it and she spread her legs, writhing beneath him, needing him as much as he craved her.

"I've missed you, Robin." He kissed the inside of her right thigh, then licked all the way to her lush, round breasts, red from his earlier assault. She held his head to them and he took each into his mouth in turn. Her hands found his erect cock and he groaned as she squeezed.

"Now," she said. "I'm serious."

Without giving him time to position himself, she rolled him again. He loved how physical Robin was, how hard she pushed him, how hard she pushed herself. She straddled him and in one thrust slid onto him, hot and wet and ready.

She gasped, and he felt her tightness.

"Robin," he began, then she moved her hips and he couldn't speak.

He pulled her to him, chest to chest, to kiss her, their tongues mimicking their lovemaking. Fast and frantic, in and out, no waiting to catch a breath. Their desire and urgency created a thick layer of sweat, bodies hot and slick, sliding together, a perfect fit.

Will rolled her back and they slammed against the couch. Her strong legs wrapped around his waist, giving him deeper access. She gasped beneath him, the slender muscles straining in her neck as her orgasm bubbled to the surface.

One look at Robin's face and he couldn't hold back. He pushed into her and released, feeling her muscles tighten around him as they came together. He collapsed onto her, kissing her neck, her ears, tasting the salty slickness of her skin.

Before she could pull away, Will gathered her into his arms, picked her up, and carried her to bed.

"Now we're going to do this right," he said.

"That was pretty all right to me," Robin said, kissing him.

"Slower, Robin. I'm going to kiss every inch of your flesh. I'm going to taste every part of your body." He stared into her eyes, greener and darker in their lust. "I'm hungry for you, Robin. I've been starving for you for seven years."

Before she could protest, or argue, or remember why she'd been angry with him — rightful or not — his lips found hers.

Will kissed her with the intimacy of a lifelong lover, slow, exquisite, full of passion and love. Robin melted into his body as if they were one body, one soul. And in their exploration, past transgressions washed away.

## TWENTY-FIVE

Will hated leaving Robin while she slept, but she was resting so peacefully he didn't want to wake her. He left her a note and slipped out at seven, found one of Mario's men outside the door, and made sure security knew he would return at ten but not to leave Robin alone.

He phoned Trinity on his way to her place.

"It's seven in the morning," she moaned.

"Seven thirteen."

"I worked the late news. And I was up until three going over the transcripts."

"I'll bring Starbucks. I need to talk to you, Trinity. It's important."

She instantly sounded awake. "What happened? Did Theodore Glenn kill again? I can meet you at the station —"

"I'll be at your place in twenty minutes. Don't leave."

"What —"

He hung up. She'd ask him a million questions he didn't want to answer yet. He'd just as soon talk to her in person.

On his way over he called Jim Gage on his cell phone. He was already on his way to the lab. "Jim, can you meet with Agent Vigo and me this morning at ten at Robin McKenna's loft?"

"I don't have anything new," he said. "I faxed my report on the Sturgeon crime scene last night. The autopsy is scheduled for this morning —"

"Carina can cover it. I need to talk to you."

"Why not my office? It's private."

"I don't want anyone in the lab hearing about this."

Jim didn't say anything.

"Jim?"

"You want me to keep our meeting off-the-record?"

"You could say that."

"Why?"

"I don't want to say over the phone."

"Is this about the Glenn case?"

This was harder than Will thought. "Are you alone?"

"Yes."

"It's about the Anna Clark case. Some new evidence has come to light. Bring the files, but don't tell anyone. *No one,* even if you trust them with your life."

"I don't like the sound of this. It sounds like my department is being investigated. And the Feds are involved?"

"Just one. You can trust him. Please, Jim. Trust me this once."

"Ten? I'll be there."

"Alone."

"Alone."

Will brought Trinity her favorite Starbucks coffee, a triple grande mocha with whipped cream.

She'd already showered and dressed, her

blonde hair still wet, combed straight back. She took the drink. "You remembered." She sipped. "Whipped cream. I gave it up last year."

Will said, "I'm sorry."

"Well, when my jeans started getting a little tight I had to cut corners."

"You are as beautiful as ever."

"This is scrumptious. I can splurge every now and then." She smiled brightly, though her sharp eyes held a hint of suspicion. "So why are you trying to bribe me?"

"Sit down."

"Doesn't sound good." She sat on her white sofa. "Give it to me straight, Hooper."

"Always."

She raised her eyebrows, but said nothing.

"I want you to run with the report that Theodore Glenn visited you the other night. Complete with his denial of murdering Anna Clark."

"Why now?"

"Because you're going to interview me at the station about it, and I'm going to emphatically state that the FBI has reviewed the evidence and concurs with the original report."

"What? You took me seriously? You re-opened the case? When did the Feds —"

He put up his hand. "I'm going to tell you

something completely off-the-record, Trinity. Because I like you and I don't want to deceive you. Glenn didn't kill Anna."

She blinked, momentarily confused. But Trinity was a smart woman, and she pieced it together quickly. "You want me to fabricate news?"

"No, I simply want you to report what I officially say. I have the Feds with me on this. I can bring out one of the top FBI profilers, have him say whatever is necessary."

"I don't understand."

He could practically see her mind working double-time trying to figure it out. "We have new evidence suggesting Glenn didn't kill Anna. The FBI agrees."

"So why's he going to lie?"

"Because if Anna's killer thinks that we're looking into the investigation, everyone involved is in danger. We also have a convicted murderer on the loose. He's killed three people since his escape. And something we've kept out of the press — so you can't report on this — Glenn broke into Julia Chandler's house on the cliffs and left a package. If she were there, he'd have killed her, too, as well as her niece who lives with her."

"But Connor Kincaid took her out of town."

"Yes, they are not just out of town, but out of the state. So we're talking high stakes here — Glenn is not going to stop. And he has help."

"Help?" She perked up.

"I'm not going to say anything more about that because it may jeopardize her life."

"Her?"

"Trinity — listen. We don't know exactly *who* is helping Glenn, but we have a list of women he regularly communicated with while in prison. We're all over them right now. But I can't say anything more about that."

"All right, all right. Off-the-record, I get that. But I don't like being used, Will. You have to give me something. I can't report a lie."

"You don't have to. I'm telling you all this because you can say no. If you do what we want, Theodore Glenn may think that you didn't work hard enough to convince us, or you aren't looking at the evidence yourself. It could put you at risk."

"You have a patrol outside —"

"Yes, and I'm going to suggest that you leave town after the report. Temporarily."

"No. No, this is the biggest story of the year. I'm not going to run —"

"Is the story worth your life?"

"Yes."

Will stared at her. That was the last answer he expected. "Trinity —"

"I'm not going to be stupid. I understand what you want. You want to deflect attention away from the Anna Clark investigation so you have time to look into the case and see who planted the evidence that led to Glenn's conviction. At the same time, you don't want Glenn to think that I'm dismissing his claims. I can do that, Will. I'm trusting you. Will you trust me?"

He hesitated, worried about Trinity's safety. "Okay." But he didn't feel good about it. He couldn't very well force her to leave town. He could, however, keep a patrol officer on her 24/7.

She sighed. "So when do we do this?"

"How about the noon news?"

"I can't get it taped that fast — unless you go down to the studio."

"I'll trust you on this. We can do it live."

Her eyes brightened. "Really?"

"Yes. But you have to promise me you'll be careful."

"And you have to promise me the scoop before any other station."

"Absolutely."

"And an interview."

"Okay."

"And a date."

He paused. Had he read her wrong? Did Trinity still have feelings for him? He didn't want to hurt her. He liked her, but not intimately. Especially now.

"I'm kidding," she said, grinning.

He must have looked relieved because she added, "You're still involved with her."

"Her?"

"Robin. Unless I'm wrong."

He shook his head. "You're not wrong."

She winked at him. "It would never have worked between us. Cops and reporters, fire and ice."

## TWENTY-SIX

Robin woke to the sun streaming in over her partition. Odd — she glanced at the clock. Nine fifteen! She never slept this late.

She rolled over, already knowing Will wasn't in bed with her. She listened to the sounds of her loft. The faint *tick-tick-tick* of the clock in her kitchen. Water running in the apartment downstairs. The general buzz of traffic three floors below. The purr of Pickles at her feet.

She felt the sheets where Will had been sleeping. Cool. He'd left some time ago. Her hand touched paper and she opened her eyes again. It was a note torn from the note-pad beside her bed.

Robin —
You are beautiful when you sleep. I had to go to a meeting, but I'll be back at ten. I'll be bringing Agent Vigo and Dr. Gage with me.
I love you.

—Will

She wasn't angry that he'd left; he had work to do. Still, she wished they'd woken up together, to see him in daylight with a clear mind and heart.

For years it had been so hard to let go of the pain of the past, but last night erased barriers between them. Maybe they had a chance. If she could just forget that horrible conversation seven years ago, delete it like she deleted spam, with a simple *click.*

Right now, she wanted to savor this blissful feeling. She almost felt guilty for feeling happy. *Almost.* But after this week of hell didn't she deserve a moment of peace? Of happiness? Of the *idea* that maybe something good might come of all this, this, this *evil* that surrounded Theodore Glenn?

Robin showered and dressed in jeans and a filmy white blouse, as if she were going into the Sin. She restrained from putting on her belt holster. She didn't want to act paranoid in her own damn apartment. Sleeping with the lights on was bad enough.

Thinking about the Sin brought her back down to earth. She had to close her business, at least for the next couple days. The idea made her ill, but she had to think about her employees. Her customers. What if Glenn wanted to go out with a bang? Have a big hostage situation? Kill not only her, but everyone in the building?

She couldn't run the risk.

She made coffee, anything to act normally.

Though she was expecting the company, the knock on the door startled her. She looked through the peephole, then opened the door unceremoniously.

Will smiled warmly at Robin. For the first time since he saw her on Monday, she looked rested. Rested and beautiful, even with the worry lines across her face.

"You remember Jim Gage, right?" he asked. "And Hans Vigo?"

She nodded. "I made coffee."

"I'll help," Will said. The kitchen didn't afford them any privacy, but at least he could say softly, "I'm sorry I had to leave, but —"

"I got your note. It's fine."

He wanted to say something else. Specifically, something to the effect of, *We're okay now, right? You're not still mad at me?* But he didn't.

Will was uncomfortable in this position. He generally decided when to break off a relationship. While he often pursued women, they always wanted to be pursued. It was safe that way. But Robin had left him when he didn't want her to leave, and now she was back but he didn't know *how* back. Forever? For tonight only?

She smiled at him, but he couldn't read anything in the smile.

Robin put a tray of coffee, cream, and sugar on the kitchen table, then sat down.

Will said, "Robin, you might want to step out of the room."

"I'm okay."

"We're going to be looking at crime scene photos."

"I've seen them."

"Robin —" He stopped. "You can walk away anytime."

She nodded, holding her coffee mug with both hands.

They were the only four in the room. Even Mario was outside the door. No leaks.

First, Will said, "Trinity agreed to run the report. Twelve o'clock news, with repeats in the evening."

"What report?" Jim asked.

"We asked Trinity to run with the story of Glenn breaking into her apartment. Then she's going to interview me at the station and I'm going to state categorically that we looked at the evidence, the Feds looked at the evidence, and Glenn is guilty, case closed."

Jim frowned. "So if Glenn didn't do it, what do you think happened? We processed that scene with a fine-tooth comb. After the Coleman crime scene, we had everyone breathing down our neck. You, Descario, the press. I even had to go up in front of the professional conduct board. I swear the scene was processed clean."

"You're not under scrutiny, Dr. Gage," Hans said.

"Then what exactly am I doing here?"

Will didn't blame Jim for sounding defensive. "We want to look at the crime scene photos and preliminary notes again. With Hans, who hasn't seen everything. That's why I asked you to bring the case files."

"I don't have any evidence, only the written reports and photos."

"But you have all the photos, correct?" Hans asked. "Not just the ones that went to the jury."

"True. I prepared a board for the jury to highlight the similarities between the four murders. As you know, because we couldn't use the physical evidence in the Coleman homicide, I needed to establish a causal link between the Anna Clark murder — where we had physical evidence — to the other three homicides where we didn't have physical evidence. That we could use," he added.

Jim opened the box, took out files, and put them on the table. "You don't honestly believe Theodore Glenn is innocent?"

"He killed Bethany, Brandi, and Jessica," Will stated emphatically. "He didn't kill Anna Clark."

Robin sucked in her breath, but said nothing. Will went on.

"We have new evidence that Theodore Glenn was physically elsewhere during the narrow window of Anna Clark's TOD."

"Then you're saying that someone planted evidence on the body? The victim had Glenn's hair in her hands."

"It could have been planted," Hans said.

Jim scowled. "Did you testify for the defense in the O. J. Simpson trial?"

Will couldn't help but grin, but when he saw Jim's and Hans' stern faces, he covered up his humor. "Look, Jim, I know this sounds wacky. But hear me out, okay?"

"Tell me straight."

Will told him everything they'd learned so far about the time line, admitting to his relationship with Robin and why he believed Glenn told Trinity the truth the other night.

"But the clincher — if none of that evidence convinces you that we have a problem here — Glenn didn't kill Anna's cat. His previous history tells us he would have hurt the animal in order to torment her, but the cat was unharmed."

"Maybe he didn't have time," Jim said.

"It's the only thing that makes sense."

"Why would he lie about this?" Hans said.

"Because he's a psychopath?" Jim said, running a hand through his hair. "If you believe that, then you also believe that someone planted evidence."

Will nodded. "Yes. Someone involved in the investigation had to have not only killed Anna, but framed Glenn."

"You can't be serious, Hooper," Jim said.

"I am. I wish we were wrong, but I don't think we are."

"Then who? Who would do this? Why?"

Jim was asking all the questions Will had been thinking about last night while he lay awake next to Robin. Who? Why?

"It had to have been a cop — or someone at the crime lab."

Jim slowly rose. "What?"

"Sit down."

"No. You're accusing *my crime lab* of planting evidence. The next thing is you'll accuse them of murder!"

When Will and Hans didn't say anything, Jim's jaw dropped. "You think one of my people killed Anna? Because we fucked up the Coleman crime scene and they wanted to get Glenn? That's pathetic."

"Actually," Hans said, "we think that whoever killed Anna planned to kill Robin, but Anna came home unexpectedly. Either Anna interrupted the intruder, or the intruder was someone she knew and trusted enough to let in. There was no sign of forced entry."

"Nor was there in the first three murders," Jim said.

Will said, "Wouldn't Anna have fought Glenn off? Not let him in? There would have been something. But we assumed that he was waiting for her when she got in. That he picked the lock or had a key, possibly stealing it out of one the girls' purses while they were working."

"He could have picked the lock at any time. Those old buildings had crappy locks."

"Let's look at the photos," Hans said. "Maybe our theory is totally off. Maybe we're wrong."

"You don't think you are."

"We don't," Will said. He glanced at Robin as Jim spread the files on the table. Robin was holding it together, her mouth tight and face impassive. It was her large, round eyes that showed how tense she was.

Under the table, he found her hand and squeezed it.

Jim spoke as if he were on trial. "You can see from the photographs that each victim was cut dozens of times by a sharp instrument. Analysis determined it was an X-ACTO knife."

"Was the weapon ever recovered?" Hans asked.

"No," Jim said. "Based on the marks, we determined that the cuts were made with the exact same type of knife — a stainless-steel X-ACTO Number 5 blade. Each incision was made precisely. You can see the initial puncture here" — he pointed to what Will knew was the beginning of the incision — "is deeper than the rest of the incision. He punctured, then sliced. It was confirmed in the autopsy."

"I see here that the first three victims were cut in excess of forty times, but the last victim, Anna Clark, was cut only twenty-two times."

"But the incisions are the same," Jim said defensively.

"It's a common knife. You identified it immediately, correct?" Hans asked.

"But the same type of knife was also used to slit the throats of the victims — a double-edged blade, three-and-a-half to four inches long, stainless steel. Very likely a butterfly knife, but I couldn't testify to that. Two killers with the same two knives?"

"Hmm."

"What? You can't see it?" Jim grabbed two of the photos. "We *know* Glenn killed Bethany Coleman, but our evidence was thrown out because of contamination. Look at the incision on her body compared to the incision on Anna Clark's body. Same length, same type of puncture, same knife."

As Jim looked at the photos, he frowned.

"Do you see what I see?" Hans asked.

"What do you see, Hans?" Will asked, honestly curious. He believed someone else killed Anna based on the time line. He hadn't seriously thought that the evidence itself could have proved something different than what was presented at trial.

"It's actually a minor point," Hans admitted. "But the depth of the cuts in Anna's body are shallower than in the first three victims. There are also hesitation marks on

Anna, but not the others. On Bethany there were two hesitation marks — but all the rest were clean. No hesitation on Brandi or Jessica. But the last victim — virtually every incision had a hesitation point."

"That doesn't prove Glenn didn't kill her." Robin spoke for the first time.

Hans' voice softened as he said, "No, it doesn't. But I think Jim sees what I see."

Will looked at the photos. At first he didn't notice anything strange at all — only the sick perversion of a psychopath.

It was Brandi's crime scene photo that gave him the first glimpse of something.

"Is that a pattern on her body?" he asked.

Hans nodded. "I think he left a pattern on each of his victims."

Will rotated the picture. He saw it at the same time as Jim said, "T.A.G."

"Tag?" Will asked.

"His initials," Robin whispered. "T.A.G. He marked the bodies of my friends with his initials."

"Robin, if you want to step out, Mario can take you —"

She shook her head rapidly back and forth, tears glistening in her eyes. "I need to see this."

Will grasped Robin's hand again.

Jim continued. "There's a pattern on each

of the first three victims, but on the fourth victim it's completely random."

"It would be virtually impossible to notice the pattern," Hans said, "because each body has a *different* pattern. Nothing to connect the three, but when you turn the photos . . ." He took out a felt-tip pen and connected the marks.

Now Glenn's initials were obvious. On all the bodies, except Anna Clark.

"I can't believe I didn't see this," Jim said.

"It wasn't clear," Hans began, but Jim waved his hand.

"Look at this." He pointed to a close-up of an incision on Anna's body.

The cut had two hesitation marks, one at the beginning and one near the end. "What's that striation?" Will asked. "It looks like a double flap of skin."

"It is," Jim said. "Whoever made this incision did it once — and hesitated twice here and here — then cut into the flesh again in an attempt to make the mark appear uniform. But the knife pulled off another layer of skin. If the medical examiner had been sharp, he would have seen something was off and further investigated the anomaly, and I think he'd have been able to tell the body had been cut postmortem. But it would be hard to prove in court because these cuts happened shortly after death."

No one said anything for a moment. "Why?" Will asked.

"Whoever killed Anna didn't want her to suffer," Hans said quietly. "They killed her right there in the foyer, as soon as she came home. I think the killer surprised Anna, and was also surprised by her. He may not have known he hadn't killed Robin until after Anna was dead."

"But then she didn't call Will?" Robin said. "That means the killer called Will. Why?"

The killer — instead of Anna — contacting Will gave him pause. Did he know the killer personally? If they were right about what had happened, it was most likely someone he worked with, someone he socialized with after work, who had killed Anna Clark, then planted evidence to implicate Glenn, showing not only a calm cold-bloodedness but premeditation.

"I don't think we have enough information to know why at this point," Hans said.

"You're a profiler," Will said, feeling the pressure. "Based on this evidence, what type of person killed Anna?"

"I think we need to approach this differently than a traditional crime scene," Hans said. "Because evidence was planted at the scene that implicated Theodore Glenn. That means that the killer had access to evidence that only those directly involved in the investigation could access. The killer knew Glenn used an X-ACTO knife — and the exact *type* of knife. That was never revealed to the press until trial. Anna's killer knew the type of double-edged knife used to slit the victim's throats."

"And the bleach," Will said. "We didn't say a word about the bleach until trial."

Jim ran a hand over his head. "There were probably thirtysome people involved in the investigation who knew Glenn's M.O., not including the D.A.'s office."

"But they didn't know about the patterns," Will said. "They assumed — as we did — that Glenn was randomly cutting his victims as a method of torture."

Jim said, "Because the marks in Anna's case were made so soon after death, scientifically there isn't much distinction between the cuts. And it would have been difficult to prove in court if we had reason to suspect another killer."

"I agree," Will said. "Jim, we're not looking only at the crime lab —"

"Yes," Jim said quietly, "you are. And now, so am I. Because your average cop isn't going to have access to Glenn's hair samples, nor know how to place them in a hand to make it appear that they were pulled out of the head in a fight."

Hans said, "According to the reports, you took a DNA swab when Glenn was first arrested after Brandi Bell was murdered."

"Yes," Jim said. "We had a warrant."

"And you searched his house."

Will said, "We had a warrant to search the premises for any personal effects of the victims, an X-ACTO knife, blood evidence, among other things. It was extensive and thorough."

"It would have been easy to remove hairs from his brush or comb," Hans said. "Never logged it in."

"It couldn't have been logged," Jim agreed. "I personally checked all the evidence after Will called me this morning. Nothing is missing."

"If someone removed hair from Glenn's house after the Brandi Bell murder," Will said, "that means that he planned to kill all along, just waiting for the right time."

"We need a list of everyone involved in the execution of the warrant," Hans said.

"It's right here." Will flipped through the report and pointed to a sheet in his own handwriting. "I logged everyone who came in and out of Glenn's house."

Hans looked at the list. "You're not here, Jim."

"I had another case."

"There're only seven people on this list, plus detectives Hooper and Sturgeon."

"What about Frank?" Jim asked. "He was an alcoholic — no offense, Will, but you know it was true. Maybe he was feeling guilty because he fell asleep the night of the Suarez homicide."

"Frank didn't have the wherewithal to pull something like this off," Will admitted. "And we searched Glenn's house *before* Jessica was killed. Something like this requires forethought and precision."

"This is an organized killer," Hans said. "The crime was planned well in advance. The killer was likely waiting in the apartment for Robin to return home after her shift. The killer was surprised by Anna, who wasn't supposed to be home that night. Sliced her throat, laid her on the floor. Had to act fast. Put the hairs in Anna's hand, closed it. Cut the body. Half as many times as Glenn. Because the killer knew he hadn't gone deep enough, recut along the same lines to try to reach the same depth as Glenn. Same type of knife, same length of marks, but a little off. After, he poured bleach over the body to destroy evidence as well as mimic Glenn's M.O."

"And there was no pattern," Will said. "If the killer surprised Anna, then the killer had to have paged me. Why?"

"That is the million-dollar question," Hans said. "And I don't have a good answer for it, not yet."

"Does this mean I had two stalkers?" Robin asked, incredulous. "First Glenn, who seems like he was obsessed with me all along and not just a lunatic? Then someone in the police department?" She rose from the table, shaking her head.

"Robin," Hans said, "you were in the public eye."

"So it's my fault . . ." she began defensively.

"It's not your fault."

"I should have seen something. Why didn't I know something weird was going on?"

"*We* should have seen something," Will said. "Don't blame yourself."

"Anna wasn't supposed to die. I was." She glanced from one man to another, her eyes resting on Will. She was trying hard to keep up her game face. "I need a minute." Robin left the room and they heard the bathroom door, the only door in the loft, quietly shut.

"She'll be okay," Will said, though he

wished she didn't have to go through this particular hell.

"There are four cops and three crime scene technicians on this list who were in Glenn's house," Hans said. He read the names.

Jim shook his head. "I can't believe — why?"

"I think this is one of the rare cases of we won't know why until we have the individual in custody," Hans said.

"Joseph Miller is no longer in my department," Jim said. "He transferred three years ago to Los Angeles."

"My office can investigate him," Hans said. "It will be easier that way, if you agree."

Will nodded. "And Officer Janice Bernstein moved up north. San Carlos, I believe. Near San Francisco."

"And the other three cops?"

"Patrick Kincaid — I almost forgot he was a beat cop back then. I was his training officer, before I made detective." Will smiled wanly. "I'll personally vouch for Patrick. And it's not like we'll be able to question him, he's in a coma."

"Is he related to your partner?"

"Brother," Will said.

"Officers Doug Holmes and Roger Supan — they're still on the force," Will said. "Supan may have made detective last year, I don't remember. Neither are in my precinct."

"Stu Hansen and Diana Cresson are both still in the lab," Jim said.

"I suggest we move cautiously on this."

"There's no motive," Jim said.

"That we know about," Will clarified.

## TWENTY-SEVEN

It was nearly eleven thirty when Will and Hans arrived at the police station. He'd already spoken with Trinity twice, and agreed to be "caught" at twelve ten right outside the rear entrance of the police station.

Will briefed his boss, Chief Causey, then went up to the e-crimes unit while Hans used Will's desk to call Washington.

He knocked on the door of Patrick's old office. Someone else had moved into it. He couldn't blame the department, but knowing everyone had gone on with their lives and his best friend was still lying in a coma hit Will hard.

"Come in," a gruff voice said.

Will entered. Doug Myers looked haggard sitting at his desk. "You left a message that you had information about the law firm associated with Glenn."

Doug handed him a file folder, a big grin crossing his face. "I got nearly everything you needed."

"Nearly? What did you find?"

"The money. Glenn paid nearly three hundred thousand to the North Bay Law Offices for legal defense. But this other corporation you had me track down? San Diego Investment Corp? Glenn's escrow accounts have transferred nearly five million dollars over the past two years to ten different accounts in and out of America, through SDIC. Corporation within corporation to hide the identity of the individuals involved."

"But you have a name?"

"Alan and Eve Reston."

"Eve?" Will asked. "Alan and Eve — Alan is Glenn's middle name. But why? Who set it up? How deep was Sara Lorenz in with Glenn?"

"Who?" Doug asked, but didn't wait for the answer. "So I'm working on blocking the accounts, but I can tell you it's not going to be easy."

"I can get the Feds on it."

"Good luck. You can probably lock down the U.S. accounts with a warrant, but some of these countries are going to take weeks or months. Or never. And he could easily move the money before then.

"I did find one local connection," Doug added.

"And?"

"The corporate filings for SDIC and the law firm are in San Diego. They have a local post office box, same zip code."

Too close to be a coincidence.

"Can I see that?"

Doug handed him the corporate paperwork. The zip code was indeed a San Diego number, identical for both — the boxes were only a few numbers off. "This is a downtown zip code," Will said as he wrote down the information and thanked Doug.

He called Hans on his way out of e-crimes.

Hans said, "I'll alert Homeland Security to flag the passports for anyone with the last name of Reston. We can't assume that they're using the same names, however."

"He could simply drive across the border," Will said.

"One problem at a time. Border Patrol is on the lookout. We have a stop on the Arizona/California border in case he plans to leave California, and others at Calexico, Tijuana, and other likely exits."

"I don't have to tell you how screwed we are if he goes to Mexico. It'll be virtually impossible to get him out, especially if he has money."

"I've already alerted my legal attaché, but you're right. If he crosses the border, we may never see him again."

"I sense a 'but.' "

"I can't see him leaving without making an attempt to see Robin."

"You mean kill her." Will swallowed heavily. "I won't give him the chance to get that close."

"I think he's torn — he's smart, knows we have Robin under lock and key. But he wants to get at her in the worst way. He may be rash, and we'll have to be expecting it."

Will wasn't about to forget it. He switched gears. "What I want to know is, where is Sara Lorenz?" Will asked. "She's the key to this, and it's like she disappeared off the face of the earth."

"If she's still alive, she's just as dangerous as he is," Vigo said.

"Why do you say that?"

"Because she'll do anything for him, and her own life doesn't mean anything to her."

"Are you sure you want to do this?" Mario asked Robin after she told him about closing the Sin.

She nodded, her stomach tied in knots. "I

have to." She had her staff schedule on her computer and all their personal phone numbers. She began calling, and for the most part everyone was understanding.

"I'll cover your wages for your scheduled hours," she told them. "I wish I could do more."

At noon she took a break and watched the news, waiting for Trinity Lange's report. She didn't have to wait long.

"Trinity Lange, reporting for KSTV outside the San Diego Police Department. Less than seventy-two hours ago, escaped convict Theodore Glenn broke into my home and admitted to murdering Bethany Coleman, Brandi Bell, and Jessica Suarez."

Pictures of Robin's friends came onscreen. Though the photos were only seven years old, they seemed so young.

Trinity came back on camera. "But in an odd twist of events, Glenn denied killing Anna Clark. In fact, he demanded that I investigate his claims.

"I encouraged him to turn himself in and address his argument in the proper venue, but Glenn left and is suspected of murdering retired SDPD Detective Frank Sturgeon, who had arrested him.

"I turned over the information to the police as well as pursued my own parallel investigation. To recap the crime, Anna Clark was killed in the same manner as the three previous victims. She was tortured with an X-ACTO knife, doused in bleach, and had her throat slit. She bled to death and was discovered by her roommate.

"One difference between the victims, as presented in court, was the fact that Anna Clark was the only one of the four women who had not had a personal relationship with Mr. Glenn. The first three victims were all ex-girlfriends of the convict, though according to testimony they had all parted amicably.

"Another difference in the crimes is that Ms. Clark was cut twenty-two times, not forty-six, forty-seven, and fifty-five times as were the first three victims. In addition —"

Will stepped out the door and Trinity spun around. "Detective Hooper! Detective Hooper, please tell KSTV viewers about reopening the investigation into Anna Clark's murder."

Will frowned, glared at the camera, then turned to Trinity and said in a clipped tone, "A joint task force between the San Diego Police Department and the Federal Bureau of Investigation has exhaustively reviewed the evidence related to the Anna Clark homicide. The FBI agrees with the evidence presented at trial. It was collected properly, the M.O. is consistent, and physical evidence places Theodore Glenn at the crime scene. His hair was found tightly clasped in the victim's hand. He may have thought the bleach would destroy all evidence, but he was mistaken. In Anna Clark's death, she fought her attacker and we are confident that Glenn was rightfully convicted.

"The Anna Clark case is closed."

He turned and walked away, the camera and Trinity following. "Detective Hooper! Any news on Theodore Glenn's whereabouts? Are you any closer to capturing him? Who is next on his list, or do you know?"

Will spun around. It was clear to Robin from the expression on his face that this part of the staged interview hadn't been planned. "We will hunt down that animal and he won't know what hit him. Theodore Glenn will be back behind bars sooner rather than later."

"Do you have any leads?"

"No comment."

Trinity wrapped up the scene as Will disappeared from camera. "To reiterate, Theodore Glenn escaped during the tragic San Quentin earthquake on Saturday where eighty-one people died, including twenty-six prisoners and four guards . . ."

Robin shut off the television.

"You okay?" Mario asked.

She nodded and resumed her calls. She'd never be truly okay until Glenn was back behind bars.

Or better yet, dead.

Carina caught up with Will in the bull pen. "Just got a call back on the woman in Anaheim, Jenny Olsen, who wrote to Glenn. Remember, we found her car at the library? The Feds paid her a visit. She started by lying, they threatened jail time, she caved. She saw Glenn on Sunday night, late — about eleven thirty p.m. Gave him her car the next morning. Swears he was a perfect gentleman and we obviously had the wrong man." She rolled her eyes. "The Feds were not amused and arrested her for aiding and abetting a fugitive."

"Anything else?"

"Mario called. Said Robin shut down the Sin. Paying her staff at least through the weekend."

Will frowned. "Closed it? Because Glenn's on the loose?"

"She's concerned about the safety of her employees and customers."

It was a smart, responsible move, but it

had to have hurt. The Sin was Robin's business, her livelihood.

Will pulled out the slip of paper he'd written the post office box number on. "It looks familiar," he explained after bringing Carina up to speed on the e-crimes part of the investigation. "The fact that two corporations affiliated with Glenn have the same post office zip code, I think we need to stake it out."

Carina opened her file on the case. She flipped through the reports. "Here," she pointed.

"Same post office that Sara Lorenz uses? Definitely no coincidence." He called Hans and clued him in. "I'm sending an undercover team over there," Will said. "And instead of picking her up, I'll have her followed."

"People don't always check their boxes daily," Hans commented.

"This is the best lead we have so far."

"I agree. I saw your interview with Trinity. I think it went well."

"I hope it doesn't lead Glenn to her doorstep," Will said.

"You beefed up her protection."

"I told her to get out of town, but she refused."

"That's all you can do."

"I can put her in prison for her safety," Will mumbled, with no intention of doing it. "Robin closed the Sin."

"I thought she would," Hans said.

"Anything more on Lorenz's cell phone?"

"We're tracing the numbers. So far, nothing has panned out."

An idea came to Will. "Doesn't the post office require a physical address on file?"

"I'm not sure," Hans said. "But I can check. I see what you're getting at, I'll see if they have any address for Lorenz or the corporations."

Will hung up and said to Carina, "Where is Sara living if she's not at the house she owns?"

"Friends? Family?"

"We couldn't find any family on her. But what if one of these corporations Doug tracked down owns property?"

"You're a genius," Carina said.

"I just hope it leads somewhere, because I'm getting nervous." Will dialed Doug's line and added to his partner, "Glenn has been quiet for too long. He's going to make a move. Soon."

Theodore paced, furious over the *pathetic* newscast. Trinity Lange put on a good show, but she had done *shit* to prove he hadn't killed Anna Clark.

The Feds had looked into the case in two days and ruled that everything was fine? Since when did government bureaucrats work that fast?

And then William called him an *animal.* Some low-intelligence four-legged nothing. He was *something,* better than the cops, better than William. Smarter. Tougher. Not limited by conforming to an inane man-made moral structure. He could do *anything.* He'd BASE jumped off the highest bridge in the world. He'd flown a twin prop in thunderstorms that would have frayed the nerves of the most skilled fighter pilot.

He could do anything. Be anything. Get away with anything.

And they called him an *animal!*

What about the women he killed? What were they? Oh, that's right, *victims.* Didn't matter that none of them were pure, that they were anything but *innocent.* But slice a couple of sleazy strippers to death and suddenly they become *innocent victims.*

Stupid fools. Framing him for Anna's murder to get him out of the way. Maybe *William* had done it. Maybe he'd killed Anna, framed Theodore, so he could have Robin all to himself.

Theodore laughed. William didn't have

the balls.

Sara came into the room. "Is everything okay?"

"No," Theodore said. He didn't elaborate.

"I have —"

A phone rang. Her cell phone. It was a disposable phone, like he'd told her to buy, but still he was suspicious.

She answered it, not taking her eyes from his. "Hello?" She listened. "Oh, are you sure? I understand. When do you think you'll reopen?" She waited, then said, "I'm sorry. If there's anything I can do, call me, okay?"

Sara put the phone down.

"Who was that?" Theodore demanded. He was too close to have the cops find him now.

"My boss." She giggled.

He stared at her, self-preservation instincts kicking into high gear.

She continued. "Didn't you wonder how I learned so much about Robin McKenna?"

He didn't respond. A cold chill crept up his spine as he realized exactly what Sara meant. "What have you done?"

She shook her head. "No, it's all fine. I didn't use this address, I used a P.O. box, different than our corporate address. I have a completely different identity over there, a driver's license, fake social, everything. I've been working at The Eighth Sin over a year, no one suspects —"

He slapped her. "I told you to tell me *everything* you were doing. You kept this from me! What were you planning to do? Keep me in the dark forever?"

"Pl-please. Listen." Sara took a deep breath, took a step away from him, her eyes bright with fear.

She continued. "Everything is fine. Just fine. I know her schedule, I know where she lives, I know everything about her. I know that she still sleeps every night with the lights on."

Theodore stepped toward Sara but said nothing.

"You wanted to scare her, right?" Sara continued, emboldened by his silence. "Well, she's scared. She closed the Sin tonight. Until further notice. Called everyone and said she was still paying us, but not to come in."

Theodore walked over to the front window, opened one of the plantation shutters, and stared at the quiet street. Bryce Descario's house was across the road, three houses down. He could have easily killed him at least three times. The guy had such a predictable routine, it would have been easy. He left between eight and eight fifteen every morning dressed in workout clothes. Returned before ten thirty. Left again at noon in business casual clothes. And so on.

But he didn't care about killing Descario. The thought didn't fill him with any emotion, excitement or otherwise. No thrill.

Killing William Hooper? Oh, yes, he felt it. Anticipation crawled up his spine, excitement spreading, giving his mind clarity and purpose. Killing Robin McKenna? He filled with heat, a blaze of intense satisfaction and *bliss*. As if watching her die would put him on top of the world, he would have the key to the universe.

But together — killing the two lovers together would be the pinnacle of everything Theodore ever wanted. A culmination of all his now seemingly childish pranks with his sister, the games he'd played with the strippers, watching William and Robin fuck like animals.

Now, he saw his true potential, what he could have if only he could get William and Robin in the same room. If only he could control them. He ran through the possibilities.

"Teddy?" Sara asked cautiously.

"You should *never* have kept that information from me." But he wasn't angry. He saw the benefit, but more than that he was looking to the future. Robin bleeding. Dying for him.

"You're right. I'm sorry."

"Let's get ready to go to Mexico. You start packing. I need to transfer some money."

"I can do that," she said. "I know —"

"I said *pack!*" He slapped her. Something in her eyes — she was hiding something from him. "Now," he added, keeping his voice artificially calm.

This was the second time she had made a comment about handling the money. What did she know that he didn't?

He was about to find out.

# TWENTY-EIGHT

Jim watched Trinity's newscast from his office. He had mixed feelings about Hooper's plan. While he understood the necessity of putting whoever killed Anna Clark at ease, he still wasn't one hundred percent confident that it was someone in his lab. Someone he'd worked with for years. Who he'd had dinner with, gone for drinks with, hired or promoted.

"You're a scientist, Jim, stop being so emotional," he muttered.

He'd re-packed all the evidence related to Anna Clark's homicide into the case file box to take home. He'd quietly contacted the Sheriff's Department, where the city arranged to store long-term physical evidence because they didn't have the room, and asked that everything relating to Glenn's investigation be sent immediately to Quantico. It was already en route. Anyone who came in asking about it would be detained.

He needed to do this work from home. He wasn't a good liar, and he didn't want to lie to his staff. And more important, he wanted the freedom of spreading the photos and reports out so that maybe he could see something he hadn't seen before.

Stuart Hansen had been borderline depressed after the screwup on the Bethany Coleman homicide. He'd taken Jessica's death personally. But could he have killed an innocent human being in order to frame a killer? Jim couldn't understand that kind of reasoning.

Hans Vigo did, but Jim expected that from the Feds. Suspicious of everyone. What he *didn't* expect was that Will Hooper would be so ready to suspect an insider. Yes, the evidence was there, and Jim could *see* that, but would Will be quick to think that someone he worked with every day was capable of cold-blooded murder? It had been Will's idea for a federal agent to follow

Stu, Diana, and the two cops — in case they recognized a local law enforcement tail.

Jim's career was on the line. Worse than that was the thought that he'd failed in the worst way. By missing something that had let a killer walk free, but more devastating to him, personally, was that he could have been working side by side with a murderer. He put everyone he knew in that role, and no one fit. Kind, smart but dopey Stuart Hansen? Career-minded Diana Cresson? All to right a wrong by committing a crime? A cop turned vigilante?

None of them fit. And if it *had* been personal against Robin McKenna, Jim couldn't help but ask why. Who that he knew would have anything against a witness? It didn't make sense.

His cell phone rang. "Gage."

"It's me, Stuart. Did you see the news? What's going on? What are the Feds up to? Did they really reopen the Anna Clark homicide?"

Responding like Agent Vigo instructed him, Jim said, "I don't know. I'm out of the loop on this one. But nothing came of it, and they concur with our findings."

"Are we all going to be fired? Am I going to be fired?"

"No one is going to be fired, Stu."

"We're worried."

"It'll be okay. Just sit tight. The cops need to find Theodore Glenn and life will get back to normal."

He was leaving with the box an hour later when he ran into Stu and Diana in the parking lot. Damn, he thought by leaving after the lunch rush he'd miss his people. "Where are you off to?" Diana asked, glancing at his files.

"I'm coming down with a bug," he said. "I'm going to do paperwork at home." His smile was strained.

"Are you sure we're not going to be in trouble?" Stu said. "With the Feds? Are they investigating you? Is that why you're leaving?"

"Stu, slow down," Jim said. "No one is investigating anyone. I told you the Feds looked at the evidence and everything is fine. Glenn was rightfully convicted."

"Any news on that front?" Diana said. "We haven't heard anything."

"We've been busy with our jobs, and that's what we need to focus on. We have a dozen cases to process from this week, I have a major trial in two weeks. Worrying about the Feds or Glenn isn't productive."

"Right," Diana said. She squeezed Jim's arm. "I agree." She motioned for Stu to follow her to the lab. "Back to work."

Will was on the phone with the undercover team surveilling the post office. They had a pair watching the parking lot, as well as a man inside watching the boxes. So far, no one matching Sara Lorenz's description had been seen, and no one had opened the boxes. The Feds had obtained a warrant to search the boxes. Nothing of interest was in any of them — only a day of mail had been delivered.

"Which means we're a day too late," Will grumbled.

"It shows that she probably picks up her mail regularly," Hans offered.

The physical address on the postal box application led right back to the house Sara Lorenz had rented to Stephanie Barr since last year.

Hans took a call while Will wrapped up his conversation. They hung up at the same time and Hans said, "We need to get over to the Sin."

"What happened?"

"We've been monitoring Sara's cell phone for real-time activity. She just received a call. From the Sin."

At the time Robin was supposed to be opening her business, she was sitting in her office while Mario and his men turned away her customers. They'd posted a sign on the door simply stating that due to an emergency, the Sin would be temporarily closed.

She called Isabelle Swann at the art gallery. "Robin! I'm so glad you called. I'm thrilled with the response we've been getting on your work. Several serious buyers have already contacted me."

"That's wonderful," Robin said. She wished she could be more excited over the news.

"You don't sound very happy about it. What's wrong?"

"My life is completely falling apart." She dropped on Isabelle virtually everything that had happened this week, from Theodore Glenn escaping — which the gallery owner knew — to closing the Sin.

"Oh, sweetie, that must have been such a hard decision."

"I didn't have a choice. And I don't have a choice in this, either. You're going to have to postpone —"

"No, I know exactly what you're going to say. I'm not postponing the showing."

"I can't risk it."

"I'll hire extra security. I have some cops that work for me off-duty. Good guys."

"It's not about the security. I've hired my own, and the police are watching my business and home, but Theodore Glenn doesn't care about that. He may decide to take out something big. Like your gallery. Holding everyone hostage or something. I don't know how he thinks. But I can't risk it."

"Look, Robin, I understand your concern. But I'm not postponing the show. If you can't come, I'll work around it. In fact, I might be able to spin it. Yeah, that's it, we'll do a video feed. You say a few words, let people ask you questions. I can make a big deal about it, so if that guy is hanging around, he'll know you're not here. Okay?"

"I don't know —"

"Robin, it'll work. I hope it doesn't come to that, but I'll make it work. I promise. I'll sell dozens of your paintings and make us both tons of money." She laughed. The prices weren't so extravagant that Robin could even think of closing her club and painting full-time, even if she wanted to, but they were high enough to warrant looks by serious investors.

"Are you sure?"

"One hundred percent."

"I'll let the police know. If they think we should cancel, I'm going to agree with them."

"Just think about it, okay? Call me Saturday. I have to go. Be careful, sweetie."

She hung up before Robin could say anything else.

She'd met Isabelle two years ago when the gallery owner came into the Sin and spotted Robin's paintings. She demanded to know who had done the work, and for two years they'd worked together to increase Robin's exposure in the art community. Isabelle had sold several of her paintings already, keeping the allure by only having one piece for sale a month. Then three months ago Isabelle announced that Robin was ready for her own gallery show. Robin went along with it.

Isabelle was also one of the only women Robin had grown close to since Glenn killed her friends, and even now Robin kept her at arm's length. As much as she could with Isabelle's natural exuberance and enthusiasm.

Did Glenn know about Isabelle? That she was someone important to Robin? How much did he know about the art show? Could he really be planning something for Sunday?

She rubbed her forehead and opened her payroll. She clocked everyone in at their normal time.

The knock on her office door startled her. "Come in," she said.

It was Will. Alone, though she heard voices in the bar. "I didn't expect to see you until later," she said.

Will closed the door, sat on the edge of her desk, his hand reaching for her face. Caressing her in a casually intimate gesture that gave her butterflies.

"I don't know how to say this, so I'm just going to tell you straight."

The butterflies turned to lead. "Wh-what?" she asked.

"Two hours ago a phone call was made to Sara Lorenz."

"Is she one of the women you're following who might be helping Glenn?"

Will nodded. "We haven't been able to locate her. The call came from here."

"Here?" she repeated. "The Sin?"

"Yes."

"That's not possible. I don't know anyone by that name."

"Mario said that you called your staff this afternoon."

"I closed the Sin until further notice." Her head was swimming. "You're not saying — I don't know Sara Lorenz!"

"She may have changed her name or appearance or both. I need you to look at her

406

picture. It's not a very good image; it's from her driver's license about six years ago."

Robin looked. The woman in the photo was a mousy blonde with brown eyes. She gave the camera a half smile. She looked *normal.* Not like someone who would help a killer.

"I don't recognize her."

"What if she went blonder? Darker? She's five foot three, one hundred ten pounds on her license. Picture her with makeup."

The picture swam in front of her, beginning to look familiar. She remembered the last time she'd identified someone off a picture — in that case, off a rough police sketch. She'd seen Theodore Glenn. Not because the sketch looked specifically like him, but the shape was his. She'd just known.

The shape of Sara Lorenz's face was familiar. Her cheekbones. Her eyes.

Dear God, someone she trusted had been spying on her for a killer. Watching her. Talking to her. Her blood ran cold. She'd never suspected her assistant manager was working with Theodore Glenn. How could anyone help him? How could a *woman* trust him?

Robin frowned, the paper rustling in her shaking hands. "I — what if I'm wrong?"

"Who do you think Sara is?"

"She *might* be my assistant manager, Gina Clover. Gina runs banquets and special events during the week. You met her earlier this week." She handed Will the picture and rubbed her temples.

*This was not happening.*

"Can you grab her personnel file?"

Robin crossed her office to the filing cabinet as if she were out of her body and watching the scene unfold in front of her. Detached. This was unreal. That Glenn had been watching her even while in prison. That a woman, knowing he was a killer, would help him.

Hands still shaking, she handed Will Gina's folder.

He flipped it open to her original application. "Rock and roll."

"What?"

"Same post office box as Sara Lorenz."

"She's supposed to put down a home address," Robin said, grabbing the file. There was a notation. *Moving.* "I remember now," she said. "She said she was living with her parents until she found a place of her own and would give me her address when she moved. But I never thought to follow up."

Will pushed her chin up, forced her to look at him. His eyes gave her strength and confidence. "We're going to get through this. We *will* find her, and she will lead us to Glenn. Don't blame yourself. Carina and I both met her earlier this week and neither of us realized Gina Clover and Sara Lorenz were the same person."

"How could she do this? To me? Why? I've never done anything to her. She was a good employee. I didn't think he'd have someone *spying* on me! What about my neighbors? Are they spying on me, too? How many people are helping him, Will? When is this going to stop?"

Will wrapped his arms tightly around her while she shook with unshed tears. Taking a deep breath, she pulled herself together. She was tired of acting like a victim, tired of feeling like her life was spinning out of control and all she was doing was waiting for Glenn to come and kill her.

"What's the next step?" she asked.

"You're going home with Mario. Agent Vigo and I are going to continue trying to locate Sara Lorenz. Carina is overseeing the stakeout at the post office Lorenz uses."

"I can't sit around and do nothing."

"I know this is hard, but —"

"You don't know!" She forced herself to calm down. She shouldn't take her frustration out on Will.

He ran a hand through her hair, held her at the neck, tilting her head to look at him. "I do know. I'll come by later tonight, okay?"

He kissed her, then led her from the office. "Gina Clover," he told the federal agent and Mario who were talking in the bar. "Mario, please take Robin home until further notice."

"Find them," Robin told Will. "And please, be careful."

Sara had stolen from him.

Theodore stared at the evidence right in front of him. Sara was smart, *shrewd* in fact, but even she couldn't hide her tracks.

He'd suspected something funny when she got jumpy about the corporate funds. But since he had the quarter million sitting right there in his offshore account, and another seven or so million in his personal account, he wasn't concerned. But when he checked his own funds, he realized she'd moved money from his account with the power of attorney he'd given her. Over the last year she'd moved nearly five million dollars to a variety of accounts both in and out of America.

And she hadn't told him.

*That* meant she planned to leave. Leave

with his money, but without him.

Or was this another one of her "good ideas," like faking an identity and working for Robin McKenna? Something "smart" that she'd insist would be "just fine." The bitch was crazy to play games with a master.

He noted all the accounts, but left them alone. If the Feds had figured any of this out, he didn't want to alert them. He'd only have one chance to transfer the funds, and he had to make sure he had a clean account for the money to go into, an account *he* controlled and not Sara Lorenz.

Not that it would matter when she was dead.

He'd get the plans out of that bitch before he killed her. Take *that* to the bank.

## TWENTY-NINE

"I can't believe we've hit another dead end!"

Will slammed his fist on his desk. They were so close — they had Sara's cell phone, two of her fake identities, the names of the two major corporations Theodore Glenn was using to funnel money, the P.O. boxes, and now nothing.

His phone rang and he snatched it up. "Hooper," he snapped.

411

"Detective Hooper?" The voice was suspicious.

"Yes?"

"This is Brian Varadian with San Diego Bank and Trust. You spoke with my manager this morning about a corporate account."

Will grabbed his notes. "Right, North Bay Law Offices."

"I cannot give you any information without a warrant, you understand."

"I have a warrant." Or he would and made a note to call the D.A., Andrew Stanton.

"Then perhaps we can meet at the bank tomorrow morning?"

"How about now?" He glanced at the clock. Eight at night.

"The bank is closed, and the doors are on a time lock. No one can enter before eight a.m."

"Eight tomorrow morning. I want everything — every transfer, deposit, withdrawal, safe-deposit boxes, whatever you have."

"As long as it is specified in the warrant, I'll give you what you need."

Will hung up and called Stanton. The D.A. said he'd have the warrant ready.

"Okay, maybe we do have a break," Will said. "Twelve hours, and perhaps we can figure out exactly where Glenn is hiding."

"How do you figure that?" Carina asked.

"If the account is paying any bills, maybe a mortgage or property taxes, there'll be some correlation between the payment and an address or account number," Will said. "We're close," he said. "I feel it."

Theodore wrote all account numbers in a small notepad, then destroyed the computer.

He could have been comfortable here in San Diego if he wasn't a wanted man. A spread in France or Switzerland, or perhaps Argentina, would have to do for a time. He had several identities to choose from, but he could no longer trust Sara. As soon as he was settled, he'd create his own identity.

He hadn't thought that running would hold excitement for him, but he felt that familiar surge of anticipation at the thought of eluding the police. It would eat at William Hooper.

That is if Theodore decided the cop would be more tortured living than dying.

Sara walked into the den and stared at the computer which lay in pieces all over the room. "What did you do?"

"What did *you* do, Sara?"

He stepped toward her.

She stepped backward. Good, she was scared. She should be.

"I don't know what you mean, Teddy."

413

"My name is Theodore."

"I — you liked —"

"I humored you when I thought you were helping. Now I find out that you've been *stealing* from me."

"No! That's not true. I would never — I love you, Teddy!"

In two long strides he had her by the arms. He shook her, her head flopped back and forth. "You funneled money from my personal account into the law office account, then moved it all over the world. Millions of dollars."

"So that wherever we go we'll have money!" she pleaded.

"Or so you could run away without me."

"No! No, no, that's not it at all. Listen to me, please."

"I'm listening."

She nodded, brown eyes wide and full of fear and hope. "I knew as soon as you escaped that the cops would freeze your account. If all the money was gone, there'd be nothing to freeze, right? And by the time they figured it out, we'd have already transferred the money to other accounts. See? See how smart it was?"

He shook his head.

"I don't believe you."

"It's the truth! I swear, I was thinking

about you."

"You were thinking about yourself. That was *my* money and I *told* you exactly what to do. You aren't smart enough to come up with your own ideas. You're mine, and now I don't want you."

He grabbed her hair and held it tight, pulling her up the stairs. She stumbled, screamed, but he didn't stop. He dragged her by her hair the last ten feet to the master bedroom, kicked her in the kidneys, and slammed the door shut.

"Teddy, please, I only —"

"Shut up!" He kicked her again. "I taught you how to hide money. I gave you access to my accounts. I *trusted* you, Sara, and you betrayed me."

"I didn't —"

He opened the nightstand where he had earlier put a knife — a sharp butcher knife from the kitchen. Without hesitation, he sliced her thigh. It was only a hair deep, but the cut stung. Sara screamed, tried to get up, but Theodore knocked her back down.

He grabbed her and tossed her on the bed. He sat on her, his left hand over her mouth, the knife in his right. She lay paralyzed with fear and he stared into her eyes. She looked back. When she saw her fate in his face, she started fighting.

He slammed the knife into her chest, over and over, a rage he'd never felt quite like this overtaking him. The surge of emotion, of adrenaline, seemed to stop time as he cut her chest open. She stopped fighting almost immediately, but he still sliced her, unable to stop.

Suddenly, he pushed himself off her, the knife still in his hands. The woman who had been Sara Lorenz was almost unrecognizable. He stabbed the knife into the blood-soaked mattress and walked to the bathroom where he showered in hot water.

He felt a million times better when he stepped out. He dressed, passing Sara's dead body without a glance.

Time to leave the country.

But he'd be back.

"Sooner," he said out loud, "than you think."

# THIRTY

Jim Gage spent all night reading and rereading the reports of all four crime scenes.

What had gone so wrong seven years ago? The politics of the time were such that lab priorities were directed from on high. And while the district attorney's office didn't oversee the crime lab, their priorities were the lab's priorities. When a case was going to trial, everything else was pushed back so that the lab could focus on the immediate.

Overworked staff, limited resources, politicians directing priorities, everything conspired against him running a perfect lab. But it was still damn good and Jim couldn't fathom that anyone on his team — people he worked with, socialized with, respected — could kill. Mistakes happened, more often than he wanted to admit, but killing to fix them?

He didn't want to believe it, but the *evidence,* the facts, showed that someone other than Theodore Glenn had killed Anna Clark.

But if Robin McKenna was the intended victim, then it was personal and not because some ill, misguided cop or criminalist was trying to right wrongs.

They'd talked around the issue earlier when he, Will, and Agent Vigo first discussed the possibility, but they had a more immediate concern than finding Anna Clark's killer. Theodore Glenn was still a threat and the major focus of their resources.

But now, at night, with nothing else on his mind, Jim couldn't help but think about the Anna Clark case and what happened. If Robin was the intended victim, then why?

He made a list of all law enforcement they'd identified, even those who had left the jurisdiction. It only made sense that someone with access to evidence had planted the hair in Anna's hand. That gave them six suspects. It was a reasonable conjecture, but right there Jim saw holes in the theory. A good defense lawyer would point out that someone else had been convicted, that the M.O. matched perfectly — except for the initials which no one had noticed for seven years. Maybe they'd intentionally connected the slash marks to make it appear they were in the form of initials? Why hadn't it been brought out at trial?

Jim could play devil's advocate with the best of them. And the truth was, there was no physical evidence that anyone other than Theodore Glenn had killed Anna. Even if they narrowed the list, without a confession they couldn't put the killer behind bars.

Something tickled the back of Jim's mind. It was that page from Anna's apartment to Will.

Will was supposed to go up to the apartment.

Was he supposed to be the intended victim? Who would want to kill both Robin *and* Will?

It brought him right back to Theodore Glenn, who had obsessed over the two of them. What if he — but the time line put him in the bar at the time Anna was killed. He couldn't have made the call.

Jim wasn't a profiler. He looked at the evidence, and the evidence just wasn't there. But the beginning of an idea began to take shape. He called Will, his voice mail picked up.

"Will, it's Jim Gage. I wanted to bounce a couple ideas off you. No rush, call me in the morning." He hung up.

Thing was, he couldn't get the idea out of his mind. Even though it was well after one in the morning on the East Coast, Jim called Dr. Dillon Kincaid at his house. Dillon was a private practice forensic psychiatrist who had consulted often with the San Diego Police Department until he moved to Washington last year.

Dillon answered on the third ring, half-asleep.

"Sorry to wake you," Jim said. "It's Jim Gage from San Diego."

"Jim. What's wrong?" He sounded more alert.

"Everyone's fine," Jim said. "I have a difficult case and wanted to run it by you."

"Hold on."

A minute later, Dillon picked up another extension. "Okay, what's going on?"

"This is loosely related to the Theodore Glenn case."

"Have you caught him?"

"No. It's about his last victim. We think someone else killed her and framed Glenn."

Dillon didn't say anything for a long minute. "That would mean someone with inside knowledge of the case killed her."

"Yes. A cop or a criminalist."

"And how can I help?"

"Will is working with a Fed on this, Agent Hans Vigo. We had a talk this morning about the intended victim being Robin McKenna. It was her roommate who was killed, but Anna was supposed to be out of town the night she died."

"Go on."

"What I can't get my mind around is that someone — either the victim or the killer — called Will Hooper at twelve fifty-five a.m. from the victim's apartment. Anna was killed within thirty minutes of that call."

"So she could have been dead or alive at that point?"

"Yes."

"What do you want from me?"

"I don't know, someone to bounce ideas off of. I feel like something is here, but I can't clearly see it."

"Let's backtrack. Tell me about Anna."

"She was a twenty-one-year-old stripper at RJ's. A lesbian, but most people didn't know that. She'd been roommates with Robin McKenna for six months. Quiet, kept to herself. She'd apparently been molested by her father for years, according to Robin. Her mother divorced him, and she and her daughter were trying to work out a relationship, which is why Anna was heading to Big Bear for a weekend with her mom. But her mother was delayed, and Anna apparently turned around and came back to San Diego, though that's conjecture."

"And Anna knew Will?"

"She would have had his number because he interviewed all the employees of RJ's during the investigation into the first three murders."

"Where's Anna's father?"

"Back east somewhere. You don't think he killed his daughter?"

"And planted evidence against Glenn? No, unless he's a cop."

"No. A middle manager at some computer company in Massachusetts."

"What about Robin McKenna?"

"She was closing at the bar that night. She was delayed — when Will saw the lights on in the bar, he went there instead of the apartment across the street."

"Wait — she was in the bar while someone else called Will from her apartment? Why did Will think that Robin had called him?"

"Because Anna was out of town."

"And a cop would just go over to the house and not call back?"

"They were romantically involved."

"Ah. So he gets the page and heads over there. I remember the Glenn case. He targeted strippers. Why couldn't he have been the one to kill Anna? There was evidence, right?"

"Yes, but — we now have new evidence. An alibi for Glenn. It's pretty tight, Dillon."

"So you don't think Glenn could have killed Anna."

"No."

"What physical evidence did you have?"

"Hair."

"Easy enough to plant. What about the M.O.?"

"On the surface, identical. Multiple cuts with an X-ACTO knife, body doused in bleach, throat slit. But looking at the evidence more critically, the cuts appear shallower than the first three victims and there are fewer marks. We also believe that the marks were made postmortem, but that'll be hard to prove at this point."

"Why wasn't that noticed at the autopsy?"

"If the coroner was rushed, it wouldn't have been obvious. Again, we're going off the crime scene photos on that one and it's a close call, especially after the bleach."

"Hmm."

"So?"

"So what?"

"Was Robin the intended victim?"

"I don't know."

"That doesn't help."

"Okay, let's play this out. Anna Clark was supposed to be out of town. I assume this was common knowledge?"

"Yes."

"So the killer would have every reason to believe that Robin would be coming home, alone, that night. So he breaks into the apartment, and either finds Anna there, or Anna arrives while he's waiting for Robin. He has to kill her."

"If Anna arrived while the killer was there, the killer would have to have called Will."

"Was the phone dusted?"

Jim looked over the reports. "Yes. Only smudged prints."

"That's odd."

Jim's stomach sank. Why hadn't he seen that before? There should have been clear prints from at least whomever used the phone last.

"The killer wore gloves. Called Will. Why did he want Will to find the body?"

"If Robin was the intended victim, the killer knew about Will's relationship with her. Wanted Will to be the one to find her," Dillon said.

"That's almost exactly Glenn's M.O.," Jim said. "Glenn got his thrills first from making his victims suffer, then watching Robin's reaction to the news when she learned they were dead."

"But Jim, Anna's killer hasn't killed again, at least not in the same manner. Which suggests that this was a personal crime. A premeditated crime of passion."

"Passion?"

"Look at Robin's ex-boyfriends, other people at the time who may have stalked her."

"It sounds too coincidental that she would have two stalkers — Glenn and this unknown killer."

"She led a public life, exposed herself in front of thousands of men. I can see how more than one might be unbalanced enough to kill."

"But to also be a cop?" Jim made a note. "At least this gives me something to go on.

Thanks, Dillon."

"Anytime, Jim. And I'll think more on it. Call me if you have anything new, I'm happy to help. But you should run the scenario by Will and Agent Vigo. He's a good guy, by the way. I've worked with him before."

"Glad for the recommendation."

Jim hung up, drew up a detailed time line and the list of suspects. He also made a note that perhaps someone in law enforcement who wasn't directly involved in evidence collection had accessed the information. It wasn't unheard of, and the evidence locker wasn't restricted to law enforcement personnel. Anyone from the D.A.'s office to cops to the crime lab could go in there and simply sign in. They could easily lie about what evidence they were viewing. No one double-checked, unless they were removing it from the locker.

And something as small as a few hairs could easily be concealed.

Ten minutes later his doorbell rang. He rose from his desk, glanced out the peephole, confused more than concerned.

He opened the door. "You could have called."

"I could have."

Jim barely noticed the gun until three bullets hit him in the chest.

# THIRTY-ONE

Will knocked on Robin's door after midnight. He'd debated going home, but he wanted to see her. She'd seemed so lost after she learned that the woman helping Theodore Glenn had been in her employ for the past thirteen months.

Mario had left one of his men guarding the door. "Detective," the man acknowledged.

Robin unbolted the door and let Will in. As soon as she closed and locked it, Will took her in his arms, her body up against the wall. He kissed her as if it were for the last time.

Her arms went around his neck and she pulled him to her, drinking in his embrace as if she hadn't seen him in years and still loved him.

With Robin, he never wanted to wait, he wanted to make love to her wherever they were, at the drop of a hat. It had been that way since the moment they first met, but he didn't want their relationship to be built solely on lust. He wanted the connection they'd begun before he blew it, the one he prayed they could find again.

"Robin," he murmured, pulling back.

"Hmm," she mumbled, her voice heavy with sleepy desire.

He kissed her neck, so white and long and soft. He felt the vibration of a moan in her larynx, so he kissed her again.

Will picked her up and carried her to her bed.

"The bed? That's a novel idea," she teased.

He didn't smile back. "I blew it with you, Robin. I won't blow it again."

Her smile faltered. "And having sex in bed has something to do with that?"

"I want to make love to you." He kissed her neck again. "I want to show you how much I love you."

"Will, please —"

"What? What's wrong?"

"Just kiss me."

"No."

She frowned. "What are you doing?"

"I'm not doing anything other than trying to fix what went wrong. I know exactly what you're doing."

She tensed beneath his body. "Do you? So smart."

"You're pushing me away."

She literally pushed him off her. "*That's* pushing you away, Will. Why are you doing this? Why are you trying to make more of us than there is? Why can't we just enjoy each other and not talk about all that other stuff?"

"Because what happens between us *is* important. It's more than sex. You know it as much as I do. I love you, Robin. You have to listen to me."

He sat next to her on the bed. She rested her head on her arched knee and looked at him, large green eyes exposing her hope. She was so beautiful, comfortable and sexy in her partial nudity. "I made a mistake by not going after you seven years ago and telling you I was wrong. Look at it from my viewpoint — I saw the M.O., I made a judgment call. I was wrong."

"You were wrong about *me*. I told you —"

"I know what you told me, and I should have believed you, but I'm a cop, okay? People lie to me all the time."

"I've never lied to you, Will."

"Do you love me?"

"What kind of question is that? How can you expect me — ?"

"Do you love me? If you've never lied to me, answer that question."

Her bottom lip quivered and Will almost felt bad for pushing her. "Oh, God, I want to, Will." Tears formed in her eyes.

He gathered her back into his arms. "I

want you to love me, Robin. More than anything. I'm not going to let you walk away this time. You mean too much to me. My only regret is that I didn't see it seven years ago. I was too self-absorbed, too scared that I was falling in love and would screw it up again."

He brushed back her hair, unable to keep his hands off her. She leaned into his caress. "I gave up the one person who would have made a real difference in my life. The one person who gave me more life, more joy, than anyone else. You're the first and only woman I'm willing to give up everything for. My job. My friends. My life. I'll go anywhere to be with you, I'll do anything to convince you that I want to live my life with you in my bed, at my side, in my heart.

"Seeing you again after seven years of drought — it brought everything into perspective. Being a cop means nothing to me without you.

"So I ask you, Robin. Do you love me? Do you love me like I love you?"

Robin couldn't hold back the tears any longer. The pain and fear and anguish washed down her cheeks and she wrapped her arms around Will. "I've always loved you, Will. From that first night, I've loved you."

She showered him with kisses. "No more apologies," she whispered in his ear. "No more what-ifs. I'm not going to run anymore."

They were naked in minutes, taking and giving everything they had, joining in the exquisite moment where you know for certain that the person you love loves you the same way.

After, Will watched Robin sleep. The peace on her face was the same as in his heart. For now, for these quiet hours before dawn, they could forget everything except each other.

But reality intruded much sooner than Will expected.

# THIRTY-TWO

Carina was already at the crime scene when Will arrived. She wasn't handling Jim's murder well, and Will didn't blame her. She and Jim had been romantically involved years ago, and they'd remained good friends.

Nick Thomas, Carina's fiancé, had driven her to Jim's house after she got the call. He stood on the periphery, giving Carina space, but knowing just as Will did that she wouldn't be able to work the case. She was too close to the victim, too emotional. Even the responding officers saw that and kept Carina from walking into the house.

Will sat in his car several minutes, his head on the steering wheel. What had they done wrong? Had their news conference backfired? Or had Theodore Glenn come out of hiding?

Nick approached his car and Will got out. "How's Carina?"

Nick shook his head. "I didn't want her to come, but —"

"She had to see for herself."

"Help me take her home."

Carina was pacing on the front lawn of Jim's house. "Finally," she snapped when she saw Will. "What were you doing? Fucking Robin while Jim was shot to death?"

"I'm going to forget you said that," Will said through clenched teeth. "Go home, Carina."

"No. I'm working this case. Jim was my friend. I thought he was yours, too."

"He is." *Was.* "Please, Carina. You're not going to be any help in this state."

"What state is that? That I care? That I want justice? If I see Theodore Glenn I'll shoot first. That bastard. That bastard!" Tears of rage and anguish coated her eyes. "He killed him in cold blood. For no reason other than the fact that *Jim was doing his job!*"

Will put his hands on her shoulders, felt the tension ripple under her skin. "See, Carina? You've already gotten it wrong because you're too close to this case."

"What in the world are you talking about?"

"Theodore Glenn didn't kill Jim. Jim opened the door to his killer. Jim knew the person who shot him."

Out of the corner of his eye, he saw the crime lab van pull up. "Carina, trust me on this one. Let Nick take you home. I'll call you and tell you everything."

"Promise?"

"Yes." Will nodded at Nick to grab Carina.

"Let's go home, Cara."

"I'm sorry," she mumbled, letting Nick escort her to their car.

Will strode over to where Stuart Hansen and Bonnie Jamison were pulling equipment out of the van. "What happened?" Both looked stricken.

"I'm sorry, but you're going to have to leave. The sheriff is on the way."

"The sheriff? Why?"

"You know the victim."

"Is this because of that report on the

news? Did Jim know something?"

"You know protocol. I'm sharing jurisdiction with the Sheriff's Department. You need to leave."

Stu looked like he wanted to argue, but he quickly packed up and he and the junior tech drove away.

Will took a deep breath before walking up to the front door where two uniformed cops guarded the house. The door was open, Jim's body on the floor, three bullet holes in his chest. The responding officers had checked for vitals, but Will himself also checked. He couldn't believe Jim Gage was dead. They'd worked so many cases together. They hadn't always been friends, but Will had complete respect for the scientist. No one was better at the job than Jim Gage.

Gloves on, Will walked the crime scene. Jim's desk had a half-eaten bowl of soup and near-empty beer bottle on it. The workspace was clear. Would Jim have sat down at his desk to eat dinner? Will doubted it, unless he'd been working on something. Something related to this case.

Something that a killer didn't want anyone else to see. Something, maybe, that Jim had called him about earlier.

*I wanted to bounce a couple ideas off you. No rush, call me in the morning.*

Why hadn't Will called him back? Or stopped by his house? Jim wasn't even supposed to be working the Anna Clark case. They'd agreed to bury it until Glenn was caught. It was supposed to be business as usual so as not to tip-off Anna's killer.

Agent Hans Vigo entered the room. "I'm sorry," he said. The man looked much older than his fortysome years, weary and gray. "I didn't think Anna's killer would come after Jim."

"It wasn't Glenn." Will stated the obvious.

Vigo shook his head. "Jim wouldn't have opened the door to him. I had a message from Jim thirty minutes before he was killed. He had a theory he wanted to run by me."

"Same here," Will said. "He said he'd talk to me in the morning."

"His theory died with him." Vigo looked at the bare desk, frowning.

"How could this happen? No one — except for Chief Causey, Trinity, and Carina — knew we'd concluded Glenn hadn't killed Anna. I watched the tape of Trinity's broadcast several times and she emphatically stated that the case was closed. We didn't put anything in writing."

"We don't know what Jim may have said or done," Hans reminded him. "He'd obviously been working on it, since he wanted to talk to both of us. Perhaps he called the wrong person. We need his phone records ASAP: from home, his cell phone, and his desk at the lab."

"Jim is responsible. He wouldn't have let anything leak."

"You don't have to defend him," Hans said. "I'm not accusing him of anything. Maybe he didn't say or do anything, it could have been something he *didn't* say or do that made our killer suspect something was wrong. We don't know."

"If Jim had an answer, he wouldn't have left a message. He would have hunted one of us down," Will said, trying to alleviate the pang of guilt over Jim's murder. "We need to backtrack, find out exactly what Jim was doing, what he was working on, who he spoke with yesterday, phone records, everything."

"Are you going to be okay on this?" Hans asked. "He was a friend."

"I'm okay." Okay to work the case, but he'd never get the picture of Jim's dead body out of his mind. "The Sheriff's Department is going to handle the evidence. I told our criminalists it was protocol, though we rarely use it."

"In light of what we've been working on,

that's wise. And I can have my people put a rush on the phone records. We should have something in a few hours."

"But first things first," Will said. "Maybe the killer made a mistake. He didn't have a lot of time to clear out Jim's office. The sheriff's criminalists may find something we can use."

"And if that fails," Will added, "we interview every crime scene investigator who's been on staff since Anna Clark's homicide."

When Will came back to Robin's apartment it was after four in the morning, but she hadn't slept much.

Robin had never seen Will looking so weary. He was beyond tired, but more than that his sad eyes registered defeat.

"What happened?"

"Jim is dead."

"Jim? The same Jim who was in my loft this morning?"

Will nodded.

"I thought — we hadn't heard from Glenn in two days, I thought maybe he'd left the country."

"Glenn didn't kill him."

"I don't understand. Was there an accident?"

Will took her arm and moved her to the

436

couch. She sat, taking his hands. "What happened?"

"Jim was killed at his home tonight. I screwed up big-time." Will shook his head, trying to make sense of the senseless. "That whole thing with Trinity this afternoon, trying to divert Anna's killer, to lead him into thinking we weren't reopening the case — it didn't work. In fact, it may have pushed the killer into action." He ran a hand through his hair and leaned back on the couch, closing his eyes. "Jim was a friend."

Robin squeezed Will's hand. "I'm so sorry. How do you know it wasn't Glenn? Maybe he saw the newscast and was angry that the case wasn't being reopened."

"We considered that, except that Jim opened the door to his killer. No sign of force. It was someone he knew. Someone he trusted. His home office was cleared out. I don't know exactly what Jim had with him, but clearly whoever killed Anna thought he'd found something incriminating."

"You need to get some sleep."

"I can't. I'll grab a couple hours later. I need to get down to the station and retrace Jim's steps. I got word on my way over here that Jim left work early. That guy never leaves early. If someone was watching him, that might seem suspicious. I won't know until I find out who spoke to him, what he said, what they saw. But what really makes this truly the worst case of my life — I know the killer. It's someone I've worked with, someone I would also open the door to without hesitation. How could I work with a murderer for years and not know it?"

Robin put her head on his shoulder and Will's hand went automatically to her hair. "I know exactly what you mean," Robin whispered.

They rested for a few long minutes and Robin thought for sure Will had fallen asleep. She debated waking him, knowing he had work to do, but also knowing he needed at least two hours sleep just to function.

He wasn't sleeping. He said, "I wish I didn't have to go."

"Me, too."

He sighed, tilted her head to kiss her. "But I'll talk to you later, let you know what's going on."

She nodded. "Take care of yourself, Will."

"Sure," he said without conviction, then left.

For three hours, Will almost forgot about Theodore Glenn. He and Hans worked side by side reviewing security tapes of the time that Jim Gage left the lab, poring over his e-mails, and waiting for preliminary evidence reports. Two detectives, Hazelwood and Dominguez, were working with them. Causey said they could have anyone else they needed.

Carina came in at seven thirty looking as crappy as Will felt. At the same time, Doug from e-crimes ran into the bull pen. "Hooper! I got something."

"I hope it's a break."

"Property owned by North Bay Law Offices in Rancho Santa Margarita. Bought a year ago — the same month that Sara Lorenz began renting out her house downtown."

Will sent Hazelwood and Dominguez to the bank to meet with the manager regarding the corporate accounts linked to Sara Lorenz and the law firm, then immediately sent a patrol and backup to the house. Will followed with Carina and Hans, calling SWAT to stand by in case they ascertained that Glenn was on the property.

The house was large, on a half acre in the gated community of Rancho Santa Margarita. Will noted that it was on the same street as Bryce Descario's house. Had Glenn been watching the other night when they stormed that house based on the note

Glenn had left for Will?

He glanced at Hans and knew the Fed was thinking the same thing.

Will motioned for four men to cover the back, and when they were in place Will pounded on the front door, gun out.

"San Diego Police Department!"

No answer.

He nodded to the two cops who had a ramming iron to break down the door. He nodded at Carina to go low.

As soon as the door was open, a piercing alarm went off.

"Take care of that!" Will shouted to one of the cops. Gun out, he scanned the entries, staircase, and corners. He motioned for the officers behind him to take different rooms. The first floor was cleared quickly.

"There's a broken computer in the den," someone shouted.

Cautious but quick, Will led the way upstairs. Cops fanned out to check each room.

"Detective!"

Will walked down the wide hall to double doors leading into the master bedroom.

Blood spatter grotesquely decorated the room, arcs of blood on the ceiling and walls surrounding the queen-size bed where a woman — who Will imagined had been Sara

Lorenz — lay shredded. A knife protruded from the bed next to the body.

"Everyone out until the crime unit clears it," Will said after two cops searched the room to make sure no one was hiding. He stood in the middle of the room with Hans and Carina. "He killed her in a rage," Will said, almost to himself.

"It seems very disorganized," Hans concurred. "Violent. With his other victims it wasn't as personal. I wonder if she said or did something that specifically upset him."

"Like threaten to turn him in?" Carina suggested.

"Maybe he thought she had," Will said. "Or he no longer needed her." He looked closely at the blood surrounding the body. "She's been dead for several hours. The blood is starting to dry."

"It looks like rigor mortis has set in," Hans said, "though without fully inspecting the body it's hard to say how long. But at least eight hours, probably closer to twelve. The coroner should be able to give us a good estimate. Were there any other properties your e-crimes team uncovered?"

"No," Will said. "Not in California. Doug's searching Arizona, Nevada, and fanning out from there."

"If this was his only safe place, why kill

her and leave?" Carina wondered.

"He's moving forward on his plan," Hans said, "whatever it is he's planned next."

They slowly walked through the crime scene waiting for the investigators. In the bathroom doorway, Will said, "He showered. He showered right here after killing her." Towels with blood lay on the floor, and a facecloth tinged with pink hung over the shower spout.

Hans said, "This definitely doesn't fit Glenn's pattern."

"Because of the overkill?" Will asked.

"Because it doesn't appear that he tortured her, at least not like his previous victims. He stabbed her to death, but it looks like it happened in rapid fashion, few defensive wounds. From everything you've told me about Glenn, he doesn't get angry."

"Unless he perceives someone as betraying him," Will said. "Like in court. He lashed out at everyone because he didn't believe he would be convicted."

"Therefore," Hans concluded, "everyone had betrayed him. Everyone lied."

"Sara," Will mumbled, "what were you doing with a killer?"

"Will," Carina said quietly. She stood on the far side of the bed.

He looked and saw what she'd found on

the nightstand. An open letter addressed to him.

William:

I had an epiphany of sorts. Perhaps it came from realizing that I, the master manipulator, was being manipulated himself. Or perhaps from the realization that we were both duped.

I didn't kill Anna Clark. I don't care whether you believe me or not, at least not anymore. I've been doing a lot of thinking about this and now realize where I went wrong. What about you?

Do you know who killed Anna? Do you know why? When you find out, take out an ad. In Spanish. Because by then I'll be fluent.

By the time you read this, I'll be in Mexico. I wish I could see your face right now.

I will be back. Tomorrow? The next day? Next year? You won't know until it's too late.

I've decided, William, who will live and who will die.

Aren't you dying to know what I'm going to do?

Aren't you dying to know when I'm going to do it?

"He couldn't have crossed the border," Will said.

Hans didn't say anything.

"Hans, you said it was covered."

"The border is a big stretch of land. If we can't keep thousands of people from illegally crossing the border into California, it's doubly hard to keep track of who's going south. All Border Patrol agents have his photo and description. They are on high alert here and in Calexico and every point in between, but you know as well as I do that it's easy to cross the border almost anywhere."

"He's lying," Will said. "He's lying so we let our guard down. Get complacent." But even as he said it, he wasn't sure Glenn *was* lying. It would fit in with his sick mind to taunt them and disappear.

"He might be lying. Let me call my people and see what I can find out." Hans left the room.

"Are you okay?" Carina asked.

"Dammit, Carina, he's playing with us. The letters, the calls."

"He wants to put you on the edge, to push you into being reckless."

"I'm going to get him. He's going back to prison, Carina."

*Or he's going to be dead.*

Crossing the border had been easier than Theodore had planned. He made sure that a camera caught him because he wanted William to know that he had eluded the cops.

Now he sat in a bar in a small village south of Tijuana and planned what to do.

On his way south he'd driven by Robin's loft. Early, well before the sun rose.

He'd parked several blocks away, in a car that couldn't be traced to him. When the cops learned about his connection to Sara Lorenz, they may eventually trace her to his phony law corporation and through that discover the truth about his legal payments. The trail was long and deep, it would take them weeks to put it all together, but eventually they would figure it out. By that time, if everything went according to plan, both Robin and William would be dead and Theodore long, long gone.

If he hadn't needed the safe house that Sara provided, he'd have left days before. Now he couldn't go back, but that was okay. He had a plan and it was going to work. The anticipation excited him.

He'd pulled out his binoculars and trained them at Robin's windows. The lights were on. Can't sleep, Robin? Scared of the boogeyman? Theodore grinned.

*You should be scared. You should be very, very afraid.*

When she passed by the window, he could only make out her figure, a dark, curvy shadow against the light. But there was no mistaking that body. He adjusted the binoculars, but the light in the loft made it difficult to see her expression. Frustrated, he left.

All the way down to Mexico he'd remembered her in the loft. Seeing her again made him want to control her. Just like he'd controlled her when she stripped onstage. Robin may never have realized it, but she was focused solely on him every time he walked into RJ's. She loathed him, despised that he slept with half the girls who worked there. Yet she watched him, knew where he sat in the audience, monitored who he flirted with and how well he tipped the other dancers.

Yes, he had always been in control of Robin McKenna whether she admitted it or not. And now, he still controlled her. She'd hired a bodyguard because of him. She closed her business because of him. She couldn't sleep because of him. William would tell her he'd disappeared in Mexico and she would change her entire life, her routine, because she'd never know when he would return.

He relished his power over her.

Send her a postcard now and again. Tell her he was coming . . . picture her as she was now, scared and nervous, watching over her shoulder.

If he had more time, he would stay in Mexico for months. Maybe a year. Wait for Robin to relax. Then — pounce.

He wanted to enjoy her squirming beneath his gaze. He wanted to watch her face while he tortured and killed her lover. He wanted to stare into her eyes as she watched the blood drain slowly from William's body. To hear her beg. To listen to her pleas.

What would she do, what would she say, to save him? Would she finally admit that he controlled her? That he had the power? Theodore would find out soon.

Impatience clawed at him. He looked around the cheap dive Mexican bar he'd staked a seat in after the old folks dropped him off across the border. *Too easy.*

He drained his beer and motioned for the pretty little *chica* to bring him another.

His plan was rather brilliant, but he expected nothing less of himself. He just needed a little time for the police to move on to other cases. Crime didn't stop, and once they proved he'd left the country, they'd have to let it go.

Robin had it in her little mind that she was a big, tough woman, yet she was nothing but a scared, aging stripper whose only power was her body.

*When he had Juliet, Romeo would follow.*

The Latina babe put the beer in front of him. *"Gracias,"* he said and smiled.

The girl beamed. She swung her hips seductively as she moved back behind the bar. One of the men glowered at him as he watched the show. Theodore stared back. The man averted his eyes. The *chica* kept glancing over at Theodore. He winked.

It would be nice to have sex with that hot little *chica,* no strings attached. Maybe he'd have a place to stay while he secured his money and worked out the details of his plan to kill William and Robin.

He smiled. He was getting away with murder and it felt good.

## THIRTY-THREE

The coroner had just gone inside Sara Lorenz's house, and Will was about to follow, when Hans waved him over. "Glenn is telling the truth. He's in Mexico."

"That's fucked. How?"

"Drove across into Tijuana at eight forty-two this morning."

"You have the exact time?"

"We have him on camera. He made a point of it."

"How? Why didn't they grab him?"

"He was in the back of a car driven by two senior citizens. The Border Patrol agents were specifically looking for a male driver fitting his description, or passenger with a female driver. They don't have the man power to pull over every vehicle. Glenn is charming, he's altered his appearance somewhat, he could have said any number of things to convince the couple to drive him across. Seriously, everyone is warned about bringing passengers from Mexico into California, but in reverse?"

Will knew Hans was right, but what was he going to tell Robin? Once in Mexico it was up to the Federal government to extradite him and the Mexican government rarely helped. The American government had no authority down there.

"I have LEGAT on it and they're going straight to the top. No playing around on this one. But —"

"But we probably won't get any help."

Hans glanced around, made sure no one

was eavesdropping. "I might have someone who can look around for us. Completely off-the-record."

"Who?"

"A friend of mine. I've worked with him in the past, he has contacts everywhere."

Will told Hans firmly, "You find him; I'll bring him back."

"You can't, Will, and you know it. But my friend can."

Will nodded. Hans said, "I'll make the call."

Robin had been trying to paint all day, with little success. Worry about her business, Theodore Glenn, the nice Jim Gage being killed in his own home — everything she attempted to create on canvas looked as bleak as she felt. So when Will came by late that afternoon, she relished the break — until she looked into his tired, worried eyes.

"I don't even want to ask, but something happened."

Will said, "Glenn slipped out of town."

"He's not here? How do you know?"

"He was spotted crossing the border into Mexico. Tijuana."

Robin blinked rapidly. "And no one stopped him?"

"I watched the security camera tape. He

changed his hair — added some gray — and he has on dark contact lenses. Very average looking. And he wasn't alone. He had two seniors with him."

"Are they okay?"

"We have an officer at their house waiting for them to return. We ran their license, we know who they are — no record, not even unpaid parking tickets. We spoke to their neighbors and learned that they go down one Friday a month to meet with some retired teachers' group. They'll be back tonight and we'll talk to them. Find out where they left Glenn, if he said anything." Will looked at Robin, rubbed her chin. "We will find him."

"He's gone." The stress of the last six days intensified. He was gone . . . but for how long? "Is the Federal government going after him?" Will averted his eyes, just a fraction, but Robin knew he was keeping something from her. "What is it? Will, what aren't you telling me?"

"It's not —"

"Don't tell me it's not important. If it's about Theodore Glenn, it's important! I need to know."

"He killed Sara Lorenz. Stabbed her to death last night."

She sat heavily on the couch. "I — I want

451

to feel bad. But she helped him. She *spied* on me."

"He also left me a letter. Told me he was going to Mexico."

"And?"

Will didn't say anything for a long minute.

"Dammit, Will, I'm not a fragile flower. Tell me!"

"He said he was coming back. I just won't know when."

Robin took a deep breath. This had been what she feared, in some ways more than facing Glenn again. Knowing he was free, waiting to pounce on her. Taking his time.

"I'm not going to let him touch you. Robin, we have everyone looking for him. The Feds have people in Mexico. We are on the border —"

"You were supposedly on the border before he crossed it, too," she snapped, feeling bad for taking it out on Will. "I'm sorry, it's not you —"

"Don't apologize. I know how you feel, Robin. I feel the same way."

She shook her head. "No. No, you don't. I've put my life on hold. I hired a bodyguard. I closed my business. I've barely left my loft. I'm trapped. All because of *him*." She didn't even want to say his name anymore. "I think that's exactly what he wants. He wants me to be jumping at shadows, looking over my shoulder, worried that he could come for me at any minute. I'm not going to live in fear for the rest of my life! Not anymore."

She stood, walked over to the window and looked down at the crowded street below. "I've been living in fear for seven years, even while he was in prison. The dark scares me because I immediately think about Anna. Falling in her blood. I sleep with the lights on like a little girl. I have a gun because I think it can save me, but only I can do that. Only I can take back my life."

She faced Will. "He's not going to have power over me anymore. I'm not going to let him." She stepped toward Will, a weight lifting from her heart. Saying the words out loud, *believing* them, made Robin feel free for the first time in years. "I've made something of my life, and I'm going to enjoy it. I'm not going to let that bastard take it away from me!"

Will grabbed her, pulled her tight against his body, his lips pressed hard on hers. She opened her mouth, tasted him, a free woman at last. Free and in love.

"Robin," he murmured. "You've never let anyone control you."

He ran both his hands through her hair

and she leaned into his caress. "I will do anything, Robin, *anything* to keep you in my life. You're vibrant. Beautiful. Smart. I'm complete with you. I would do anything for you. Mostly, though, I need you."

She touched his face. "Will —" She kissed him. "I'm glad we found each other again. Older and wiser."

He rested his forehead on hers and she breathed in his warm scent. "I have to go."

She nodded

"Being involved with a cop isn't easy. It's not a regular nine-to-five job."

"Neither is running a nightclub."

"I want to share everything with you, Robin, but some of it isn't pretty."

"You certainly don't have to tell me that."

"No, I don't." He paused. "How long are you going to keep Mario around?"

"I told Isabelle — who manages the art gallery — that Mario would handle security for the event."

"Good."

"But Sunday is Mario's last day. I'm not going to have a bodyguard for the rest of my life. I can't live like that."

"You'll have me."

"That I can live with."

It was six when Will arrived back at the station. Carina had already written up the report on the Sara Lorenz homicide. "During the canvass," she said, "neighbors said that Sara was friendly, kept to herself, and told everyone she was an attorney. In fact, she was a paralegal but has been putting herself out as a lawyer. Doug found more money and the Feds are locking it down. Dominguez and Hazelwood met with the bank manager this morning, with a warrant from Stanton, and we now have all the bank records and contents of a safe-deposit box."

"Busy day for everyone, not just us," Will said. "What was in the box?"

"You're not going to like it." She slid over a folder.

Inside were copies of photographs of Robin. They'd been taken over time, over at least two years. "Sara," Will said.

Carina nodded. "Sara kept a journal of Robin's movements for the last twenty-six months, much more intensive in the last year since she started working at the Sin under the name of Gina Clover. There were also letters from Glenn to Sara about how to circumvent the system, how to create corporations within corporations, things like that. We have a good chunk of their correspondence and Doug is going over it now to create a better time line."

"We know the gist of it." Will looked through the pictures. Robin at the art gallery. Robin at work. Robin at the gun range. Many of the photos were taken from a distance. Some from odd angles, as if Sara had used a camera phone at waist level. "Sara was probably sending Glenn photographs to help gain his trust."

"Lot of good that did her." Carina rubbed her eyes.

"Go home," Will told her. "It's been a long couple of days. The Feds are tracking Glenn in Mexico, we can't even take a shot at him down there."

"Jim's killer is still out there."

"And we can't do anything about that at six o'clock on Friday night."

"What about you?"

"I —" He didn't want to tell Carina he was working on Jim's case. She would insist on staying, but she was going through an emotional wringer. "Just paperwork." Not a complete lie. "If anything breaks, I'll call you."

"Promise?"

"Absolutely."

Carina left and Will found himself alone in the task-force command center. It had been set up to track Glenn, but right now Will spread out his file on Anna Clark's murder. Why had Jim called him? What had he wanted to talk about? Jim's message hadn't sounded urgent, but Will wouldn't forgive himself anytime soon for not responding to it immediately.

The door opened and Hans walked in. Closed it behind him. "Got something."

"And?"

"Gage's phone records. He made a call last night to Dillon Kincaid. I assume you know him."

"Yes, I didn't know you did."

"I worked with him on a case last year. I saw the 202 area code and called the number. I was surprised when he answered."

"I wonder why Jim called him."

"And talked for twenty-six minutes. We started talking, but I think you need to listen in. He's waiting for our call."

Hans put the phone on speaker and dialed Dillon's number. He answered on the first ring.

"Hi, Dillon, it's Hans with Will Hooper."

"How are you doing, Will? How's Carina holding up?"

"She's okay. I just sent her home. I didn't know we'd be talking."

"You can fill her in later. I feel awful about Jim. He was a good guy, one of the best investigators I've ever worked with."

457

"We're going to have a huge hole in the department," Will agreed. "Why did Jim call you last night?"

"He wanted to run through something that was bugging him. And I've been thinking about it all day. Hans filled me in on the differences in the crimes Glenn confessed to and the Clark homicide. What I keep coming back to is Jim's thought that the cuts were made postmortem."

"Which means what? That the killer didn't want the victim to suffer?"

"Yes. The killer wanted to kill her, but not torture her. There was no pleasure in the act of killing. Killing was a means to an end. And especially since Anna wasn't the intended victim. If you're right and everyone involved in the case knew Anna was going to be out of town, then the killer was surprised when Anna showed up."

"There was one more thing about Anna's crime scene," Will said. "Glenn always tortured his victims in their bed, then moved them to the front door before slitting their throat. But there was no evidence that Anna was even in her bed that night."

"That fits in with your theory that the killer was waiting for Robin," Dillon agreed. "The killer surprises Anna, subdues her — according to Hans she was petite, so it would have been easy for someone of virtually any size to slit her throat. Then, to make it appear that Glenn killed her, the copycat makes incisions in her body with an identical weapon. Jim said that it appeared that the marks were made twice?"

"Yes," Will said. "We talked about that yesterday, that the killer traced and deepened the marks. But the coroner at the time didn't make note of anything odd."

"Sometimes, we only see what we expect to see," Dillon said sadly.

"We're no closer to figuring this out," Will said. "I need to interview the seven people Jim spoke with between clocking out and going home. I'll drag them all down to interrogation —"

"Good idea," Dillon said. "But I think I can do you one better."

"How so?"

"Jim was hung up on why you were paged. Pagers started going out of fashion even back then. Everyone had cell phones. But I think the person didn't want to talk to you. The person wanted you to come to the apartment and find the body. You, Will, specifically you."

"I don't understand what you're getting at, Dillon."

"The killer was angry with you. I told Jim

last night that this sounded like a premeditated crime of passion. I suggested that he look into Robin McKenna's ex-boyfriends, regulars at the club, anyone who may have wanted her dead and planned on using Glenn's M.O. to do it. But not just anyone could have access to Glenn's hair samples and, according to Jim, no one in the media knew about the bleach until the trial. That was insider knowledge."

"Not to mention using the exact type of knife. Those details weren't revealed until trial either," Will interjected.

"This murder was a crime of passion, but it was directed at you, Will," Dillon said. "The individual has an above average IQ. Methodical, organized to the point of being borderline OCD. Narcissistic — not in the same way as Theodore Glenn who believes he's above everyone, but to the extent that this person categorizes people as worthy and unworthy. That is how Anna's death was justified, even though she wasn't the target. Anna was unworthy because she was a stripper — it wasn't a 'real' job in the eyes of the killer. In fact, the killer probably has disdain for working-class professions and individuals. But more important, this individual dislikes women in general. And this is what is key:

"I'd stake my reputation on the fact that the killer is a woman. She identified solely with her father, and would have followed in his footsteps. If she's a cop, her father was a cop. If she's a CSI, she has an advanced degree and her father was a doctor or scientist of some kind. She worshipped her father and is an only child, possibly a child the father wanted to be male and couldn't keep those feelings from her. She internalized that and concluded that women were inferior."

Will leaned forward but couldn't speak. Dillon was describing a woman he knew. As Dillon continued, Will's fear grew.

"Her mother was a weaker figure in her mind, likely a homemaker," Dillon surmised. "She may have gone back to work at some point and took a working-class job because she had no formal education, something that would embarrass the killer even if it was satisfying to the mother. She will have no close female relationships. Her female colleagues will not like her and she will exclusively socialize with her male colleagues. She is attractive, professional, and a perfectionist. She will have clocked in as much overtime as she can, not for the money but because her job is her identity.

"Will, you personally know this woman.

And there's a fifty-fifty chance you had a sexual relationship with her."

# THIRTY-FOUR

"Diana Cresson," Will said.

His stomach churned. How could he accuse a woman he'd worked with for more than a decade, a woman he'd *slept* with, of murder?

But as Dillon explained the profile, Diana came to mind and stayed. Diana was the only woman in Jim's department Will had dated. She was meticulous — a wonderful trait in a criminalist. She was a dream in court, formal and professional. Her father was a biologist for a prestigious university on the East Coast, where she grew up. Will couldn't remember her ever talking about her mother.

Could Diana have killed Jim? Shot him in cold blood? A man she'd worked with for years?

"Did you have a relationship with her?" Hans asked.

"Years ago, shortly after my divorce. Hell, I had relationships with a lot of women after my divorce. They were all short-term, but we always parted on friendly terms. Including Diana." Could he peg her as a killer?

"So your relationship with Diana was before Robin?" Hans asked.

"Yeah. It ended a year or more before I hooked up with Robin."

"How?" Dillon asked.

"As friends. We both had busy careers. My job always came first. We've had drinks after working on a case, in a group, ever since. I didn't hurt her or dump her for someone else. That's not my style."

"Will, you're not up for trial here, don't get defensive," Hans said.

"I'm not defensive, I'm angry! How could I have not seen it?"

"No one did."

"Why? Why on earth would Diana want to kill Robin?" As Will said it, he realized the truth. "She knew about my relationship with her."

"You said your partner knew?" Hans asked.

"Frank brought it up all the time, until I lost my temper when he got crude." Will shook his head. "So Diana found out? But is that a motive for murder? I've dated other women since Diana, and they're all alive."

"To Diana it is," Dillon said. "In her mind, you preferred a low-class, unworthy woman over her."

"Robin is *not* low-class," Will said.

"I'm explaining how Diana sees Robin. Robin was a stripper, correct? Diana would put her in the same class as a prostitute. And you, Will, are a detective. A noble profession, someone intensely dedicated to his job. In fact, your job always came first and that was how she justified your breakup. She could come in second to a job. She could not come in second to an inferior woman."

Hans interrupted. "But if she doesn't like women, how could any other woman be acceptable to her? Wouldn't she look at the other women Will dated as inferior?"

"Possibly, but I know Will and I'd guess most of his relationships were discreet and the women had some sort of professional career. Correct?"

"True," Will acknowledged.

"But closely on the heels of Diana's failed relationship with Will came his relationship with Robin, and it grated on her. She watched for signs that you were now unworthy of her devotion. If you looked tired, it was because you had been with Robin the night before. She built up a fantasy in her mind that you preferred Robin to not only her, but to your job, and that was unacceptable. A serious relationship would take you away from your destiny of being a cop. You couldn't be a good cop and be in love — in her mind.

"But there's something else. Anna Clark wasn't the first woman Diana killed. If you go back into her past, there will be at least one more. Probably in college."

"We don't have enough evidence to arrest her," Will said. "Stanton will never give me a warrant based on a profile."

"Was she one of the people Jim talked to yesterday when he was leaving?" Dillon asked.

"Yes."

"Call everyone Jim spoke with yesterday and have them come in. Call them into an interview room separately, ask what they talked to Jim about, and then let them leave quickly, walking past the room where everyone is waiting. In and out. Diana goes last. If Carina can put on her game face, have her in the room asking the questions. If Carina can pull it off — make it seem like Diana is not a suspect — it will put Diana at ease, since it was common knowledge that Jim and Carina used to live together. And if Carina can let down her guard a bit, tell Diana how hard she's taking Jim's death, it'll bring on Diana's guilt. She killed Jim because she thought he was a threat to her — that he knew something that would lead back to her. But she didn't want to do it. It will bother her because Jim was one of the good guys in her mind, and the more salt you can rub on that wound, the greater chance she'll confess or slip up. But Diana will not confess to a woman, so I'd suggest after Carina asks the questions, you go in — maybe find an excuse to send Carina off — and push her."

"Thanks for your help, Dillon," Hans said.

"Anytime. And again, I'm sorry about Jim."

Hans disconnected the phone and Will slammed his fist on the desk. "Diana."

"You couldn't have known."

"Why not? I slept with that woman. I liked her. I wouldn't have believed she could do something like this."

"We still don't have proof. We need the gun."

"She's not stupid enough to keep it lying around her house."

"Has ballistics come back on the bullets?"

"The coroner performed the autopsy this afternoon, the bullets are already at the sheriff's forensic lab and they're rushing it. We'll have the report by tomorrow. They'll work all weekend if they have to."

Will paced, bouncing ideas off Hans. "Diana isn't stupid. She's not going to use her own gun, even if she has one."

"She could have taken something out of the evidence room," Hans suggested.

Will nodded. "I'll have Hazelwood look into that, see if she signed anything out. But if it's a gun that has been used in a crime, we'd have the ballistics on it for comparison.

"But," Will continued, "she framed Theodore Glenn for Anna's murder, maybe she'll try to frame someone else."

"We need to get all seven of those individuals in and talk to them," Hans said. "And check to see if any of them has a concealed carry permit."

Will glanced at his watch. "It's after eight. Let's get everyone together and see what happens. On the QT. We don't want Diana thinking she's a suspect."

Will made the call to Hazelwood to contact the seven people seen speaking with Jim as he was leaving the lab yesterday, then he called Chief Causey at home and filled him in. Causey would contact Stanton to give him a heads-up and work out a reason to get a warrant. Then Will called Carina, filled her in on his conversation with Dillon, and told her the plan. She assured him she could play the part.

"I want her to fry," Carina said. "I won't screw it up."

Will was waiting on two more people — including Diana — when his cell phone rang. It was Officer Diaz, informing him that the couple who were seen driving Theodore Glenn across the border had just arrived home. Damn, he wanted to talk to them, but right now Jim's murder was the priority. Instead, he sent Dominguez out.

Then Trinity's number popped up on his caller ID. He almost didn't answer it, but he'd promised her a scoop.

"Hooper."

"So I can see why you didn't call me as soon as you found out Jim Gage had been murdered in his own home. You were busy investigating a crime. And maybe I can overlook the fact that you didn't give me a heads-up that the Sheriff's Department was working the crime scene because that's logical — Gage was in charge of the city's crime lab. His own people shouldn't be processing his blood. Got it. But you couldn't even call me and tell me Theodore Glenn wasn't a suspect? That he fled to Mexico? You promised me, Will, and it's barely been twenty-four hours!"

"Trinity, it's been hell over here. I'm sorry

press relations wasn't at the top of my to-do list. How'd you hear about Glenn?"

"That's not fair. I helped you, and you don't even throw me a bone. And I'm not telling you my sources, but the fact that the nice cop outside my town house told me he was leaving because Glenn was in Mexico and he'd been pulled off babysitting duty kind of clued me in."

Will bit back a retort. He understood why Trinity was mad, but dammit, he was at a critical point in the investigation. "Off-the-record, Trinity."

"No."

"Then I'm not saying anything."

"You're an ass!"

"I'll give you something, but you can't report on it until I give you the okay."

"Not good enough."

"It'll have to be."

"Dammit, Will! If you think I'll ever be your messenger to the public again, ha! Never! You're a liar, Will —"

Will watched Diana walk into the bull pen and Detective Hazelwood approach her with a warm smile.

"Okay, I'll give it to you."

Silence. "What?"

"We have a suspect in the Jim Gage homicide."

"In custody?"

"No."

"Who?"

"I can't tell you that until the suspect has been arrested. You know that."

"Is it the same person who killed Anna Clark?"

"That's a big jump," Will said.

"No, it's not. If Theodore Glenn didn't kill Dr. Gage, who would? Maybe someone who thought Gage had information that would incriminate them? Maybe your little ploy yesterday didn't work."

"Don't go there." Will still wasn't certain he wasn't partly responsible for what happened to Jim.

"Sorry." Trinity sounded sincere. "Well?"

"Let's say that the suspect is also a person of interest in the Anna Clark homicide."

"Fair enough. And I can run with this?"

"Run."

"Ciao."

Will put his finger up to ward off Hazelwood when his fellow detective indicated everyone was ready. He called Causey again and clued him into his conversation with Trinity so the chief wouldn't be surprised by the media coverage, then walked down the hall to where the seven employees in the crime scene lab who had spoken to Jim

470

yesterday were waiting.

"Thanks for coming in, I appreciate it. This won't take long, we're simply retracing Dr. Gage's steps yesterday and you all spoke to him right before he left the office."

"I just said good-bye," one of the clerks, a timid young woman, said, biting her thumbnail.

"Then why don't you come in first?" He smiled easily and escorted her down the hall.

Carina was already in the room. She'd showered and looked fresh, but dark circles framed her eyes.

Will quickly went through the first five individuals, then called in Stu Hansen. This was getting tricky, because Will knew Stu and Diana were friends and had worked together for years. "Thanks for coming in tonight, Stu."

"I can't believe he's dead. I heard you don't think it was Theodore Glenn. Why? That doesn't make sense. Glenn threatened Dr. Gage several times. He —"

"Whoa, slow down, Stu. You spoke to Dr. Gage twice yesterday. On the phone in his office, then again as he was leaving."

"Yes."

"What was the phone call about?"

Stu frowned. "Why?"

"We're trying to figure out what Jim might have been working on."

"I told him I didn't like the Feds coming in here and looking at our evidence, like we did something wrong. We didn't do anything wrong, not on the Anna Clark case. We went by the book. Textbook."

"We know," Will said. "Like I told the reporter, we have no reason to believe anyone other than Theodore Glenn killed Anna Clark. This is about Jim, not a seven-year-old murder. Do you know what was in the box Jim was carrying with him when he left?"

"Box?" Stu frowned, glanced to his left as if trying to remember.

Will put a photo in front of him taken from the security camera. It showed Jim talking with Stu and Diana outside the exit leading to the parking garage. "This box."

"I really didn't think anything about it."

"You didn't notice it at all? It's large. He's carrying it with both hands."

Stu shrugged. "It was a case file box."

"Did it have anything written on it?"

"Not that I noticed — wait. Yeah, there was. The boxes are marked with the case number. Jim's arm was covering the number, but it was an older case — the first two numbers tell the year and it was '01,' and I guess I thought why was he working an old case, especially since that's the same year the strippers were killed."

"You automatically equated a case file from 2001 as being related to the Theodore Glenn murders?" Will questioned.

Stu shook his head. "I don't know, it was on my mind. After Glenn told that reporter he didn't kill the Clark woman, and then the press conference and the Feds getting involved — yeah, it was on my mind." His eyes widened as he made a connection. "You don't think Jim's murder had anything to do with that case?"

"We simply want to know what work he took home with him," Will said.

"It was Glenn. It had to be. No one else had a reason to kill him."

Will switched gears. "Do you own a personal firearm?"

"No," Stu replied, eyeing Will suspiciously. "Why?"

"I'm just asking."

"No, you're fishing. I've worked in the lab for a dozen years and I know how interviews are done. Do you think one of *us* killed him?" Stu looked disgusted. "What's with you? I think it was Glenn, we all do, and you're not even considering that possibility?"

473

"We have strong evidence that suggests Glenn did not — could not — have killed Jim."

"What?"

"I can't discuss that with you."

"Am I a suspect?"

"Should you be?"

"Do I need a lawyer?"

"Do you?"

Stu stood up. "I don't have to be here."

"No, you don't. But you're an employee of the San Diego Police Department and Chief Causey has given me the authority to interview anyone under his command who may have information about the Jim Gage murder. If you refuse, you will be put on administrative leave pending an investigation. You may have your union representative in here with you, if you do not want to answer our questions without him present."

"I —" Stu looked flustered.

Will asked, before Stu requested anyone, "What did Jim say when you and Diana spoke to him for two-and-a-half minutes when he left work yesterday?"

"I really don't remember." He closed his eyes. "I told him I was worried someone would be fired. He said he was out of the loop, that the Feds looked at the case and didn't think it should be reopened."

"Anything else?"

"He wasn't feeling well and was going to do paperwork at home."

"Did Diana say anything?"

"She asked about Glenn, if there was any news on him. Jim said there wasn't. That's it. That's all I remember."

"Thanks, Stu."

"That's all?"

"Yes, just be available."

Will looked at Carina. "You ready?"

She nodded.

Will escorted Stu out. Diana was still sitting on a bench in the hall, a file folder open, working on something. She looked up and gave them a half smile. "Everything okay?" She glanced at Stu — who looked flustered and upset — her brows furrowed.

Will nodded. "No problem. You can go in, second door." He sounded casual. "I'll just be a minute."

Diana gathered her material and started down the hall.

Will escorted Stu to the door, ignoring his questions, which were variations on the same theme: Were they firing anyone? Why wasn't Glenn a suspect?

His cell phone rang as he made it back to the interview room. He walked past, to the adjoining room, where Hans was listening to Carina's interview with Diana.

"Everything okay?" Will asked quietly.

"Exactly how Dillon predicted it would go."

Will answered his phone.

"Dominguez here. I just spoke with Roy and Edna Stein. Nice couple. Too nice. Glenn was standing at a closed gas station early Friday morning next to a silver Honda Acura near the on-ramp to I-5 three miles from the border. He waved them over and asked if they had a cell phone because the gas station was closed and his battery died. They offered to give him a ride because they don't carry cell phones, and he told them he was a journalist writing an article about illegal border crossings and he needed to meet a contact in Tijuana. They happily drove him down there."

"Why?"

"To quote Mrs. Stein, 'He was a polite young man and had credentials.' "

"Did you tell her who he was?"

"Yes, and she didn't believe me. She thinks we're mistaken."

"Where did they drop him off?"

"The HSBC Bank on Avenida Revolucion."

"And he didn't ask for a ride back?"

"They offered, but he said he'd be down

there for a few days and would have a friend pick him up when he was done. He gave them twenty dollars for gas — offered more, but they declined."

"Do they still have the twenty dollars?"

"No, they bought gas with it."

"Get over to that gas station where they picked Glenn up and check out the story. If the car is there, have it impounded." He hung up, told Hans what he learned.

"I'll text message my buddy. He's already down there."

Will listened to Carina in the room. She was just chatting now, talking about Jim as if commiserating with a girlfriend, casually sitting across from Diana. "You know, I'm really going to miss him," Carina was saying. "We broke up years ago, but we were always friends."

"He was a terrific lab director," Diana said. "Very smart, serious, a complete professional. Did you need anything else? It's late and I still have paperwork to finish up."

"I don't know what's keeping Will. He'll only be a second, I'm sure."

Diana glanced at her watch, tapped her fingers on the table. She didn't look Carina in the eye, seemed on the verge of saying something, then closed her mouth.

"I think she's primed," Hans said.

The door opened and Chief Causey walked in along with District Attorney Andrew Stanton. The chief looked tired. "Are you one hundred percent certain she killed Dr. Gage?"

"I know she killed Jim. I can't prove it yet," Will admitted. "I have Hazelwood in the evidence room — the lab techs and criminalists routinely check in and out evidence. Nothing may come of it, but she doesn't have a CCP or a registered gun."

Hans said, "I don't think she expects to be under scrutiny. You may very well find evidence at her home."

"I have a judge waiting to sign a warrant," Stanton said. "I need something more than Dillon Kincaid's profile — and frankly, it needs to be tangible. Hard evidence."

"The sheriff's crime lab is working double-time on this," Chief Causey said. "They are combing through fibers and trace evidence. I've talked to the sheriff personally and he understands the sensitivity of the situation."

"If they find something from Diana, she could claim that she'd been in Gage's house before."

"But it would be enough for a warrant," Stanton said. "I'm going to listen in with the chief."

Will nodded. "Hans, let's nail her to the wall."

## THIRTY-FIVE

Will walked into the interview room and Diana began to stand. He smiled and motioned her to remain sitting. "Have you met Special Agent Hans Vigo?" Will asked her.

"I heard someone from the FBI was around," she said.

Hans extended his hand, shook Diana's, and Will said to Carina, "Can you please follow up with Border Patrol?"

He handed her a note. The note told her to watch with the chief and when he gave her a signal — running his left hand over his head — to come in with a note and hand it to him. Will knew he had to play Diana very carefully because she knew all the tricks.

When Carina left, he took Diana's hands and squeezed, as if he were supporting her through a difficult time. "We're all going to miss Jim. How are you holding up?"

She shrugged. "I'm shocked."

Will dropped her hands and flipped open his notepad. "We've asked everyone about conversations with Jim the day he was killed. I know you already spoke to Carina, but we're trying to figure out what he was working on. He took a box with him from the office —" Will slid the security photo in front of her. "We can't find it. It's not in his office, his house, or his car. We've retraced his steps and know he went directly home from the office. Do you know what he was working on?"

She shook her head. "He didn't say. I didn't ask. Jim always brought work home. I think we all did."

"They sure don't pay us enough to work from home," Will commiserated.

Diana's words were careful, measured. "I'm curious why you don't think Theodore Glenn killed Jim. It's the most logical conclusion. He threatened him in court, just like the others."

"Of course we looked at Glenn first. But Jim let his killer in. There was no sign of forced entry. No sign of a struggle. Jim opened the door and his killer immediately shot him. No hesitation, just *bang-bang-bang,* three bullets to the chest."

Diana looked down at her hands and let out a long, shaky breath.

"I'm sorry," Will said. "I should be more sensitive. You and Jim were friends."

"We were colleagues," Diana said. "He was my boss. I had a lot of respect for him."

"We all did." Will paused. "Carina is not taking his murder well."

"They lived together, didn't they?" Diana asked.

"Yeah, for three years. So you don't know what was in the box?"

She shook her head.

"Was there any writing on it?"

She didn't say anything.

"Diana?"

"There was a case number."

"Did you recognize it?"

"No. It was recent, it started with an '08' which meant it came from this year."

"What was he working on in the office?"

"Primarily the Frank Sturgeon homicide this week, and of course he supervises dozens of cases. I had a gang shooting I processed two days ago, and it has been keeping me busy."

Gang shooting. Will remembered hearing about it, though he'd been focused on Glenn's escape. Four dead gang members in an alley. He wondered if they'd recovered any firearms.

He gave Carina the signal and asked, "Have you ever been to Jim's house?"

Diana froze at the question. "I — why?"

"You were friends."

"Colleagues."

481

Will smiled. "I go to a lot of colleagues' houses."

"I've been there a few times."

"When was the last time?"

"Why does this sound like an interrogation?"

Carina walked in, handed Will a note. He 'read' it — it was blank — then scribbled *check status of guns in gang shooting* and handed it back.

"When was the last time you were at Jim's house?"

"I don't see what that has to do with anything," Diana said, her face tight as she watched Carina leave.

"Diana, why won't you answer the question?"

"It sounds like you're accusing me of something. I thought we were friends, Will. I thought you respected me."

Hans spoke for the first time. "Diana, I've reviewed your personnel files and you have an exemplary record."

"Why were you looking at my personnel files?"

"We looked at everyone in Jim's department," Hans said.

Diana stared at Will. "You said the Feds weren't involved."

"I never said that."

"On the news. You said the Feds reviewed the evidence and that we processed that stripper's crime scene properly."

"It was processed properly," Will said, staring Diana in the eye. "But Theodore Glenn didn't kill Anna Clark."

Diana's face paled. "We found evidence at the scene."

Will continued as if Diana hadn't spoken. "Jim knew Glenn didn't kill Anna. He also knew someone in his crime lab did. I think he had a hard time facing people he trusted knowing that one of them was a killer. So he took the case file home. We know he had the files at his house because he spoke with Dr. Kincaid in Washington about the case only twenty minutes before he was killed in cold blood by someone he trusted."

During Will's speech, Diana's lip began to tremble. She whispered, "I — I can't believe it."

"Right now, the Sheriff's Department is processing trace evidence found at the scene. They have hair and fiber samples that do not belong to Jim. Right now, my partner is sending the guns in your gang shooting to the Sheriff's Department to compare with the bullets removed from Jim's dead body. Right now, my only question for you is, why the hell did you kill Jim?"

Diana wasn't expecting the accusation. Her hands were shaking as she pushed her hair behind her ears. "I — I didn't!" Her denial rang hollow.

Will leaned forward. "Do you realize that your actions are going to set killers free? Do you realize that you've contaminated not only Anna Clark's crime scene but every case you've processed? Every killer, every child molester, is going to file suit and our entire department is going to be under scrutiny. We will be blowing our budget defending cases that should never come up for appeal. You did this, Diana. And why?"

"I — I don't know what you mean. I didn't do anything. I didn't do *anything!*"

"Stanton is in the process of getting a warrant to search your house. We don't need a warrant to search your desk or the lab." On the fly, Will made up a story. "Right now, while my partner is pulling the guns from the gang shooting, Detective Hazelwood is going through your desk."

"You can't do that!"

Will raised his eyebrow. "You work for the government. Everything in your office is government property."

"I want an attorney."

That surprised Will. He thought for sure she would continue to deny her guilt until she broke down.

"You're not under arrest," Will said carefully.

"But I'm a suspect, aren't I? I can't believe you think I could do something like this, Will. After everything between us, you just threw it away. For what?"

The non sequitur didn't make sense. "I threw what away?" he asked.

"Us!"

"Is that why you planned to kill Robin? Because I had a relationship with her?"

Diana glanced at Hans. She realized she'd said something wrong.

"I don't know what you're talking about, Will. Who's Robin?" Her face went blank.

Will played along. "Robin McKenna was Anna Clark's roommate."

Diana leaned back in her chair, waved her hand in the air. "Another stripper."

"She found the body. She testified at Glenn's trial."

"I don't remember. But I trust your word."

She seemed too calm, too composed. Had Dillon been wrong in his analysis? Will didn't think so: Diana had killed Jim and Anna. But maybe he needed to work her over more subtly. Play along with her biases. Make her think that she had a compatriot.

He sighed dramatically. "That entire case was a low point in my life."

"How so?" she asked.

"Come on, I'm sure you felt the same way I did. I mean, the victims were *strippers*. Probably prostitutes as well."

"There were five calls for solicitation at RJ's in the year prior to the first murder," Diana said.

Will didn't react to the information Diana shared, but it proved that she remembered far more about the case — and Robin — than she'd admitted.

Will shook his head. "I don't know what I was thinking getting involved with one of them."

"You're a man," Diana said. "They know how to lure good men into their trap. You're lucky she didn't get herself pregnant. Trap you."

Will didn't dare look at Hans, wished he had Dillon to play off of. *Get herself pregnant.* There was something there . . .

"Yeah, lucky indeed. But good riddance, right?"

"Can I go?"

Will opened his notepad, fumbled around. "Yeah, just — oh. Hey Vigo, look at this."

Hans leaned over, nodded solemnly. "Hmm."

Will was showing him nothing of importance, but said to Diana, "You said the case box Jim was carrying was from 2008?"

She nodded.

"Dammit, I can't believe I missed this!" He slammed the notebook shut. "Stuart Hansen lied to us. I need to bring him back."

"Stu?" Diana paled. "He wouldn't lie."

"I didn't think so, but he swore up and down that Jim was carrying a case box from 2001." He leaned forward. "Diana, we have evidence that proves Theodore Glenn didn't kill Anna Clark. Now I know who did. Hansen."

"Stu couldn't kill —" She stopped, and Will almost saw her mind working. "I can't believe it. Why would he?"

"He screwed up the Bethany Coleman crime scene," Will said coldly. "If it weren't for his mistakes, we'd have nailed Theodore Glenn after the first two murders. Frankly, I wanted him fired. But Jim defended him, defended his entire team. And then Stu kills him."

"Stu? No —"

"We know that Jim took home the Anna Clark case files."

"But then Stu was telling the truth, they were from 2001 —" She stopped.

Will leaned forward. "Then you were lying."

"You're wrong."

"You said the case files were from 2008."

"I was mistaken."

"You were certain."

"I — no." She took a deep breath. "I don't know what you're talking about, Will. You just said that Stu killed Jim —"

"Stu was under surveillance," Will said.

"He could have slipped out."

"So were you."

"What? You had *me* under surveillance? I'll sue you! You can't —"

"Yes, we can. And you know what? You could have slipped out as well. You *knew* we were on to something. Jim never leaves the office early. He had a difficult time thinking that someone he knew and trusted had killed an innocent woman and framed Theodore Glenn. He had to get out of the building, look at the evidence, see what he could find. His only mistake? Running into you outside in the parking lot. When you saw the 2001 case files you panicked. Thought Jim had figured it out, or would figure it out. You went to his house, shot him, stole the files."

"No!"

He ran a hand over his head, then

slammed it on the table in front of him. "Yes! You killed Jim. Why?"

"I didn't! And you have no proof. Do you think I'm this stupid? Do you think that I don't know you're trying to get me flustered? Why are you doing this to me, Will?" Tears clouded her eyes.

Carina walked in and silently handed Will a note, not looking at Diana. Carina had written *Fry her.*

Will watched Carina leave. "We have the warrant."

"What?" Diana exclaimed.

"Stanton found a sympathetic judge. We have enough to search your house —"

"No! I'll get it thrown out. You can't prove —"

"What can't I prove, Diana?"

"Don't do this to me, Will."

"I'm not doing anything to you," Will baited her. "You killed Anna Clark and planted evidence to implicate Theodore Glenn. Not because you cared one way or the other about his victims or whether he went to prison, but because seven years ago you wanted Robin McKenna dead."

"No."

"Dammit, Diana! Tell the truth for once! We're going to find everything. Did you already destroy the case files? It doesn't matter, because those were copies. The FBI has the originals. What about the gun? You don't own a gun, but you have access to guns. I will personally test fire every gun in lockup until I find the gun that killed Jim Gage. Starting with the gang shooting you investigated this week."

Diana's mouth opened and closed repeatedly. "No, no, no," she mumbled. "It's not like that."

"Then what the fuck is it like, Diana? You killed Jim for the thrill of it?"

"No!" She was shaking. "I didn't — I didn't want to hurt anyone."

"I don't believe you. You wanted to kill Robin McKenna, didn't you?"

Diana's face hardened. Her eyes flashed with hatred.

"You were screwing her! You were jeopardizing your career for a slut. You were all discreet about us, didn't want anyone to know we were sleeping together, but with her? You didn't care who knew. I can't believe you picked her over *me*."

Will stared at Diana, furious that he hadn't seen what she was capable of. "You killed Anna because you were waiting for Robin. You'd planned on framing Glenn all along, but you called me from the apartment. Why?"

"Theodore Glenn killed her," Diana whispered, frantically trying to hold on to the web of lies. "He was convicted of her murder."

"You went to Jim's house because you saw that he had the box of files from the Anna Clark homicide. You figured out that he was looking into the case, even though I specifically told the press that the case was not being reopened."

"No."

"Stuart Hansen has already told us that he saw the case number on the box and it was a 2001 case number, not a recent case number as you said," Will repeated, pushing Anna hard.

"I — I must not have seen it right. Or Stu's lying. Why aren't you asking Stu these questions?"

"You went to Jim's house. Premeditated. You took a gun out of evidence and shot him when he opened the door. Then you went into his office and took the case files. You had to know what we knew about the Anna Clark homicide."

"No. No. No. I want an attorney and I want an attorney right now!" She crossed her arms and stared at the table.

Carina walked in. "I have the ballistics report." She handed it to Will, then glared at Diana Cresson. "Jim Gage was a good man and a good friend and you will burn in hell for killing him."

Will stared at the report. This wasn't another fake out, but the Sheriff's Department really came through. Jim was shot with the same gun that killed one of the gang members in Diana's case. The gun itself was missing. Though it had originally been logged in to evidence at the scene, it was not currently in the evidence room or in the lab.

The case wasn't airtight, but Will had enough. And with a warrant, he was confident he'd find enough evidence at Diana's house to turn over to the D.A.

Knowing who killed Jim Gage didn't make him feel better. The case was solved, but a good friend had been killed in the process. Will would live with the weight of Jim's murder for the rest of his life. And though he knew Trinity's broadcast had nothing to do with Diana's decision to kill Jim, if only Will had found another way to handle the case maybe Jim would still be alive.

"Carina, would you like to do the honors?" he said quietly to his partner.

"Diana Cresson, you have the right to remain silent. Anything you say can and will be used against you in a court of law . . ."

# THIRTY-SIX

Will hadn't planned on returning to Robin's that night. It was after two in the morning when he found himself in her building.

Chief Causey had called off all police surveillance in light of Glenn's flight to Mexico. With the budget crunch, the over-time was already stretching their thin re-sources even thinner. And while Will under-stood the chief's decision, he sensed that Glenn would return sooner rather than later. Will was relieved to see that Mario had kept one of his men on Robin's loft.

He tapped lightly on the door, exhaustion weighing heavy on his heart and mind. How was he going to explain to Robin what hap-pened with Diana? How could he tell her that his ex-girlfriend planned to kill her because of some twisted obsession? How could he admit he never suspected while he dated and worked with Diana that she was capable of cold-blooded murder?

How was he going to explain the D.A.'s decision about prosecution?

Robin answered the door moments later. She wore a paint-smeared smock and held a brush in one hand. Her nose had a dab of blue on the tip. He couldn't help but smile.

"You're painting."

"Yes. I feel alive." She leaned forward and kissed Will. "When was the last time you slept?"

"I don't remember. I have six hours before I have to go back."

She crossed the room to her studio space, recapped her paints, and pulled off her smock. He followed closely, needing to hold her. His lips touched hers and he caught her breath with his mouth, pulling her into a sizzling kiss. A kiss that reached deep inside him. A kiss that meant more than a prelude to sex. A kiss that said *I love you, you're mine, I'll never let you go.*

He pulled back, then went in at the opposite angle. Robin wrapped her arms around his neck, melting in his arms. He was home. Wherever Robin lived was home to him now. It didn't scare him, it didn't send him running for the door, instead it gave him a sense of love, hope, and the future that he'd never had before.

If Robin had doubted Will before, she didn't now. How could she when he devoured her with such passion?

He scooped her up in his arms and carried her around the partition to her bed. He put her down, lying down beside her, his hands in her hair, his mouth delicately touching her lips. The quiet emotion sang to her soul. She sighed blissfully.

Sex between them had always been rough and tumble. Even the other night, after seven years, they devoured each other as though starved. Tonight was different: Will set a slow pace, an intimate approach that she'd never experienced with him before.

His mouth trailed down to her neck where he planted small, wet kisses along the sensitive curve of her throat. She was torn between pushing him to go faster and harder or urging him to keep drawing out the pleasure. She wore a tank top, and his tongue played with the tops of her breasts, riding the edge of her shirt, dipping long licks down, making her moan in anticipation.

"Will," she gasped, reaching down to pull off her top.

"Let me." He grabbed the bottom of her shirt in his fists and slid his hands up her body, his mouth following the path of the shirt as he removed it, landing once again on her mouth.

Robin wrapped her arms around his neck and pinned him to her, their embrace hot, deep, slow. Her hands rumpled his hair, moved down to his shirt, and she yanked it up.

"I need to feel your body against mine,"

she told him. "I want you naked. Now."

"Patience, sweetheart."

His kiss stopped her from arguing, and he pulled off his shirt quickly, his body hot to the touch, his chest rippling with barely controlled passion. She wanted him, like this, pelvis to pelvis, chest to chest, lips to lips, all night. She sensed he held back, and she urged him to move faster.

He leaned up, looked down at her face. He was as flushed as she. "I am going to make love to you, Robin. Slowly. Not one inch of your skin will be untouched, unkissed, unloved. I will show you I love you."

"I know you —"

"*Shh.* Let me do this for us, Robin."

She nodded, unable to speak as he leaned forward, in anticipation of another breathless kiss. Instead, he moved down to her breasts. His mouth claimed one while his hand squeezed the other. No small caress was this, he focused his entire attention on her chest until her skin glistened and she gasped. Then he switched, his hand fondling her now-sensitive nipple while his mouth worked on the other. Her hands kneaded his head, his shoulders, everywhere she could reach. She reveled in the heat his body generated, in how he made her feel.

His tongue left a hot, wet trail from her

chest to her navel. He popped open her jeans and slid them down her hips, pulling them off with her panties, his mouth skimming over her most sensitive area, just enough to make her shiver in excited anticipation. "Will," she breathed, unsure if she'd spoken aloud or not.

Then her jeans were off and on the floor, and Will was kissing her feet. He moved up, so slowly, so patiently. She'd never seen Will patient, not in bed. She loved their fast and furious lovemaking, but this was so much more intimate, more meticulous and loving, that he took her breath away.

Lightly, he bit her calf. Nibbles, followed by deep kisses. She gasped, involuntarily spread her legs when he licked under her knees, then his bites moved up her inner thigh, skipping over her very wet spot, and down the other inner thigh.

"You're torturing me," she gasped.

"I'm loving you," he said, then spread her legs and devoured her.

She arched her back, not expecting the orgasm to hit her so quickly. She held on to Will as she came down, but he didn't let up, bringing her back up fast.

"All's fair," she moaned and pushed him off her and rose to her knees.

Will loved so much about Robin, including her love of getting physical in bed, but seeing her naked, kneeling on her bed in front of him, her hands on his shoulders, satisfied expression mischievous, gave him a rush. It had been all he could do to hold back and not penetrate her. Holding back with this sexy woman was a challenge, but one that obviously pleased both of them by the look on Robin's face, and the heat spreading through Will's body, pooling hard between his legs.

She unbuttoned his jeans and pushed them down, freeing him. He tried to push off his pants, but she held his hand, took his fingers and put them in her mouth, one by one. In and out. His thumb. His index finger. His middle finger. Once she got to his pinky he was shaking and more than ready to bury himself in her.

Then she took the other hand and did the exact same thing until he had to close his eyes. But the sensation of her mouth on his fingers alone was just as stimulating as watching her.

She pushed him down. With his jeans half off he couldn't easily move, and she apparently liked that because she smiled at him. "Let's see how you like it," she murmured.

"I like it," he answered and she laughed, then slid her mouth on his quivering dick.

Just like she did for each of his fingers, she did it again, only longer, deeper, with her hands on his ass, brushing against his balls until he couldn't hold back.

"Robin," he cried, his hands fisting in the blankets as he came.

She rose, a goddess in the soft light of her bedroom, her dark red hair wild around her face, her chest heaving, her body wet and sexy from exertion.

"Now," she said, "we're both ready to go slow." She pulled off his jeans and laid on top of him. His arms wrapped around her and he kissed her. First slow and easy, then faster, more urgent.

Will rolled Robin over so he was on top, spread her legs, and slowly sank himself into her.

Robin sucked in her breath, her entire body on fire as Will filled her. They lay there without moving, wholly connected, mouth to mouth, chest to chest, thighs to thighs. Even their feet touched and she had never felt so completely wrapped in love, had never felt so desirable. He covered every inch of her body, she didn't know where she ended and he began.

Slowly, he began to move within her. Patiently. As if they had all the time in the world. *This* was making love, *this* was intimacy. She looked into Will's eyes, so dark smoky blue now in his passion that they looked black as night. He stared at her, his lips only inches from hers, his body rigid with forced restraint.

She moved her body to match his rhythm and quickly, too quickly, they both neared their peak. Her eyes drooped and Will kissed her. "Look at me, Robin." She opened her eyes as her orgasm rushed toward the finish line.

"I love you," he said, then fell on top of her as they rode each other over the edge.

Will pulled Robin to him and they lay spooned together in her disheveled bed.

"I had to see you," Will whispered in her ear.

She squeezed his arm, which was draped over her bare stomach. "I'm glad."

"I don't want to lose you."

"You're not going to. We talked about this earlier."

His chin touched the top of her head. Something else was going on here.

"What's wrong?" She tried to turn to face him, but he held her firm against him.

"I like holding you, Robin. You feel good here in my arms."

"Tell me what's bothering you."

"Where do I start?"

She ran her hand up and down his forearm. He'd looked so tired when he came in earlier. "Sleep. You can tell me later."

"I arrested Diana Cresson tonight."

"The criminalist?"

"She killed Jim." Will's voice cracked at the end.

"Oh God." That meant . . . "Theodore Glenn didn't kill Anna. You were right." All these years she had blamed the wrong person. It didn't make Glenn less guilty, it just meant he hadn't killed her friend Anna. She didn't know what to think, how to feel about this.

"I didn't want to be right, Robin. Not about this. I wanted to believe Glenn killed Jim because it would have been easier. But Diana — she worked for Jim. She was his friend, his colleague."

"She was *not* his friend," Robin said. "The woman must be unbalanced to do something as awful as that."

"She is as sane as you and I, Robin, only her idea of right and wrong are warped."

Will swallowed, continued. "I've always been honest with you about my past relationships. I've dated a lot of women. I guess — hell, I don't know. I screwed up somewhere. I never knew how to keep a relationship going. I was never in it for the long haul. My marriage fell apart because I was really married to my job. So after Wendy, I dated a lot, never got serious. Never, until you."

"I don't need to know about your past, Will," she said. And she didn't. As far as she was concerned, what was happening now was what was important, not the past. "I haven't been a saint."

"Hear me out. Please." He swallowed again. "No relationship lasted more than a couple months with me. Not after Wendy. I dated Diana. And let the relationship fade away like everything else. The job always came first for me. I liked Diana, but it didn't click."

He squeezed her tight and his voice cracked. "It's my fault, Robin. She planned on killing you. I don't know what I would have done then."

Robin absorbed the information. "Me? Why? I never did anything to her."

"I always prided myself on being discreet in my relationships, but with you — God, Robin, I thought about you all the time. Frank knew about our relationship and he had a big mouth. Dillon Kincaid, a forensic psychiatrist we consulted in this case, believes Diana had a fixation on me, and when I left her to focus on the job in her mind that was acceptable. Then I started seeing you. She viewed all women as inferior. But us, together, seemed to set her off."

"Did she — did she tell you this?"

"No, but her interview was convoluted. She was on the verge of confessing when she lawyered up. I have to tell you, Robin, they're going to cut a deal with her. We have her on Jim's murder — she used a gun she'd processed earlier this week in a gang shooting, and there's trace evidence that the Sheriff's Department will likely be able to tie to her. They are going to send some people to search her house in the morning — we felt it would be cleaner if they served the warrant."

"What kind of deal?"

"They're not going to try her for Anna's murder."

"I don't understand," Robin said slowly.

"The D.A. is going to offer her a deal — she confesses to Jim Gage's murder, waives her right to trial, and she'll be given life without parole in a federal penitentiary. Agent Vigo is working out the details on that right now. It's tricky, but they think they can cut it."

"Why is it tricky?"

"If we bring her to trial for Anna's murder,

every case she ever processed will be under scrutiny. Hundreds of violent predators will file an appeal, and many will win. She planted evidence. We don't have the time or resources to fight all those cases. But if we can keep it in-house, have her plead out, seal the records, we won't face such an onslaught."

Robin didn't know what to say. Intellectually, it made sense, but emotionally she wanted justice for Anna.

"There're some huge political considerations . . ."

"Politics?" Robin slid away from Will, rolled over and faced him. "She's getting away with Anna's murder because of *politics?*"

"She's not getting away with anything. Please try to understand. Don't you see that every single one of her cases is going to be called into question? Hundreds of convicted criminals — murderers, child molesters — are going to claim they were framed or that the evidence was tainted because she handled it. We may already have that problem, but the D.A. is working an agreement with the Feds to review all case evidence that Diana Cresson handled. We need time. None of us believe that she contaminated any other crime scenes — Anna's murder was personal. But try telling that to a jury."

"It's not fair." Robin's bottom lip trembled. Will touched it with his thumb.

"You're right. None of this is fair. I wish I had a better answer for you. I wish that bastard Glenn was in prison. I wish I had seen Diana for what she was years ago. I wish I had figured it out before Jim ended up dead."

She reached for him, rubbed his shoulder. "I'm sorry. I know you've done everything you can."

Robin wished Anna could be avenged, that her killer would go to prison for killing her. But she would be satisfied that Diana Cresson went to prison, period. At least she knew what really happened. That would have to do.

Will pulled her back to him, flesh against flesh. "When you walked out, I tried to replace you, but you are irreplaceable. I was miserable and didn't know it until I saw you again, saw what I had so callously tossed aside. I didn't know what we had until it was gone, Robin."

"And we have it back." She kissed him.

"God, yes." He kissed her again, his hands fisting in her tangled hair. "Yes, Robin, we have it back, in spades."

"I love you so much, Will Hooper. And

we'll get through this. I promise."

"I should be saying that to you."

"You have. In words and deeds." She cuddled into his chest. "You need sleep."

He rolled over on top of her. "I want you more."

# THIRTY-SEVEN

Will met with the Sheriff's Department personnel at Diana Cresson's house Saturday morning in Lemon Grove, a suburb of San Diego. He was observing only. Hans was supposed to meet him there, but he was a no-show and didn't answer his phone.

Chief Causey, however, arrived along with the assistant sheriff. These two murders — Anna Clark's and Jim Gage's — had the potential to seriously damage the department. "If I can suggest, sir," Will said, "use Trinity Lange to defuse the situation. Give her something good. Like a confession on the Gage homicide. We don't have to discuss the Anna Clark murder — those are wild accusations by an escaped convict who killed a mother, a guard, and a retired cop."

"Stanton is going to work the media," Causey said, "but I know you owe that reporter a bone. I'll talk to the D.A. about it."

"Thanks, Chief."

A sheriff's criminalist came out of the house with a bag. He approached the three of them, speaking to his supervisor. "We found a box of case files that matches the description of the box missing from Dr. Gage's house. We also found this." He held up a plastic bag with a notepad in it.

Will recognized Jim's small, block printing. At the top of the paper was written: *Dillon Kincaid 10:05 p.m.* Beneath were notes from the phone conversation Dillon told him about. Key phrases were underlined. *Robin McKenna intended victim. Why call Hooper? Did call come before or after murder?*

There were several pages of notes.

"We also found shoes that tested positive for blood. We'll expedite the test to verify a match to Dr. Gage."

"Any journals?" Will asked. "Notes of any kind?"

"We're still searching," he responded. "We have a computer specialist working on a laptop. Files have been recently deleted, but he believes he can retrieve them."

Will's phone rang. It was Hans. "Any news on Glenn?" Will answered.

"My contact Nico tracked Glenn to a bar on the south end of Tijuana," Hans replied. "The owner said a man matching Glenn's description went home with his waitress last night. Nico broke into the apartment and Glenn was gone. The waitress was uncooperative, but Nico learned he'd missed Glenn by twenty minutes."

"Shit," Will muttered. "Did the owner tip him off?"

"Could be. Nico is getting close. We'll get him. Are you at Cresson's house?"

"Yes. We found the missing case files and other incriminating evidence."

"I just spoke with Dillon Kincaid and he said she'll probably have a journal or diary that will be a justification of all her actions."

"There are deleted files on her computer they are retrieving right now. Are you going to meet me downtown later?"

"I wish I could stay for a couple more days, but I'm driving to the airport as we speak."

"Heading back to D.C.?"

"Not yet. Three fugitives were spotted north of Salt Lake City, possibly heading to Idaho, Montana, or even crossing the border into Canada. I'm meeting up with another agent who specializes in fugitive apprehension and hopefully we'll catch their trail."

"I heard on the wire that there's a major storm coming in."

"That's why I have to jump on the next

flight. With Glenn out of the country and Cresson behind bars, I don't know how much help I'll be to you."

"Who do I contact to find out how to extradite Glenn when your guy Nico finds him?"

Hans paused. "There won't be any extradition issues. Nico will bring him back. I didn't go through LEGAT on this. If I went through the bureaucracy, they'd still be negotiating with the local authorities and Glenn would be long gone. Trust me."

Will understood exactly what Hans was doing, and he owed him a big one. "I appreciate it, Hans. But I'm worried about Robin. I can't expect her to lock herself in her loft for the rest of her life."

"I gave Nico your contact information. He'll be in touch as soon as he has information on Glenn. The local FBI office is working with your D.A. regarding a plea agreement with Cresson."

"It was good working with you, Hans."

"Likewise, Detective. If you need anything, let me know."

"Catch the other bastards."

"You got it."

Robin went to the art gallery Saturday after lunch to talk to Isabelle about the showing the following day. She was still running high after her night with Will. Finally, her personal and professional lives were going well. She had a man she loved — who she believed with her whole heart loved her right back — and her dream of being a professional artist was within her grasp. Her club was reopening tonight and she was offering half-price drinks to bring people in. If this night went well, the two nights she'd lost because of Theodore wouldn't hurt her business at all.

Isabelle greeted her with a hug. She was a petite version of Snow White, Robin had always thought, with dark hair and milk white skin. Her brown eyes practically glowed, and she wore her designer clothes with flair and confidence.

"I am *so* excited about tomorrow! I have several serious buyers who have expressed interest in commissioning you for work, and a new high-end hotel wanting two murals for their dramatic beachside entry."

"You've been busy," Robin said, outwardly calm but inwardly jumping up and down.

Isabelle laughed. "Let me show you what we've done."

For the next hour, Isabelle walked through the gallery and showed how they were highlighting Robin's work with special lights

510

and dramatic black backdrops that made the bold colors on white canvas really pop.

"I can't thank you enough."

"Thank me? You're going to help me make a name for myself as a keen eye for new talent. At least that's what I'm hoping the art critic will say when he views your work tomorrow."

"Oh, God, I'm going to panic." For months, this date had been so far off. But, it was actually happening tomorrow and Robin hadn't had time to think about it because of the hell Theodore had put her through since his escape.

"You'll be fine," Isabelle said. "You already have fan mail." She reached into her desk drawer and handed Robin an ivory envelope. "This came in today's mail. You did see that big feature in the arts section of the paper on Thursday, right? I'm expecting a fantastic showing."

"Wow. Thanks." Robin hesitated opening it.

"Come on, don't I get to share in the praise, too?"

She smiled. "I'm just not used to this."

"Get used to it."

Robin ripped open the envelope and slid out the heavy note card.

Her stomach turned sour when she recognized the handwriting.

My Robin,

I'm leaving for a while, as I'm sure your boyfriend told you. Are you fucking William again? Of course you are. You're a slut, like all of them. They wanted me to screw them. They loved it. You know they begged for me. They wanted me. They knew how powerful I am.

You were supposed to be mine. What made you think you were so much better than me? You're nothing but an animal in beautiful clothes. What will you do when you find William dead? I hope you don't kill yourself like Juliet. I want that honor.

By the time you read this, I'll be in Mexico. Free. Think about that. I'll be free. You'll never be free as long as I live. Someday I'll come for you. You'll never know when. Tomorrow? Next month? Next year?

Sleep well, Robin. Sleep well with the lights on.

Theodore

P.S. Sara did her job very well, otherwise I wouldn't have known you are still scared of the dark. As well you should be, because the next time the lights go out it will be William's body you trip over.

Robin read the letter as if she were in a tunnel, everything in the periphery black. Fading.

*The next time the lights go out it will be William's body you trip over.*

He wasn't gone. He knew where she lived, where she worked, where her art was shown. He would come back and hurt her, hurt people she cared about.

Dear God, why? Hadn't she been through enough?

"Robin?" Isabelle sounded as if she were speaking from far away.

Was she supposed to be scared for the rest of her life, thinking that Glenn could come back at any time? Certainly after a few weeks the police would have more important crimes to focus on. Glenn had money and brains. He could disappear for months, years, until he felt like tormenting her. Send her a card now and again. Keep her scared. Keep her on edge. She'd never live in peace with that bastard free.

Before she realized what she'd done, she'd torn the card up in small pieces.

"No!" she shouted. "I'm not going to live

in fear for the rest of my life!"

She looked at the pieces of paper in her hands and realized she'd destroyed evidence. She wasn't thinking straight. "Do you have a manila envelope?" she asked Isabelle, her voice tight.

With a frown, Isabelle found one in her desk. Robin dropped the pieces into it, then said, "I'm sorry. It's him. Just trying to hurt me."

Her eyes burned with unshed tears as she called Will. "Theodore Glenn sent me a letter. Dammit, Will, when is it going to stop?"

# THIRTY-EIGHT

Leaving Robin at the club, even with Mario and his team keeping an eye on her, was the hardest thing Will had done, but D.A. Stanton had called him personally to come down to the station.

A plea agreement was on the table and Diana refused to sign it until she talked to Will. He didn't want to talk to her, but had no choice. The sheriff's crime scene unit had re-created her deleted files. She kept a computer journal of two murders, other than Anna Clark. Dillon had been right — she had killed before. But he'd been wrong about the victims.

For all Diana's talk about her father the biologist, he was dead. She'd killed him and his young lover — a teaching assistant — and staged it as a murder-suicide. It had been ruled that the teaching assistant killed him when he allegedly broke it off with her, then killed herself in a wave of remorse.

Diana's journal admitted to both murders.

He hated leaving Robin vulnerable only to sit across from his warped former lover who had wanted Robin dead, but Will had no choice. This was his job, and he would do anything legal to put Diana Cresson behind bars for the rest of her life.

They sat in a room normally reserved for defense attorneys and their clients, Diana across from him, in jailhouse orange, and shackled. Her face was devoid of makeup and her blonde hair hung in a limp ponytail. Her eyes, however, glowed with an appeal for something. What, forgiveness? Understanding? She would get neither from Will.

"I knew you'd come," she said, smiling brightly.

"I didn't have a choice. You refused to sign the agreement unless I did."

"We always have choices, Will."

"What do you want from me?"

"Everything I did, I did for the right reasons."

"You can't believe that, Diana."

She nodded vigorously, her eyes glistening. "I'm sorry about Jim. I'm really sorry about Jim. But he knew about me."

"No, he didn't."

She blinked. "He was looking into the Anna Clark case. He told me to my face that no one was reviewing the evidence, but then he walks out of the building with all the case files? He never leaves early. I didn't want to kill him, but I had to get those files back."

"The FBI had copies of all those files. And nothing in the files incriminated you for Anna's murder. What they did tell us was that someone other than Theodore Glenn killed Anna. Jim discovered that the cuts on Anna's body were made postmortem."

She frowned. "I didn't want to kill Jim. I had to."

"You didn't have to kill Anna Clark."

She waved her hand as if swatting a fly, her shackles rattling. "Who cares about her?"

"She had a mother who cared about her. Friends."

"Friends like Robin McKenna?"

The viciousness that suddenly crossed Diana's face surprised Will. "I wanted to kill that slut, not her lesbo roommate. Anna

516

came in unexpectedly. I had no choice."

"Why did you call me after you killed Anna?"

"I didn't."

"Someone paged me from the apartment."

"When Anna came in, I was already there. I was getting ready for Robin, and I didn't expect her for another thirty minutes. I told Anna that I was processing evidence in Robin's closet. She didn't believe me, walked over to the phone and paged you before I could stop her. I didn't want it to go that far, I didn't intend to kill her, but I had no choice. She paged you so I hit her with my gun. She was stunned, and I dragged her to the entry and slit her throat. Just like Glenn did to his victims. I had it all planned, except I didn't expect Anna. Robin should have died, dammit!"

"Why did you want to kill Robin?"

"She took you away from your job. She was a whore, Will. She didn't deserve a good man like you. If she were dead, you could focus again on your career. Your future. You could have been chief of police someday, Will."

"I never wanted to be in charge, Diana. That was something you got in your head."

"Why'd you do it, Will? Because she was easy? Because she would do anything you

517

wanted? Men are so shallow, they'll give up anything and everyone for a good fuck."

Will refused to discuss his relationship. "The Sheriff's Department found the journals you attempted to delete. You admitted to killing your father and his lover."

"I did not kill anyone. I don't know what you're talking about."

"The police in Massachusetts are going to reopen the case."

She shrugged.

"You killed your own father. You never told me he was dead, Diana. You talked about him as if he were alive."

She didn't respond, playing instead with her fingernails. They'd been bitten to the quick. Still, she picked.

"You were furious that your father betrayed your mother. That he slept with another woman —"

Diana slapped her handcuffed hands on the table. "My mother? That stupid twit? She trapped my father into marriage. She got herself pregnant."

The conversation from earlier came back to Will. *You're lucky she didn't get herself pregnant.*

"So he married her and they had you."

"My father loved me. He wanted me. We had a wonderful life, even with her around.

Then came *Tiffany.*" She spat out the name. "That little whore seduced my father. He was going to leave me!"

"Fathers don't leave daughters," Will said.

"He spent more time with her than me! I watched them in bed. He was nearly fifty years old and fucking a twenty-three-year-old grad student! He spent all his free time with her. And then he cancelled our winter ski trip. We went every year for two weeks during winter break, and he cancelled it. He *lied* to me. Told me he had to write a paper for a big journal. And you know what? He didn't! He spent every day, every night, with that bitch."

Will could all too easily picture the young Diana feeling betrayed by her father, walking in, shooting him. Framing the girlfriend. Killing her. Even then, smart.

"Are you going to sign the plea agreement, Diana?"

"Do you want me to?"

"Yes."

"Will you visit me in prison?"

The thought made him physically ill. "No."

"Are you sleeping with Robin again?"

"That's none of your business."

"She's going to suck the ambition right out of you."

"Maybe I don't have the same ambitions you have."

"Then I should have killed you, too." She said it with such calm assuredness that Will didn't know how he could even respond.

He slid the papers over to Diana. "Sign it."

She faltered, for just a moment, and Will saw the scared, vulnerable woman inside. Then her stone expression returned, she grabbed the pen, and signed. "Don't think I'm done with you, Will."

"Yes, you are."

Will stood and walked out with the papers without another word to Diana Cresson. He tossed the agreement at Stanton and said, "Done."

"Thanks for coming down, Detective," D.A. Stanton said. "We are expediting the agreement to try to keep this mess under wraps, make sure her past cases aren't put under any unwarranted scrutiny."

"The reporter Trinity Lange knows all about the Anna Clark homicide," Will reminded him. "She's expecting an exclusive."

"I can handle Ms. Lange," Stanton said. "She'll get an exclusive and more provided she doesn't mention Anna Clark in the same report as Diana Cresson."

Will didn't like that Diana wasn't going to be prosecuted for Anna's murder, but he understood why.

The chief frowned. "Is everything kosher, Hooper?"

Will glanced at the closed door. "At least she'll never get out of prison."

Whoever was tracking him was smart. Too smart.

Theodore patiently hid in the alley. He detested the foul stench of rotting food and feces, but it was the only place he could hide that provided him with a view of the restaurant where he'd spotted the man for the second time.

His tail was six feet one, broad and lean, with longish black hair pulled back. He looked half Mexican or Cuban, a little like that bodyguard Robin had hired, except thinner and wiry. He didn't act like a cop, but more dangerous.

Theodore did not like being the prey.

He still had the gun Sara procured for him, since carrying the rifle was too conspicuous when he'd crossed the border with the old folks. He'd also picked up a second gun from the waitress he'd fucked the night before. Had her boss not called and warned her that someone was on his way over he would have been caught.

Theodore wouldn't go down without a fight, but had no intention of losing any fight.

He hadn't wanted to go back to San Diego for at least two weeks. He'd planned on crossing into New Mexico, then slowly working his way back to San Diego. Give Robin enough time to go half crazy, wondering when he would come for her.

But that damn asshole had been following him all day. Twice he'd almost got him. Twice Theodore had slipped away. But the cop, or whoever he was, was sly. Cunning. Theodore didn't think he'd leave Mexico alive if he were caught.

Instincts propelled him forward. Every scent, every sight, every sound was crystal clear. But it wasn't the sound or sight that saved Theodore's life. Instead it was a touch, a prickly sensation on his skin. He *felt* the door behind him opening. So slowly that it made no noise.

He rolled across the alley just as the whiz of a bullet brushed past his head.

The bastard definitely wasn't a cop. He was an assassin.

Theodore jumped onto a Dumpster and without hesitation grabbed onto the balcony above him and smoothly pulled himself up.

Decades of mountain climbing benefited him now as he scaled the old, crumbling brick building. Up, up, up. Grab the next balcony. The lack of safety equipment coupled with the assassin pursuing him gave Theodore a burst of adrenaline that topped everything, even murder. He survived by his own wits and skill, his brains, his strength, his superiority.

From the corner of his eye he saw his pursuer on the building, gaining on him. Fuck that, the bastard moved up the face like a real-life Spider-Man.

Theodore swung over to a narrow window ledge. He took out his gun and fired at the man below him. *Pop, pop, pop.*

Then he kept moving, his fingers raw from the rough stone. He reached up for the roof ledge and rock crumbled. He didn't look back, didn't know how close the assassin was, but he must have stalled him for a few seconds.

That was all Theodore needed. He pulled himself up onto the roof, rolled low, jumped up, then ran, leaping across two roofs until he saw a balcony with the window open. Perfect.

He jumped onto the balcony and through the open window. He ran through the rooms until he found a door and let himself out before the owners could even catch a glimpse of him.

He found himself on a street four blocks over from the alley where he'd been hiding from the man who wanted him dead.

Time to disappear.

# THIRTY-NINE

"It's beautiful," Robin told Isabelle when she walked into the gallery early that afternoon with Will on one side and Mario on the other. The day was overcast with a fifty percent chance of rain later that night, but for now it was dry.

Her excitement from yesterday had been squelched by the message from Glenn, but she was determined to continue with her plans.

*You'll never know when. Tomorrow? Next month? Next year?*

Glenn's words haunted her, but he was right. She wouldn't know when. And she refused to be a prisoner for the rest of her life.

"Isn't it?" Isabelle beamed, a little wary of the two tall, armed men. "I decided the halogen lights worked best with your bold colors."

Twenty-six paintings were on display in

all different sizes, with two dramatic eight-foot murals framing the entry. Each painting had its own special lighting. A caterer had been hired to serve champagne and hors d'oeuvres and they were setting up in the small kitchenette in the rear of the gallery.

"Get ready, Robin. The guests are arriving," Isabelle said excitedly and left to greet them.

"I'll man the door," Mario said. "I have one man on the back and two working as caterers."

"Glenn's not coming here," Robin said. "It's still daylight."

Will forced her to look at him. "He wrote that to scare you."

"He wants to kill you." She swallowed her fears and nerves. "I'm sorry."

"Don't apologize. He's a master at psychological torture. But you're stronger than that. I'm not leaving your side, Robin."

"For the rest of my life? We both have jobs. You can't be with me every minute of every day. And maybe that's what he wants, to get us both together —"

"Stop." Will put his hands on her face, his expression firm, sharing his strength and confidence. She breathed easier.

"Okay."

"This is your big day. Don't let that ass-hole ruin it. We have very competent people looking for him. We're not dropping this. He killed two cops, Robin, don't forget that. Cop killers don't walk."

She nodded, held his hand against her face. "I'll be okay."

Will watched Robin all afternoon. After her moment of fear at the beginning of the art show, she'd put on her game face and was gracious, polite, and professional. He saw through her act, but the performance gave her confidence and strength. He was proud of her.

The gallery was packed, the event obviously a success. As the crowd thinned out, his cell phone rang. It was an unavailable number. He picked it up as he moved to a quieter corner, his eyes still on Robin. "Hooper."

"Nico. The target has fled."

"What?"

"The target is no longer in Mexico."

"What happened? Where is he?"

"I had him in sight twice. The first time he scaled a building and escaped through an unsecured apartment. But I learned where he eluded me. A few bribes later and I had word where he was headed. Almost had him again on a dirt road outside Tijuana. He shot a woman to buy himself time. She would have died if I hadn't stopped to put on a field dressing.

"I never had him in sight again, though I tracked him to Calexico."

"When?"

"Two hours ago."

"And you lost him there?"

Silence. "I couldn't cross the border. I called in a favor and have him identified as boarding a Greyhound bus heading for San Diego. Number 177 arriving at the main bus terminal at eleven-oh-six p.m."

Will wrote down the information. "Thanks," he said, then realized Nico had already cut off the call. In the back of his mind he wondered who the hell Nico really was and how someone as straightlaced as Hans Vigo had hooked up with him.

Will had no intention of waiting for the Greyhound bus to arrive in San Diego. He called in the information to Chief Causey to expedite putting together a SWAT team to apprehend the bus en route, then he told Mario what was going on.

He pulled Robin into a semiprivate corner behind one of her canvases.

"What's wrong?" she asked, searching his face.

He rubbed her arms. "I have a lead on

527

Glenn. I have to go."

Her brows furrowed in worry. "Be careful."

"Mario is going to take you home and stand guard until I get back." He kissed her short and hard. "I love you."

Will rode with the unmarked SWAT van east on I-8. It had begun to drizzle in San Diego, but as they drove the sky cleared up. Commander Tom Blade was on the radio in the back. "ETA twelve minutes," he said.

"Do you have a visual?"

"The CHP is tracking the bus discreetly. We don't want to alert Glenn or the other passengers that something is wrong. They have an unmarked pair of vehicles playing tag team with surveillance. Bus dispatch has ordered the driver to pull off at Exit 30 and feign illness. Protocol requires that all passengers disembark if the driver leaves the bus. We're five minutes behind the bus."

"Make sure the CHP knows how dangerous he is."

"They're aware."

Something nagged Will. Why would Glenn get on a bus? He'd know he was trapped if anyone saw him. Bus terminals had similar security as airports. He wouldn't be able to bring a gun on the bus, and Will didn't see the bastard going anywhere unarmed.

Nico sounded confident that his information was correct, but he didn't personally witness Glenn boarding the bus. Will was relying on information from an informant he hadn't talked to.

"Where's the passenger manifest?" he asked Blade.

"There're nine adult males on board traveling alone, and four traveling with a companion."

"I need names."

"It's on the computer." Blade jerked his thumb.

Will scrolled down the list on the SWAT laptop. Nothing jumped out at him. He had Glenn's fake names, the names Sara Lorenz had created for him. None were on the list, nothing even close.

"He's not on the bus."

"I don't have time for this, Hooper. ETA is six minutes. The bus has just pulled off the road. CHP is in place. We're going off your information, dammit."

"He was there, I'm certain of it." At least as certain as he could be based on his conversation with his mysterious informant. "But he got off somewhere. Did the driver stop anywhere after leaving Calexico?"

"Their dispatch said there were no scheduled stops between Calexico and San Diego."

"What did the driver say?"

Blade instantly saw the potential problem. "We determined that the safest course was not to engage the driver in conversation but to get everyone off the bus as quickly and safely as possible."

Will listened to Blade with growing dread. "Dammit, Blade, he got off the bus. Somehow, he got off and we don't know where the hell he is."

Bus passengers were detained outside the suburb of Alpine off I-8. A light drizzle rained down as the passengers hovered under a fast-food awning, but Will barely noticed.

Theodore Glenn was not on the bus. He was not among the passengers. And he stood listening to the old bus driver with fear.

"We was only on the road twenty minutes when the old man complained he was sick. I left him at the Motel Six right outside Calexico."

"Do you normally stop the bus if someone is ill?"

" 'Course not, we got a toilet on board. But he looked white as a sheet and said it was his heart. I didn't want him croaking on my watch."

"What time was that?"

The driver made a point to look at his log. Will grabbed it from him. There was no mention of a stop outside Calexico. The log indicated no stops until this one.

"Did you stop or not?"

"Look, if I make an unscheduled stop, I got this huge pile of paperwork to deal with, and the guy was sick and —"

"What did he look like?" Will interrupted, keeping his voice low and even.

"Old. Least sixty, sixty-five. White hair. Lots of it, but white as snow. He'd have been tall if he wasn't so crouched over and walking with a limp. Coughed the entire time. No one wanted to sit near him. I was glad to dump him off."

"Did you see him get on the bus?"

The driver shrugged. "Sure."

"Are you certain?" Will asked, his voice rising.

"Yeah, I did," the driver said, defiant.

Will strode over to the group of passengers waiting to continue their trip.

"Raise your hand if you remember the stop at Motel Six where a sixty-year-old white-haired man was let off the bus," he asked them. Virtually all of them raised their hand.

"How many of you would be able to recognize that man?"

A couple people put their hands down, but most kept them up.

"How many of you saw that man board the bus?"

After some hesitation, one by one the hands went down. The only hand remaining was a young boy of about ten.

Will went over to him. "What's your name?"

"Keith Gomez."

"Are you traveling alone, son?"

He nodded. "My mom and dad got divorced. I come on the bus to visit my dad every other weekend. I'm going back home to my mom. She's going to be worried if the bus is late."

"We'll explain it to her, Keith. You saw the white-haired man board the bus.?

He shook his head.

Will frowned. "You kept your hand up. I thought you understood that meant that I wanted only those people who saw him get on the bus."

"He didn't. See, there was this other man. He was sitting in the back, right next to the bathroom door. As soon as the bus started to go, he went in there. He was coughing a lot. He was in there a long time. Like ten minutes. When he came out he looked different. He had brown hair, then he had white hair. He saw me staring and winked at me."

"Do you remember anything else?"

"He was coughing a lot and told Fat Ernie — the bus driver — that his ticker wasn't good. What's a ticker?"

"It's slang for heart," Will said.

"So Fat Ernie dropped him off. Ernie said it was to sleep off a bender. What's a bender?"

"When someone drinks a lot of alcohol in a short period of time. What did the white-haired man look like before he entered the bathroom?"

The kid shrugged. "Brown hair. Sort of old, like you."

Will unfolded Glenn's mug shot and put it on the table in front of the kid. It instantly grew moist in the drizzle. "Is this the man you saw?"

The kid nodded. "Yeah, but he looked a little different. I think that's him."

Will stood and walked over to Blade and the others. "He's not going to be at the motel, but someone should check it out. I'm going to check the bus. The kid said

Glenn changed his appearance in the bathroom."

Will boarded the bus and went straight for the bathroom. Pulling on gloves, he went through the trash. He found a receipt and bag from a costume shop in Calexico. On the bag Theodore Glenn had written:

By the time you read this, I'll have Robin.
Hurry home, William.

# FORTY

Robin stared at the gun in her hands. She'd been holding it since the last time Mario checked in with her. He was outside her door, the only entrance and exit into her third-floor loft. One of his men had made sure all the fire escapes were secure and watched the doors into the building and underground parking garage.

Quiet. Too quiet.

Will hadn't called, but she couldn't expect him to from the field. He was working. How could she do this every day he went to work? Worry that he wouldn't come home?

*Stop.* She was making excuses. On the surface, because of her fear that what she and Will had was too good to be true; but deep down she knew it was because she feared Glenn would make good on his threats. That he would kill Will. And her. That this entire ploy was a ruse to put Will within Glenn's reach. Dear God, if he killed Will . . . A groan escaped Robin's lips. Though intellectually she understood that she wasn't responsible for the deaths of her friends seven years ago, in her heart she knew Glenn's obsession with her had contributed to the murders.

She turned her gun over and over in her hands. "I will kill you, Theodore Glenn. I promise, I will kill you."

Pickles leapt onto her bed and made her jump. He purred loudly and massaged his paws on her lap.

She stared at the lamp in her room. Even if she turned it off, she still had the small light in the kitchen on. She hadn't really tried to be in the dark since the last time she freaked out, and that was years ago.

She turned off the lamp.

Her apartment plunged into darkness. Pickles meowed as her grasp on him tightened. She let go and he jumped down, running under her bed. Her breath came in quick gasps. She tried to focus on the dim light coming from the kitchen, but it seemed to be moving farther and farther away. Her heart raced and she frantically reached out for the lamp, fumbled, knocked it onto her carpet.

"No, no, no!"

On her hands and knees she found the lamp and turned on the switch. It flickered and came on. She righted the lamp on her nightstand and hated herself for her fear. Dammit, she was thirty-one years old! She'd faced belligerent customers, hurtful boyfriends, and Theodore Glenn in court. Back then she had testified against him with less palpable fear than she had right now when submerged in darkness.

Isabelle had suggested a psychiatrist would be able to help with her phobia, but Robin didn't want to admit that it was a mental problem. How could she expect Will to sleep every night with the lights on? Last night she knew, even after his exhausting week, that he'd been awake half the night.

For Will, she would find a way to get over this. Maybe with him in her bed, she wouldn't need a light to feel safe.

"Sorry, Pickles," she said to the cat still hiding under her bed. She put the gun down on her nightstand so she could take a hot shower. Water always made her feel better. The ocean, the bath, the shower, didn't matter what, water was soothing.

Halfway to her bathroom, the light went out. Damn, the bulb must have been loose when she knocked the lamp off the table. She felt her way toward the bathroom door to flick on that light. Her heart was beating rapidly, but she felt like she was in control. A start.

Until her hand reached the light switch, turned it on, and nothing happened.

No bathroom light.

No bedside light.

Not even the kitchen light above the stove glowed.

She breathed deeply, but couldn't seem to catch her breath. She felt along the wall toward the partition that separated her bedroom from the rest of the apartment.

*Thump. Thump.*

What was that?

She drew her breath in to scream, but it came out a croak. She couldn't even scream! She didn't care if Mario thought she was a fool, she just wanted light. Any light.

As her eyes adjusted to the dark, the distant glow of the streetlights below cast odd yellow shadows across her ceiling. A shadow moved outside her bedroom window.

*Just the wind. Come on, Robin! It's just the wind! You're three stories up.*

Rain in San Diego was rare, but it had been drizzling for most of the evening. The clouds obscured any moon that might have been out. A mist hung above the streets.

*Thump.*

*Click, click, squeak.*

"Mario!" Her voice couldn't shout above a whisper, it was as if her throat had been sewed tight and she was trying to scream through a pillow.

Her alarm. Yes! Her alarm would alert her security company. Any time the power went out, a silent alarm went off and the security company would send someone if they couldn't reach her by phone. Her phone didn't work when the power went out.

She needed to hide.

*Just get to the door! Dammit, Robin, Mario is somewhere in the building. Get to the door and bang on it. Make noise!*

She was at the edge of her partition. To the left was a wall, to the right open space, then her living area which contained two sofas facing each other. A large lamp was on the side closest to her bedroom. If she knocked it over, it would crash on the hardwood floor.

A sob escaped her lips. She was pathetic. Scared of a blackout. It was the first rain of the season, for all she knew the relay station had been flooded or something. San Diegans didn't handle rain well.

*Scrape, thump.*

Cold, damp air rushed into her loft.

Her bedroom window was open. Someone had opened it.

Everything happened so fast, she didn't have time to scream. She felt like her lips were thick and she moved in slow motion.

She started for the door, sucking in air to scream, then stumbled over the end table, falling hard on the floor. The air rushed from her lungs, the wind knocked out of her.

For two seconds she couldn't move. Then she got to her knees.

"Robin?"

It was Mario on the other side of her door.

She opened her mouth to call out to him, then someone slammed her back down to the floor, forcing the air from her lungs with a rush.

She kicked backward, made contact with hard flesh. Her attacker grunted, grabbed her hair and yanked her head back. Any farther and he would have broken her neck. She couldn't swallow.

Cold metal touched her throat. A sliver of pain shot through her body, as if her neck had been burned. Warm blood slid down her skin.

"One word and I'll kill you."

*Theodore Glenn.*

"Robin!" A key turned in the lock. Mario had a set of keys, but she'd slid the security bolt. To make her feel safer. Instead, her own fear had trapped her inside with a killer.

Glenn yanked her up, his left arm tight around her waist, his right hand holding the knife to her throat. He moved soundlessly through her apartment toward the open window.

Robin felt like laughing hysterically — or breaking down in tears. For years she'd trained with a gun. Took self-defense classes, qualified for a concealed carry permit, practiced drawing her gun quickly.

But when she saw the shadow, her only thought was to run. She didn't even think to grab her gun on the nightstand. Fight or flight, and she'd chosen flight without consciously thinking about it. How pathetic was that?

Mario banged on the front door.

*Crunch.*

Glenn pulled her to the window next to her bed, the rain blowing into her room, dampening everything.

Her nightstand was to the left of the window. She needed to buy time for Mario to get in. As Glenn maneuvered her through the window, she reached down, feeling for her gun.

Her fingers skimmed the barrel.

Glenn pulled her to the ledge. She reached out for her gun. A pain unlike anything she'd felt sunk into her side.

"Don't think about fucking with me, Robin," he growled in her ear.

He also had a knife in his left hand, and this one had cut into her side. Her head swam, her fingers slid across the gun, and suddenly she was pulled onto the narrow ledge of her building with Glenn.

She should push them both over. Kill him with her.

*Will.*

She pictured her lover finding her broken body on the street below. She couldn't do that to him. Just as important, she didn't want to die.

*Bide your time. He could have killed you inside. He had the opportunity, but he didn't.*

The drizzle had turned to a steady fine rain, and in only a few seconds Robin was damp. Out of the seven days of rain San Diego got every year, why did one have to be tonight?

Theodore held her tight. He pocketed his knives and held her tight with his right hand. She fought, bit his hand, and tried to jump back in through the window.

He backhanded her, and her head hit the brick facade. She shook it, the pain intense, blood dripping into one eye, and hadn't yet recovered when he forced her onto a rope ladder he'd hung from the roof.

"Stop being stupid, Robin."

From below them, Robin heard noise in her apartment. She slowed her ascent, but Glenn picked her up and put her over his shoulder. She was looking at the sidewalk below, and it was rapidly moving farther away as Glenn practically ran up the shaky ladder. He wasn't even holding her, had balanced her on his shoulder, and she found herself grabbing his shirt, fearful of falling headfirst onto the concrete more than three stories below.

When he reached the roof, he held her legs tight against him and ran, walked right onto the roof of the building next door. She cried out, screamed, kicked — anything to get away. He was too strong. Dammit, so was she! She was a dancer, she lugged kegs in from storage. She fought twice as hard, reaching around and clawing his face.

"Argh!" He threw her off his shoulder and kicked her in the jaw. She rolled on the gravel roof, stunned. He hauled her up again and whispered in her ear, "You'll pay for that, Robin," as he hoisted her back over his shoulder.

The fall had disoriented her and she shook her head to clear her thoughts. They were on yet another roof. How had they gotten there? Had she blacked out for a minute?

She heard sirens in the distance. Glenn laughed. "Too late."

They were at the edge of the building. He was going to throw her off. Was that his plan? All that drama for *this*?

Something white was coiled on the edge of the roof. A rope. What was that for?

He took her off his shoulder, but didn't let go of her arm. Robin jerked away, stumbled, but Glenn didn't loosen his grip. He attached the rope to his belt, grabbed her by the waist, and jumped right off the building.

"She's gone."

Will listened to Mario tell him how Theodore Glenn had kidnapped Robin right from under his nose. SWAT director Tom Blade was pushing one hundred miles an hour to get them back to San Diego as fast as possible.

He didn't want to believe that Glenn had

gotten to Robin so fast, but it fit the time line. Hell, he had hours to plan it. He may have had it all worked out days ago. Waiting for the right time.

The only thing Will was certain of was that Glenn would kill Robin. The question remained as to where and when.

Will pictured Sara Lorenz's shredded body and the rage that had caused it.

*He'll kill her soon. He won't be able to stop himself.*

Will closed his eyes, focused on the messages Glenn had left for him and Robin. His twisted desire to watch his victims suffer. His taunting of Will. His talk about Romeo and Juliet.

*Romeo and Juliet.* Robin wasn't dead, not yet. Glenn wanted him to think she was, so Will would do something stupid, blinded with grief. But Will knew Glenn wanted to kill Robin in front of him. That would buy him precious time.

Glenn had the opportunity to kill Robin in her apartment. Why didn't he?

Because Will wouldn't have found her. Mario would have seen her body first. That wouldn't have given Glenn any satisfaction. He planned on taking Robin somewhere where only Will could find her body.

*Hurry home, William.*

"Commander Blade, take me to my house. Now."

# FORTY-ONE

Robin's head throbbed and though she tried to keep alert on the drive, she knew she had passed out for at least a few minutes. When she woke, they were parked in an area that seemed familiar. It wasn't until she was out of the car, heard the waves rolling up the quiet beach, and recognized the row of closely built homes, that she knew exactly where she was.

Will's place.

Glenn pulled Robin across the middle of the front seat and out his door. He had a bag slung over one shoulder, and she didn't want to think about what was in it. Knives? Bleach? What had he planned for her? He was parked two houses away, and kept a knife at her back to prevent her from screaming. She was just as fearful of other people's lives as she was of her own. If someone tried to help her and Glenn killed them . . . she didn't want to think about it.

But the street was empty. Nearly midnight on a wet Sunday night. No one to help. No one to see her struggle.

She opened her mouth to scream and his

hand covered her lips. She bit him. He continued to hold her tight.

"Whoa, girl, save the festivities for bed."

Bed? What did he plan on doing? Raping her? She almost laughed. Rape? This was all about power? Control?

Of course it was. Ever since he walked into the club, a year before he killed Bethany, he'd been trying to control Robin. His quiet manipulation. The way he watched her. The women he dated — all friends she cared about.

He'd always been trying to control *her*. And his lack of control over her had set him off.

She struggled. She was strong, a dancer, a fighter. She could run fast, faster with her life in danger. Just get away . . .

She kicked back, connected with his balls, and pulled away from him.

He grabbed her leg and yanked hard. She hit the grass, her head bouncing off the ground. If he hadn't hurt her earlier, she might have had the strength to get away. Dammit, Robin!

She struggled and cried out and he put a long piece of duct tape across her mouth.

Before she knew it she was inside Will's place.

The last time she'd been here was the day

he asked her for the second time if she had been sexually involved with Theodore Glenn. She'd walked out right after that, never to look back except in her dreams.

The house was the same, for the most part. A few pieces of furniture looked new, but he still had the barely worn white Berber carpeting. One thing that drew her eye was a familiar painting hanging on the main living room wall.

It was one of hers, a piece Isabelle had sold over a year ago.

A rush of emotion filled her. For a split second, warmth and love strengthened her.

She would survive. She had to, not only for Will but herself. To keep the rare love they had alive and burning.

Glenn slammed the door shut, bolted it. "We're home, Robin."

She struggled against the duct tape. He removed it in one pull and she gasped from the pain.

"I saw you fuck him right here." He pulled her through the living room, past her painting, to the small dining table next to the kitchen. "I stood on his patio and watched. You couldn't see me because it was dark. That night I killed Jessica. That night I imagined killing you."

She swallowed uneasily. She remembered

that night with Will. They'd been desperate lovers, so needy for each other. They hadn't waited to go upstairs. The clothes came off and they made love on the table.

It made her physically ill to know that her sexual relationship with Will had been observed and exploited. Glenn had watched them here, at the bar, where else? How could she have been so blind to his obsession before?

"You couldn't get off on your own, you had to watch other people having sex?" she spat out, bracing for a blow.

Instead he laughed. "You like to perform. You knew all along I was there."

"Like hell I did!"

"You fucked him for me."

"I love Will."

Glenn's face reddened, and he said in a low growl, "Really. That's why you've had such a successful relationship for the last seven years. Remember, I had a spy on you. But I know Will is obsessed with you."

"You're the obsessed freak."

"I would have gotten away with all of it if someone hadn't fucked up that crime scene."

"What?"

"You identified me off that sketch, all because you didn't like me," he said, angry.

"It was you."

"But the cops had nothing on me," he said as if she hadn't spoke. "Nothing. The evidence was thrown out after I killed Bethany, and there was nothing to tie me to Brandi or Jessica."

"Except someone caught you leaving Brandi's house!"

"That was your lies. And I had an alibi for Jessica."

"A drunk cop who fell asleep. You took the damn picture!"

He laughed, played with the knife in his hands. "But I didn't kill Anna. Someone planted evidence after killing her. And *that* is what sent me to prison. I should never have been convicted. My plan was brilliant. Perfect. They'd never have caught me."

She shook her head. "All this because I wouldn't sleep with you?"

He backhanded her so fast she didn't realize it until she was on the floor, tasting blood in her mouth.

"You thought you were better than me. I would have made you a queen. I would have taken you out of that pathetic strip joint and made you *somebody*. But you would rather flirt with seventy-year-old drunks than a young, virile man like me."

"I'd rather flirt with anyone than a twisted

fuck like you."

She pulled herself onto her knees, shook her head to get rid of the ringing.

"You think you're so smart. Bethany thought you were — and I quote — 'a total bitch' because you told her she shouldn't be sleeping with customers. And Brandi was jealous — she wanted your body, your hair, your attitude so badly. She wanted to *be* you."

"You're wrong." Robin pulled herself up and leaned against the kitchen counter.

"She was six years older than you, already on the downswing. She wanted me because I made her feel young and sexy. You should have seen her face when I tied her up. At first she thought it was just another sex game and she got excited. Until I carved into her tits. She was the first I used bleach on. Do you know what it feels like when bleach is poured on an open wound?"

Robin couldn't help but picture Brandi lying tied to her bed, bleach poured over fresh wounds. She shuddered uncontrollably.

Glenn opened his bag and Robin jumped, swaying. Tried to run, but her head felt thick. He easily grabbed her, yanked her arm toward him and made a shallow two-inch cut on her forearm. She screamed out.

He held her arm while he pulled out a small jug of bleach, pushed down on the cap, twisted, and it popped off.

"Feel for yourself, Robin."

She screamed when the caustic liquid hit her open wound. Glenn grabbed her mouth and held tight. She bit him, tears streaming down her face from the pain. He didn't let go.

"You thought you were better than me. That you could get rid of me. Never, Robin. From the moment I saw you, we had a bond. I would have been the best lover you ever had. I would have taken care of you. I'm rich, Robin, and I was rich then. Still, you shunned me. For what? A loser cop?"

Slowly, she breathed in through her nose as the pain dissipated.

"I'd have preferred to have William watch me fuck you then kill you, but he'll have to live vicariously. I'll make a tape."

He pulled out a digital video camera from his bag. He placed it on the table and brought her over to the living room — only feet from the front door.

That was his plan all along. To kill her where Will would walk in and find her. Right here, in his house. Romeo finding Juliet.

She couldn't let it happen like this. If

Glenn was going to kill her, she had to find a way to get out of Will's house. She didn't want him to be tormented by her murder for the rest of his life, like she'd suffered after Anna died.

Only worse. Because Will loved her.

She glanced at her painting that hung on Will's wall. It was a beach scene, one of her favorite to paint. Vivid shades of blue and green, rolling waves, a bright sky, and a couple holding hands in the heat of the afternoon. It reminded her that what had been lost was now found. He'd chosen one of her favorites.

She didn't want her blood on that painting. It may be the only thing Will had to remember her by.

"For seven years I've been planning how to make you pay for your testimony, Robin. You pulled my name out of thin air after seeing that worthless sketch. If anyone should be dead, it should be you. I should have killed you when I had the chance: in the bar when you and William went at it like a couple of rabbits. Is that what turns you on? Sex in public?"

Glenn restrained Robin by wrapping her wrists together with duct tape, then using a rope to tie her wrists to the coat closet doorknob.

She kicked at him, barely made contact, and he laughed.

"I hear you're scared of the dark, Robin." He flipped off the entry light and they were plummeted into darkness.

She screamed until another piece of tape was stuck to her mouth.

"All you needed to do was come home with me."

Her shirt tore, and a sharp pain crossed her body from her navel to her breast. She couldn't scream, but her back convulsed in pain and her legs scrambled. She pulled herself up, but with her arms tied to the door she was stuck.

"All you had to do was let me fuck you. You would have liked it. Brandi used to beg me for more. She couldn't get enough. She was devastated when I broke up with her. But you knew that, didn't you? Your *friends* told you everything. Did Brandi tell you how she liked being tied up and spanked? Did Bethany tell you how she liked it from behind? Did Jessica tell you how we had sex in your apartment when she was on break? Anna had given her the key."

Robin tried to ignore Glenn. He wanted to torment her emotionally. The pain across her midriff stung, but began to subside.

"The only thing I regret was not videotaping my kills. My mistake. I won't make it again."

He put the camera on her face, the video flash almost blinding her. "That's good. Show me your fear, Robin. Show me your pain."

He poured bleach over her new cut and her body convulsed, moving as far away from him as she could. Tears streamed down her face.

She felt the duct tape slip. Just a fraction. She had hope. Maybe her sweat was loosening it, or the rope was cutting into it, or both. Something was giving, and in the dark Theodore might not notice.

She twisted her wrists together, felt the tape slip a little more.

Glenn set the camera up to one side, the light on her body, not her face. He stood and seemed to be pacing, but she couldn't see him. Then his voice came from halfway across the room. "I wanted to take you. For me. All me. When I fucked Sara, I pictured you. I put her dress over her head and it was you. When I fucked Brandi, it was you. Always you. You wouldn't get out of my head. You'd bewitched me, I couldn't stop seeing you and I hate you for that. I couldn't stop coming to RJ's. And then you spurned me. Treated *me* like I was some substandard pervert while *you* were ripping your clothes off for horny men who jerked off in the bathroom thinking about you!"

His voice grew closer, louder, and he kicked her in the thigh. She sucked air in through her nose, a mewling noise escaping from her throat.

"The whore in Mexico, I thought of you. I fucked her hard and wanted to choke her to death because of you. I hate you. I hate you for forcing me to take chances. If it weren't for you, I would be halfway across Mexico by now. If you would just get out of my head, I'd finally be free!"

Robin yanked one raw wrist out of the makeshift restraints as Theodore's shoe connected with her stomach. The wind was knocked out of her and she couldn't catch her breath.

Then he was on top of her and whispered in her ear, "When I killed Bethany, I told her it was because of you. When I killed Brandi, I told her you were fucking the detective in charge. That it was because of you that she had to die. Because you treated me like scum. When I am the smartest person you have ever met."

Robin's other wrist slipped free. She clasped her hands together, pulled them back like she was holding a baseball bat, and as hard as she could swung her fists into the side of his head.

She won that round through the element of surprise.

*Run, Robin!*

He grunted, shifted just enough that she could slide away.

A weapon. Where did he put his knife? That bag of his. On the table. It was closer than the kitchen.

She scrambled to her knees and crawled. Her hand brushed against the bottle of bleach.

"Bitch, I'll slice your throat —"

She pulled herself up the wall, bottle in one hand. She moved to the right, toward him — hoping he'd think she was still moving toward the kitchen. The video camera light was aimed on the other side of the room, making this side even darker in the shadows.

She hit the light switch, blinking in the brightness, startling Glenn enough for her to splash bleach at him. He couldn't get his arms up fast enough to block most of the cleanser from hitting his face.

He screamed and paused only momentarily, blocking the front door. She ran toward the back, ripping the duct tape off her mouth so she could scream.

He was right behind her.

Will didn't wait for backup.

It was him and Blade. The rest of SWAT was less than five minutes behind, but five minutes was the difference between life and death.

His house was dark, a faint, foreign light filtering through the closed blinds. What was that?

But other than the light, he could see nothing unusual about his place. Had he been wrong? Had Glenn deliberately tricked him? Had he wasted precious time by coming here first?

Suddenly, the interior lights went on. He heard a deep, guttural cry — a man? — then, as his hands were on the doorknob, a piercing female scream.

Gun out, Blade at his back, Will kicked open his own door and went low and to the right. Glenn had a knife in his hand and was about to throw it at Robin's back as she ran toward the rear of the town house.

"Down!" he yelled.

Robin dropped to the floor at the same time that Glenn spun around and aimed the knife at Will. He and Blade fired simultaneously.

One bullet hit Glenn in the arm, but he'd

anticipated the gunshots and dove behind Will's couch.

Did Glenn have a gun?

"Robin! Stay down!"

She crawled in the kitchen, behind the counter. As long as she didn't move, Glenn couldn't see her, Will hoped.

Robin didn't say anything.

Will looked around and saw the blood in the foyer, bloody handprints on the white walls. The smell of bleach permeated the room.

How far had Glenn gone? How much blood had Robin lost?

If Will went for Robin, Glenn could kill him — either by shooting him, or throwing a knife.

Blade was behind a table he'd flipped on the right; Will was in the narrow hall off the foyer that led to his upstairs. He could see the couch Glenn hid behind, but he couldn't see the kitchen.

Could Glenn see Robin?

"Come out with your hands up!" Will shouted.

The low voice of laughter made Will's blood run cold.

"Not exactly how I planned it," Glenn said, "but she's still dead."

Will's ears buzzed.

"Will!"

He heard Robin from the kitchen. She sounded strained, but she was alive. Alive, not dead. Glenn had wanted him to react, to do something rash.

"You're not going to leave alive unless you throw your weapons out and stand up, hands behind your head."

"She is dying, Will. I sliced her from her navel to her breast. She's bleeding to death. I can sit behind here all night long. By the time you have the courage to come for me, precious Juliet will be dead in a pool of blood on your kitchen floor."

"Don't, Will," Robin called from the kitchen. "Don't listen to him. He'll kill you."

She didn't sound herself, but that could be from fear.

Will stared at the bloody handprints. So much blood. Too much.

Robin was alive now, but for how long?

He glanced at Blade. Held up his fingers. *On three, cover me.*

Blade nodded.

*One.*

Will glanced around the corner. A small spatter of blood was next to the couch where his bullet had hit Glenn in the arm.

*Two.*

He pictured the layout of his kitchen, the

likely place Robin would hide — behind the center island. It was a solid block of wood.

*Three.*

Blade fired rapidly over the table while Will rounded the corner and skirted along the wall toward the kitchen.

A hand with a knife came over the top of the couch aimed right toward him.

From Will's left, gunfire. He jumped, turned his gun toward the sound.

Robin, white as a ghost, leaned against the wall, firing directly behind the couch, emptying the .45 into Glenn who still cowered there.

The knife fell.

Robin slid slowly down the wall. Will quickly glanced at Glenn — he was dead, his eyes staring at the ceiling.

"Blade!" Will shouted and motioned toward Glenn's body.

He holstered his own gun and knelt at Robin's side, gently resting her body on the carpet.

She struggled to get the words out. "Is he —"

"He's dead."

"You sure?"

"Absolutely."

"Good."

She closed her eyes.

"Robin, don't go to sleep."

"I'm okay."

He almost laughed. "You're not okay." Glenn hadn't been lying when he said he'd cut her chest. Blood seeped from the red wound, but it was her arm that he was worried about. Blood rapidly flowed from a two-inch cut on her arm.

He tore off his shirt and wrapped it tight around her forearm, then pulled his T-shirt over his head and applied pressure to her chest.

A siren sounded in the distance.

Blade came over. "He's dead, Hooper."

"Damn straight," Robin muttered. "I didn't practice at the range every week to miss."

"This doesn't look like your gun," Will said.

"He left it on the table." Robin's voice was weak.

"Ambulance?" Will asked Blade.

"On the way."

Robin's face was cut and bruised, blood coming from her mouth and one ear. She was having a difficult time breathing.

"Hang in there, Robin."

"I'm not going anywhere," she said faintly.

"You'd better not."

"You bought my picture."

At first Will didn't know what she meant. Her left hand vaguely pointed toward his living room wall. He looked, saw the beach scene he'd bought last year after hearing her work was available at the gallery.

"I thought it would look nice in my place." That wasn't the total truth. "I missed you, Robin. Looking at it every day reminded me of you."

"I love you, Will."

# FORTY-TWO

*Two weeks later*

Will watched Robin closely to make sure she didn't overdo it. He hadn't wanted to come to the wedding — Robin had only been out of the hospital for a couple days — but she'd insisted.

"Carina is your best friend. You can't miss her wedding."

By the look on Robin's face, the formal Catholic ceremony had been lovely. Will didn't pay much attention to it, watching Robin for signs of fatigue.

"Stop it," she said as they walked into the reception at the Kincaid family house an hour later.

"You want to go home?"

"No. Stop treating me like I'm about to break. I'm okay, Will. I'll let you know if I need to go home, I promise."

He relaxed. Some. "If you promise."

He'd almost lost her. Again. She'd lost so much blood after the showdown with Glenn.

But that was over.

Nick and Carina came up to them shortly after the newly married couple arrived in the backyard. "I'm so glad you came," Carina beamed at Robin. "You haven't met my husband, Nick Thomas."

Robin smiled. "The wedding was beautiful."

"Thank you," Carina said.

Will hugged his partner. "You've never looked more gorgeous, Cara," he said affectionately. He shook hands with Nick. "Congratulations."

"It was perfect," Carina said.

"Almost," Nick said, his face clouding a bit. "If only Patrick could have been here."

Carina nodded. "I prayed every day that he'd be back up and around in time for my wedding. We even considered postponing it, but what would that do? Put Nick and me on hold on the slim chance that Patrick recovers? When? This month? This year? Five years from now?" She glanced at Will, her dark eyes glistening. "Don't wait, Will. Love, and life, needs to be your priority."

She took both Will and Robin's hands into hers and squeezed, then walked off with Nick to talk to the rest of the guests.

"Robin —"

"You don't have to —"

"Shh." He looked around the crowded backyard. All the Kincaids were here. Even Dillon Kincaid's elusive twin brother hovered around the periphery. All Will wanted was a quiet place to talk to Robin.

"Come with me," he said, finally spotting a place to escape.

In the side yard, wisteria climbed a trellis, giving privacy to a bench. Will sat Robin down, then knelt in front of her.

She grinned. "Don't do that, Will."

"What?"

"You'll get your pants all dirty."

He shook his head. "I love you, Robin."

"I know. I love you, too. We're missing the —"

"Shh." He cleared his throat, glanced up, saw the scar on her throat.

*Theodore Glenn almost killed her. You almost lost her, Will. Why are you wasting time now?*

"Marry me."

Damn, that came out pathetic.

"Is that a proposal?"

He ran a hand through his hair. "Yes."

When she didn't say anything right away, his heart skipped a beat. "We can wait —" he began.

"I don't want to wait. Of course I'll marry you, Will."

He sighed in relief, pulled a small box from his pocket. "I've been carrying this around with me for the last two weeks. I was going to ask you to marry me when you were in the hospital, but that wasn't really romantic. This isn't all that romantic, either, but —"

"It's the perfect time," she said, grinning like a kid, as she took the box from his hand.

Her face lit up when she opened it. The solitary deep blue sapphire sparkled in the sunlight. "Oh, Will."

"I remember once you told me you thought sapphires were prettier than diamonds. But if you want a diamond, I can trade —"

"Stop right there. I love sapphires. And I love that you remembered."

Tears coated her eyes.

"Don't cry. I can't stand to see you cry."

"They're good tears."

"I didn't know there was such a thing."

She nodded, leaned forward, and kissed

him. She tasted like heaven. And she was going to be his wife, his friend, his lover. Forever.